Murder, Forgotten

DEB RICHARDSON-MOORE

LION FICTION

Published by
Lion Hudson Limited
Wilkinson House, Jordan Hill Business Park
Banbury Road, Oxford OX2 8DR, England
www.lionhudson.com

ISBN 978 1 78264 311 1
e-ISBN 978 1 78264 312 8

First edition 2020

A catalogue record for this book is available from the British Library

Printed and bound in the UK, September 2020, AMN01

Deb Richardson-Moore, with her trademark skill to yank readers in from the first sentence or two, tells a compelling whodunit that makes the reader wonder: can a writer/artist's intense, immersive creativity be dangerous? Although the book's description says Julianna, the blockbuster mystery writer and immediately sympathetic character, is losing her memory, Richardson-Moore unleashes twists from the start. Is Julianna's memory really slipping away or has she fallen so deeply into her made-up worlds that real-life murder actually becomes inevitable? Is that the real mystery?

Writing with her delightful turns of phrase, Richardson-Moore not only makes you wonder about that; she also makes you become the detective who must solve this richly multilayered mystery: what in the world happened here, and in what real world did this murder actually happen?

A delicious premise vibrantly told.

John Jeter, author of *Rockin' a Hard Place* and *The Plunder Room*

Deb Richardson-Moore has woven a masterful tale of mystery and suspense in her latest book, Murder, Forgotten. *With superb pacing, she takes us on a page-turning journey from the coast of Scotland to the South Carolina shore. Her cast of characters with their many secrets will keep you guessing whodunit right to the end.*

Sally Handley, author of the *Holly and Ivy Mystery* series

Deb Richardson-Moore is a former journalist and a former pastor in Greenville, South Carolina. Her first book, *The Weight of Mercy*, is a memoir about her work as a minister among homeless people.

She and her husband Vince are the parents of three grown children. To find out more about Deb, go to her website: **www.debrichardsonmoore.com.**

Online reviews are always appreciated.

Also by Deb Richardson-Moore

NON-FICTION

The Weight of Mercy: A Novice Pastor on the City Streets

FICTION

The Branigan Power Mystery series:

The Cantaloupe Thief

The Cover Story

Death of a Jester

To the real Annabelle,

who ensured I had no visitors during the writing of this book

Acknowledgments

Thank you to my earliest readers – including the supremely enthusiastic Madison Moore and Elaine Nocks. You ladies kept me going.

Thanks to later readers Lynne Lucas, Lynn Cusick, Vince Moore, Bronwyn White, Mary Jane Gorman, Mary Beth McFaddon, Martha Lyon and Nancy Pendergast. Book friends are the best friends.

A big thank you to my editor Jess Gladwell, and to the enduring and patient members of my writers' group: Wanda Owings, Susan Clary Simmons, Jeanne Brooks and Allison Green. And thanks to Scott Simmons, who drove Susan and me to Killer Nashville while this book was in progress.

Unlike my previous books that were greatly helped by sabbaticals, this one was written in stolen moments. I am grateful to Vince and Dustin, who didn't complain when I wrote during vacations.

Carl Muller has continued to offer his quiet wisdom when legal questions arise. Truly a gentleman and a scholar.

And as always, my greatest thanks to Vince, Dustin, Taylor and Madison for sharing their lives and their love.

PART I

Chapter 1

Julianna climbed into the back seat of the waiting Volvo, square and black and unremarkable until she sank into its plush leather. The wind lashed through the crowds on the pavements as they stumbled against their luggage, called for taxis, grabbed children. Edinburgh Airport, though smaller than most she passed through, sported the same cacophony of noise and movement, and Julianna wasn't up for either. She sighed with gratitude upon entering the warm car.

Margot slid into the front seat beside a stranger, then turned and smiled wearily. "You remember Evan, don't you, Julianna?"

She looked into the rearview mirror where half of the driver's face was reflected. The stranger spoke. "How are you, Mrs Burke? It's been awhile."

Perhaps he was familiar. She met so many people. She'd learned long ago to listen for clues. Often someone would drop his own name in the first few minutes of conversation if you waited. A name or, if not, at least a city or an event or a book title or a spouse's name. You smiled and nodded until you figured it out. She never wanted someone who knew her to suspect she didn't know him. Though increasingly she didn't.

"Of course, Evan," she said, picking up on Margot's pointer. That was a big part of Margot's job these days. "How are you?"

"Fine, ma'am. It's good to have you back in East Neuk."

"Mr Burke will be joining us next week," she said, shivering as she looked at the steel gray sky. "Though it doesn't look much like golfing weather, does it?"

She didn't notice the look that passed between the two in the front seat; didn't see the question that arose in Evan's reflected eyes. "Aye, that's for sure. It's been a brutal winter."

Julianna closed her eyes against the airport traffic for what seemed only moments, but when she opened them again, rain was spitting on the windshield, and they had crossed the frigid waters of the Firth of Forth. Now they were passing barren fields with the waist-high stone walls that lined miles and miles of these winding roads. It had been too long, she thought – too long since she and Connor had been back to this eastern coast of Scotland where her writing career began.

Twenty years ago they'd discovered the stone house – or castle, as they laughingly called it – along the Fife Coastal Path, almost exactly halfway between Crail and Anstruther. Connor had wanted to play the fabulous golf courses of Scotland with the natives – who could've been his cousins had his ancestors not "crossed the pond", he'd claimed. But he didn't want to travel solo or to be alone every night. Truth be told, Connor never wanted to be alone.

She'd been halfway through her first book and said she could write anywhere. So he'd booked them into the turreted house of gray stone because of its reasonable rental price in April, before any semblance of warm weather arrived. At a desk overlooking the North Sea, Julianna had been invigorated. The book was set in her native Charleston, and somehow, with only her memory to rely on, the setting came alive more vividly than when she was actually writing in the Deep South.

After her third book, they'd bought the house in Scotland.

Her eyes flicked to Margot, who was turned again to the back seat, apparently awaiting an answer. "I'm sorry. What?"

"Evan said his wife has potato soup and sourdough bread waiting for us. Doesn't that sound good?"

Did it? She supposed so.

Margot must have sensed her confusion. "Sheona knows what we need on a day like this," she said smoothly, indicating the gathering darkness and rain, which was pounding harder.

"Ah, yes, right. Soup." Julianna did remember Sheona, a pretty little thing who came in upon occasion to cook, when she and Connor didn't feel like going out. But had she already decided not to go out? She looked at the rain and the trees permanently bent by these winds. Well, good decision if she had.

Julianna saw Evan's eyes squint in the mirror. She attempted a smile. "Margot, you did pack my laptop, didn't you?"

"Of course." Her assistant hesitated. "Why?"

"So I can write, silly. Why else?"

"I packed it so you could keep up with the news from Charleston."

"I can do both."

"I… I'm just surprised. That's all," said Margot.

Julianna laughed. "Why else would I come to Scotland in March?"

Again, a look passed between the two in the front, but this time Julianna caught it. She hesitated. "Margot?"

The young woman turned and faced her. "It's just that you and Dr Fitzgerald and Liza Holland thought it'd be good for you to get away. You hadn't said anything about writing."

Julianna frowned. Charlie Fitzgerald was her longtime neighbor and family physician. He was always offering advice. But Liza Holland? Why would she weigh in? Julianna did remember the silver-haired neighbor who lived six doors down. They walked their dogs together and compared notes about what had possessed them to adopt Shiba Inus, a highly anxious Japanese breed. They apologized repeatedly as the dogs tried to attack every other dog on Sullivan's Island. But why would Liza Holland think she needed to get away?

Julianna puzzled over the question for a minute, then lost interest. She laid her head back and closed her eyes once more. She was tired, so very tired. More tired than the plane trip from Charleston to Philadelphia to Edinburgh warranted. A tiredness that had crept into her brain and made thinking difficult. She needed to talk to Connor. She relied on him, personally and professionally. It'd been this way for the twenty-two years of their marriage, years in which he'd become much more than a husband; he had become her first reader and business manager and publicist and travel agent, dealing with editors and publishers, bookstore owners and hoteliers.

For one thing, he encouraged her wanderings. That's what they called it when Julianna's mind left the prosaic world of victims and killers and weapons and alibis to arrive at the furtive twists and psychological turns that so captivated her readers.

Her first wandering had occurred in this very place, in the house overlooking the North Sea, when Connor returned from an afternoon of golf to find Julianna gone. He'd told her the story a hundred times, and she'd repeated it a hundred more. He'd opened a beer and poured her a glass of white wine, sure she'd be back at any moment. But as the long and chilly day stretched toward sunset, he'd grown worried and, guessing correctly, had hurried down the coastal path in the direction of Anstruther.

He overtook her within the first mile, and with relief suggested they continue on for the village's famous fish and chips. But his relief soon gave way to puzzlement at Julianna's passivity. He tried to engage her in conversation, and she smiled and agreed with everything he said, but her eyes were glazed, trance-like. He was beginning to be alarmed when she tripped and went sprawling. Connor rushed to help her up, and she looked at him in surprise.

"What are you doing here?" she asked, then looked around and laughed shakily. "What am *I* doing here?"

"I found you on the path," he said, the incoming tide crashing on the rocks below. "Are you all right, Jules?"

She smiled. "I know exactly what happens next," she said. "And exactly how to set it up."

She insisted they turn around immediately, without dinner. Back in the stone house, Julianna worked feverishly through the night, jotting down the numerous changes she would make in the manuscript, crafting the ideas that would make her plodding story soar, deleting entire sections and writing new ones. They'd talked about it in the years since, named it: Julianna's *wanderings*. When her subconscious or her soul or her spirit or her muse or whatever the heck you called it took over her conscious writing self and saw possibilities that simply weren't there before. It was not so much a silencing of her inner critic as it was a releasing of her inner genius. In the trance of wandering out of the day-to-day, Julianna was able to access complex mysteries that swayed critics and readers alike.

She'd like to wander now, she thought peevishly. She always awoke from those episodes energized and excited about the next twist in her novel. She might stay up for eighteen to twenty-four hours straight, pounding out sentences and paragraphs and pages that made critics swoon, and made readers stand in line on the days her books went on sale, even in this sorry day of online publishing. She shook her head, felt the satisfying weight of a book in her hand. But wait. She wouldn't wander now. There was no book, no plot, no mystery to be worked out. Or was there?

She opened her eyes and stared at the rain, pounding now, shrouding the countryside like the inside of a charcoal coffin. Odd metaphor, she thought idly. Could an entire view be reminiscent of the *inside* of a coffin? And why charcoal? Didn't Charlestonians prefer highly polished cherry to burnished metal? When was the last time she'd been to a funeral anyway? Recently, it seemed. *Focus, Julianna.* Was she working on a book?

She honestly didn't know. She felt as if she was in that strange land between sleep and wakefulness, when the sticky remnants of a dream were so overpowering that she wasn't sure who she was, who she was married to, or where she lived. Part of her wanted to fight to the surface to answer the questions. Part of her wanted to sink deeper and ignore them. The latter won, and she fell asleep.

Julianna startled awake at the slam of two doors in quick succession and found herself alone in the plane. No, not the plane. The Volvo, of course. She heard the trunk open and squinted to see a man – what had Margot called him? – carry her suitcases through a doorway where a young woman stood. He bent to kiss her. Then Liza Holland's face was at her window, and she was startled again. Liza opened the door and the cold wind off the North Sea whipped in.

But this face was younger, and the hair a swirl of flying red curls, not silver. Julianna peered more closely.

"Julianna, are you all right?"

"Oh, Margot, of course. I was just, ah, dreaming." She was ashamed of her confusion. No reason to confess if she didn't have to.

She took Margot's arm and let the younger woman lead her across a drive of pea-sized pebbles to the brightly lit kitchen. Sheona – see? She remembered just fine – greeted them with a smile, and hurried to close the door behind them before the wind could rip it off its hinges. She took their coats, shaking off the rain and hanging them in a room beside the kitchen.

"Evan's taking your luggage to your room, and supper's on the stove," she called. "I'm so glad to see you, Mrs B." Bustling back to the kitchen, she looked as though she wanted to hug Julianna, but resisted. Instead, she patted her arm awkwardly. "I've been praying for you."

Julianna stopped for a moment to study Sheona's face. What did that mean, she was praying for her? It might mean something or nothing. Back home, people said they were praying for you, or "Have a blessed day!", like they said good morning. Many – many! – put the blessed-day refrain on their voicemail greeting. Frankly, it annoyed Julianna, though that wasn't the kind of thing you expressed aloud in South Carolina.

Sheona was smiling tentatively. Maybe she meant she was praying for their safe travel. Julianna returned her smile and let it go, patting Sheona's arm with a well-rehearsed "thank you, dear". That got her through a great many encounters when she wasn't quite sure what was going on. Because of her celebrity, chances were good the remarks were complimentary. A vague "thank you, dear" covered a lot of territory, Connor assured her.

She looked around the kitchen and wished Connor were here already. They'd have a glass of wine in the solarium before they got to the soup or whatever it was Sheona had cooked. They'd talk about the flight, how the writing was going, whom he'd played with today. But no, he wouldn't have played in this driving rain, she thought, looking out of the kitchen window into impenetrable darkness. The wind fairly roared off the sea, and rain attacked the windowpane like machine-gun fire. Even a golfing fool had his limits.

But wait. She struggled to clarify her thoughts. If they'd flown today, he couldn't have played anyway. And she couldn't have written. She'd never been able to write on planes.

She sighed. Margot was looking at her, and Sheona was busying herself at the stove so she wouldn't have to look. That much was clear.

Julianna pulled herself together. "I understand you have made soup for us," she said. "How very kind."

Sheona and Margot looked relieved. "Yes!" said Margot with more enthusiasm than potato soup usually warranted. "Let's eat!"

The soup was indeed delicious but the two generous glasses of cabernet sauvignon were what Julianna needed. She felt more relaxed, mellow. So what if she couldn't remember every little detail of every single day? She lived in parallel worlds.

There was the workaday world of Sullivan's Island in the warm and shabby beach house where she'd been raised. Her pine-paneled office overlooked the side yard of the Atlantic Avenue home, and a screened-in porch perched above the dunes to offer a view of the mighty Atlantic Ocean. She padded barefoot back and forth with her laptop and coffee to write passages in each place, depending on her mood and the mood of the ocean. Next door lived the Fitzgeralds, good friends and an unending source of hilarity for her and Connor. Meg and Charlie never told their horde of adult children who was visiting when, so there were screaming matches in the driveway and on the exterior decks during long, sodden drinking parties.

The workaday world also included book signings and university lectures and launch parties, the exhausting and necessary marketing side of the business that followed every release. That had been fun in the beginning, but it had grown close to unbearable. Connor had taken on the nuts and bolts, but when it came to facing readers, she was the commodity, she was the celebrity, she was the creator, she was the one they wanted to hear, to see, to touch. What had been exciting at first became grueling, and then foreboding. All those people, they wanted her advice, her celebrity, as if her success might somehow rub off on them, her glitter might sprinkle into their lives.

And then there was the world inside her head, the world of twisty plots and dark traumas and characters who lived and breathed as surely as those noisy Fitzgeralds next door. But what those characters did and had done to them was the key. *How did a genteel Southern lady come up with this stuff?* critics repeatedly asked. *Are you not afraid?* Connor's friends echoed. She and Connor had laughed out loud when they read thrill-master Gillian Flynn's acknowledgment of her husband: "What do I say to a man who knows how I think and still sleeps next to me with the lights off?"

"Oh, I sleep with a night light," Connor assured his friends. "And a sand wedge."

That was Julianna's cue to add to their shtick: "If a little fear keeps him in line, so be it."

But that had been when she had clarity between her worlds – when she might lose a few hours deep in thought at her laptop, sure, but a ringing phone or a doorbell or the barking of her Shiba Annabelle would rouse her.

Lately that clarity had blurred. When she was deep into a plot, it might take her several minutes to surface, not unlike a diver kicking free of the ocean's pull. That's how she felt sometimes when she re-emerged on her porch, as if she was gasping for air, surprised, relieved even, to find herself in familiar surroundings. She was always glad if no one was around, because she didn't want anyone to see the time it took for reality to click into place.

Parallel worlds, she thought, finishing her second glass of wine. She lived in parallel worlds – one literal, one literary. That meant she had twice as much to remember as most people. No wonder some of the details got lost. Totally understandable.

Julianna glanced around the dining room and found that she was alone. But there was an empty glass and plate across from hers. Margot, she remembered triumphantly. She heard movement in the adjoining kitchen and Margot returned, hoisting a nearly empty bottle of wine.

"Want the last few sips?" she asked.

"No, you go ahead," Julianna replied. "I think I'll go on to bed. I'm beat."

"I won't be far behind you."

"Margot, what day is Connor coming? I know you've told me, but I'm rather hopeless with times and dates." She smiled. "As you well know."

Margot looked stricken. Julianna felt dread rush into the pit of her stomach, but she had no idea why. She waited for her assistant to speak. "Margot?" she repeated.

"Julianna, honey, we've talked about this. Connor's not coming."

Chapter 2

Logan Arnette opened the plastic-windowed door of her Jeep Wrangler and allowed her mother's dog to hop out. "You're home, Jezebel."

The fawn-colored dog looked at her suspiciously, then barked. She seemed to know that Logan had deliberately mangled her name.

Logan reached into the back seat and retrieved her overnight bag, along with canvas totes that held the dog's bowl, canned food and leash. "Surely you can make it into the house unleashed," she told her. "I don't see any animals that need attacking between here and the door."

Annabelle curled her tail haughtily and climbed the splintered steps to the entrance before turning to wait for Logan. But Logan wasn't rushing. This was the beginning of a weekend in her family's old beach house, and she planned to savor it. Of course, it took only a glance next door at the Fitzgeralds' gloriously updated house with wraparound decks of splinter-free faux wood to rouse her irritation. Why wouldn't her mother renovate this Moby Dick of a house? That's exactly what it reminded her of – some creaky old monstrosity that would've suited Captain Ahab. Oh, she knew it was built in the 1950s rather than the 1850s. But still.

She gazed up at the weathered gray shingles and darker gray shutters in need of painting. She and her brother Harrison endlessly suggested renovations or, better yet, a sale. Then her mother could buy on nearby Marshall Boulevard, one of those sunny, post-Hurricane-Hugo mansions that actually reflected the South Carolina coast rather than dreary New England.

But Julianna was immoveable. And with their stepfather Connor shrugging off their suggestions, they had no chance. He would have eventually come around; Logan was sure of it. But now he was gone.

Logan shivered in the early March breeze and reached into the Jeep to grab a sweatshirt. A gray cloud the color of the house scuttled across the sun, and the temperature seemed to plunge ten degrees. She hurried up the steps and unlocked the door, watching Annabelle charge off in search of Julianna. She turned to the security console, tapping in the code she'd recently memorized. It was a gleaming new addition, out of place in this dim entrance. Out of place chronologically, too. It had been installed *after* Connor was killed. *After* detectives had satisfied themselves they'd gotten every shred of evidence from the crime scene and allowed Julianna to move back in.

Logan knew Julianna could never have arranged the installation of the security system. Margot had emailed her the code, so surely it was Margot's doing. With Connor gone, Logan was counting on Margot to save her from dealing with her mother on a daily basis.

She dropped her overnight bag on the speckled linoleum in the kitchen and dumped Annabelle's things in the adjoining laundry room. She headed for the oceanfront porch, the saving grace of the place, the selling point should she ever convince Julianna to part with it. But the chances of that had diminished the minute Connor died. As if her mother weren't attached enough to her childhood home, now it was the house she'd shared with Connor. How she'd loved that man. Certainly loved him more than the children who'd come along before. Logan and Harrison agreed on that – one of the few things they had ever agreed on. Connor had married their mother when Harrison was thirteen and Logan nine.

The substitution of one stand-offish stepfather for one absentee father had meant little to either child at first, though the money was better after Connor came along. Harrison and Logan suddenly had their pick of toys and books and clothes, and eventually cars and colleges. It was much later, once the self-absorption of her teen years had passed, that Logan began to recognize Connor as so much more.

Logan gazed out over a yard of bristly grass and sandspurs, a line of dunes and the gray waters of the Atlantic. The street and its houses were set back from the ocean, but this porch was perched high enough to give an unobstructed view of the coastline. As she watched, the sun emerged from behind a cloud and magically turned the water's sandy gray to glittering blue. She took a deep breath. She loved this beach, loved this vista, even if she'd prefer to have it from a more palatial homestead. She smiled as Annabelle bumped her leg, apparently realizing that Julianna and Margot weren't around, and Logan was it as far as food supply went.

"So you've figured out who's got the can opener, huh, Jezebel?" Logan patted the dog's head and walked back to the kitchen to feed her.

In two recent visits to the house, she had avoided the narrow hallway off the kitchen that led to her mother's office. On these occasions she'd been able to see its doorjamb from the kitchen doorway, crisscrossed with yellow tape screaming *Crime Scene.* Sticking her head into the hallway now, she could see that the tape had been removed. She edged to the office and looked in.

Logan's great-grandfather and grandfather had built this house, and at one time, before the notion of "man cave" caught on, the room had been her grandfather's den. Knotty pine covered all four walls and ceiling, creating a pockmarked, red-hued box that wasn't to Logan's taste – or anyone else's in the twenty-first century, she was pretty sure. But Julianna had loved her father and loved visiting his den, where they talked books. *Moby Dick*, no doubt, Logan always thought when her mother told the story.

Julianna had been a late-in-life baby and inherited the house while still in her thirties. She made the beloved den her writing study, keeping every shelf and every book that had belonged to her father and only swapping his recliner for a handsome desk and writing chair, his cracked leather sofa for a colorful chintz-covered one. From this unassuming room had come an unlikely string of successful thrillers. Logan shook her head. She had never told her mother, but she was a huge fan, eagerly awaiting each masterful book, amazed that the woman who was so vacant and flighty and scattered in real life was so incisive and focused on the page. But maybe one was necessary for the other, Logan sometimes thought. Maybe to be as good as Julianna was as a writer robbed her of an ability to function as a mother.

Averting her eyes from the upholstered chair by the window, Logan walked to the shelf reserved for Julianna's books. *Charleston at Dusk*. That was the one that started it. Her mother and Connor had been newly married then and had flown off to Scotland, leaving her and Harrison with their severe grandmother on their father's side. The old lady demanded that Logan wear a dress for dinner every evening; she made Julianna look like Donna Reed.

Logan continued down the shelf, running her fingers along the hardback spines: *The Mango Thief*, *The Palm Rustler*, *A House Built on Sand*. Logan recalled the thrill of reading each one, the tales so compelling that she lost any sense of knowing the author. *The Relentless Tide*, *Murder on the Marsh*. She remembered the jolt that inevitably occurred as she finished each book, thinking, *My mother wrote this? How in the world?*

In Charleston, of course – heck, in the entire state, the entire country – Julianna was a big deal. But here on Sullivan's Island, where her family had lived for generations, no one cared. Or if they did, they took pride in pretending they didn't. Here she was still Julianna, that Montague kid who rode her bike down Atlantic Avenue, and clambered over the cannons at Fort Moultrie. Her neighbors afforded her privacy, because that was what well-mannered Southerners did.

Logan halted her bookshelf journey. Maybe that was her mother's attachment to this ramshackle house. Maybe she worried that if she took on the trappings of a more opulent residence, it would endanger her privacy, her seclusion, her comfortable anonymity in this place.

Still, a bathroom with Italian marble would be nice.

The thought reminded Logan that she wanted a shower before settling in for the evening with a Netflix movie and a glass of wine. She heard a shout and turned to the window to see two young boys riding their bikes in the Fitzgeralds' driveway. Her eyes reluctantly fell on the chair below the window, rescued years ago from an unused guest bedroom and re-covered in a vibrant Laura Ashley print. Like a squirrel on the roof, her brain scrabbled to avoid thinking about what had happened in that chair, and rushed, instead, to the chair itself. For if her mother spent no money *on* the house, she had no problem with splurging on items *in* the house. Elegant fabrics, expensive rugs and luxurious towels overlay warped cabinet doors, aged floors and rusted enamel tubs.

Logan's eyes stubbornly refused to settle on the chair's flamboyant print in pink and red and indigo and green, roving instead to the abstract oil painting on the adjacent wall that repeated its colors. Her eyes fell to the identically upholstered sofa beneath the painting, then slowly, slowly, returned to the chair. The police had taken the seat cushion, but the matching floral print persisted underneath and on the seat back. She saw it now, the rust-brown stain marring the pink and red.

Connor's blood. The emptying of so much blood that his life had ended. Just like that.

Logan spun abruptly and left the office, suddenly desperate for that hot shower.

Three hours later, she huddled beneath a blanket on the porch, listening to the palms scratch against the house as the wind rose, watching the moon stripe the distant heaving water. Her movie forgotten, she sipped from a delicious red blend she'd found in Connor's wine rack. That was one thing they'd always found to talk about, she and her stepfather. Connor was no wine snob, but he had loved to discover new reds at wineries when he and Julianna traveled, and to introduce them to Logan when they returned home.

She glanced around and saw a Tom Clancy hardback on a side table. That had to be his. This was Julianna's house, but Logan couldn't imagine it without the stepfather she'd known for the past twenty-two years. He'd inhabited these spaces as surely as her mother had.

On an impulse, Logan got up and walked to the living room, then mounted the unadorned stairs to the top floor. Julianna and Connor had shared the largest room, but the house was built before master bedroom suites were compulsory. Amazingly, Julianna, or maybe Connor, had covered its paneling with grasscloth. The comforter on the four-poster bed picked up the browns and taupes and olives from the wallpaper, making the space a tranquil backdrop for a collection of watercolors by local artists, including two of Logan's own.

As Logan entered, her bare feet sank into thick carpeting, and she stood for a moment before her paintings. One was a sunset over the marsh, the sky glowing orange and pink and purple. The other was a scene of the beach in front of this house, but it was on an overcast day, so the canvas was dominated by grays and dark blues. Seeing her work unexpectedly always jarred Logan. With her guard down, she grudgingly admitted these paintings were good.

She walked to Connor's side of the bed, and was surprised to see another of her works hanging above his nightstand. She hadn't realized this was where he'd hung it. A face remarkably like her own stared back at her, her mother's face of years before, blonde hair whipped by a fierce wind, aquamarine eyes echoed in her jacket and in the sea behind her, cheeks flushed, and a smile caught halfway between a laugh and a surprised shriek. Only the nose was wrong, she noted. Her mother's was straighter than she'd captured it.

She'd painted the portrait from Connor's favorite photograph, taken near the couple's house in Scotland. She'd nervously given him the canvas as a Christmas gift the year before last. His astonished delight apparently hadn't been faked since he'd hung the portrait where he'd see it every morning and every night.

Logan thought of another canvas, another face, turned against the wall of her studio. It'd been intended as a gift this past Christmas. She'd held back out of… what? Pique? Hurt? It was likely that she'd waited too long.

Lowering her gaze, she noted another Clancy book on the nightstand, along with a John Hart and a Ruth Ware. Scoping out the competition?

She hesitated for a moment. Surely the deputies had already been through it. There was no privacy for the deceased. She tugged open the nightstand's single drawer, and found a deck of worn cards sporting the Budweiser logo. Connor had taught her and her best friend Britt to play poker with these cards. She found a book light and plugged it in. It clicked uselessly. That was so like Connor. He never threw anything away.

She rummaged through the rest of the detritus – CDs, pencils, notepads, a telephone book from 2004, orphaned cables and chargers. She saw a yellow envelope and recognized her own handwriting. Puzzled, she opened it, but as soon as she saw the silly birthday card, she recognized it as one she'd sent her stepfather during her senior year in college. She opened it, knowing the words penciled inside before she read them.

"If I haven't thanked you properly for what you've done for our family," she read in her rounded cursive, "I want to do it now. Thank you, Connor. For everything."

There were no other cards in the drawer, no Christmas cards, no Valentines, no more birthday greetings. This was the one he'd saved, as stilted as its message was. A lump rose in her throat.

She shoved the drawer closed and opened the door beneath it. It held an orderly stack of three-ring binders. She opened the top one, which was filled with a neat sheaf of copy paper. "The Mango Thief," read the top page. "By Julianna Burke."

Logan slid to the floor and flipped through it, her excitement rising at seeing her mother's original manuscript. She'd never seen one before. Julianna and Connor, and eventually their team of editors and publicists, kept them closely hidden until publication. Logan read the hardbacks like everyone else, though hers did have unique autographs – "To my darling daughter" and such. And of course, *Charleston at Dusk* had been dedicated to her and Harrison and Connor. But an original manuscript? Logan had never thought to ask.

She pulled out more of the notebooks. *A House Built on Sand. The Palm Rustler. The Relentless Tide. Murder on the Marsh. Charleston at Dusk.*

How odd to see the famous books on these humble printed pages. She counted seven binders. But her mother had published only six novels.

She flipped open the last one. There was no title page, no acknowledgments, no dedication.

"It wasn't that Martin Engler wanted to die," she read. "It was simply that he didn't care any more."

Logan's heart began to beat faster. Was this a new book by her mother? She'd had no idea she was close to finishing one. She rifled to the last page. The number 190 was tagged at the bottom. Above that, after the final paragraph, were the tantalizing words "Chapter 28", followed by blank space.

Logan sat back against the bed. An unfinished manuscript. Is this how Connor had read along as her mother wrote?

In the days following Connor's death, Logan had spent more time with her mother than in the past several years. Julianna had gone to stay with her neighbor, Liza Holland, and had moved through Liza's house like a ghost – or a mental patient. She had appeared vacant at the funeral, with Margot hovering at her elbow to cover her lapses with both local mourners and New York publishing executives. Just last week, after deputies allowed Julianna back into this house, Logan had brought dinner. Through all that, her mother had never mentioned a new book.

But then she wouldn't have. She was spacey at the best of times. After Connor's death, her sleep became more disrupted, her empty stares more pronounced, her answers more nonsensical. Frankly, Logan had been relieved when Margot whisked her out of the country.

But if you didn't have to deal with the real Julianna Burke, the thought of a new Julianna Burke mystery was delicious. Logan would snuggle into bed sooner than she had planned and see what Martin Engler's problem was.

But first she had to lock up downstairs. She stood, nearly tripping over Annabelle, who'd followed her into Julianna's room unnoticed. The dog whimpered.

"I know, baby girl," Logan said. "Your mama will come back. I promise. But you get to sleep in my room tonight. How's that?"

Annabelle trotted out of the room and dashed to Logan's childhood bedroom. She sat at the door, looking up expectantly.

"Back in a flash," Logan assured her.

She walked down the stairs and through the living quarters, turning off a living room lamp, rechecking the security alarm, and locking the door that led from the kitchen on to rickety side stairs. Circling back, she saw the glow from her mother's office. She knew she'd left a light on, but the hairs on the back of her neck bristled nonetheless. She'd never been afraid in this house, not once, not even as a teen left alone overnight when her mother and Connor remained in Columbia or Greenville or Asheville after a book signing. "The neighbors are *so close*," she'd whined in her successful campaign of persuasion not to be dragged along. But those close neighbors hadn't prevented Connor's murder. For that matter, neither had the other two people in the house.

Logan took a steadying breath and returned to the office, the black binder still in her hand.

She reached to turn off the desk lamp, but then thought about this treasure she'd unearthed in Connor's bedside table. What else might there be? Resolutely turning her back on the blood-stained chair, she pulled open the slender top drawer of her mother's desk. She felt guilty for a moment. Though she'd talked to her distracted mother from the office doorway or slouched on the couch as a teen seeking permission for one thing or another, she'd never been alone in this space. Julianna had not forbidden it – the family simply understood that the study was her private place. Even Connor entered only as work-related Connor, not as husband Connor.

Feeling like a snoop, Logan peeked at the contents of the drawer and found an orderly arrangement of paper clips and pens, nail files and miniature staplers, lip balms and reading glasses.

She sat down in her mother's chair and pulled open a file drawer on the right side of the desk. A neat array of labeled folders hung on metal tracks. "Invitations" read one. "Speeches." "Guns." Logan glanced inside that one and found pictures of various guns, their barrels and stocks and triggers painstakingly identified. She ran a finger along the other files, came to one full-to-bursting marked "Mail/Fan". Behind it was another one, slimmer, marked "Mail/Ideas".

She opened the second folder and pulled out a handwritten letter with a yellowing newspaper article paper-clipped to it.

Dear Mrs Burke,

I am your biggest fan – well, at least in these parts.

Logan looked at the dateline on the article: Altoona, Iowa. She removed it and turned the news page over, taking care because of its age. The reverse side included the top of a page, so Logan could tell it came from the *Des Moines Register* on July 7, 2002. Seventeen years ago. She returned to the letter.

I loved, loved, loved Charleston at Dusk and eagerly await more of your novels. When I saw this in our local paper, I thought of you and how it might make a good story in your hands.

Logan picked up the newspaper article again. "Man Electrocuted in Freak Accident" read the headline. The reporter had played it straight, probably because his Midwestern editors wouldn't allow him to make light of a death, no matter how bizarre.

An Altoona dentist died Tuesday after an opossum apparently crawled through the basement window of his Easter Lake house and gnawed through the protective covering of a hairdryer cord, according to the Polk County Medical Examiner. When Dr J. V. Gravley turned on the dryer, the exposed wires came into contact with water on the sink counter, electrocuting him, said ME David Lang.

Lang said the teeth marks on the cord matched that on other cords in the cabin's boat shed. He also located a brush pile with a nest of opossum babies.

Gravley had been alone in his fishing cabin at Easter Lake for a long Fourth of July weekend, said his wife, Alicia Gravley. He frequently stayed alone in the cabin, fishing and catching up on his reading, she said. He had built the rustic retreat and was looking forward to remodeling it in his retirement.

Gravley was formerly Chairman of the Board of the Greater Des Moines Dental Society, President of the Altoona Rotary Club and an active golfer at Fox Run Country Club. He is survived by his wife and two sons, Carter and Cleveland Gravley.

Logan laughed out loud at the ridiculous story, not bothering to read the concluding paragraphs in which residents of Altoona testified to what a great man Dr Gravley was. But the article triggered a faint memory.

She returned to the letter:

Of course, the question people in Altoona are asking is, "Why was Dr Gravley drying his hair at a lonely, rustic fishing cabin?"

Who was he trying to look good for?

Was the lovely Alicia tired of her husband's long weekends away? Had they coincided with a certain dental assistant's absences? Or, for that matter, were the sons disgusted with their father's behavior?

The gossip will continue in these parts because that idiot medical examiner is satisfied with his possum theory.

And who knows? Maybe it did happen that way. But I thought you might get a kick out of it.
Sincerely,
Rhonda McIntosh, Iowa's Biggest Julianna Burke Fan

Logan placed the letter and clipping on her mother's desk, all thoughts of the black blinder forgotten. She rose and stood before her mother's bookshelf, running her eyes along the titles. There was something about a chainsaw cord with peanut butter on it…

She picked out *The Palm Rustler*, her mother's darkly comic novel about a loving, middle-aged couple who received a large inheritance. Logan remembered the plot before she reached the page she was looking for. After getting the windfall, the two bought new cars, a huge house, and a vacation home. As they began to spend, and climb socially, they subtly changed. Eventually each began to suspect the other of infidelity and believed the other was going to take the money and disappear. They began to consider ways of killing each other, passively at first, not entirely sure it was what they wanted to do. That's when the wife dabbed peanut butter on her husband's chainsaw cord, knowing that squirrels had easy access to their garage.

Nothing happened at first, Logan remembered, and she'd been sure from the tone of the novel that the couple would realize their mutual misunderstanding and get back together. In fact, they were headed that way when a huge rain came and brought down a dead tree in the back yard. When the husband went out to dismantle the tree, the combination of frayed cord and standing water electrocuted him, horrifying his wife as much as anyone.

Logan leafed through the book, recalling how Julianna had carefully set the trap and manipulated the reader's emotions. Logan located the incident and re-read several pages, recalling the gut punch the episode had provided on first reading.

She leaned back in her mother's chair. So Julianna's peculiar idea of getting squirrels to assist in a murder had come from a reader. A real-life newspaper article. What about that?

Logan returned to the folder and read through another clip, this one from Sacramento, California. She shuddered in distaste at the description of a Lizzie Bordon-style murder. To her knowledge, her mother had never used it.

A third clipping told of a hit-and-run death that authorities in rural Maine had solved only two years after the event. Great fodder for somebody's novel, Logan thought, but her mother hadn't got around to it.

The fourth clip, however, startled her. It was closer to home, from Raleigh, North Carolina, and was a well-written, three-part newspaper series. A woman had killed her seventeen-year-old daughter when the girl stumbled on to an old crime from her mother's past. Logan stared at the three broadsheet pages allotted to the real-life murder. That was the plot of *A House Built on Sand,* though the daughter had become a son and the story was set in Charleston rather than Raleigh.

Logan spun around in the chair, her mind reeling. She had assumed her mother's novels sprang straight from her imagination. There was nothing wrong with taking the kernel of a story and running with it. After all, the books were made over the course of 350 twisting, turning pages, not in the plot summary. Still, she'd had no idea that readers sent in ideas.

She returned the papers to the folder and slid it into the file drawer. She'd come back later, perhaps, to match up clippings and how they made their way into her mother's books. Or maybe not. She wasn't sure how she felt about it.

She grabbed the black binder and clicked off the lamp, her lingering nervousness at being alone in the house trailing her up the stairs. Luckily it was matched by her eagerness to see how Martin Engler fared in her mother's hands.

Chapter 3

Julianna woke to the wind rattling the windows. This old stone house was unshakeable, but the windows, well, what could you expect when the North Sea flung March winds at them?

She got out of bed and went to the ocean-facing window, in search of the Isle of May. The story she loved best about this stretch of wild, eastern seaboard involved the Blue Stane, or stone, at the entrance to the kirk of St Mary's in Crail. Legend had it that the devil got so mad when he learned the church was being built that he stood on the Isle of May and hurled the boulder across the water. There was even a little sign in Crail that told the story, a naked blue devil dancing beside the text.

With the sun sparkling on the water, Julianna could indeed make out the small island in the distance. Funny, but her mind seemed clearer this morning. She didn't know if it came from a good night's sleep or if it was that the dreaded sundowners tripped her later in the day, but she definitely felt clearer. She'd talk that over with Connor.

A chill slithered up the back of her nightgown, then a cold dread hit her chest like an anvil. Oh, no. That was what she'd had to face last night. Margot had told her that Connor wasn't coming because Connor was dead. She had screamed in outraged disbelief and fear, she recalled with embarrassment.

How could she possibly have forgotten finding Connor in her office, bleeding, bleeding? She thought it was some sort of hemorrhage until she saw that most unbelievable sight: her very own blood-covered letter opener on the floor. The woman who had made millions writing such scenes didn't recognize it when she saw it in real life.

How could she possibly have forgotten the funeral, the horrible ordeal of all those people coming at her, all those people hugging her and patting her and crying against her neck, all those people whose names and faces she couldn't place?

She closed her eyes, gathered her strength. How long ago had that been? Margot said that Connor died on February 22, she was pretty sure. She reached for her purse and pulled out her daily planner. It opened to March 9, but the page was blank. She flipped back to March 8, and there in Margot's handwriting was the word "Scotland". Okay, two weeks then. Connor had been gone for two weeks.

She took a moment to let the grief wash over her with a pain so physical it made her want to retch. She drew a deep breath and allowed another moment for self-pity. The worst thing about losing her memory, she thought, was that she had to keep reliving the fresh pain of Connor's loss. How many days had she woken to face the loss with a piercing newness? Most of them, she supposed.

She yanked her nightgown over her head and pulled on a pair of sweatpants, a hooded sweatshirt and heavy socks. She ran her hands through her ash blonde hair, cut stylishly short. In the kitchen Sheona had coffee ready, and Margot and Evan were already eating.

"Good morning, Mrs Burke," said Evan, standing to leave. The women smiled a greeting. Julianna felt everyone waiting – probably to see if she knew them.

"Good morning, Evan. Sheona. Margaret." She smiled mischievously. "Oops, I mean Margot." She saw their eyebrows shoot up. "Now, now, don't get excited. I have all day to forget you."

The three of them laughed. Julianna poured her own coffee, and Margot pushed a pill across the table toward her. "Your gingko."

Julianna swallowed the pill with a sip of coffee, and accepted a piece of toasted sourdough bread and orange marmalade from Sheona.

"What do you want to do today, Julianna?" Margot asked.

"I want to look online and see if the sheriff's office has turned up anything. Then take a walk, maybe up to Crail."

"I've been online this morning," Margot said. "Nothing yet."

Julianna tried to remember talking to the Charleston County Sheriff's investigators. Surely she had. She hated to admit to her confusion, but curiosity won out. She waited until Evan left the kitchen and Sheona was busy in another room. She slid her chair directly across from Margot and leaned forward.

"Can you tell me about my interviews with the detectives? I'm having trouble remembering."

"Sure," said her assistant. Margot could've come from this part of the world, her mane of curly red-gold hair pulled into a loose ponytail, and freckles liberally sprinkled across her pretty face. With her frequent and easy smile, she looked even younger than thirty-four. She had moved from the South Carolina foothills to attend the College of Charleston, and as so many graduates did, opted to stay in the coastal city. Connor had hired her two years before, stealing her from a wedding planner after observing her efficiency at a neighbor's extravaganza. She had been an English major and a Julianna Burke fan, so she leapt at the opportunity. Julianna questioned how long she'd want to stay cooped up with a couple old enough to be her parents. Connor said the speeches and book tour appearances provided plenty of stimulation. Julianna wasn't so sure.

Margot was of the same generation as her children, but Julianna related to her differently. She seemed older, somehow, more poised, more organized, and certainly more thoughtful.

Now the young woman sipped her coffee. "How can I help?"

Julianna smiled at her fondly. "First, I want to apologize for my behavior last night."

Margot shook her head. "No, Julianna. I understood what was happening. The flight, the rain, the strain on you was terrible."

"I know, my dear. But the histrionics cannot have been easy for you, and I do apologize." She paused for a moment as a wave of memory passed over her. That was how grief felt in these moments of lucidity – like huge waves hitting her over and over, dragging her underwater, hammering her until she couldn't catch her breath. Could forgetting be any worse? She didn't see how. She smiled tremulously.

"So, what did the detectives want to know? And how did I answer them?"

"Well, they talked to you the evening…" Margot looked into her coffee cup. "The evening it happened."

"I called them?"

"I did. You ran up to my room and told me to call 9-1-1."

"So you were in the house too?"

Margot cocked her head. "Yes, I live there, remember?"

"Of course. I, ah, just didn't remember if you were home. It was on a Friday, right?"

Margot nodded. "I left you working on the porch. I had come to see if you wanted an afternoon pick-me-up – coffee or tea or a pina colada." Both women smiled. One of the bonuses Margot brought to the job was bartending. She blended several specialties, from mojitos to watermelon sangrias to frozen pina coladas. Happy hour was a cherished summer tradition for Julianna and Connor and the neighbors they invited over.

"But in February?" Julianna asked.

"Actually, yes. It was one of those freak warm weeks. You had people over the afternoon before and I'd made our first batch of margaritas this year. The Fitzgeralds. The Satterfields. Liza Holland and her friend. You seemed to really enjoy the drinks, so I thought you might like one that day too."

"And did we have one?"

"No." Margot hesitated. "To tell you the truth, I'm not even sure you heard me. You were really hunkered down over your laptop."

"Doing what?"

Now it was Margot's turn to look surprised. "Working on your novel."

"So I *am* in the middle of a novel?" Margot continued to look ill at ease. Julianna sat back, speculating as to what her assistant wasn't saying. "It's okay. You can tell me."

Finally, Margot blurted, "I think you were in the middle of a 'wandering'."

"Oh, I see. What makes you say that?"

"Well, this is going to sound silly, but you have this look you get when I mention a pina colada. You look roguish, younger, like a college girl playing hooky. You once told me that you and your girlfriends skipped class on the first beautiful day each spring and laid in the sun on your dorm roof and made frozen drinks. You kept the blender in your room because you lived beside the rooftop door."

Julianna smiled, remembering those long ago days stretched out on beach towels on the flat surface that served as their personal sundeck. That's why she and her buddies requested third-floor dorm rooms. Who *were* the girls? Martha, she recalled. Nancy. Stefanie with an "f". Jackie. Karen. All of them students at Wake Forest University in Winston-Salem, North Carolina. She was on a memory roll.

Margot was speaking again. "Anyway, when I asked on that Friday afternoon, you looked up and your eyes didn't look quite right. Kind of glazed over. You said, 'No, thank you,' and returned to your keyboard. I honestly didn't think you'd taken in what I asked. I'd never seen you like that before, but I'd heard you and Mr Burke talk about it." She shrugged. "I thought it might be that wandering thing, anyway."

Julianna tried to picture the scene Margot described. Of course she knew her favorite writing spot on the screened porch, knew the long table kept clear of papers because of the constant breeze, knew the way she absently reached for a coffee mug or a sweating glass of iced tea or a chilled glass of Chardonnay. But she couldn't picture a warm day two weeks ago or Margot asking if she wanted a pina colada. Where was that memory? Her newfound confidence began to waver.

"Go on," she said.

"So I went to your office to speak to Mr Burke. He was lying on the sofa with his laptop on his stomach – you know how he used to do that?"

Julianna nodded, her eyes suddenly filling with tears.

"We talked about the invitation from the University of South Carolina for the spring."

Julianna's chin jerked up. "You didn't accept, did you?"

"No, no. Everything… happened. I emailed them that you couldn't make it."

Julianna was unsure she'd ever be able to speak publicly again.

"We only talked for two or three minutes, Mr Burke and I," Margot continued. "Then I went to my room and worked on details of some events we *had* accepted. For next fall and beyond. Then I lay down for a nap."

Julianna nodded to encourage her.

"It was getting dark when I heard you walking through the kitchen. You know how that floor squeaks even if you're barefoot? I think that squeak is what woke me up. Then just a minute or so later, you ran up to my room, shouting, 'Call 9-1-1!' I called on my cell then tried to ask you what had happened, but you couldn't answer. You just screamed, 'Connor! It's Connor!' and ran back downstairs. So I told the dispatcher I thought it was a heart attack. I couldn't think of anything else it could be."

"A heart attack?"

"Yeah, that's why the fire department came to the house. They're first responders."

"I didn't know they did."

"Yeah. I followed you downstairs. That's when I saw Mr Burke." Margot paused, recalling the blood-soaked scene. "And so I called 9-1-1 again and told them it wasn't a heart attack but a stabbing. The Sullivan's Island police were right behind the fire truck."

Julianna waited for Margot to say more, and when she didn't, asked, "So someone came into the house between you speaking to Connor, and me finding Connor in my office? How long was that?"

"Maybe an hour and a half." Margot sighed. "I guess I slept pretty hard. Anyway, I didn't realize all this until later, but apparently Sully's police chief is in transition. They've got some new guy coming in from Pennsylvania."

"Pennsylvania? My word."

Margot laughed, relieved at the momentary break in tension. "And I hear they have Yankees in Atlanta."

Julianna slapped at her hand. "Go on."

"When the interim chief saw that the victim was Mr Burke, he called the mayor, who told him to call the county sheriff for back-up."

"Ah. Lance Royston. Did he come?" Julianna tried to recall seeing her old high school friend, but couldn't.

"He did come. Later. His detectives arrived first. And they were more than a little skeptical that neither of us heard anything. But I honestly didn't and I assured the one I talked to that you were 'in the zone' and didn't either."

"Did I tell them that?" Julianna asked. "That I didn't hear anything?"

Margot nodded.

Julianna had a sudden vision of a slim black woman in a taupe suit and low heels. "Wait, I talked with a woman in the living room, didn't I?" she said, fragments coming back.

Margot looked up. "Yes, that's right."

Julianna closed her eyes and pictured the high-ceilinged living room of her beach house, paneled in the ubiquitous knotty pine, but soaring twenty feet at its apex. She had kept her mother's huge fishing net on one wall, dotted with starfish and sand dollars and shimmering aqua sea glass. It was totally 1960s, her daughter Logan complained, but Julianna liked it.

Now she could see the detective inspecting the net, then taking a seat on the striped couch that picked up the aqua of the sea glass. She tried to hear herself addressing the woman: Detective? Officer? But she drew a blank on the name.

Margot seemed to read her mind. "Detective Cynthia Giles talked to you. Detective Brad Lancaster talked to me. They separated us pretty quickly."

"I can't remember what I told her."

"When the first officers on the scene talked to us, you were struggling. Understandably," Margot added hastily. She paused, choosing her words carefully. "You told them that you didn't hear anything – not me talking to Connor in your office and no one coming in the front door. At first they didn't believe that was possible.

Then they separated us. Detective Lancaster took me, and Detective Giles stayed with you. Ultimately, Harrison and Logan and I told them about your 'wanderings'. I hope that was all right. It seemed the best way to protect you."

"Protect me?"

Margot looked uncomfortable again. "I don't think they ever suspected you of killing Mr Burke. Not really." Julianna looked at her in horror. "But they couldn't believe that you – or I for that matter – didn't hear some sort of commotion. That's the puzzling part. How someone came in so quietly and killed Mr Burke without raised voices or arguments or anything else to alert me and you. I can't answer that."

"And fingerprints?"

Margot looked miserable. "Yours, of course, since it was your letter opener. But apparently Mr Burke pulled it out and smeared any new prints that were on it. So there were only his and yours."

Julianna looked at her in horror, a realization dawning. "He pulled it out?"

Margot drew a deep breath and nodded. "That's one of their theories – that he was sleeping on the couch when he was stabbed. That's why we didn't hear voices. Then he staggered over to the chair by the window and pulled the letter opener out. That's where all the blood was."

Despite the coffee, Julianna felt her energy flagging. Maybe it was the dismal nature of the conversation. Or maybe it was the heaviness of her grief. She glanced out of the kitchen window and wasn't surprised to see that the blue sky had disappeared, and a cloud bank of iron gray was all that was visible. Scotland's weather tended to change hourly, if not more often.

The worst part was seeing her future – whether here on this frigid coast or in the humid subtropics of Sullivan's Island – spool endlessly before her. Knowing that she had to get through the rest of her life without Connor. That life held no interest for her any more, no spark. She tried to remember what she'd been like two weeks ago, and couldn't. Tried to remember what she'd been writing, and couldn't.

That woman was gone, as surely as Connor was.

Her head drooped and she decided to return to bed rather than walk to Crail.

"Oh, one more thing," Margot said. "The detectives asked over and over why Annabelle didn't bark."

Julianna frowned. "Why didn't she? She barks at everyone." She looked around in confusion, and her voice took on a hint of panic. "Wait a minute. Where *is* Annabelle?"

"She's fine," Margot said. "Logan's got her." She paused to give Julianna a moment to calm down. "But the night it happened, she was with you when you came up the stairs. Apparently she was on the porch with you the entire time."

"Annabelle didn't hear someone enter the house?" said Julianna. "That's not possible."

Margot gave a rueful grimace. "That's what the officers thought. I would've thought the same thing." The women eyed each other, contemplating the implication of Margot's words.

"Do they still think that?" Julianna asked. "Do they suspect one of us?"

Margot started to say something, then stopped. She seemed to reconsider. "Well, they allowed us to come here, which tells me no. But they have our address and phone numbers. If they give the word, we have to return within twenty-four hours."

"That's rather strange, isn't it?"

"Well, given that you *are* Julianna Burke, they figure you're not going to go unnoticed in Scotland for long. Plus, Dr and Mrs Fitzgerald and Liza Holland spoke to Sheriff Royston last week. They guaranteed our return if there's any reason he needs us. And I think they lit a fire under him to find the real killer."

Julianna stood shakily. "So now Lance Royston knows about my memory too. We went to high school together, you know. Did I already tell you that?" She closed her eyes, but it only made her dizzy. "I suppose it will be only a matter of time before the media catches on." She looked around as if she'd forgotten why she was in the kitchen. "Did I take my pill already?" Margot nodded.

"Thank you, Margot. For telling me all this." She started to leave, shuffling as if she'd aged ten years since waking. She thought of something, and turned. "Have I asked you about this before?"

Margot looked uneasy for a moment, then nodded. "Every morning," she said.

Chapter 4

Logan awoke on Saturday to a single ring of the doorbell followed by the high-pitched frenzy of Annabelle's barking. When her heart stopped pounding, Logan hurried down the stairs in irritation, yelling for the dog to shut up.

She flung open the door to find Annabelle on the other side of the storm door. She stared in bewilderment for a moment, then opened the door for Liza Holland. "I forgot how much your Maxie looks like Annabelle," she laughed. "It's unbelievable."

The trim older woman in cycling pants and sweatshirt smiled. "All these brown ones look alike," she said, as a fawn-colored Shiba Inu with the same white forehead and foot markings as Annabelle nosed her way into the house. "Is it okay for her to come in? Julianna lets her."

"Sure," said Logan, throwing the door wide. "Can I offer you coffee?"

"If it's no trouble."

Liza Holland unsnapped Maxie's leash, and the two dogs sniffed each other before bounding through the house and into the kitchen. Logan opened the door for them to go on to the porch, and they jumped on to Annabelle's couch. "I agree with them," Logan said. "Best seats in the house."

Liza perched on a stool at the U-shaped kitchen counter. "I just stopped by to see if you want me to walk Annabelle," she said. "I was doing it before Julianna left for Scotland."

"Really? That's awfully nice of you." Logan filled the coffeemaker with cold water, then spooned coffee into the basket filter. "My mother said you guys walked together."

"We did… before," Liza said. "But Julianna hasn't been up to it, and Shibas are terribly high energy. They ramble around the house at night if you don't walk them. But I don't have to tell you that, since you've had her at your place."

"Yeah, I learned the hard way." Logan took two mugs from an antique kitchen cabinet that had been her grandmother's and placed them on the chipped tile counter. "But we very much appreciate you doing that."

"So how's Julianna doing? Have you heard from her?" Liza brushed her silvery-white hair out of her eyes, which were an iridescent shade of blue. She didn't wait for an answer. "I cannot imagine the pain she is in. The way she talked about Connor wasn't the way most women talk about their husbands. Best friend, husband, business partner. It was like she lost everything in one fell swoop."

"Yeah, I know," Logan agreed. "I haven't talked to her, but I got an email from Margot. She said Mother is very much the same – clearer in the mornings and gradually getting worse as the day wears on." She shrugged. "I'm afraid that whatever was going on with her memory has been magnified by losing Connor."

"She told me that Charlie recommended gingko supplements. Are they not helping?"

"Dr Fitz?" Logan asked. "I didn't know. But I suppose they can't hurt. She was so much worse before she and Margot left. Harrison and I are hoping that getting out of this house will help." Logan poured the coffee and slid a mug to Liza.

"And the sheriff's office?" asked the neighbor. "Any progress?"

"They're not telling us. Those two detectives who questioned Mother are coming by this morning to see me and Harrison. Again. What time is it anyway?"

Liza looked at her watch. "Nine o'clock. Do you need me to leave so you can get dressed?"

"No, they aren't coming until ten. I'm glad for the company. Catch me up on island gossip."

Liza threw back her head and laughed. "You know I wasn't born here. I'll never be an insider."

"Be that as it may, what's going on with the Satterfields? And Mullenses? And Fitzgeralds? I need to know we're not the only subject being discussed."

Liza laughed again. "You are bad, my girl. Let's see. I haven't seen the Mullenses all winter. They go to Key West for four months. But the Satterfields and Fitzgeralds were right here two weeks ago, the night before… Well, you know."

Logan turned from where she'd been rummaging in the refrigerator for milk. "No, I don't know. Mother had a party?"

"Not really a party. More like happy hour." Liza shifted to get more comfortable on the wobbly stool. "You may remember we had a real warm week in late February. Margot makes those yummy drinks that we guzzle all summer. But she called and said Connor and Julianna wanted us over for a preview of spring. She made margaritas and we all brought salsa and chips and guacamole. It was fun." She looked sad for a moment. "Who knew it was the last time?"

"Who was here?"

"Charlie and Meg Fitzgerald. Dick and Sunny Satterfield from across the street. My friend Fred Manigault from Mount Pleasant. He was at my house because we had plans for dinner, but we came here instead. Oh, and that woman from your mother's publishing house."

"What woman?"

"You know her. She was back for the funeral."

"There must've been fifteen people from her publisher at the funeral."

"Yes, but this was someone Julianna and Connor worked closely with. I think she even spent the night here. Early fifties? Black hair? Loud?"

Logan grinned. "That's got to be Renata O'Steen."

"Yes, that's the name."

"Did the detectives talk to all those people?"

"I'm sure they did. I know they talked to Fred and me and the Fitzgeralds. But Renata left the morning after the margarita party for

New York. Since she was already out of town when Connor was killed, I don't know whether they tracked her down or not."

Logan twisted the mug in her hands. "I'm not sure I'll have anything more to tell them."

Liza looked at her without answering, waiting quietly, intentionally, her blue eyes kind. It struck Logan that the older woman was a good listener. Maybe that's what Julianna prized in her.

When Logan didn't follow up, Liza said, "Why would you think you wouldn't have anything to tell them? They need to know about Connor – who he was, what he did, who he knew. From everything I've heard, you and he were buddies. Anything you could tell them about him would help."

"Yes," she said slowly. "But they asked about that before. Our relationship, if we got along, things like that. We were okay. But my mother and I not so much. I hadn't been out here for six months before he died."

"I didn't realize. Why was that?"

Logan shrugged. "No real reason. I mean, we didn't have a fight or anything like that. It was just that my mother was wrapped up in her writing. And Connor. She didn't have a lot of time for me."

Liza nodded solemnly. "Not even Christmas? No, that's right. They were in Florida." Liza continued to look at Logan steadily, and Logan expected her to protest on Julianna's behalf. Instead she said, "Mothers and daughters have complicated relationships. They often leave things unsaid and undone without realizing it."

Logan looked up from her coffee mug. "What did she tell you about me?"

"Oh my goodness, what didn't she tell me? 'Logan is smart. Logan is beautiful. Logan is a talented artist but she doesn't know it yet. Logan is sensitive. Logan is kind. Logan is a good cook. I don't think Logan reads my books.'"

Logan let out a bark of laughter. "*What!?* I don't know which is weirder! That she thinks I'm a good cook or that I don't read her books!"

"So you don't cook but you do read?" Liza smiled.

"In a nutshell, yeah." Logan shook her head in perplexity. "I'm probably her biggest fan. And she doesn't even know it, huh?"

"No, she doesn't," Liza said, touching Logan's arm briefly. "You might want to tell her."

"If it's not too late," said Logan. "I'm not sure it would register now." She wiped a T-shirt sleeve across her eyes. "Have you read her novels?"

"I hadn't before I moved here," Liza admitted. "I'd heard of Julianna Burke, of course, but I wasn't a mystery fan. But when I found out she was my neighbor, I began reading them. And I'd contend they are not simply mysteries. Your mother elevates the genre."

"What's your favorite one?"

"That's hard to say. I loved *Charleston at Dusk*. But I'd have to say *A House Built on Sand* was my favorite."

"Ah, the jolly subject of filicide." Logan remembered the newspaper clippings from Julianna's files and thought about mentioning them. Would that be disloyal to her mother?

"What?" asked Liza. "You look like you want to say something."

"I found a folder in her file drawer," Logan said slowly. "Apparently readers send her clippings of real-life murders in the hope she will use them in a book."

"Yes, she mentioned that."

"She did?"

"Sure. When you walk as much as we do, you talk a lot."

Logan relaxed. "I just never knew that some of those things really happened. I thought they came from her imagination."

"Well, believe me, to turn a 3,000- or even a 10,000-word newspaper article into a 100,000-word book takes plenty of imagination," said Liza. "She may have borrowed the smallest grain of an idea, but it was her talent and discipline that turned it into a pearl." She smiled. "You see why I'm not a writer. My metaphors are rather mundane."

Logan laughed. "I guess you're right."

"Do you feel it's somehow cheating to use ideas from real life?"

"Oh no, not at all. It just feels odd to think I know her plots and characters so well and didn't grasp something as central as that."

Liza finished her coffee and slid off the stool, placing her mug in the scratched enamel sink. "Let me get going so you can get dressed for your detectives. I'll be glad to take Annabelle and bring her back in a little while."

"That would be great," Logan said, calling for the dog. "The more that chick gets tired out, the better."

After Liza had left, Logan ran upstairs and dressed in jeans, a lightweight taupe sweater and flip-flops. She pulled her sun-streaked hair into a ponytail and brushed on a little mascara. She had her mother's fair coloring and petite build, while Harrison took after their burly dad.

There were framed photos of her and Harrison in her old bedroom. She could see Rivers Arnette in his son's face. She didn't know her father well and didn't care to. Her mother never talked about him, so most of what she knew came from Harrison and an occasional cryptic comment from Grandmother Arnette. Rivers was her youngest son, wild and handsome enough to turn the head of the bookish Julianna Montague when they met the summer after her junior year at Wake Forest. Rivers was a drinker and a gambler even then, but the prominent Arnette family was able to buy him out of trouble. Julianna found him dashing and exciting, and they married the spring she graduated.

But marriage didn't suit him. His vices got worse, and he ran to fat. He had little interest in his children and, after a while, little interest in coming home. The couple divorced when Logan was two. The senior Arnettes, whose other sons were a bank executive and a lawyer, seemed relieved when he left Charleston.

Logan had seen her father exactly twice during her twenties, when he returned home for his parents' funerals. She was embarrassed by the large, ambling man, his face marked by broken blood vessels. She didn't like seeing him, because her embarrassment led to incredulity that he'd been married to her mother, which led to guilt for feeling that way. When she could get past the guilt, she recognized that she too was glad he'd left Charleston, and glad his leaving had provided an opening for Connor Burke to enter their lives.

The doorbell rang, and she was grateful Annabelle was gone so she didn't have to hear the piercing yap. Coming up the oyster-shell driveway behind Detectives Lancaster and Giles was Harrison, beefy and red-faced and irritable.

"Detectives, it's good to see you," she said, going over their names in her head. Brad Lancaster was blandly handsome and stone-faced, dressed in the navy blazer and khaki slacks that was the business-casual uniform of the Lowcountry. Cynthia Giles was African-American and athletic-looking; Logan got the feeling that her conservative gray pantsuit would be history the minute she was off duty. "You remember my brother, Harrison Arnette."

Harrison barely acknowledged them, slumping into a wing chair and propping his boat shoes on the matching ottoman. Logan left them sitting in silence and went to the kitchen for the fresh pot of coffee she'd brewed. She filled four mugs and placed them on a whimsical fish-shaped tray along with spoons and cream and sugar. The detectives waited politely as she re-entered the living room, while Harrison wore his habitual scowl. He was her only brother and she loved him. But she found that dealing with him from afar was preferable to having him nearby. Not unlike her mother.

"Okay, how can we help you?" she asked, handing around the coffee mugs and motioning for everyone to help themselves to cream and sugar.

Detective Giles launched right in. "Remind me what it is you do, Ms Arnette."

Harrison laughed. "You better ask what she hasn't done," he said. "It won't take as long."

Logan shot him a withering look. "I'm a receptionist at a medical office," she said.

Detective Giles looked up mildly. "And from what your brother says, you've had other jobs?"

"Well, yes," she said, reddening. "Dog groomer. Waitress. Marketing rep. Retail clerk. Art gallery manager."

"She's an aspiring *artiste*," Harrison put in. "Unfortunately, it doesn't pay the bills."

She tried to ignore her brother. "I currently work for Drs Littlemeyer and Johns in Charleston. They're internists."

"And how long have you been with them?"

"Eighteen months."

Harrison hooted. "That's a record, isn't it, Sis?"

Logan clamped her lips to prevent herself from answering him. Detective Giles turned to him. "And, Mr Arnette? You're a real estate developer?"

"That I am."

"Do you build on Sullivan's Island?"

"Don't I wish? If you can talk my mother into moving, we can tear this place down and build a real house." He waved in disgust at the fishing net on the wall of knotty pine. For the first time, Logan felt a twinge of disagreement with her brother. Maybe this old house ought to stay just the way it was, she thought, if for nothing more than to frustrate him.

"In your previous statements," continued Detective Giles, "you indicated that you were at your separate homes on Friday evening, February 22. What we wanted to follow up on this morning is to get impressions of your mother and her assistant and the neighbors."

"Sounds like a blast," Harrison muttered.

"We are still puzzled," said Detective Giles, "as to how someone entered the house without Mrs Burke or her assistant, Margot Riley, hearing anything."

Harrison snorted. "Margot, I'll grant you," he said. "That's a mystery – if she didn't do it. But didn't you get the memo about our mother being a space cadet?"

The officers didn't react. "We heard from you two and Dr Fitzgerald that your mother has memory problems," Detective Giles continued. "Perhaps even dementia. That doesn't explain not hearing the door open or your stepfather being stabbed to death." She looked at them both directly.

"I don't know what we can tell you," Logan said. "We weren't here."

"Can you tell us about your mother's neighbors?"

Harrison looked interested in spite of himself. "Her neighbors? You think Connor outraged somebody with a loud lawn mower or weed whacker?"

"We don't know what to think," Detective Giles answered calmly, her dark face and hazel eyes betraying no trace of annoyance. Yet. "But we know that Mr and Mrs Burke held a gathering here the night before Mr Burke's death. And we wondered if something happened that led to his murder the next day."

Harrison dropped his feet to the floor and leaned forward. "First I've heard of a 'gathering'. Did you know about that, Logan?"

"Yes. Liza Holland mentioned it. The Fitzgeralds, the Satterfields, Liza and a man she's seeing, and Renata from Ironwater."

"What was Renata doing down here?" Harrison asked. Logan shrugged and turned to Detective Giles. "I really don't know. Do you?"

"We've talked to Ms O'Steen," she said, looking unsure about revealing information. She glanced at her partner. "She said she was consulting with your mother about a book she's working on."

"Mom's working on a book?" Harrison asked, looking dumbfounded. "I didn't think she was up to it."

Logan only nodded, unwilling to share what she knew of the half-completed manuscript lying open, waiting for her return, on her bedroom floor.

"So, the neighbors?" Detective Giles prodded.

"Well, let's see," said Harrison. "Old Fitz and his wife are boozers, and they have a passel of maladjusted kids who are waiting for them to die so they can tear each other apart over the oceanfront property."

"Harrison!" Listening to him belittle her was one thing, but Logan loved the Fitzgeralds. Their daughter Britt was her best friend, and she had spent a lot of time in their home. She turned to the detectives.

"Ignore him. Dr Fitzgerald is our family doctor, and Meg is great. We grew up with their family."

Harrison persisted. "Dick Satterfield comes from old Charleston money. His wife, Honey or Bunny or After His Money, showed up from the big city to show us hicks how it's done. She sits on the board of the symphony and talks about it incessantly."

Logan translated: "Mr Satterfield is a perfectly nice man who married Sunny, from Atlanta, I think. She was a talented violinist and now helps the symphony raise money."

Detective Lancaster tried unsuccessfully to hide a smile behind his coffee mug. Cynthia Giles shot him a warning look.

Harrison kept on. "Renata O'Steen was originally Mother's agent, but she went to work for her publisher, Ironwater, and became sort of her editor and liaison. Of course, the even better connected Connor – who up and married the author – represented a challenge for her. If we're looking for a murderer among the party guests, my money's on Renata."

Logan threw up her hands. "Renata and Mother have been close for Mother's entire career. No way she'd do anything to hurt her."

"Well then," said Harrison, "that leaves the lovely Liza Holland and her mysterious beau." He turned to Logan. "Who'd she bring? That gay guy with the designer house?"

"She said his name was Fred Manigault. He lives in Mount Pleasant."

"Fred Manigault! I know him! He owns that restaurant on the marsh. The Mangrove. Funny he never mentioned he was consorting with Lady Liza."

Logan rolled her eyes and waited for the detectives to say something. But they were carefully noting every crazy thing Harrison said. She supposed they rarely got such unfiltered opinions.

A knock on the door diverted everyone's attention. Before Logan could get up, the door opened and a slender hand slipped in, unhooking a leash. "She's home!" called a woman's voice. "I won't disturb you."

Annabelle charged into the living room, nails skittering across the wood floor and barking madly. "Give her a minute," Logan instructed.

"She'll calm down. It's okay, girl. Come over here." The dog took up watch beside Logan's chair, her tail down and her eyes on the detectives and Harrison.

"You'd never know I was family," Harrison grumbled. "She hates me as much as she does you guys."

Detective Giles looked at Detective Lancaster and a silent message passed between them.

"That was something else we wondered about," said Detective Lancaster, slipping into the conversation for the first time. "The dog."

"As in why does our mother have such an obnoxious dog?"

Logan imagined that Detective Lancaster would like to punch Harrison's smug face. "No," he said calmly, "as in why didn't the dog bark when someone came into the house and killed Mr Burke?"

Harrison looked at Annabelle. "Good question," he said, serious for the first time. "She barks at everybody who comes to that door."

Logan thought of something. "There's a storm door at the front," she said. "Mother and Connor sometimes left the front door open to let in the afternoon sun. So maybe Annabelle saw who was coming in and knew them."

Harrison shook his head. "It wouldn't matter. That dog barks even when Mother comes in."

"Well, Harry," said Logan, deliberately using a name he hated, "I'm not sure you're the best judge of that. You're never here."

The detectives remained silent, watching the siblings. Harrison smirked. "Well, *Sis*," he said, using a nickname she hated equally, "you're the only one I can think of that Annabelle *wouldn't* bark at. So I guess that makes you or Margot or Mother the prime suspect."

For a long moment, everyone looked at the Shiba sitting alert at Logan's side. "Mr Arnette," said Detective Lancaster, skimming over Harrison's accusation, "earlier you mentioned your suspicion of your mother's assistant. What can you tell us about Margot Riley?"

"Ah, Margot's okay, I guess." Harrison seemed bored with his earlier game. "But who knows? She hooked her wagon to Mother's star, and it was fading. Maybe Connor was trying to fire her."

"That's ridiculous," Logan interrupted. "Connor was not trying to fire Margot. Mother needs her more than ever. We all do."

"And why is that, Ms Arnette?" asked Detective Lancaster.

"Isn't it obvious?" Harrison answered instead. "Our mother's losing her mind."

Chapter 5

Julianna woke for the second time, groggier than she'd been before. She looked at her watch on the bedside table: ten minutes past noon. The sun was shining brightly for the moment. She made her way into the adjoining bathroom, modernized and painted a cheery aqua. She stopped as her mind sought the memory the color evoked. *Jewelry?* she conjectured. *Decorative bottles?* She couldn't quite retrieve it.

She washed her face and applied foundation, powder and lipstick, noting the wrinkles around her mouth, eyes, and neck. She attempted a smile, which helped a little. She applied mascara to frame her blue-green eyes, then wet her fingers and ran them through her hair with a bit of gel. She saw a bit of light gray at the roots, disguised by the ash blonde but visible. She'd need to go to her hairdresser soon. Connor always said she didn't look her age, but it was catching up with her, that was for sure. She looked down at her heavy sweats. They would be necessary, and probably a coat, scarf, and woolly hat as well.

She walked through the kitchen and spied a note propped against the salt shaker on the butcher block table.

Julianna,

Please don't leave without me. I'll walk to Crail with you.
Margot

Julianna decided she didn't want company, so she walked quietly into the mud room. She found outer garments hanging beside the door, including Connor's shiny waterproofs. She ran her hand down one sleeve and placed her face in the jacket, but he wore it over his clothes, and it held no scent of him. When was he coming anyway? The days got so muddled. She'd have to ask Margot when she got back.

She opened the door on to a patch of pea gravel, the glare from the North Sea nearly blinding her. She ducked back inside and found sunglasses in a jumbled basket by the door. She pulled the door shut without locking it, and set off on the Fife Coastal Path, just steps from the doorway.

From this vantage point, the path allowed a glorious view of the sea and rock-strewn grassland plunging to it. The path undulated, for a while perching at cliff height above the water, then plummeting to dissect pasture-like stretches. Admittedly, the terrain was steep and rough, but back in the States it wouldn't have mattered. Developers would have been plonking houses all over this landscape. That was what appealed to her and Connor. Scotland remained stubbornly rural, with tiny fishing villages rather than giant resorts dotting its seaside. Serious golfers flocked here for serious golf, but it wasn't a place you came for beaches or sun or crowds.

Julianna trudged for over a mile, chilled by the wind in the elevated places, but more comfortable when the path dipped. She walked with her head down and hands stuck deep in her coat pockets, her mind blank, scarcely noticing when she passed the red sandstone outcroppings that hid the Caves of Caiplie. She and Connor had explored the caves, or *coves* in Scottish, where Christian monks and pilgrims had sheltered in the ninth century. There was a time she'd been moved by the wild beauty of this ancient land, so unlike the flat coast of South Carolina. But not today. Today she felt heavy, dull.

She looked up when she reached the stone walls of Crail Harbour, and followed the trail above it. The boats that hadn't gone out for the day were mired in tidal mud. She recalled seeing the harbor for the first time and being amazed at the muck-bound boats. Then the tide had turned and the water surged back inside the walls.

On arriving in Crail, she chose a cobblestone street lined with rows of houses to climb to the main road, walking up and up and up, pausing to catch her breath and note the colorful painted doors. *Logan would like this,* she thought with a sudden pang that broke through her weariness. Her daughter painted lovely seascapes and marsh scenes, but she had no confidence in her work.

She rounded the final residence and emerged on to the High Street, making her way to a cozy teashop. A bell on the shop door jangled, and Julianna sank gratefully on to the chair nearest the door, piling her coat and woolens on another seat at the small table. She was suddenly so tired that her muscles trembled, and when she picked up the menu, it quivered.

When the young waitress came, Julianna ordered a hot chocolate and a blueberry scone, then sat in exhaustion, hoping the snack would perk her up. She looked around the light-filled shop, hung with vibrantly painted scenes of the fishing village and photographs of St Andrews, a few miles down the road. Connor played the famous course often, and they'd returned many evenings for drinks or dinner along the cobbled streets that surrounded the fifteenth-century university. Was he playing there today? She couldn't remember. Wait a minute. Had Connor even arrived yet? It seemed that maybe they'd flown separately this trip. But why would they do that? Julianna was too tired to figure it out. The waitress placed a thick ceramic mug before her, along with steaming cocoa in a metal pitcher. Julianna poured the hot liquid and sipped before turning hungrily to the scone. She was halfway through when she realized her trembling had ceased and she was feeling better. She slowed down in order to relish the food, and glanced out of the window. Few people were on the High Street and they were probably locals, she thought idly. Tourists didn't arrive until much later – folks from the west coast of Scotland, or England, or even the States and Asia.

In fact, why was she here now? She thought back to that morning and could see the planner she'd pulled from her purse. March 9. The season for some occasional warm days on Sullivan's Island. And yet here she was in Scotland, where winter would keep its unyielding grip for another three months, at least by her standards. Connor must have talked her into coming early. Maybe there was a tournament he wanted to play.

Satisfied, she leaned back in her chair and looked out of the window again. She saw a knot of people gathered in front of the bed and breakfast across the High Street. She looked on curiously, but the bystanders blocked her view of what was happening.

She poured the last half-cup of chocolate, which was still pleasantly warm. Did she want to walk back to the stone house and work on her book? Where was she with that? She thought hard, but couldn't come up with her storyline. Where was Margot? Julianna looked around as if she might have misplaced her assistant. Margot could catch her up.

But no, that wasn't what Margot did. Connor. Connor was the one who kept up with the plots, encouraged her to focus, even suggested which characters might surge to the forefront. Julianna's breathing grew shallow, then more rapid. Why couldn't she remember her book? And where was Connor?

A sudden vision from the night before flashed across her mind: Margot kneeling by her dining room chair as Julianna screamed and screamed. As if from a distance, she could hear her own shrieks that Connor was not coming, that he was dead. Margot was hugging her, trying to prevent her flailing, but there was something else, something she was whispering. What was it?

"Ma'am, are you all right?" The young waitress was back.

Julianna's head jerked up, but her eyes were unseeing. It was Margot's pale face before her. She strained to hear Margot's words: "We came," she whispered. "We came…"

"Ma'am?" An older woman stood behind the waitress, twisting a dishcloth in her hands. Julianna stared at them blankly. The older woman stepped forward and touched Julianna's shoulder. "Are you all right, dear?"

Julianna tried to block her voice. She wanted to hear Margot. *If Connor's dead, why did we come?*

"We came…" Margot reluctantly whispered, "we came… because the sheriff thought you might be in danger too."

Julianna was suddenly overheated and used her cloth napkin to wipe the perspiration off her forehead and upper lip. The older woman handed her a glass of water, and she gulped it. She panted for a few more moments, heart pounding, until her breathing gradually slowed. Finally, her heart slowed as well.

She looked up with a mixture of bafflement and embarrassment. "I'm so sorry. I'm fine. Thank you." And then witlessly, "The scone was delicious."

The women nodded and backed away, clearly relieved that their customer wasn't going to pass out in the tearoom. The waitress waved at the commotion outside. "At least they's already here, the medics are. In case you need 'em, ma'am."

Julianna's eyes swung once more to the gathering across the street. The waitress was right. Paramedics were loading a stretcher into a white ambulance with green and blue blocks along its side. One of them turned to shake the hand of a man who remained crouched on the ground. He must've been tending the distressed person until they arrived.

The man stood and slapped the orange and yellow herringbone pattern on the rear doors. Then he turned and faced the teashop. He was wearing a British driving cap, a long black coat and black leather gloves, but Julianna recognized him instantly.

She bolted from her chair and flung open the shop door. A blast of cold jolted her as she stepped on to the pavement. She ran across the High Street and pushed through the stragglers, who were beginning to disperse as the ambulance pulled away.

She looked left and right, and not seeing the man in the black coat, rushed into the bed and breakfast. The parlor was empty.

Julianna stood, her mind racing. Her book's central character surfaced in her head, fully formed. Martin Engler. A psychiatrist who was told a terrible secret by a patient. A secret that the patient couldn't have known would be personal for Dr Engler.

Minutes ago she had nearly been in the throes of a panic attack because she couldn't remember her plot, couldn't remember her main character. What had jarred her memory? Julianna looked around wildly once more for the man she had seen – the man who apparently had come to the aid of an ill man right on the High Street in Crail.

Her neighbor, Charlie Fitzgerald.

Chapter 6

Logan climbed the stairs to her neighbor's front entrance, marveling at the difference the enclosing of the ground floor made to the house's grandiose appearance. Where her mother's house had its original wooden stilts with only a maid's quarters and a storage room underneath – gray, gray, and more gray – the Fitzgerald house sported a three-story façade of coral stucco. And instead of her mother's creaky wooden stairs, she was walking up an expansive staircase of concrete edged with brick, with enough room for five abreast on each curved step.

Logan remembered when the Fitzgerald house had looked almost exactly like the Burke house. She'd spent many a night here with Britt in a corner bedroom with a sloped ceiling. But Britt was now a family medicine resident in DC, and Charlie and Meg had literally raised the roof so that all the top-floor rooms had nine-foot ceilings. Or higher. Practicing in nearby Charleston paid well, she thought with an appreciative glance at Meg's new furniture on the streetside porch.

She rang the doorbell. Meg, dressed in yoga pants that did nothing to hide her ample rear, answered the door. "Logan!" she cried, enveloping the younger woman in a squeeze. "How good to see you! Come in the house."

Logan relaxed into Meg's effortless hospitality, as she had since she was a child. "Have you heard from your mother?" asked the older woman.

Logan shrugged. "That's kind of why I'm here," she said, following Meg into her bright kitchen and accepting a cup of coffee. She pulled a high-backed stool from the gargantuan island and sat. "I hardly know how to ask this. But is Dr Fitz home?"

Meg shook her head, her tousled auburn curls bouncing. "No, he's at a conference in New York. Why?"

"Mother just called, rather insistent, saying she saw him in Crail."

Meg grimaced. "Oh, Logan, I'm so sorry. I know Charlie hoped that getting Julianna away from the place where Connor died would help. It sounds like she's more confused than ever."

Logan couldn't let it go. Her mother was so sure she'd seen her longtime friend and physician. Meg was looking at her with concern.

"Start at the beginning," she said, "and tell me everything."

Logan felt a measure of the peace she had always felt in this house, the warmth that Meg had exuded when she and Britt suffered the inevitable slights of middle school, the broken hearts of high school. How many times had she wished that Meg, rather than Julianna, were her mother?

"Well, from the *very* beginning," Logan said, taking Meg up on her invitation, "you know that Mother was distant when I was growing up. We talked about that."

Meg smiled and nodded, just as Logan remembered her doing on all those summer afternoons when she and Britt came into a very different kitchen, sand on their feet, the smell of coconut sunscreen on their skin, gulping bottles of sports drink. Meg was always around with a smile and a snack and, more often than not, a toddler on her hip.

"Your mother's a writer," Meg offered. "People like that live in their heads in a way the rest of us don't."

"Whatever," Logan said, sounding like her middle-school self. "I long ago resigned myself to her and Connor being a team. A rather impenetrable team. Harrison and I felt like outsiders in ways Britt and your other kids never did."

Meg raised an eyebrow but said nothing.

"But that wasn't all bad. When I began to notice that Mother's memory was slipping, I was glad to let Connor handle it. After all, those two had handled her life and career for years without me. But

I had no idea of the extent of it until these past two weeks, watching poor Margot try to negotiate everything." Logan looked up. "I even felt relieved when Margot took her off to Scotland. Is that awful?"

"Well, it's human," Meg said.

"I'm feeling guilty now, like I need to get involved in her doctor's appointments and how she's going to live, going forward. But I hardly know where to start. So when she called, saying she'd seen Dr Fitz in Crail, I thought, well, that was one place to begin."

Meg nodded. "I can't tell you much except that Charlie is definitely not in Scotland. We can call him in New York, if you like."

"Yes, that would be good."

"I can't tell you anything I overheard between Julianna and Charlie," she continued. "Patient confidentiality and all that. But anything she told *me* that I think you should know, I'll be glad to share."

"Thanks, Meg. I'm really out of the loop. I didn't even know little things – like her taking gingko, until Liza Holland mentioned it."

"Can't hurt. You can research it online if you like. And fish oil. Unfortunately, as you probably know, there's no treatment for dementia."

Logan's head jerked up. "Does she actually have a diagnosis of dementia?"

Meg looked as if she'd like to take her words back. "I shouldn't have said that. I was making a leap. You need to prepare a list of questions and go with Julianna the next time she sees Charlie. You don't need me crashing around in the middle of this like a bull in a china shop."

"You don't crash," Logan said with a smile. "Maybe you're a little bullish. But I am beginning to realize I need to be involved, however much I don't want to be." She sighed. "How often did you see her, Meg?"

"It depended on the season. We did a lot of happy hours in the spring and summer and fall. But when we saw her in late February – the day before Connor died – I hadn't seen her in probably four months."

"What did you think when you saw her in February?"

Meg stood to reheat her coffee in the microwave. "Honestly? I thought she'd gone downhill."

"Just since last fall?"

"Yeah."

"I hadn't spent any time with her for six months," Logan said. "That's why I was so taken aback these past few weeks. I didn't know what was normal and what was grief-related."

Meg sat back down. "Don't beat yourself up, Logan. She'd learned so many coping tricks, it was hard to tell what was going on."

"What do you mean?"

"She and Connor and Margot seemed to have a kind of shorthand. So when a topic came up, Connor or Margot had a way of reframing someone's question or comment. It was pretty subtle, but I got the feeling it was intended to give Julianna time to catch up. Of course, I could have been imagining it."

"I doubt it, Meg. You've known Mother for what, thirty years?"

"Something like that." Meg paused, her eyes wandering to the bank of windows that provided a view of the ocean. "But you know, Logan, now that I'm recalling that afternoon in February, something occurs to me." Meg was silent for another moment, a crease appearing between her brows.

"Something about Mother?" Logan prompted.

"Sort of," she said slowly. "And Connor. Someone asked Julianna what she'd been working on all winter. Connor laughed and said it had taken almost all season to come up with a title. We, of course, clamored to know what it was. But Julianna looked kind of dazed. I actually wondered if she had forgotten it." Meg stopped again, as if re-creating the scene in her mind. "Connor said, 'You don't mind if I tell them, do you, Jules? It's never too early to generate buzz.' And Julianna said, 'I guess not. But keep in mind it's a working title.'"

Logan waited. "And?"

"And Connor said it would be called *Murder, Forgotten*."

Meg and Logan sat over their coffee, as Logan tried to fit the title with the first chapter she'd read the night before about Dr Martin Engler. The manuscript was riveting, but she had underestimated how tired she was. She fell asleep after ten pages, and woke in the middle of the night with the lamp on and her hand caught in the binder. "*Murder, Forgotten*, huh? Yikes. Did anybody laugh?"

"No," said Meg. "But there was an uncomfortable silence. I think Connor realized it and jumped in to tell us about the book."

"What did he say?"

"He said it was a doozy, maybe shaping up to be her best ever. That, of course, got everyone's attention. But your mom's publisher friend, Renata, did *not* look happy. She said, 'Careful, Connor. You don't want to give too much away.'"

Logan nodded, interested.

"But a little while later, Renata went to the bathroom. And Sunny Satterfield said, 'Quick, Connor. Tell us what the book's about.'"

"And did he?"

"A little bit. Let's see if I can remember. He said it was about a psychiatrist who is treating a man and finds out something about the man's daughter. And somehow it relates to the psychiatrist's own past. I'm not clear on the details. Connor didn't have time to say anything more before Renata came back and shut him down."

"It must be set in the days when psychiatrists had time to listen to patients," Logan said.

Meg laughed. "You're right. Charlie complains that they don't do much more than push meds these days. He suggested that afternoon that Julianna make the guy a psychologist or counselor instead. But she said no, he was a full-blown psychiatrist. It was like he was real and already living in her head." Meg smiled fondly. "She really has a terrific talent, you know."

"That she does." Logan stood to place her cup in the sink, and abruptly remembered why she'd come over. "Can we make that call to Dr Fitz now?"

"Sure." Meg walked into the living room to retrieve her cell phone.

She held it to her ear as she walked back to the kitchen.

"Hope I'm not disturbing you," she said, nodding at Logan. "Charlie, Logan is over here and said she received a disturbing call from Julianna. She thought she saw you in Crail, Scotland." She listened for a few moments, smiling sadly. "That's what I told her. Okay. See you then." Meg laid her phone on the island. "He's on a break from the conference and will be home tomorrow night. I'm sorry, Logan."

"No need to be sorry," she said, standing. "Like I said, I'm afraid Mother is getting worse. I'll talk to Margot as soon as they get home." She hugged Meg again, wondering what it would be like to have her as a mother. Then she felt guilty for thinking it.

Out on the street in front of the Fitzgerald house, Logan contemplated what to do next. She wanted to get back to her mother's manuscript. But Meg's conversation about the final evening of Connor's life had left her curious about the people who were there. Could something have happened that led to Connor's death the next day?

Who did Liza say was present? Charlie and Meg Fitzgerald. Dick and Sunny Satterfield. Liza and her friend Fred Manigault. Margot. Renata O'Steen. Mother and Connor.

She gazed at the Satterfields' crisp, white-brick house directly across the street. The house sprawled over two lots and was lushly landscaped with hardwoods and palms, and azaleas that would burst into bloom in a few weeks. She decided to pay a quick visit.

After ringing the doorbell, Logan heard a disembodied voice and looked to her right to find a shiny speaker in the wall. "It's Logan Arnette, Sunny," she said loudly, wondering when the Satterfields had added a speaker system. She heard the sliding of a deadbolt, unusual on this street. It occurred to her for the first time that the neighbors might be nervous at the thought of a killer walking into the Burke house, unheeded, unseen. Had Meg's door been similarly bolted? She didn't remember hearing it scrape, but Meg might have seen her coming up the steps.

Sunny's appearance startled her. Ordinarily the woman matched her name, bouncy and effusive with shoulder-length blonde hair and a year-round tan. But now she looked drawn and pasty, her eyes darting nervously over Logan's shoulder.

"Logan!" she said with relief, her manners taking over. "What a pleasure. I've just put on tea. Will you have some?"

"Thanks, Sunny, but I've been drinking coffee with Meg. I've had plenty."

Sunny ushered her inside, locking and bolting the door behind her. The Satterfields' black lab, Buster, whined, and ignoring Logan pawed the door. "Okay, boy, you can go out. Just a minute, Logan." Sunny led the big dog to the French doors that opened on to a rear deck. Unbolting and unlocking one, she let him bound out. She looked around sheepishly. "I know he's glad you're here."

Logan looked at the woman she had once thought so glamorous. "Sunny, is everything all right?"

"Dick's out of town," she said, laughing nervously. "I like to keep Buster in here with me when I'm by myself. Silly, I know."

"I don't remember you doing that," Logan said. On the contrary, Sunny was known in the neighborhood for working in her yard in a bikini or short shorts, garage and doors and windows flung open wide.

"Well, you remember me before we had a murder across the street."

Logan looked at her. "I'm sorry. I've been so consumed with my family that I guess I hadn't considered what a murder meant to everyone else."

Sunny motioned her to the kitchen, and Logan took a seat at a breakfast table set in a bay window overlooking the back yard. A bottle of bourbon sat beside the sink and Sunny poured some into a mug, added a tea bag and boiling water. "Sure you won't have some?" she asked.

Logan shook her head. She hadn't known Sunny to drink in the middle of the day either.

Sunny pulled out a chair across from Logan, holding her hands around the hot mug as if to warm them. Her voice was nearly a whisper. "This neighborhood always felt so safe. And to think that someone walked right in – in broad daylight – and stabbed Connor. It's just… it's just ruined *everything*." She took a big gulp of tea. Logan didn't know what to say. Sunny took another drink and sat up straighter. "I'm sorry, Logan. That sounds terribly narcissistic, I know. Dick says it's not about me. But I don't know how to…" She flapped her hands helplessly, her unspoken words hanging in the air. Again, she strained to pull herself together. "How's your mother doing?" she asked. "I think that was the saddest funeral I've ever been to."

Logan remembered the crowded sanctuary in the Methodist church down the road, Margot's tears, Julianna's confusion, Harrison's anger, her own emptiness. The day had been gray and cold, with a fierce wind whipping through the Spanish-moss-laden trees in the churchyard. Altogether dismal.

"Hard to tell." Logan wagged her hand to indicate indecision. "She's in Scotland, you know." She paused. "Did you see her much over the fall or winter?"

"Not really. They were in Florida over Christmas, weren't they?" Sunny continued without waiting for an answer. "I walked with her and Liza a time or two when I didn't have Buster with me. Those Shibas of theirs don't want any other dogs around. And I think I saw her sometime around Thanksgiving."

Logan had spent Thanksgiving with three of her work colleagues and their friends. She had waited until the last moment for an invitation to dinner with her mother and stepfather, but it never came. "How was Mother when you saw her at Thanksgiving?"

"She seemed fine," Sunny said, drinking deeply from her bourbon-laced tea. "Why?"

"I mean, did she seem forgetful? How did her memory seem to you?"

Sunny looked blank. "Well, Julianna is always a bit spacey. That's just her artistic side, don't you think? Some of my musician friends are the same way."

"Well, how about when she and Connor had you over two weeks ago for happy hour? Did you notice anything then?"

"The day before Connor was killed?" Sunny seemed to withdraw. Logan wondered if her newfound fear would keep her from remembering anything else. But Sunny had a thoughtful look on her face. "Well, now that you mention it," she said, "it did seem like Connor and Margot answered for her several times when people asked her questions. I knew she was deep into a novel, so I didn't think anything about it. Connor did tell us a little bit ab–" An ear-splitting bark sliced through the room. Sunny jumped up with a cry, knocking her chair over and backing away from the bay window. Logan stood and saw a squirrel racing up a tree, Buster circling beneath.

"It's okay, Sunny. Buster's after a squirrel."

She gave a shaky laugh. "I'm sorry. I guess I'm on edge."

You think? It was all Logan could do not to say it out loud. "When is Dick coming home?"

"Tomorrow."

"Does he…" Logan didn't know how to ask this tactfully. "Does he know… how anxious you are about being alone?"

Sunny shrugged. "He installed the front door speaker and new deadbolts."

Now that Logan was standing, she wanted to take the opportunity to leave. But she had one more question. "Sunny, is there anything you can think of that seemed off that last afternoon you were at Mother's house? One of the guests talking about anything that struck you as odd?"

"You mean besides Renata looking like she could kill Connor?" Sunny caught herself and slapped a hand over her mouth. "Oh, I didn't mean that literally."

"What *did* you mean?"

"Connor and Julianna told us the title of the book she's working on. *Murder Forgets*. Or something like that. So of course we were dying to hear the plot. Connor was trying to tell us and Renata would not allow it. Then she left the room for a minute and I asked Connor to spill more details." She giggled. "He would have too, if that Yankee Ice Queen hadn't sailed back in."

"So she was really upset?" asked Logan.

"Seemed to be."

"But not enough to harm Connor?"

Sunny giggled again. "For giving away the plot of a book? That would be crazy, wouldn't it?"

Logan raised an eyebrow in assent. "Nothing else struck you?"

"Well, you have to realize I was probably on my third Margot margarita by then. Nothing much was striking me."

Logan couldn't think of anything else to ask. When Sunny realized she was leaving, she stopped her. "Wait until I get Buster back in." She opened the back door and called the Labrador. That was when the incongruity struck Logan.

"Sunny, if you're concerned about the murderer coming back," she said, "you must think Connor's murder was random. Not pointed specifically at him."

"I wouldn't say that." She tucked a piece of lank hair behind one ear. "We never think it could be someone we know, do we? Until it's too late."

Chapter 7

Margot spun her laptop around so Julianna could see Logan's message. "She went to the Fitzgeralds' house," she said, pointing to Logan's email. "Mrs Fitzgerald said Dr Fitz is at a conference in New York. They called him there."

Julianna sat back, stewing. Margot had expressed doubt the previous evening, telling her that Charlie Fitzgerald couldn't possibly be in Crail, telling her that Logan, five time zones behind them, would visit next door to prove it. They'd gone to bed before hearing from Logan, but her email was waiting when they woke.

But Logan hadn't proved anything, had she? She and Meg might think Charlie was in New York, but that didn't make it a fact.

She leaned forward. "Ask Logan if they called his hotel room or his cell."

Margot shot her a surprised look, then dutifully typed in the question and sent it to Logan. "Done," she said. "Now what?"

Julianna sighed. "Coffee." She got up and helped herself to the pot that Margot had brewed. She felt Margot's eyes on her back as she poured, and turned to face her, sipping from her heavy mug. "What?"

"I don't want to nag," said Margot, pushing a pill across the table, "but if you'd gotten me like I asked you to before walking to Crail, this would be a moot point."

Julianna's temper flared for a moment, then subsided. "You're absolutely right," she said. "You would have seen that it was Charlie, and we wouldn't be having this conversation."

But was the man on the High Street Charlie? In the clear light of a new day, was she sure that she'd seen her next-door neighbor? She remembered her trembling and anxiety in the teashop, enough to bring the concerned owner to her table. Had her untrustworthy mind juxtaposed a stranger acting in a medical capacity with her physician back home?

She snatched the gingko pill from the table and cocked her head. It was a capsule filled with brown powder. Julianna smiled at her assistant as she gulped it. "I'm sorry I've been such a pill."

Margot laughed. "Never. What's on the agenda for today?"

"Actually, I'm eager to get back to my book."

"Really?" Margot said with genuine surprise. "Julianna, that's wonderful." She paused, choosing her words carefully. "I know that Mr Burke worked closely as your first reader. If you need me to take on any of that, I'll be happy to."

Julianna pulled a yogurt from the refrigerator and sat across from Margot. She stared at her silently. "You know, that's not a bad idea." She ripped the foil off the top and plunged her spoon in and stirred. "Did you bring the binder with the pages?"

"No, that was Mr Burke's area," Margot said. "Where do you keep it?"

Julianna looked blank for a moment. "In my office?" she spoke largely to herself. "No, that's not right." She closed her eyes, picturing Connor lying on her office couch, laptop on his stomach. A wave of pain hit her so hard it felt like nausea. She heard herself laugh and say to her husband, "That looks so uncomfortable. How can you possibly read like that?" He only grunted and grinned at her.

But he wasn't reading her pages. He read book reviews and schedules like that. How did he read her book pages?

Her eyes flew open. "He read them in bed," she said. "The binder is in his bedside table. Back home."

"In that case," Margot said, "email me the manuscript and I'll read it on my laptop."

"I will," said Julianna. "But let me read over it first. It's been so long since I worked on it that I need to catch up myself."

She ate her yogurt, idly looking out of the kitchen window at the rain drumming against the house. There was a heavy rain in this new book. Who was caught in the downpour? Oh yes, Martin Engler. The family doctor. No, the psychiatrist.

Her mind returned to the teashop, to gazing out of its window on to a crowd of bystanders and a Scottish ambulance. She'd been unable to retrieve a memory of her book until she thought she saw Charlie Fitzgerald. Did that mean something? Or was it a random synapse firing at the word "doctor"?

In a moment she'd go to her desk in the study – the desk shoved up against a large picture window overlooking the gray waves crashing with whitecaps. At least, it'd be that way for a while. Maybe it would be calm and blue this afternoon. Scotland was like that. She'd drape a blanket over her shoulders in order to feel cozy and comfortable on this wind-lashed day.

She pictured the scene, and herself in it. She pictured herself trying to access the manuscript from her files. But what was the name of the file?

"Margot?"

Her assistant looked up from her laptop. "Hmm?"

"Do you remember the name of my book?"

"*Murder, Forgotten*. Great title."

"But is that how I filed it?"

Margot gave her a quizzical look. "No, your manuscripts are marked 'First Novel', 'Second Novel' and so on. You said you never have a title when you start, and usually change it a couple of times as you're writing. So this one should be filed as 'Seventh Novel'."

Julianna sighed in relief. "That's right." Finishing her breakfast, she refilled her coffee mug and headed for the study. "Wish me luck."

"You know I do," said Margot. "I cannot wait to read the next Julianna Burke novel."

Julianna raised her head to find the Atlantic Ocean calm and turquoise. But the wide, white beach had disappeared and been replaced by a rocky, plunging coastline. She looked around in bewilderment, and reached for her coffee cup. It was cold, not even lukewarm.

She turned and looked around the room she was in, not screens at all but aged plaster, interspersed with book-lined shelves. *Scotland*, she recalled. She shook her head as if the physical act would clear the fog.

But it wasn't fog so much as it was total immersion in another time, another place. Dr Martin Engler lived in the wine country of northern California, an idyllic and wealthy setting that she and Connor had explored before she set out to write this story. She pictured them now in their rented BMW convertible, splurging on the bed and breakfasts of Napa Valley and sampling pinot noirs and cabernet sauvignons and heavy merlots at outdoor tables next to the wineries. Trouble was, she could taste-test only three glasses a day before she was tipsy. Connor was a little better, so she'd sip from his glass by the day's last stop.

She gazed toward the kitchen. Where was Connor anyway? She wanted to discuss Martin Engler with him. She stood to stretch her cramped back. How long had she been reading? There were some parts of the book that were familiar and some parts that seemed new. That was the joy of taking a little hiatus. You could read your own manuscript as if it were someone else's.

Martin Engler was one of her best creations, she realized with satisfaction: complex, tortured, neither good nor evil, merely a man caught in a trying situation. Where had she conceived of him? She couldn't remember a time that he didn't exist in her head. But that wasn't saying much, she admitted.

As a psychiatrist, he heard other people's secrets. And one day a man came in with a terrible secret, a dark secret, about his unhealthy desire for his own daughter. The patient wasn't a particularly bad man. In fact, that's why he'd come to Dr Engler. He wanted to be relieved of this desire, through medication or hypnosis or whatever it took. The secret he was keeping from his wife and sixteen-year-old daughter was taking a toll. The girl would be in the house two more years before leaving for college. He had to find a way to get through those two years.

Julianna sat back down and checked the number at the bottom of her last page: 190. Well over halfway. This was the point at which she liked to get Connor's input. What questions did he have? Was there a character he was particularly interested in? Where did he think the story would end? If he got it right, she knew she had given away too much.

Thrillers and mysteries were elaborate puzzles, but there was an unspoken contract between reader and writer. The ending needed to surprise but be plausible. A character dealt with only fleetingly couldn't pop up as the murderer. A detective or amateur sleuth couldn't simply think up a solution. There had to be events or clues that helped point to it.

That's what she treasured about Connor. The basics could go unspoken between them.

She could see him sitting up in their bed on Sullivan's Island, reading glasses pushed on top of his messy hair, pen in hand, saying, "Jules, I'm not getting why Dr Engler cares so much," and she'd known she hadn't adequately conveyed Martin's back story. Sometimes that was a problem. Martin Engler existed so fully formed in her imagination that she assumed the reader could see him, hear him, understand him, too. Connor, as first reader, could point out where she hadn't yet made the case.

The fingers of a memory were scratching at the back of her mind. Connor had said that exact thing about Dr Engler – that he didn't know why the psychiatrist cared so much about this particular patient. When had he said that? She tried to picture what Connor was wearing – flannel pajama pants or boxer shorts? But all she could see was his blue T-shirt. Was the comforter on the bed the winter one or the summer one? She closed her eyes, and the heavy olive and brown brocade swam into view. It was winter. Had she re-worked the book after his comment?

She couldn't remember. She tried to recall what part he had underlined as he questioned Martin's motivation. Something about Martin following his patient in the driving rain to see where he lived, to get a glimpse of the daughter. She scrolled back to the section.

Connor had been right, she thought now, having read the pages cold. Martin's actions did seem over the top. Because the reader didn't know at this point that Martin Engler and his wife had given up a daughter for adoption sixteen years before. The reader had no way of understanding the depth to which the patient's story affected him. She hadn't corrected it yet. Why not? What had she been doing that prevented her from an immediate rewrite? She'd have to ask Connor.

Julianna stood to stretch again, acknowledging her fatigue. Nothing unusual about that. Reading 190 pages took a lot of concentration and left little energy for starting anew. Some days were catch-up days.

She was ready for a glass of wine and some socializing. She wandered into the kitchen and didn't see Connor or Margot. She opened a bottle of Malbec and poured it into one of the huge globe-shaped goblets she loved. She peered out of the kitchen window. The sun was behind the house now, but it still glimmered on the sea. Maybe Connor hadn't returned from the golf course yet. A wave of irritation washed over her. She needed to talk about her plot.

Well, the next best thing was to take a walk. Sometimes she could work things out as she walked.

Leaving her wine on the kitchen counter, she searched the mud room and pulled on Connor's down jacket and woolen gloves. She let herself out, retracing her path from the day before, drawn once more to Crail. Maybe she could find Martin Engler and learn why he was in Scotland. No, not Martin Engler. Charlie Fitzgerald. Her neighbor. She needed to know why Charlie was in Scotland. Had he followed her? That made no sense. He could see her every day back on Sullivan's Island if he wanted. Unless… The thought was too complicated and she lost it.

She'd go back to where she'd seen Charlie, across from the teashop. Maybe she'd see if he was registered at the Golf Hotel, the most imposing building on the High Street. She and Connor often enjoyed meals in the hotel's unadorned dining room – smoked haddock from nearby Pittenweem, steak pie, local seafood chowder, sticky toffee pudding.

She trudged past the Caves of Caiplie, as she had the day before. But today, the imposing boulders caught her attention. Looking up at the hulking sandstone carved by centuries of pounding waves, she wanted to see the view of the North Sea from their zenith. She scrambled up the grassy hillside and circled around until she reached the uneven rock that provided the roof for the caves. At some points below, there was grass, but at others a scattering of rocks. So a fall could mean a twisted ankle, or it could mean a crushed skull.

Julianna stepped gingerly on to the high rock and was surprised by the force of the wind. She staggered and spread her feet, clawing for balance. Up here, the view was magnificent, or would be if she could gain her footing. But the wind was unceasing on this exposed outcropping and lashed at her until she fell to her knees. A sharp pain shot through her legs. The view forgotten, she wanted off this rock.

She inched backward, the wind roaring in her ears and deafening her to any other sound. She didn't hear the man come up behind her – didn't see his long black coat flapping or his driving cap pulled low on his head. She didn't detect his presence until he laid a hand firmly on her back. Julianna whipped her head around.

Martin Engler! she realized with surprise. No, that was impossible. The stranger bent to look at her, but the cap hid his face. The pressure on her back grew. Was he pushing her? He reached for her hand, seemingly to help her up. But was that only so he could shove her more easily?

Fear clutched Julianna, and she flattened herself against the rock and screamed. The sound was lost in the wind, but that same shrieking wind caught a corner of the man's cap, and Julianna saw a look of shock cross his face. She realized he had been on the High Street the day before – the man she thought was Charlie Fitzgerald. But he wasn't Charlie, was he?

Julianna's panic overwhelmed her, and her thoughts rocketed back to the night in the dining room. "We came," Margot had whispered, "we came… because the sheriff thought you might be in danger too." She *was* in danger, but it hadn't stayed behind on Sullivan's Island. It had followed her to this remote coast of Scotland. She closed her eyes and screamed again.

Suddenly, the pressure on her back was gone. Julianna thought the wind must have caught the man's coat, forcing him from the rock. She whirled, seeking another glimpse of his face, but instead saw a flying tangle of red hair and slender white hands reaching for her.

"Julianna!" yelled Margot. "I've got you."

Margot's arms encircled her waist and she helped her crawl slowly backward, the wind stinging their faces and whipping their hair into unseeing eyes. Mercifully, they felt the rock give way to grass. They continued their backward retreat into a depression in the ground, protected from the wind and its noise. Breathing heavily, Julianna twisted to look for the man who had threatened her. He was walking rapidly toward Crail, his hands thrust inside his trouser pockets, coat flailing behind him.

"Did you see that man?" she gasped.

Margot nodded mutely.

"He tried to push me. You saved me."

Margot looked doubtful. "Are you sure? I thought he was trying to help you."

Julianna looked at her in surprise. "Help me?"

"Yeah, he was trying to help you up. That's what it looked like."

"Then why did you shove him away?"

"I didn't. I got there and reached to help you. And he sort of nodded and left." Margot gazed after the man. She turned back to her employer. "Do you know him?"

"Yes. No. I don't know." Julianna felt as if she might cry out of frustration. "He's the man I saw in Crail."

Margot stood and pulled Julianna to her feet. "Well, then he definitely wasn't Dr Fitzgerald. I didn't get a look at his face, but Dr Fitz would've spoken."

Julianna looked at her sharply. *Would he?* She clamped her lips in a tight line. The women trudged toward the Fife Coastal Path that would take them home.

"Do you want to tell me why you left the house without me?" Margot asked.

Julianna thought about the question. Why had she? "I… I'm not trying to be difficult, Margot. I think I was trying to…" She trailed off and shrugged helplessly. "I don't know what I was trying to do."

Margot slipped an arm around her shoulders and gave her a hug. "I'm just glad you're all right."

They walked the rest of the way in silence. When Julianna opened the kitchen door, she sensed the emptiness of the house. "Where is everybody?" she asked.

"Evan and Sheona don't work on Sundays."

"But where's Connor? Is he back yet?"

Margot shot her a look and tried to change the subject. "You were really engrossed in your writing earlier this afternoon," she said. "Ready to send me those pages?"

Julianna stopped in confusion. "Send *you* the pages?" she repeated. "Why would I do that?"

Margot stared at her steadily, sadly. "Oh, Julianna," she said.

Chapter 8

Logan woke up on Sunday morning from a dream about her mother. She lay still beneath the floral lavender comforter of her childhood, trying to ascertain if it were a dream or a memory. She was twelve, and she and Britt were, unusually, having a snack on the Burke porch because Britt was afraid of getting co-opted to babysit for her siblings. Julianna came out of the kitchen, barefoot, in shorts and a flamingo-covered T-shirt, balancing her laptop and a glass of iced tea.

"Girls!" she cried, placing everything on her porch writing table. "What are you up to today?" Her mother was happy, excited, in a way that even pre-teen Logan recognized: her writing was going well.

"Hiding out from the rug rats," said Britt.

Julianna laughed. "Good practice for when you girls have your own. Right, Logan?" Her mother actually walked over and kissed her on the forehead.

But Logan wasn't going to be bought that easily. "I'm not having kids," she said.

Julianna looked surprised. "Oh? Is that right? Why?"

"Because I–" At that moment, they heard the distinctive tromp of Connor's golf shoes on the kitchen floor. Julianna didn't wait for Logan's answer, but spun and ran. Through the glass door, Logan could see her mother wrap her arms around her husband's neck. Pointing through the door, she said to Britt, "Ew. That's why."

Memory, Logan decided. She hopped out of bed and checked her email. She read Margot's question asking whether Meg had reached Dr Fitz's hotel room phone or his cell.

"Judging by how quickly she made the connection," Logan typed, "it had to be his cell."

She knew exactly what Margot was after. Dr Fitz could've answered his cell phone from anywhere. Even Crail.

But that was nonsense. Dr Fitz was in New York.

What if he wasn't? Why would he follow her mother to Crail?

An image surfaced, unbidden, in her mind: Sunny Satterfield locked in her house with poor Buster. Had Meg been unafraid of a random neighborhood killer because she, unlike Sunny, knew who it was? She brushed the preposterous thought aside. The Fitzgeralds had lived next door to Connor for the entire twenty-two years of his marriage to Julianna. What possible motive could they have to kill him now? Noisy lawnmower – like Harrison said? Weed whacker? Ridiculous. She got irritated with her brother all over again.

She padded downstairs, Annabelle at her heels. "You know, Jezebel, I think you'll be better off here than at my place. Let's stay, shall we?" It was true. The dog had never relaxed at Logan's apartment, leaping up every time she left the room or answered her cell phone. Logan figured she could stop by her apartment after work the next day and pick up more clothes.

She fed the dog, made a half-pot of coffee and retrieved *The Post and Courier* from the driveway. Then she ate a bowl of cereal and spent an enjoyable hour on the porch with the newspaper. It was still only 10 a.m., so she decided to go to morning worship at Chapel by the Sea. She showered and dressed in fitted slacks and a sleeveless eyelet blouse from her mother's closet. She patted Annabelle goodbye and walked the few blocks to church, enjoying the unseasonably warm day and studying the mix of old, renovated, and new houses.

Her favorite house on the street was a Key West-style cottage, its porch and railings painted green and soon to be overrun with pink bougainvillea. She could see only three blooms this early in the season. Give the sun-loving vine another couple of weeks and it'd be a flower riot.

She also liked the stately white house with black shutters and a red door, fronted by huge azaleas and ancient oaks dripping with Spanish moss. She knew that come April Mrs Agerton would place a pot of red geraniums in every empty space.

There were other houses as worn as her mother's – they'd been shabby chic before the term existed – and not many for rent. Sullivan's Island was a world away from the touristy Isle of Palms next door, connected by the slender Thompson Memorial Bridge over Breach Inlet. Sully's was a place of deep history, and deep family roots like the Montagues'. Connor Burke had been an interloper, granted admission only because of his marriage.

Logan reached the church cemetery and found Connor's grave near the Montague plots. The ground bore signs of being freshly dug and turned. The marker wasn't in place yet, but Logan knew what it would say, because she'd ordered it. *Connor Randall Burke – Beloved husband, father, friend.*

No "stepfather", she'd decided at the last minute. He was more than that. She had fully expected him to walk her down the aisle someday in this very church. She laughed at herself. Well, yeah, that would require a groom somewhere in the picture. What she wanted, she realized, was a marriage like her mother's and Connor's. A union of two against the world.

She'd thought that was what she had with Mark Zefferelli, an art professor at the College of Charleston, whom she'd met when she managed DeeAnn's Art Gallery. He'd curated a show of grad students' work, and she was in charge of mounting it. By the time the six-week show ended, she was in love.

Mark was from Wyoming, new to the Carolina coast, and she'd shown him the hidden treasures of her hometown. Crabbing in the tidal marshes. Hole-in-the-wall breakfast diners. The delights of Piccolo Spoleto. And, during a beach weekend while Mother and Connor were traveling, Fort Moultrie and the plentiful fried seafood at Sullivan's.

Mark was enthusiastic about Logan's art, and visited her home studio often, borrowing her paintings to share with his students. They even cleared space for his easel, and spent many weekends happily working, then breaking in the evening to share a bottle of Bordeaux on the side porch of her duplex.

For the entire school year, she'd thought he was as in love with Charleston as he was with her. Until the night in his apartment when she'd found a letter from the dean at Pepperdine University in Malibu, California. It seemed he'd applied for a job there the next year.

For a while, in a daze, she planned what she'd say when he asked her to come along. Would she uproot and move to the other side of the country? She supposed she could paint anywhere. But weeks passed and he never asked.

Mark was, in many ways, like Rivers Arnette, always looking for the next big thing. He assured her that he loved her. He even loved Charleston. He just hadn't seen all of life, all of the country, he intended to. When the school year ended, he was gone. And she was left with a simultaneous ache and shattered self-confidence.

Logan stood in the peaceful graveyard, shaded by giant oaks already bursting into leaf. It was too cool in the shade, so she hurried to a section of sunny pathway.

"Logan, is that you?" She spun around, startled. The Rev Marsha Philpot crossed the graveyard that separated the parsonage from the sanctuary, a black robe and colorful stole draped over one arm, papers clutched in the other hand. "I hope you'll be joining us today," she said.

"Pastor Marsha, yes, I will be," Logan said. "I'm dog-sitting for a while."

"Please, just Marsha," said the woman who wasn't much older than Logan. "How's your mom doing?"

Logan waggled her palm in the now-familiar signal for "not great".

"I didn't get a chance to speak to you at the funeral, but I am so sorry about your stepdad. Sometimes the family can get lost when there are so many mourners."

"You did a beautiful job," Logan said honestly.

"It helps when you know the deceased," Marsha said. "And Connor had been a faithful member for my entire four years here. In fact, I need to ask you something."

Logan waited.

"Connor and Julianna created a fund to pay a stipend for a seminary student to intern here each summer. Connor took an active interest in going through the applications and helping me choose the intern. I'm up against the deadline. Would you want to help?"

Logan hesitated, running through excuses in her mind. She couldn't think of anything she'd rather do less than slog through boring student resumes. She swallowed, stalling. "Is anyone else on the committee?"

"It was three of us – Connor, me, and Liza Holland. We need a tiebreaker."

Logan smiled weakly, not seeing a way out. And working with Liza and Marsha wouldn't be so bad. "Sure, all right," she said. "I work eight to five weekdays, but other than that I'm pretty flexible. And I'll be staying on the island until Mother gets home."

"Wonderful!" Marsha said with a smile. "If you'll give me your email address, I'll send you the meeting time. This is a real help. Thank you."

Logan scribbled her contact information on a piece of paper Marsha held out, then the pastor waved and hurried into the sanctuary.

Following Marsha with her eyes, Logan saw Liza Holland approach the church entrance with a handsome middle-aged man. Liza spoke to Marsha, then raised her head, obviously seeking Logan.

Logan waved, and Liza headed over with her companion. "Logan," she said with a smile, "I'm so glad you're going to help us with this intern thing. This is my friend, Fred Manigault. Fred, this is Logan, Julianna and Connor's daughter."

Fred Manigault held out his arms. "I'm a hugger. Do you mind?"

Strike one, Logan thought. He also wore loafers with no socks, a Lowcountry style she'd never embraced. *Strike two.* Logan reluctantly stepped into his clinch. "Nice to meet you," she muttered, her speech muffled against his seersucker jacket.

"I'm so sorry about your dad," he boomed. "Great guy. Great guy."

"Oh, did you know Connor?" Logan asked.

"Everyone knew Connor Burke," he said jovially. "He and Julianna came out to The Mangrove several times. And we'd been at their house right before… well, you know."

Logan grasped at the reference to The Mangrove, remembering Harrison's remark. "Yes, my brother said you owned a restaurant."

"Harrison likes it for business meetings," Fred laughed loudly. "He knows I'll do what I can to lubricate his clients and make them think he's a big wheeler dealer."

Logan darted a look at Liza, whose face remained expressionless. Logan wondered what she was doing with this blowhard.

"Logan," Liza said, "I'm sure Marsha will be calling you this week about the applications. I really am glad you're going to help us." She nudged Fred's arm. "I hear the organ. We'd better go inside."

Logan followed them, speculating as to whether Liza had been married before moving to Sullivan's Island, or if she'd dated much since arriving. From everything Logan had seen, she was intelligent and educated and poised. Was Fred the best she'd found among the men around here? It didn't bode well for her own walk down the aisle, she thought dryly.

On Monday morning Logan woke early, unsure as to what traffic between the island and Charleston would be like on a weekday morning. She fed Annabelle, wondering if Liza had a key to her mother's house in order to take her for a walk. She'd need to ask.

She opened the door to the porch so the Shiba could spend the day on her favorite wicker sofa. "You truly lead a dog's life," Logan told her. "People pay big bucks to vacation in a place like this."

Annabelle barked and hopped on to the couch. Logan grabbed a cup of coffee for the road and left by the front stairs. As she climbed into her Jeep under the house, she heard the rumble of a garage door. She peered into the Fitzgeralds' driveway and saw Dr

Fitz backing his Cadillac SUV out of the garage. She ran over and waved him down. He climbed out, a smile on his tanned face, his salt and pepper hair thick and well cut.

"Logan, what a delightful surprise!" he said, hugging her. "Meg told me you were here for a while."

"Good to see you too, Dr Fitz. How was New York?"

"Boring. But I really was there, and not Scotland."

"I know," she said with a shake of her head. "Meg suggested that I come with Mother next time she has an appointment. I feel like it's time I got involved."

"That's an excellent idea," he agreed. "If the whole family knows what's going on, it's better all around."

"Okay, I won't keep you," she said. "Thanks for all you are doing for my mother."

"Don't mention it. She's been a friend for as long as I can remember. A good friend. I'm so sorry about Connor. He was her rock."

"He really was, wasn't he?"

"Yes, and a good friend to us, too. Dick Satterfield, Connor, your boss and I had a standing foursome."

"Yes, Dr Littlemeyer mentioned it," Logan said of the senior physician in her office.

"Though Sam and I don't quite have the freedom Connor and Dick have schedule-wise. Or had, I should say. By the way," he said with a wink, "I was with Sam Littlemeyer in New York this weekend."

Logan felt her face coloring at the veiled invitation to confirm Dr Fitz's whereabouts. He stepped back into his SUV and reversed out of the driveway with a wave. Logan slung her purse over her shoulder and returned to her Jeep. She did remember that Dr Littlemeyer had left town for a conference, though she'd not bothered to inquire where it was.

The drive to her office near the Medical University of South Carolina Hospital was only ten miles but, as she'd feared, the trip took half an hour. She met the junior partner, Dr Augusten Johns, in the parking lot. Though she never called Dr Littlemeyer anything but Dr

Littlemeyer, Gus was an old high school friend. When they were alone, she called him Gus.

She caught him as he pulled a briefcase, gym bag and travel coffee mug out of his car. "Can I help you carry something?" she asked.

"You bet," he said, handing her the coffee. "I'll spill it, sure as the world."

"Gus," she said as they crossed the lot, "where did Dr Littlemeyer go this weekend?"

"Medical conference in New York. Why?"

"Just curious. My neighbor, Charlie Fitzgerald, mentioned they'd been at the same one."

Gus laughed. "Maybe at the same conference, but I doubt they were in the same sessions."

"Why not?"

"Because Charlie Fitzgerald uses those conferences as a front to get some on the side."

Logan stopped so suddenly Gus's coffee sloshed at their feet. "Hey," he protested, "I could've made a mess all by myself."

Logan barely heard him. "Are you saying Dr Fitz is having an affair?"

"*An* affair? More like affairs, plural."

"Gus, are you serious?" Logan felt her heart plummet.

"Yes. At least according to Sam. I certainly don't run around with them. I mean, they're my dad's age."

"How long has this been going on?"

Gus shrugged. "I have no idea. I knew Britt, of course, in school, but I didn't meet her dad until I went into practice with Sam. He's pretty good friends with Charlie and has made several comments over the years about his running around."

He turned and saw Logan's stricken face. "I'm sorry, Logan. Did I say something wrong? Does he mean something to you?"

"He was my next-door neighbor growing up. His wife is like a second mom, and Britt is my best friend. I had no idea." She thought for a minute. "Do you think they know?"

"No clue. Never laid eyes on his wife."

They passed through the heavy glass door into their office lobby, and parted ways. Logan settled at her desk with a sick feeling in her stomach at the thought of such a huge secret in the family she'd idolized.

Harrison called in the midst of the Monday morning rush, when all the patients who got sick over the weekend were calling for appointments or simply showing up. Logan misplaced her headset when she went to copy a bill, and developed a crick in her neck from holding the phone against her shoulder. She finally retrieved the headset, but not before both her hand and shoulder were aching.

"Hey, Logan, can you join me for dinner tonight?" Harrison rumbled. "My treat."

Logan was suspicious. Harrison never invited her to dinner. "Why?" she asked bluntly.

"Can't I do something nice for my sister?" he asked. "Plus, I think we need to make a plan for when Mother returns."

Logan couldn't argue with that. "I'll need to go to the beach house first to let Annabelle out," she said.

"I can do that," he offered. "I've got business today on the Isle of Palms."

"All right then," she agreed. "You got a key?"

"Yep."

"So when and where for dinner?"

"Six-thirty at The Mangrove," he said, hanging up before she could respond.

The day was so busy, as Mondays usually were, that Logan had little time to think about what Harrison wanted. Probably a way to get the beach house, she mused as she grabbed a bowl of broccoli cheddar soup for lunch. She then chided herself for being uncharitable. It could be that he was as shocked by their mother's precipitous decline as she was.

The office manager asked if she could stay to help with the crush of patient files, so Logan didn't leave the office until nearly five-thirty. She drove to her scruffy duplex on a gentrifying street beyond the hospital campus. But then what street around there wasn't gentrifying? She worried that she'd soon be priced out of her rental. She packed a suitcase with clean underwear, pajamas and her last two sets of clean blue scrubs for work. She shook her thick hair out of its ponytail. It was straight for now, but a few minutes near the marsh would have it curling and frizzing. She changed into close-fitting black jeans and a lightweight sweater, adding a bangle bracelet and matching earrings when she remembered that The Mangrove was relatively swanky for a beach restaurant.

She returned to I-26, but exited before Sullivan's Island, trying to remember the back roads that led to The Mangrove. She'd been there only once, on a girls' night out in mid-summer. They'd started out on the deck overlooking the marsh but had been run inside by mosquitoes. Those giant bloodsuckers wouldn't be a problem this early in the season.

She arrived five minutes early, pulling into a sandy parking lot with boats docked on one side, the multi-decked bar and restaurant on the other. She spotted Harrison's black Mercedes, and pulled in next to it. The gleaming Mercedes and the dirty Jeep kind of said it all about their priorities, Logan thought, bracing herself for the evening.

Instead of immediately entering the restaurant through an oversized door of oak and etched glass, she veered on to the walkway that ran alongside the restaurant's outer wall. No diners were at the outside tables, and she paused a moment to enjoy the view. The tide was in, and the brackish water lapped and sucked at the plank decking. There was a small green island, perhaps forty feet away, and she watched as a great blue heron landed with a swoosh of its wings. She heard rather than saw a fish break the surface and then splash back down. Sometimes she thought these evergreen inlet views were more magnificent than those of the nearby beaches. She preferred these scenes, anyway, for her paintings.

She reluctantly retraced her steps and entered the restaurant, more sleek and polished on the inside than its exterior would suggest.

Harrison and Fred Manigault sat at a table overlooking the water, their heads bent together. Fred saw her first, and rose with a shout. "There she is!" he cried, enveloping her in a hug.

Harrison stood as well. "Inside or out?" he asked.

"This is fine," she said. "It's getting a little chilly out there."

"What will you start with?" asked Fred. "A glass of Prosecco? A cocktail? Our martinis are shaken, not stirred." He laughed at his own joke.

Harrison looked at Logan. "Shall I order a bottle of red? That's your favorite, isn't it?"

Logan frowned. "No, I've got to drive back to the island. Go ahead and get your bourbon or whatever you want. I'll have a glass of that Prosecco Fred mentioned."

Harrison nodded and Fred walked to the bar to place their order. A waitress quickly appeared with water, a bread basket and complimentary shrimp cocktails along with their drinks.

"Comped appetizers?" Logan raised her eyebrows when the waitress was gone. "You must come here a lot."

"It's good for business to stake out a few restaurants where you know you won't be unpleasantly surprised," he said.

Logan took a deep sip of her bubbling wine. "Ah, that's good after a long day." She twitched her shoulders to get the last of the kinks out. "What's on your mind?"

"Obviously Mother," he said. "But let me hear about what's going on with you first." He took a long pull of his bourbon. "Dating anyone? Painting going well?"

Logan stared at him. Something really was going on. He normally showed no interest in her life, but now his face was set in an expectant smile. Only his jiggling loafer gave him away.

But she'd play along, she thought, reaching for a piece of bread. "Not much to tell," she said. "I've dated one of our pharmaceutical reps a time or two, but nothing serious. And I'm working on paintings for a collective show of Lowcountry watercolorists at DeeAnn's." When Harrison looked blank, she added, "The gallery where I used to work."

"Oh, yes," he said smoothly. "DeeAnn's. I showed her ex-husband some properties after they divorced."

She let her brother prattle on about his business and dating and mutual friends, noting that the waitress brought another Prosecco before she had finished the first glass. Harrison wasn't being very subtle. The waitress returned, and they ordered the house specialty, crab cakes. Harrison droned on, asking inane questions that showed his ignorance about her art.

"Look, I can't stay late," she said as their entrees arrived. "What did you need to talk about?"

She saw Harrison's gaze land on her first glass of Prosecco, still half full. She could sense him giving up on the idea of getting her to relax.

"Obviously," he said again, "it's about Mother." His large face appeared sorrowful. "I can't believe how much she's deteriorated."

"Since when?"

"What do you mean?"

"When's the last time you saw her before Connor died?"

"Christmas, I guess."

"They weren't here over Christmas."

"They weren't? Then Thanksgiving."

"Did you have Thanksgiving with them? I didn't."

Harrison squirmed. "We weren't all together at Thanksgiving?"

Logan laughed. "Maybe it's your memory that's at issue."

Her brother had the grace to assume a hangdog look. "I admit I've not been the most attentive son. But you have to admit that she and Connor didn't particularly want us around." Logan shrugged. Harrison continued, "Whenever I saw her – I guess before Thanksgiving – she was her usual spacey self. But nothing like the zombie I saw after Connor died. I mean, at the funeral I wasn't a hundred percent sure she knew me, Logan."

Logan's mind went back to the wind-whipped graveyard, her mother leaning on Margot's arm, vacant and disoriented as black-clad people descended upon her like crows. "Thank you, dear," she heard her mother say over and over, as if in a trance.

"I wonder if Dr Fitz prescribed something," she said. "Don't doctors do that when someone's had a shock? Tranquilizers to get them through the first few days?"

"That could explain it," he said. "But I went by Liza Holland's a couple of times afterwards, when she was staying there. She wasn't any better. I hope she's improved when she comes back from Scotland, but what if she isn't?"

"I guess we need to get more involved in how she's going to live," Logan answered. "I'll start by going to her doctor's appointments. I haven't been in the loop."

"Then you'll agree with what I'm suggesting," Harrison said, signaling to the waitress for another bourbon. "I think we should seek Power of Attorney – for healthcare and finances. Sooner rather than later."

"Hmm. So are you saying you want to be given Power of Attorney in the event that she is incapacitated? Or you want to declare her incapacitated now and take over her affairs?"

Harrison paused, eyeing his sister. "From what I've seen the past two weeks, I think it needs to be effective immediately. I think if both of us talked to her and Charlie Fitzgerald, we could go ahead and take over."

Logan shook her head. "It's too soon," she said. "We haven't even talked to Dr Fitz or Margot – or Mother, for that matter. At this point, it's impossible to tell what's grief and what's dementia. Or if she even has dementia."

"*If* she has dementia?" Harrison barked. "Are you kidding me?" The veneer of politeness had slipped from his face. "Come on, Logan. She's loony tunes."

"We don't know that. She lost her husband, Harrison. That affects people in different ways. You're not supposed to make any important decisions for a full year after you lose a spouse."

Harrison gulped his bourbon, his face reddening. "A full year? No way."

"Why?" she demanded. "What is it you would do with a Power of Attorney anyway?"

His eyes slid away. "Make sure she is taken care of properly."

"As in a nursing home?"

"Maybe."

She leaned across the table. "You want the house," she said, pointing her fork at him. "That's what this is all about, isn't it?"

"Logan, you've always said the same thing. Don't you think it's time we did what the Fitzgeralds have done to their house? Or raze the place and start over?" He lowered his voice. "Nice houses in that area can go for six or seven mil. They're not making any more beaches."

"I wanted to once, I'll admit it," she said. "When we were living there. But it's her home and she can do with it what she wants. And we have to give her time to grieve Connor before making decisions about her mental stability." She re-aligned her cloth napkin on her lap. "And I am *not* going to rush her into signing over Power of Attorney to you or me or anyone else."

"Fine," Harrison said, grabbing the check and lurching to his feet. "Suit yourself. But when we get stuck in some kind of legal and medical limbo and can't do what we need to do, remember it was your decision."

He stomped off to pay at the bar. Logan remained seated. *Might as well finish this delicious meal*, she thought, reaching for the second glass of Prosecco. She was aware that she was enjoying herself more after Harrison's exit when another figure slid into his vacated chair. Her heart sank.

"I hate to see a pretty woman sitting alone," said Fred Manigault, signaling to their waitress to remove Harrison's plate. His black hair was slicked back, and his dark eyes drilled into hers. Logan wondered again what Liza saw in him. "That didn't go well, I take it," he said.

"It wasn't for the lack of plying me with good food and wine," said Logan. "Does that actually work for anyone?"

"Sure," said Fred with a chuckle. "Maybe not so much with family members."

"While you're here," she said, "I've been trying to talk to the people who were with Mother and Connor the day before he died. Trying to see if they saw or noticed anything out of the ordinary."

Fred sat back, making a temple with his hands. "Like what?"

"I have no idea," she said. "Why don't you start with how you came to be there?"

"That's easy. Liza and I were going to dinner. When I picked her up, she had gotten a call from Margot, inviting us over for happy hour. Liza was already elbow deep in guacamole dip, so it was a done deal."

"You didn't want to go?" Logan asked.

"It's not that," he said slowly. "It's just that every time Liza and I plan to go out, we end up with her neighbors."

"That's weird."

"Yeah, I think so too." He gazed out over the water, barely differentiated from the deep purple sky over it. A string of white deck lights reflected on the black water.

"How long have you two been dating?" Logan asked.

"Four months or so." He turned back to her. "But like I say, precious few actual dates. Lots of neighborhood get-togethers. Especially with the Fitzgeralds and the Satterfields."

Logan was quiet, the beginning of a question tickling her mind. But she had no idea how to ask it. Or even of whom to ask it.

"Look," said Fred suddenly. "I know Liza's out of my league."

Logan's eyes widened in surprise. She was unwilling to share that she'd thought the same thing. "Well, she's a little older than you, I guess," she stumbled.

Fred waved the comment away. "Only three years. That's not it. She's sophisticated and smart and – what's the word? – graceful. Or gracious. What my mother would call 'a lady'. I don't mind telling you, that's not who I usually date. Ask the former two Mrs Manigaults."

Logan felt the door had been opened. "So why *is* she dating you?" she asked.

"Good question," he said, leaning back in his chair and absently patting a waitress's behind to get her attention. The woman whirled around, and Fred tapped Harrison's empty bourbon glass without speaking, oblivious to any implication of harassment. "I have wondered if she was using me for show."

Ah, there's the old Fred. Logan hid a smirk. "What would she be trying to show?"

"I put that wrong," he said without smiling. "I wondered if she was using me as – how should I say this? – a prop."

"A prop." Now the question wasn't tickling any more. It was banging insistently.

Fred looked forlorn as the waitress brought his drink and placed it before him, stone-faced. He continued, "Yeah, like she needed a date and it didn't matter who it was. At the very best, she isn't interested in me like I am in her." Now that it was out, Fred sank into his chair and drained half his bourbon in a single gulp.

"Do you have any idea if there's someone she *is* interested in?" Logan asked.

"Yeah," he said, tossing back the rest of his drink. "That damn Charlie Fitzgerald."

Chapter 9

It was still light outside when Julianna went to bed without supper, exhausted from crying. She woke hours later, the wind howling around the stone house. But Julianna was so accustomed to the wind that it was background noise. That wasn't what had woken her. No, it was a skittering sound, and there it was again.

She got out of bed and pulled on heavy socks, then made her way out of the bedroom and across the living room. The sound came again, right outside the front door, as if someone were flinging something against it. Julianna tensed, listened again, then relaxed as she realized the wind was hurling pea gravel against the front and kitchen doors.

Calm now, she went into the kitchen to rustle up something to eat. She turned on a pendant light over the sink, causing her reflection to stare back at her from the window. She smoothed her spiky hair, and turned to the refrigerator, shivering, in search of Sheona's leftover potato soup. "Ah, just the thing," she said, pouring it into a saucepan and turning on the gas stove. She poured a glass of milk as well, and laced it with chocolate syrup. Then she decided that would be better heated too. She transferred the milk to a thick ceramic mug and placed it in the microwave.

The wind continued to bang against the stone house, so Julianna turned off the pendant light to see into the night. It took her eyes several moments to adjust. In the light provided by a half-moon and a breathtaking array of stars, she could see the sea shimmering, moving, reflecting, like something alive. Closer, she saw the bulk that was the Volvo. Irresistibly, her gaze was drawn skyward. She would love to see the night sky unimpeded, but not at the cost of getting battered by that wind.

She turned to see how the soup was doing, and saw movement out of the corner of her eye. Instinctively, she moved away from the window. She stood against a solid section of wall, wondering what she had seen. An animal? A trick of the light?

She crept to the kitchen door with its small window, slowly rising on tiptoe to peer out. A figure leaned against the far side of the Volvo, cigarette in hand. It was the red glow of the cigarette that had caught her attention.

Julianna pulled back. Was it Connor? No, no, Connor was dead. She wasn't sure of the details, but she knew Connor was not in this house. Evan? Sheona? She stretched to stare out again and saw wild hair glinting silver in the wind. It had to be Margot. No one else had that long, wild hair. She pounded on the window to get her attention.

"Julianna?"

She jumped. The voice came not from outside, but from behind her. Heart pounding, she spun around to find Margot entering the kitchen, flipping on a light, yawning.

"Are you all right?"

Julianna yanked her eyes back to the window. "Turn off the light, Margot. Somebody's out there."

Margot did as she was told, and joined Julianna. "I don't see anybody," she said.

Julianna searched frantically for the person, but there was no one, and no lit cigarette. "Margot, do you smoke?"

"Occasionally," she answered. "Why?"

"Were you outside?"

"Lord, no."

Julianna touched her assistant's hair. It was warm and bed-messy. There was no way she had stood in a frigid wind.

She was looking at Julianna with concern. "Did you have a nightmare?"

Julianna sighed. There was the lifeline Margot was so good at throwing her. Her galloping heart slowed, and she took comfort in the familiar young woman by her side. "Yes," she said. "I suppose I did." She resolutely turned her back to the window. "Want to join me for a double warm-up – soup and hot chocolate?"

"Um, yeah, hot chocolate sounds perfect."

The sun was bouncing off the North Sea and into her bedroom when Julianna woke the next morning. She lay in bed, testing her memory before getting up.

Connor is dead, she thought, feeling a familiar wrenching in her chest. Logan has Annabelle. Harrison is in Charleston. Charlie and Meg Fitzgerald live next door. Dick and Sunny Satterfield live across the street. Pastor Marsha conducted Connor's memorial service.

Her stomach somersaulted at that memory, and her mind scurried to move on. She had stayed with her friend Liza down the street on Sullivan's Island for several days. But why? Something about Sheriff Royston, she thought. That memory was hazy.

She had talked to investigators from the sheriff's office in her living room about finding Connor in her study. But did she really remember that, or did the image come from Margot telling her about it? She couldn't tell the difference. She was pretty sure she hadn't seen her old friend, Lance Royston, though Margot had mentioned that her neighbors had spoken to him.

She was here in her Scottish house with Margot because… well, she wasn't entirely sure why they were here. But she had read through her manuscript yesterday, tweaking here and there. Her heart accelerated a little as she remembered the adrenalin rush of discovering such a promising beginning to her story.

She threw off the covers. There were gaps for sure, but for the most part she felt clear-headed. What caused the fog to roll in as the day wore on? Her energy had always been higher in the morning, but now she might have no choice but to write when her mind allowed it.

After pulling on clothes, she walked into the kitchen to find Margot and Sheona. "Do you fancy some eggs, Mrs B?" asked Sheona, turning from the sink.

"I do fancy some eggs, indeed," she said. "And some of that sourdough bread, if you have any left. I got into your soup in the middle of the night, and it was excellent."

Sheona smiled and handed her a mug of coffee. "I'm so glad, ma'am."

"You seem chipper this morning," Margot said, sliding a pill across the table.

"I do feel a little better," she said, picking up the gingko capsule and examining it. "Did you bring my vitamins and calcium? And fish oil?"

"Vitamins and calcium are on the counter." Margot pointed. "But I didn't see fish oil when I was packing."

"It may be in the kitchen at home."

Julianna started to take the gingko, and stopped. Maybe its bitter taste would go down better with wine later. She slipped it into the pocket of her sweatpants, and took a multivitamin and a calcium tablet with her coffee. After breakfast, she fetched a blanket from the back of the living room couch and, draping it over her shoulders, settled at her writing desk. She returned to the trouble spot that she recalled from the day before in chapter six, when Martin Engler stood in the rain outside his patient's house, looking for a sign of the man's daughter.

But no, this wasn't the trouble spot. She simply hadn't set it up properly. She scrolled back through chapter five, then chapter four, and found the place to insert a flashback so the reader would know that something was niggling Engler's conscience. She didn't spell out what had happened to his baby sixteen years earlier, but alerted the reader that *something* out of the ordinary had occurred, and it haunted Engler.

Satisfied, she raised her head and found a different vista from when she'd started. Menacing gray clouds obscured the sun, and the wind had picked up once more. She looked at the clock on the corner of her laptop and was surprised to find that it was past noon. But she knew she was in Scotland, and she knew Connor wasn't coming. And for the first time, she found herself missing Annabelle.

Impulsively, she clicked on her email account, intending to ask Logan how she was getting along with the dog. But there were 415 unopened emails. She stared at the list, her heart sinking. These must be from people she genuinely knew, because Margot handled the public correspondence.

She opened one and skimmed it. "So sorry for your loss..." The cover artist for her books.

And another. "We all loved Connor..." Her cousin Angie.

And another, so long it made her feel tired just looking at it. Maybe a couple from church? She wasn't sure.

"Margot!" she called.

"Coming!" Margot came from the direction of the solarium.

"I just looked at my emails. Any suggestions?"

Margot leaned over her shoulder. "Four hundred and fifteen? Ugh. And I've fielded another two thousand."

"Are you kidding? Then I don't want to ask for your help with these. I should know them all. Which is not to say I will." She sighed.

Margot dropped into a nearby wing chair. "My advice is to answer twenty a day from people you want to answer. No one is going to get upset if they don't hear from you. They know you're grieving, and don't expect social niceties."

"Are you sure?" Julianna asked. "You're giving me permission to blow people off?"

Margot laughed. "I am. Blame it on me."

"Thank you, dear," she said with a devilish smile.

Margot laughed again. "That's the spirit. Ready for some lunch?"

"Why don't we walk down to Anstruther for some fish and chips?"

"Ooh, yes, I'm up for that."

"Give me one second to email you the manuscript."

Margot said quietly, "Are you sure?"

"Sure I'm sure. Didn't we talk about this?" Julianna hit the send key. "There you go."

"Thank you, Julianna. I won't let you down."

Julianna showered, determined to dress in something other than the sweatpants she'd worn since she arrived. These old Scottish houses had few closets, so she opened the ornate armoire she and Connor had purchased. She stood for a moment, not seeing its contents, a memory rolling over her.

She and Connor had been driving the winding roads of East Neuk on a brilliant summer day, stopping for lunch at a castle that had been converted into a private club. Connor always knew people who knew people, so it was no surprise that he had an open invitation.

They sat by a window that overlooked a manicured lawn where two couples were actually playing croquet. They laughed about the movie-style quality of the setting, and ordered criminally overpriced burgers and handmade potato crisps and shared a chilled bottle of chardonnay. It wasn't Connor's usual drink, but he knew she liked it. She could hear his teasing: "You know, whenever I drink wine instead of beer, I like the buzz. You need to insist more often."

And her answer: "Got it. I insist you drink wine."

Nobody at the club knew Julianna Burke, at least not by sight, so their privacy was complete. Julianna got tipsy and giggled all afternoon. It was one of those unplanned and unexpected interludes, a perfect afternoon, made all the more so by its randomness.

When they left the castle-turned-club, they ran across an estate sale at a grand old farmhouse outside Kingsbarns. The elderly owners, who were moving south into England, allowed potential buyers to see the furnishings exactly as they sat in the huge and drafty rooms. The massive antique armoire was in the master bedroom, and she and Connor recognized instantly how well it would fit in the house they'd purchased on the Fife Coastal Path. While Connor negotiated a price with the husband, Julianna could see the sorrow in the old woman's eyes. Impulsively, Julianna hugged her.

"It's not going to America," she whispered. "It will be right down the road. We'll give it a good home." The wardrobe was delivered later that week.

Julianna opened it now to see what Margot had packed. Plenty, she could see, noting the rod of hanging pants and sweaters and tunics, and the row of shoes and boots on the cupboard floor. She wondered how long she and Margot planned to stay. She searched her memory for a clue, but came up empty. Again, she felt a pang of missing Annabelle. She pulled out a pair of flat-soled black boots, close-fitting black pants and a heavy sweater of black and red.

She dried her hair and applied make-up, then walked into the living room and found Margot on her laptop. "Still answering email," she said, without looking up. "I want to get my quota done so I can concentrate on your manuscript later today."

"Let me give you the same advice you gave me," Julianna said. "There's no law that says we have to answer it all within a certain time limit."

"Well, I'm cutting and pasting replies for these people we don't know," Margot admitted. "But I think it's good to answer your fans." She looked up with an excited smile. "Especially with a brand new Julianna Burke mystery in the offing!"

"Still a ways to go," Julianna said. "Let's hit the trail."

They pulled heavy coats from hooks in the mud room, and walked into the early afternoon sun, which disappeared sporadically as clouds raced across the sky. The wind was brisk, but not enough to disturb the pea gravel as it had last night. "Wait a minute," Julianna said, crouching beside the Volvo to see if she could make out indentations on the passenger side. But the pebbles lay smooth. She glanced around for discarded cigarette butts, but the driveway was clean. Had she imagined someone out here last night? Though she felt clearer today, her mind was stubbornly elusive. She wasn't ready to trust it yet.

She and Margot turned right, heading to the village of Anstruther. "I always remember Mr Burke talking about your first wandering along this path," said Margot. "Do you remember where you tripped?"

"I do. Not because I really remember it, but because we came this way so often afterwards, and Connor mentioned it every single time. He was nothing if not predictable." She smiled sadly, the longing for her husband a physical ache in her chest.

Margot was in a chatty mood, Julianna could see. Well, she owed the girl as much energy as she could muster. Margot was stuck out here on the east end of nowhere with a dotty woman who offered no companionship.

"Have you had a wandering while writing *Murder, Forgotten*?" Margot asked.

Had she? Did she remember coming to suddenly on the island porch with no recollection of where she'd been? Did she remember a black hole while walking the beach and emerging with a solution for Martin Engler?

She thought about it so long Margot thought she hadn't heard. "Julianna?"

"Oh, sorry. I was thinking about your question. I honestly don't know." She turned to her assistant. "You might know better than I. Did you notice if I worked in a huge stretch all at once, not eating? Did Connor mention anything?"

"I'm not sure either," Margot said slowly. "But you know I was gone a good bit over the holidays. And then you guys were in Florida alone, and I think you were writing there." She paused. "But I told you a few days ago that I thought you might have been wandering the afternoon Mr Burke was killed. Something wasn't quite right when I spoke to you on the porch."

Julianna nodded. She did remember Margot mentioning it, but it seemed a long time ago, not days. She tried to envisage herself on the oceanside porch, hearing Margot's offer of a pina colada. She couldn't.

"It's possible, I suppose," Julianna said. "And then maybe I rushed in to tell Connor about it. And that's when I found him dead." It made sense, but she had absolutely no memory of such a thing.

The women walked on in silence for a while, huddled in their coats against the cold breeze. The coastal path dipped and they passed a lonely cottage that an acquaintance in Anstruther rented out. Julianna pointed to it. "That place rents for the equivalent of $160 a night in mid-summer. Can you imagine what it would pull in on the South Carolina coast?"

"It wouldn't *exist* on the South Carolina coast," said Margot. "It'd be torn down and built four stories high."

Julianna nodded. "You're right about that – especially if Harrison had anything to do with it."

The path climbed again, and when they reached its highest point, they stopped to look at the sea, calm in the distance and lapping gently on the beach far below. Julianna gestured to a blackthorn tree, its limbs bent landward from the unyielding wind. "It was right about here where I fell and snapped out of my first wandering." She gazed out to sea. "I was in the middle of *Charleston at Dusk* and struggling with that feeling of 'This is awful. This is boring. No one is going to read this. Why am I wasting my time?' And suddenly out here, four thousand miles away, the plot opened up, and I knew exactly what that ol' Charlestonian Dinah Mansell was going to do." She laughed.

Margot looked surprised. "Do you really remember?"

"Who knows?" said Julianna. "I remember Connor telling the story a million times. And hearing myself repeat it to book clubs a million times." She looked around. "It's hard to tell what is original memory and what I've added."

She stood still for a moment, then turned slowly until her back was to the sea. She looked down at her boots. "For instance, what did I trip over? A rock? A tree root?" She pointed to the blackthorn. "Did that tree have roots on the path twenty-two years ago? I have no idea."

She kept turning slowly as an idea began to form. She tried to grasp it, but couldn't.

Her eyes swept from the North Sea to the Fife Coastal Path to the lonely tree. What memory was trying to claw its way out? She pictured her much younger self sprawled across this piece of dirt, Connor leaning to pick her up, his face anxious. She pictured her exhilaration, because after all, according to the Julianna Burke legend, that was the moment her career took off.

"What is it?" Margot asked.

"I don't know," she said. "Something I'm trying to recall but it isn't coming. Something about this place."

She finally gave up. "It won't come with me dwelling on it," she said. "I know that much."

"Then let's find the world's best fish and chips. I'm starving."

They walked on, the path descending and then becoming a boardwalk between high grasses, until they reached Anstruther, a much larger village than Crail due to its gentler terrain. Here boats docked and pendant flags flew and the Anstruther Fish Bar was ready and waiting. The women walked into the unpretentious restaurant and ordered its heralded fish and chips. They chose a small metal table for two overlooking the harbor and dug into the delectable fried meal.

"It's been awhile since I walked two miles," Julianna said.

"You walked to Crail your first day here," Margot reminded her. "Same distance, isn't it?"

Julianna cocked her head. That seemed so long ago. "You're right. I guess I was thinking it'd been awhile since I walked with Liza back home."

Margot wiped her lips with a napkin. "You seem different today," she said. "Better somehow. Maybe those gingko pills finally started working. Dr Fitz said it might take a while for them to build up in your system."

Julianna started to tell her that she hadn't taken the pill today, but something stopped her. "How long have I been taking them, Margot?"

"Now you're testing *my* memory," she said. "Since December? January? I'm not sure."

"You know, what might be helping is that my memory isn't so taxed here," she said. "I don't have all those people coming at me."

"True," mused Margot. "Speaking of which, when you feel up to it, we can go over your schedule for this spring and summer."

"No!" Julianna spoke so abruptly that the family at the next table glanced over. She lowered her voice. "No. I want you to cancel everything all spring and all summer."

Margot started to protest, but Julianna held up her hand. "I want to focus on the book. I want to grieve Connor properly and decide who's going to do all the things he did. That may take far beyond spring and summer. Maybe I'll cancel all appearances until next year."

Margot looked stricken. "But you have—"

"People will understand," Julianna interrupted. "This is our window that they *will* understand. If I go back on tour now, I'll have to keep going. No." She shook her head. "No appearances until after this next book is out. It will be fine."

Margot took a deep drink from her water glass. She looked as though she wanted to argue, but instead she asked, "Do you want to tell Renata and the folks at Ironwater, or shall I?"

"You tell them. They'll call me if they have a problem with it."

Julianna leaned back in her chair and gazed out at the fishing boats bobbing in the harbor, missing Connor who had sat across from her at this very window so many times, sipping a beer, people watching, boat watching.

Margot looked down at her empty plate. She had never seen this decisive side of Julianna. She wasn't sure she liked it.

Chapter 10

Marsha Philpot called a meeting Wednesday night to go over the intern applications. Logan walked Annabelle after work, then strolled the few blocks to the white clapboard chapel. Clean-up was still going on after the mid-week supper, and a few study groups were meeting. Pastor Marsha led Logan and Liza into her office, where she'd cleared a table for the printed applications.

"How did you separate them?" asked Logan upon seeing three stacks.

"On whether they've completed first year, second year, or third year in seminary," Marsha answered. "Everything else being equal, we prefer them to have completed the second year."

Liza added, "First years are a little green. Third years are busy looking for a permanent job and may be taking Chapel by the Sea as a back-up. So we might get abandoned."

"Okay," said Logan, "lead the way. But Marsha, you're the one who has to work with the intern. I think your voice should carry the most weight."

The pastor shrugged. "I'm a big believer in the wisdom of the church body. So whenever possible, I like consensus."

The three women divided up the applications and settled into Marsha's comfortable seating area to read. For the next hour they passed pages back and forth until they narrowed it down to two second-year students: a woman from Duke Divinity School in Durham, North Carolina, and a man from Candler School of Theology in Atlanta. Liza slapped the two applications on Marsha's desk. "We'll leave the rest to you, my dear. You may need a spare if one of them has already landed a spot elsewhere."

"Who would turn down Sullivan's Island?" asked Marsha. "I thought I'd died and gone to heaven when I got this appointment."

"And has it been everything you hoped?" Liza said, turning to find her purse. She didn't notice Marsha's hesitation before answering, "Yes, of course." But Logan noticed and wondered what was behind it.

Well, she'd had one church member murdered, and apparently another church pillar was a serial philanderer. But would Marsha know that? Or did the parishioners of Chapel by the Sea keep their minister insulated from the uglier parts of their lives?

Logan wasn't even sure she believed the stories about Charlie Fitzgerald. After all, he was handsome and wealthy and professionally respected. Maybe the stories had grown out of jealousy. But Gus Johns wasn't the type to care about all that. He genuinely believed that Charlie cheated on Meg. Often.

It made Logan sad. Sad for Meg. Sad for Britt and her brothers and sisters. And yes, sad for the younger, innocent Logan who had spent so much time in that house, believing it to be the safest, happiest place on earth.

She and Liza waited until Marsha had turned off the lights in the fellowship hall and locked the doors. The pastor headed toward her house beside the cemetery, and Liza and Logan turned on to Middle Street, pulling their sweaters tightly around them in the chilly night air. "I saw Fred Manigault Monday night," Logan said, "when I was having dinner with Harrison."

"Ah, how was it?"

"Yummy crab cakes. But Harrison left in a huff, which is par for the course."

Liza laughed. "Family! What are you gonna do?"

"How long have you been dating Fred?"

"Four months or so. I was having lunch with some women at his restaurant, and he charmed all of us. I was delighted when I was the one he called."

Logan was surprised, but didn't know how to ask anything else without revealing that she and Fred had discussed Liza. "If this is none of my business," she said slowly, "say so. But do you think it's serious?"

"Too early to tell," Liza said cheerfully. "But it's possible. He's a great guy."

Logan clamped her lips shut to keep from saying something she'd regret. Liza's version of the relationship certainly differed from Fred's. She longed to ask Liza what she saw in the loud, twice-divorced restaurateur who was bucking for a sexual harassment charge from his waitresses. But there was no way to ask without offending her. So Logan kept quiet.

"So, what's the news from your mother?" Liza asked, turning on to the cross street Station 22, which would take them to Atlantic Avenue.

Logan smiled grimly in the dark. There was the opening to her second question. "Something very odd," she said slowly. "Mother thought she saw Dr Fitzgerald on the main street of Crail." She tried to catch Liza's reaction in her peripheral vision. But Liza simply turned to her with what appeared to be sorrow.

"Oh, Logan, no. She's hallucinating?"

Logan hadn't thought of it in those terms. "I suppose so. Apparently, Dr Fitz was at a medical conference in New York."

Liza made a soft clucking noise. "I am so sorry. I guess we all hoped that getting away from the place where Connor died would help."

"We all?"

"Yes, me and Charlie and Margot." When Logan didn't respond, Liza continued, "When Julianna stayed with me, she seemed quite... quite confused, I guess you could say. She kept asking when Connor was coming back. The only thing that seemed to calm her down was Annabelle. Of course, being in a strange house, Annabelle followed her around the whole time, so that worked out." She paused. "But you know all this. You saw her that week."

Logan nodded. "So you and Dr Fitz recommended the trip to Scotland. Did you talk to him quite a bit about Mother?"

They passed beneath a streetlight, and Liza's face reflected puzzlement. "He didn't share anything confidential, if that's what you're asking. I simply told him what I observed so he could make a sound medical judgment." She waited for Logan to say something, and when she didn't, added, "Sheriff Royston was surprisingly agreeable."

Logan stopped. "Why 'surprisingly'?"

Now Liza looked flustered. "Because a murder investigation was underway. And the two people in the house when it occurred wanted to leave town. That's not usually allowed."

"But Sheriff Royston knows Mother. And she didn't really 'want' to go anywhere. That decision was made for her."

"Exactly. I think that's why the sheriff was okay with it."

They resumed walking, reaching Liza's house a few steps later. She turned to face Logan, her hand on the white picket gate at her entrance. "Logan, have I said something to offend you?"

A range of emotions passed through Logan. This woman had been gracious to her mother, but if she was having an affair with Charlie Fitzgerald, Logan *was* offended, on behalf of Meg and Britt if nothing else.

"Are you having an affair with Dr Fitz?" she blurted out.

Liza's face registered surprise. Then she burst into laughter. "Me and Charlie? Heavens, no. As I said, I am quite smitten with Fred." She paused, her laughter trailing off. "Where did you get such an idea?"

Logan couldn't tell Liza it was from her own boyfriend. She shrugged. "I don't know," she said. "I'm sorry if *I've* offended you. It just sounded like you two spend a lot of time together."

"I assure you that any time we've been alone was about getting Julianna cared for." Liza looked embarrassed again, and Logan picked up the unspoken criticism.

If Julianna's children had stepped up, Liza and Charlie Fitzgerald wouldn't have had to take charge.

Chapter 11

Julianna dreamed of Martin Engler. When she awoke, she instinctively reached for the notepad and pen beside her bed and began scribbling without pausing to think or edit. She had seen Martin coming out of a sleazy strip club, while unbeknown to him his wife watched from across the street. The scene had dissolved and the couple were on the deck of their Atlanta house. *Atlanta?* she questioned, but dutifully wrote it down. They were having a barbecue, and their house and yard were filled with people, and Annette – Julianna had renamed her yesterday, and the new name made its way into the dream – broke down and began hurling accusations at Martin as everyone listened in horror. The dream ended with Martin slipping away, leaving the house, as Annette's friends comforted her. A blue heron grabbed a steak from the grill and flew away, somehow squawking without releasing the meat.

She sat up in bed. Okay, the heron would have to go. And she was perfectly happy with her northern California setting. But what was Martin Engler doing in a strip club? She hadn't created him as that kind of character.

She closed her eyes and tried to re-enter the dream, to no avail. Sometimes dreams brought ideas, not as fully formed as those accessed during her wanderings but occasionally making a connection worth noting. She had been struggling with Annette over the past few days, hence the name change from Alyx, though that accomplished nothing. What if she had Annette witness Martin's investigation into his patient's life and misconstrue it? She could get angry and leave Martin for a few days. As the child's biological mother, Annette would have to come back at some point, but their temporary separation might allow Martin some wiggle room to stalk his patient.

"Might work!" she said as she lay back down to begin her morning memory ritual, a roll call of the people in her life. Connor's name triggered the customary clench of her heart, but today, so too did the names Logan and Harrison. Had she been a good mother to them? She'd never asked herself that, but she didn't see them often. She and Connor were… what was the word? *Enough.* She and Connor were enough. Harrison was like his father, something of a bully. But was that nature from Rivers Arnette's genes, or nurture from her?

And Logan was… what? More fragile than Harrison, but who wasn't? Logan was an artist. Very much like Julianna herself, in fact, except more down-to-earth. Less scattered. She genuinely liked Logan, but Logan didn't seem to want to be around her. Her daughter had more in common with Connor. Connor had an easy way about him that Logan had responded to. Julianna thought for the first time of how her daughter might be grieving the loss of her stepfather. Her heart pinched. Had she made a mess of things, loving Connor to the exclusion of her children? What a horrible thought.

Her mind refused to dwell there, and skittered to the other names. Margot. Sheona. Evan. Charlie and Meg next door on Sullivan's Island. Leo and Peggie on the other side. They were in their eighties and ventured out only once a day, at sunrise, to toddle down to the beach. Dick and Sunny across the street. The gay couple Layton and Carson next door to them. Margot usually included them in their impromptu happy hours, but they hadn't been at the last one, had they? Pastor Marsha and her husband, Ben or Browne or something. Liza, but what was the name of her boyfriend? Frank? Manny? She couldn't come up with it. *Go on.* Renata. And who else at Ironwater? Justin, Christine, Rob, Arnold, Sheila – no, Susannah.

She breathed deeply. No one was going to put her on *Jeopardy*, but she didn't feel as foggy as this blasted Scottish weather. She crossed her room and yanked back the drapes she'd closed the night before. Another gray day. She abruptly longed for the Carolina sun.

She pulled her pocket calendar out of her purse, and looked at the days she had crossed off. Today was Friday, March 15. The Ides of March. "Beware, beware," the soothsayer had warned Julius Caesar. "Beware the Ides of March."

But the worst had already happened, hadn't it? Her precious Connor was dead. What could be worse?

Her mind returned to the first night of this visit. She flashed on a vision of herself at the dining-room table, screaming, screaming that Connor was dead as Margot tried to still her thrashing arms. And when it made no sense that she had left Sullivan's Island at such a time, Margot had a response. What was it? She strained to hear. Something about her friend Charlie. No, not Charlie. Lance. Lance Royston.

"We came," Margot told her, "we came… because the sheriff thought you might be in danger, too."

At the time Julianna had been so wrapped in her grief that the thought of danger slid off like an errant raindrop. But now she took the thought out and examined it. The sheriff thought Connor's killer might come for her? But all she did was write. All in the world she did was write.

An uneasy feeling crept over her. Had she angered someone by her neglect? Harrison's red and infuriated face swam before her, demanding she fix up the house or sell it or do *something* to capitalize on the value of the real estate. She'd dismissed him with a wave of her hand. "This is my home, Harrison," she'd said unthinkingly. Maybe he thought it was his home too.

Logan's voice came to her from one particular telephone call: "You and Connor are going to be gone for Christmas? I guess I thought since we didn't have Thanksgiving…" Her daughter's voice trailed off. She cringed at the thought that she might have hurt Logan, might have made her feel second best. *But you don't kill someone out of jealousy. Oh no? How many of your books have jealousy as the motive for murder?*

Julianna shoved the memories away. Remembering wasn't all it was cracked up to be. She stood and reached under her mattress. Four gingko pills. She hadn't told Margot she wasn't taking them. Why was that? When she'd regained some of her focus and energy, she'd gone online and read about the supplement, looking for side effects. Nausea. Restlessness. Diarrhea. Dizziness. Headaches. Nothing that really pertained. She didn't see how the pills could hurt… but still. Margot had noticed her improvement and credited the gingko, but Julianna wanted to talk to Charlie before she took any more.

She was eager to get back to her book, so she found Sheona in the kitchen and told her she'd start with coffee and stop later to make her own breakfast or lunch. Sheona showed her the casserole dish that held their refrigerated dinner, then left for the day.

Julianna settled into her writing chair, warming her hands with the coffee mug. Alyx/Annette was definitely the problem, she thought, before she even opened the manuscript file. Martin was wasting so much time sneaking around, making excuses for his absences, lying to her, that the reader would lose the thread of the most important thing – Martin's obsession with his patient's daughter.

Julianna closed her eyes. She couldn't force a wandering, but she could allow her mind to drift. What did Annette look like? Was she blonde or brunette or red-headed or a color that didn't exist in nature? Was she fat, thin or average? Was she genial or controlling, calm or nervous, friendly or friendless? What kind of work did she do? What kind of mother was she?

Julianna's eyes flew open. Maybe that was the key. Martin and Annette were highly successful professionals. They had put up a baby girl for adoption early in their marriage – no, before their marriage – when they were earning their degrees and were financially strapped. A baby would've ruined everything. But later, when they tried to start a family, they couldn't conceive. Or Annette miscarried. Or something. So actually, Annette might be even more invested in the plight of this sixteen-year-old girl than Martin was. She would become his partner in murder, rather than someone to be kept in the dark.

Because, of course, the patient's endangered daughter would turn out to be the daughter they'd given away.

Julianna grinned and took a sip of her coffee. It was stone cold. How long had she been sitting here? She walked into the kitchen to re-heat her drink, her mind still in northern California, picturing the sleekly turned out Annette, her dark hair caught in a neat bun low on her neck, clicking on two-inch heels to a well-appointed office. A business executive. Or an attorney, perhaps. That's how she could access the adoption records.

Bringing Annette in as a major rather than peripheral character would take a massive rewrite. The Englers' twelve-year-old son would have to be eliminated too. But it felt right to Julianna. It felt true. Actually, it felt *very* true. Was this the plot of a book she'd read or a movie she'd seen? Heavens, she hoped not.

She paused as she returned to her desk. She could see hikers on the rock-strewn coastal path between her property and the sea, two figures so well bundled she couldn't tell age or gender. As she watched, one of them tripped and the other grabbed an arm to right him. Or her. A thought tried to push into Julianna's consciousness – the same thought that had tried to surface yesterday when she was on the coastal path with Margot. The place where she'd had her first wandering.

Julianna squinted into the distance, trying to force the wisp of memory to gel. She gave up in frustration, and dropped into her chair.

She opened her file and saw the title, "Seventh Novel". She'd need to go all the way back to the beginning to flesh out Annette. She was ready to call up the manuscript when she saw another entry right below it: "Seventh Novel – Murder Scene". What was that? She sometimes wrote ahead when a scene was vivid in her mind; it gave her something to aim for, to write toward. She didn't remember writing ahead on this book. But lately, that meant nothing.

She clicked on the entry and saw that it was short, a mere two pages. As her eyes darted down the screen, she grew rigid. In the scene, Martin Engler went to confront his patient because their sessions had convinced him the man was on the verge of molesting his daughter. He found him asleep on a sofa in his home office. On an impulse, frantic that the daughter he had given up for adoption was in danger from this man, the psychiatrist grabbed a letter opener and stabbed him.

Julianna began to breathe rapidly. She stood so abruptly that the chair fell over with a bang. She clamped her hands to her mouth to keep the screams inside. She grew dizzy from hyperventilating and staggered to a nearby wing chair, where she fell, gasping for air. She bent and, with a groan, placed her head between her legs.

Now the memory from the coastal path came roaring back – it was the connection she was seeking, the connection between the wandering then and the wandering Margot thought she witnessed the day of Connor's death. No one knew what Julianna did during her wanderings, least of all Julianna. She'd "awakened", for want of a better word, on the coastal path, on the beach at Sullivan's Island, in the Chapel by the Sea cemetery, on the Fitzgeralds' deck, and once in Charleston's Battery Park, having no recollection of navigating her Lexus SUV there.

Julianna leaped up to see when she'd written the murder scene. February 21: the day before Connor's death.

Oh, dear God, what had she done?

She sat for another ten minutes, trying to calm down, trying to picture herself wander-walking into her office and finding Connor asleep, trying to picture her creation Martin Engler finding his pedophile patient asleep in his office. Had the scenes run together in her confused mind? Had she played out this murder scene on the screen before her?

She stood, trembling. Then, fists clenched, she went in search of Margot. She found her in her usual spot in the solarium, answering emails.

"Margot, get us plane reservations. Right now. We're going home."

PART II

Chapter 12

Logan was waiting at the airport in Charleston when an exhausted Julianna and Margot arrived late on Sunday afternoon. The waits between connections were horrific, Margot had confided via email, but Julianna insisted they start out immediately.

"On a positive note," she had written cryptically, "your mother does seem better."

Not that Logan could tell as Julianna walked wearily toward the baggage carousel. She looked thin and drawn and unsure of where she was going. "I don't think she's slept in forty-eight hours," Margot whispered.

Logan hugged her mother, who clutched her a little longer than Logan expected. "I've got Annabelle in the car," she said. "I hope it's okay to have her in your Lexus."

Her mother seemed to perk up. "Goodness, yes! She isn't going to hurt that old car. Thank you, Logan."

Logan and Margot grabbed the heavy suitcases, while Julianna took the laptop bags and purses. Logan left them and the luggage on the sidewalk while she ran to the parking deck to retrieve the car. When she pulled to the curb and Annabelle saw Julianna, the dog leaped to the front seat, emitting the ear-piercing squeal that owners of the breed call the "Shiba scream". Julianna reached for Annabelle through the open window as the dog's tail lashed Logan's face. "Jezebel!" she protested. "Get in the back seat."

The dog happily complied when Julianna joined her, stepping into her mistress's lap and licking her face until they merged on to I-526.

"We definitely want to avoid downtown today," Logan said.

"Why's that?" Margot asked.

"St Paddy's Day."

"Is it? I've completely lost track of time." She turned to Julianna in the back seat, but the older woman had already closed her eyes, Annabelle's head in her lap.

"That turned out to be a pretty quick trip, didn't it?" Logan said tentatively. "You guys usually stay longer in Europe."

Margot jerked her head to indicate she didn't want to speak in front of Julianna. "Yeah, our departure was pretty sudden," she said. They heard a slight snore from the back seat. "I'm not surprised she's out. She's got to be done in."

They drove in silence for a moment. "Any news on the investigation?" Margot asked.

Logan shook her head. "I really don't know. Those two investigators have been back to the house, and Renata left a message that they'd called her in New York. In fact, I need to call her back."

"So they're focusing on the people who were there the day before."

"Among other things, I'm sure," Logan said. "Such as a transient walking through the neighborhood. I guess that's what I'm hoping – that someone came in to steal something and Connor surprised them before they could. It's too awful to think it's someone we know."

"But how would Annabelle allow a stranger to come in?" Margot said with a glance at the dog.

"How would Annabelle allow *anyone* to come in without pitching her usual fit?" responded Logan. "It makes no sense, unless…" She paused. "I just thought of something. Was the door between the kitchen and the porch closed? If it was, I suppose it's possible that Annabelle didn't hear anything inside the house."

Margot thought back to the warm afternoon three weeks earlier. "I think I left it open after I talked to Julianna. But she could have shut it after I left." Margot looked doubtful. She glanced toward the back seat to make sure Julianna was sleeping, then lowered her voice. "Julianna's been asking me lots of questions about that afternoon, whether I think she was wandering."

Logan looked over sharply. "Was she?"

Margot raised her palms. "I don't know. I'd heard her and Mr Burke talk about those episodes, but I'd never seen one. I told her I thought she looked kind of dazed and vacant, but…" She stopped.

"But what?"

"But she'd seemed more like that all the time," Margot said, shooting a look at the back seat.

Logan nodded. "You know," she said pensively, "maybe the three of us need to sit down and put our heads together. I mean, we know all the people who were in the house the day before. The investigators don't. We may know more than we think we do."

Margot nodded so hard her red curls bounced. "That's a great idea," she said. "Are you going to stay on at the house?"

"If it's all right with Mother, I will," said Logan. "At least until we see what she's going to require medically and living-arrangement-wise. I know you were hired as her professional assistant. It's not fair to dump nursing duties on you."

Margot sighed with relief. "I'll do whatever you need me to, but I'm glad to hear that. I don't have training for anything but bridal hysteria."

Logan laughed as they pulled into the driveway on Sullivan's Island. Turning the car off, she turned to face Margot. "I know you don't. And it's been unfair of us to expect you to. You've bailed us out these past three weeks, and Harrison and I are grateful. But it's time for us to step up."

Margot opened her door. "Like I said, anything you need. We'll work it out."

Julianna went straight to bed while Margot unpacked. Logan settled into her mother's office to return Renata O'Steen's call.

"Hi, babe!" said her mother's longtime editor. "How are you holding up?"

"Okay, I guess. Mother just returned from Scotland."

"Already? That was quick. How is she?"

"Well, she was so tired, it's hard to tell. She slept in the car and went straight to bed once we got home. But Margot says there's been some definite improvement. I've got my fingers crossed."

"That *is* good news. What do you think is next?"

"I want to get her into Dr Fitz's office this week to gather all the information I can. I've been pretty much AWOL on her condition. So I want to hang around for a bit and see what she's going to need in the way of assistance."

"Don't you have to work?"

"Yes, but I can be here every evening. And I'm going to take a couple of vacation days this week."

"Sounds good. Logan, I called for two reasons. One, of course, was to see who you want me to talk to about the book Julianna is working on. We have it tentatively scheduled for release in fourteen months – as next summer's blockbuster. I know that date is probably not feasible now, but I always coordinated with Connor. So will I talk to Margot? Or you? Or to Julianna herself?"

"Let me get back to you on that, Renata. Give me some time with Mother this week."

"Okay. The other thing is your little sheriff's office down there. They've called me three times."

"Really?"

"Apparently, they do not think this was some random break-in."

"I'm sorry to hear that," Logan said. "Did they say why not?"

"Nothing was taken, according to you and your mother and Harrison. And while you evidently have transients in Charleston, they generally don't venture on to your island unless they've landed jobs on your endless beach house renovations. The deputies tell me they have interviewed and dismissed all those folks. So they are delving into Connor's business dealings, at least at Ironwater. We have no way of knowing what they are doing with his other associates."

"I don't know that he *had* other associates," Logan said. "Mother's career was pretty much a full-time job for both of them."

"That's not surprising," Renata said. "In that case, it sounds to me like the investigators are equally interested in your neighbors down there. At least, from what they've been asking me."

"What *did* they ask you?"

"Let's see. How everybody got along on that afternoon at Julianna's happy hour. What we talked about. If I sensed any undercurrents."

"And did you?" asked Logan. "Sense undercurrents?"

Renata hesitated. "That's hard to say because I don't know those people well except for Connor and Julianna and Margot. So I don't know what was normal behavior and what was off."

"But people are people. Did you pick up on anything?"

"I thought that Sunny chick from across the street was a little ditzy. Kind of giggly for a supposed symphony virtuoso. Her husband was nice enough. And of course, I like Meg. I'd met her before."

"Sunny mentioned that Connor and Mother told everyone the title of the new book and you weren't too happy about it."

Renata gave her bark of a laugh. "You know how we like to keep that under wraps. Ironwater likes to control every little piece of marketing and publicity and roll-out. A new Julianna Burke release is the biggest thing going." She sounded forlorn. "I hope Connor's death doesn't throw your mother completely off her writing."

Not wanting to comment on that, Logan moved on. "Go back to the detectives' questions," she said. "What did you tell them about everyone else?"

"Not much. Are you looking for something specific?"

Was she? It wouldn't hurt to ask Renata. She wouldn't spread Sullivan's Island gossip.

"I was curious if you thought something might be going on between Dr Fitz and the neighbor down the street, Liza Holland."

Renata laughed again, this time in genuine amusement. "I know ol' Charlie gets around," she chuckled. "Julianna told me that years ago. But that's not who Liza Holland was after."

"So you think she *is* interested in Fred Manigault?" Logan asked.

"Hell, no! Liza Holland was after your stepdaddy."

Logan was shocked into silence. She turned this piece of information over, trying to see if it made sense.

"Logan, are you still there?"

"Yes. Yes. You surprised me, that's all. What in the world makes you think that Liza was after Connor?"

"Oh, doll, that woman is not your typical Southern belle. She's got big-city moves. I could tell a mile away that poor schmuck she had in tow was a decoy."

Logan hardly knew how to ask the next question. Even to her own ears, she sounded like a squeaky little girl. "Renata, do you think there was anything between Liza and Connor?"

Renata waited a beat too long to answer. "I wouldn't think so, Logan. Connor was always devoted to Julianna, and I have no reason to believe anything changed."

Logan was reluctant to push the uncomfortable conversation further. But she did want to say one more thing. "You do know that Liza took Mother in when the house was a crime scene? She walked Annabelle and was a good friend to her."

Renata harrumphed. "Probably felt guilty," she said. Then she relented. "Logan, don't listen to me. You know your people better than the dreaded New York editor who swoops in. If you say Liza is a good friend to Julianna, I'm sure she is. She did have a crush on Connor, but that's not to say she acted on it."

Logan suddenly remembered Pastor Marsha in the church cemetery, listing the three people on the intern selection committee. Marsha, Connor and Liza. Connor made sense, because he'd funded the position. But what was Liza doing on the committee? And who had invited her? Marsha? Or Connor?

Renata cleared her throat as if she were about to wind up the conversation.

"One more thing," Logan hurriedly interrupted. "I don't mean to sound rude, but what were you doing down here that day anyway?"

"Seeing what was up with my golden goose!"

"What?!"

"The book," Renata said. "Your mother had 170 pages when I talked to her at Thanksgiving and only 190 by mid-February."

"That doesn't sound right." Logan knew that her mother spent up to a year planning and researching and traveling in anticipation of writing a book. But when she sat down to write, she pounded out a first draft pretty quickly. "What did Connor say?"

"That was just it. I couldn't get a straight answer out of him. And when I talked to Julianna on the phone, she sounded out of it. So I flew down to see for myself." She paused. "I spent the night, and I don't mind telling you I got worried. When I talked to your mother, she kind of looked right over my shoulder, if you know what I mean. But she had half of a truly great book." Logan imagined that Renata was shrugging in frustration. "I don't want to give up on it," she continued. "But if we get a year out from the release date and I'm not sure we'll have a book, we'll need to pull the plug."

"So you want a firm answer by mid-May."

"Right. And Logan, don't misunderstand me. Connor's murder changes everything. If Julianna can't finish the book, everyone at Ironwater will understand. We need to know, that's all."

Logan said her goodbyes. She swiveled to face the upholstered chair with its cruel stain, thinking she should have thrown it out before her mother returned. Renata was right. Connor's murder changed everything. And her family couldn't move on until they knew who was behind it.

Chapter 13

Julianna woke at 5 a.m., surprised at the darkness outside her window. She gradually realized she was home in her own bed, her body clock on Scottish time. And then the memory of Connor set in, sharp and piercing. She closed her eyes, willing herself back to sleep. It was no good.

She glanced over at the lounge chair that served as Annabelle's bed. Upholstered in olive brocade to match the comforter, it was a once-handsome piece that was now covered by an unsightly throw that did little to ward off dog hair. Annabelle was sleeping soundly, but the moment Julianna swung her feet to the floor, the Shiba was at her side. "Nothing wrong with your hearing, baby girl," Julianna said, stroking her head. Then a darker thought surfaced: maybe the reason Annabelle hadn't barked on the afternoon of Connor's murder was because there was nothing to hear. No one entered the house. Julianna felt physically ill and bent to bury her face in the dog's neck. "If only you could talk," she murmured.

She wanted to sit down with Sheriff Royston today, to learn details of his investigation, to piece together the foggy days leading up to Connor's death. After reading her fictional scene that could have, quite bluntly, served as a blueprint for Connor's murder, she was scared of what she might find. But she had to know. And her memory being what it was, she didn't know how much time she had.

It was too early to contact Lance, so she walked barefoot in the familiar darkness down the stairs, through the living room, and into the kitchen. She was about to flip on the kitchen light when she heard a scraping sound from the adjacent hallway. Someone was in her office. A thought flashed through her mind, unwilling words wrenched from Margot on a stormy night in Scotland. "We came… we came… because the sheriff thought you might be in danger, too."

Her heart began beating uncontrollably, a cyclone whirling inside her chest. Beside her, she could sense Annabelle tensing a moment before she charged into the narrow hallway, her barking tinged with high-pitched hysteria, her nails sliding across the pine floors.

"Whoa, girl!" she heard from her office. "It's me."

Julianna took a breath to slow her galloping heart and walked through the dark hallway into the brightly lit office. Margot was tugging on the blood-stained chair by the window. "Did I wake you?" her assistant asked in dismay.

"No, I was in the kitchen when I heard you. What are you doing?"

"Trying to get rid of this chair before you return to your office."

"How very kind. I can help."

"Are you sure?"

In reply, Julianna bent to place one hand under the chair's arm and one hand beneath the seat, and they half dragged, half carried it down the hall until they reached the kitchen. They scooted it across the linoleum and through the side doorway, where it lodged on the landing and blocked their exit. "You know what?" said Julianna. "We're never going to use this again. Let's chuck it down the stairs."

Margot giggled. "You got it," she said, turning on the outside light, then crawling over the chair to the deck behind it. She gave the chair a shove, and it toppled legs over seat, landing on the sand below with a thump. Julianna and Margot followed it down the steps, and dragged it to the trash receptacle. "If we block the trash can with it," Julianna said, "they'll know to pick it up."

Margot peered into Julianna's face, partially lit by the single exterior lantern. "Are you okay?" she asked.

"No," she said softly. "My husband was murdered, and I don't know why."

Logan came downstairs at 7:30 to find her mother and Margot sharing coffee and *The Post and Courier.*

"Can I fix you some eggs and toast?" Margot asked. "That's what we had."

"You are not going to wait on me," Logan said firmly. "I can get my own breakfast."

"Suit yourself. Coffee's made."

Logan pulled bran flakes and raisins from the cabinet, and added skim milk from the refrigerator. She watched her mother out of her peripheral vision and noted that she seemed to be reading the newspaper like a… well, like a normal person. She tried not to let her hopes rise.

"You're going to work, aren't you?" Julianna asked.

"Actually, I'm taking some vacation days to see how you're doing and what you need. I hope that's okay with you."

"I hate to make you miss work, but that is *more* than okay with me," Julianna said. "I want to see Lance Royston today. Want to come?"

Logan was surprised, both at her mother's perspicuity and at the thought of seeing the sheriff. "Yeah, I guess. But why the sheriff instead of his investigators?"

"Well, he's an old friend," Julianna said hesitantly. "And something he told Margot made me think he's got his eye on this… on Connor's death." She swallowed.

"What'd he tell you, Margot?" Logan asked.

Margot looked uneasy. She glanced at Julianna. "Do you mean about going to Scotland?"

Julianna nodded.

"He thought it was a good idea that we were going," Margot said, twisting her coffee mug. "In case your mother was in danger too."

Logan's eyes widened. "*What?!* Why would you be in danger, Mother?"

Both Julianna and Margot held up their hands. "I doubt that I am," Julianna started. "That's why I want to talk to Lance."

Margot added, "I think the problem is, they don't know *why* Mr

Burke was killed. And with your mom's celebrity status, they don't know what else might be possible. That's all. They simply don't know."

Logan sat back on her stool. "Well, this is something new and horrible," she said. "Have you made an appointment?"

"I left a voicemail," said Julianna. "I wouldn't expect him to come in before eight-thirty or nine."

As if on cue, her cell phone buzzed. Julianna peered at the number. "I see he's an early riser," she said, grabbing the phone and walking into the living room.

Logan leaned toward Margot, lowering her voice. "Before she gets back, can you tell me what went on in Scotland?"

Margot leaned across the counter until their heads were only a foot apart. "At first, it was very much like it was here," she said quietly. "She was a little clearer in the mornings, and would ask me to go over the details of what happened. Then by afternoon she was looking for Mr Burke to come home from playing golf. There were a few incidents where she got real agitated – once when she thought she saw Dr Fitz in Crail. Once when she thought a man tried to push her off the top of some caves. And once in the middle of the night when she thought I was outside in the driveway."

Logan's eyes widened, but she knew they didn't have much time, so she didn't interrupt.

"But after a few days, she seemed to get better," Margot continued. "I have no idea why. She wanted to write and almost seemed excited about working on her book again. Kind of like the old days." She threw up her hands. "Maybe Dr Fitz's idea to get away helped. Who knows?"

Logan nodded to encourage her to go on.

"But then I don't know what happened. She was working on the book one minute, and the next she was demanding that I get us flights home. Like I said, I don't think she slept from mid-day Friday until she fell asleep in your car Sunday afternoon. She was agitated again, but it seemed different. I can't explain it." Margot looked off into the middle distance, then refocused on Logan. "All I know is, the entire way home she asked me to repeat the details of the day Mr Burke was killed – what he said to me, what interactions the two of them had, where she was, what she said, what doors were locked and unlocked."

Logan leaned back. "What could be going on with her?"

"She also asked about the day before."

"About happy hour?"

"A little about that. But more about where she'd been writing that day, what I could tell about her demeanor, whether she seemed happy with the writing. Things like that."

"That's odd. What did you tell her?"

"Not much. Since it was warm, she had taken her laptop on to the porch for the first time probably since November." Margot shifted her eyes and Logan got the impression she was withholding something.

"And?" Logan asked.

"And she was *supposedly* writing on the porch."

Logan continued to stare at her mother's assistant. "Renata mentioned that she wasn't getting much done," she said slowly.

Margot shook her head unhappily. "That's putting it mildly. Logan, the thing is, I almost never saw your mother writing any more."

Julianna came back into the kitchen, interrupting their conversation. "Lance can see us," she said. "Everybody get dressed. Margot, it might be helpful if you came too."

Logan rinsed the dishes as Julianna and Margot headed upstairs. Then she followed and changed into the dressiest slacks and top she'd brought from her duplex. After she'd brushed her hair and put on make-up, she slipped into Margot's room, closed the door and took up the conversation where they'd left off.

"What was she doing if she wasn't writing?" Logan whispered.

Margot pulled on black ankle boots. "She sat at her desk in the study all winter. And she moved to the porch that day in February. But whenever I went to ask if she needed something, she was staring off into space."

"Did Connor know?"

"He had to. He was the one who read her manuscripts and made suggestions. I heard him talking a lot about Martin Engler. That's her main character."

"I know. I read the manuscript."

"You did? How?"

"I found it in Connor's bedside table."

For the first time, Margot smiled. "What did you think? Isn't it crazy good?"

"Yeah, it is," Logan agreed.

"Anyway, that's why Renata was down here in February. Apparently, she wasn't receiving pages like she wanted." Margot stood and ran her fingers through her long curls. "You now know everything I know. I'm kind of glad."

"Me too," said Logan. "As I said before, it's not fair for you to shoulder all the burden."

The women descended the stairs to wait for Julianna in the living room.

Sheriff Lance Royston was close to six feet tall, handsome in a rough-hewn way, with hair more gray than brown, and hazel eyes flecked with gold. He came around his desk to hug Julianna, then shook hands with Logan and Margot.

"Logan, you are the spitting image of your mama when she was in high school," he said in that drawl spoken nowhere on earth outside Charleston. *You ah thuh spittin' image of yoah mama…*

"How are Sherry and the boys?" Julianna said with a nod at the photo on his desk.

Royston's eyebrows shot up. "You remember them?" he asked gently. *Remembuh.*

"Of course I do, Lance. She edited the yearbook, and I had the newspaper. We were together all the time."

Royston glanced at Margot and Logan. "All right," he said slowly, a puzzled look on his face. "Why don't we sit down?" He gestured to a comfortable seating arrangement with a sofa and wing chairs covered in navy and green plaid. "Anyone want coffee?"

"We've had plenty, thank you," said Julianna, taking the lead. "Lance, I'm sure you're aware of my memory problem, so I won't try to hide it from you. Mornings are better for me, and I appreciate you agreeing to see us on such short notice."

"Of course, Julianna. And I must say, I am so glad to see you, um, feeling better."

She cocked her head. "What do you mean?"

"I mean you seem much more… coherent than when I saw you a few weeks ago."

Julianna looked confused. "We talked that night?"

He glanced from Logan to Margot. "At some length." Julianna looked to Margot as if for confirmation.

"They separated us for questioning," Margot said. "I knew the sheriff came in, but I didn't know if he talked to you or not."

"My memory must be worse than I realized," Julianna said. "I'm sorry, Lance, but I don't remember seeing you at all. But that's my point in coming today. I remember almost nothing from that night or that day or the day before. I was hoping you could fill in some gaps."

"I'll be glad to tell you anything I can," he said. "Where shall I start?"

"Do you have any suspects?"

He hesitated. "That's the one thing I can't share. Sorry."

"I thought as much," she said. "Just checking."

"I can tell you that we – and our colleagues in the Sullivan's Island PD – talked to every construction crew that's been on Sully's or the Isle of Palms since January. Every roofer, tiler, drywall hanger, carpenter, painter, fence installer, and landscaper. Every transient hired, every slacker fired. We came up empty."

"That took a lot of manpower," she said. "Thank you."

"No thanks necessary. That's what we do. I'm just sorry it hasn't led to an arrest yet. But we will get him, Julianna. I promise you that." He paused and got up to rifle through some notes on his desk. "I did want to clarify one thing, though I'm afraid I know the answer."

"What's that?"

"Who has keys to your house?"

Logan and Margot looked at each other. "I never even thought of that," Logan groaned. "The whole neighborhood does, don't they, Mother?"

Julianna nodded. "We all travel a good bit and water each other's plants, take in the mail and so forth."

"That's what I was afraid of," he said. "So who specifically?"

Julianna counted off her fingers. "Meg next door. Leo and Peggie on the other side. Sunny. Liza for the dog. Joan Agerton."

"Pastor Marsha?" asked Margot. "Didn't Mr Burke give her one?"

"I don't know. Maybe."

The sheriff sighed and walked back around to the seating area. "One of the challenges of policing in the South," he drawled.

"But Lance, surely you can't suspect any of those people," Julianna said. "They've known Connor for decades. They're practically family."

"Oh," interrupted Margot. "And Harrison."

"Of course," said Julianna. "And Logan." She smiled at her daughter. "Who, I'm glad to say, is staying with us for a while."

"In other words, anybody you've ever known has a key to your house," said the sheriff. "Great." He clapped his hands. "So how can I help?"

Julianna steeled herself. "Can you take me through the entire evening from your perspective? I've worn Margot out with questions, but I'd like another view."

"Sure." He grabbed a folder from his desk and laid it open on his lap. "The first call from your house came in at 5:47 p.m. The caller, identified as Margot Riley, said it was a possible heart attack. EMS and Sullivan's Island Fire Department were dispatched. At 5:50 p.m. a second call came in, also from Margot, amending it to a stabbing." Royston sounded as if he was giving information at a news conference, but Julianna didn't mind. "The fire department arrived in your driveway at 5:50, the same time Margot was making her second call. When they learned it was a stabbing, they were ordered to wait until Sullivan's Island Police cleared the scene. They were at your house by 5:51." He looked at the women over his reading glasses. "Believe me, people in Charleston don't get that kind of response time.

"The sheriff's office got a call at 6:10 from Sully's interim police chief Len Redding asking for back-up. Homicide Detectives Giles and Lancaster responded, arriving at 6:35." He paused. "I gotta tell you, it made it easier for us to have them invite us in. Doesn't always happen that way."

When the women were silent, he continued, "When I heard that the victim was Connor Burke, I drove over too. I was coming from North Charleston and didn't get there until after 6:40. By then my detectives had you and Margot separated.

"Margot told Detective Lancaster that she'd been asleep, and woke up when she heard you moving around the kitchen. Then you ran upstairs screaming Mr Burke's name, which is when she made the first call.

"You said you'd been writing on the porch until the light faded. You'd gone into your office – you couldn't remember why – and found Mr Burke. Detective Giles said that you seemed to be in shock and couldn't answer any more questions." He stopped for a moment and added, "She was adamant that you weren't refusing to answer but that you seemed unable to. When I arrived, I talked to you with Detective Giles present. I thought at first it was shock too. But then Miss Riley told Detective Lancaster that there were memory issues."

Julianna interrupted. "Where? Where did we talk?"

"The living room. Miss Riley was in the kitchen."

Julianna tried to picture her old friend seated on the yellow-, white- and aqua-striped sofa in her living room, but she couldn't. "Did I say anything to you, Lance? Did I know you?"

He didn't have to think. "Yeah, you knew me. You called me by name. But you weren't able to answer my questions – why Connor was in your office, if anyone else had been in the house that day, things like that. But you repeated one thing several times."

The three women waited.

"You said, 'Why don't you ask Dr Engler?'"

Julianna recoiled as if she'd been slapped. The sheriff watched her closely. Margot and Logan looked from each other to Julianna.

"At first, I had no idea who that was," he said. "I asked Dr Fitzgerald next door if he knew, and he didn't. And Dr Fitzgerald said he was sure that *he* was your and Connor's only physician."

Julianna scarcely breathed.

"It was only when my detectives talked to Renata O'Steen that we learned that Dr Engler was a character in your novel. At that point, we started thinking that maybe you were trying to tell us that Connor's murder had to do with your work. That's when I suggested to Margot that it might be a good idea for you to leave town for a while."

Julianna slowly let out her breath. "You thought I was in danger."

He nodded. "Connor was killed in your office. I thought it was possible someone had intended to find you there and Connor surprised them." He shifted in his seat. "In fact, I was surprised to get your call this morning. What are you doing back so soon?"

Julianna shook her head, not answering, her mind reeling. The sheriff might be worried about her life being in danger, but all she could envision was herself, walking trance-like into her office and finding her husband asleep on the couch. In her confused state, had she thought he was a character in her novel, a man on the verge of molesting his adopted daughter? Could she have enacted her own fictional murder?

Chapter 14

Logan offered to take Annabelle for a walk in the late morning sunshine that was warming up the day nicely. She wanted time to think. She wasn't sure what she'd witnessed in the sheriff's office. On one hand, her mother seemed more cogent than she had in the weeks before leaving for Scotland. But she certainly reacted strongly to Sheriff Royston's mention of Dr Engler. What could that mean? She'd read the incomplete manuscript she'd found in Connor's bedside table, but the plot about a psychiatrist exploring a patient's intentions toward an adopted daughter seemed unrelated.

Annabelle stopped to sniff Sunny's mailbox. "Buster been here, has he?" Logan asked.

She tugged the leash and they moved on. Now that her mother's condition didn't seem nearly as dire as she'd feared, she wanted to concentrate on Connor's death. Who would want her stepfather dead? No one really benefitted financially. Her mother would inherit, but she was already wealthy. Harrison's face flashed momentarily before her eyes. Could removing Connor have brought her brother one step closer to getting their mother out of the beach house? She shook her head as if to dissipate the idea. That was madness.

So, if not money, what? Did something happen with the neighbors the day before? Logan turned and looked back at the Satterfields' weed-free lawn and pristine white house, then across the street at the Fitzgeralds' imposing beach palace. Did those longtime friends see or hear something that afternoon that changed their easy relationship?

Or Renata? That happy hour crowd represented an odd mixture of different facets of Connor's life. Was it coincidence that Julianna's writing had hiccupped to a halt? Were he and Renata united in their worry about Julianna's ability to finish the novel?

Logan walked on, scarcely noticing the cross streets numbered as coastal defense stations. This barrier island was no stranger to the darker side of human nature. Some forty percent of slaves bound for North America from Africa had come through Sullivan's Island. No one knew how many men, women, and children landed here in chains and were rushed into so-called "pest houses" for quarantine, to keep the ruling class safe from disease. The gloomy history was documented on plaques at Fort Moultrie, a few blocks farther.

Logan turned her face to the sun and allowed her mind to roam freely. That worked well in her art studio. Perhaps it would allow her to connect the unseen forces swirling beneath the surface – forces that led to her stepfather's death.

She pulled her cell phone from her pocket and texted Britt Fitzgerald, knowing she might not hear back until that night. *Where's my best friend when I need her?* To her surprise, she got an immediate response: "Between rounds but may have a big surprise for you toot sweet."

Logan smiled at their old joke from French class and slid the phone back into her pocket. She arrived at Liza's tasteful two-story house of sky blue, with wrap-around porches and white picket fence. She stopped to let Annabelle smell every fence post, no doubt recognizing Maxie's scent. Logan remembered Renata's comment that Liza had nursed a crush on Connor.

What if his death had nothing to do with Julianna's writing or with money? What if it was some sort of lovers' quarrel, gone terribly wrong?

Logan stared at the house, willing it to give up its secrets. Then she had an idea. Yanking Annabelle's harness, she headed to the Methodist church and veered through the cemetery. The Philpots' parsonage had a rear window raised to take advantage of the mild day. She could hear music and muted voices, punctuated by the shrill voice of a child. She circled around to the front of the bungalow and looped Annabelle's leash around a dogwood tree. She mounted four stairs to Pastor Marsha's front porch, the white paint on its wooden rails peeling. Chapel by the Sea's property committee needed to get on to that.

Answering her knock, a balding man no taller than Marsha Philpot opened the screen door and held out his hand. "Logan, I'm Baron Philpot. I met you at your father's funeral, but I doubt you can remember everyone." He had a friendly smile, and bulging calves that suggested he was the rider of the bicycle on the porch.

"Thank you, Baron. You saved yourself from being called Mr Philpot."

"That's better than Mr Reverend Philpot. Come on in." Then raising his voice, he called, "Marsha! Someone to see you."

Marsha came from the kitchen, barefoot in T-shirt and shorts, a dark-eyed toddler balanced on one hip. "Alana, this is Miss Logan. Can you say hi?"

The child giggled and buried her face in her mother's neck.

"Need me to take her while you talk?" Baron asked.

Marsha looked at Logan, her eyes asking if they needed privacy.

"Not at all," Logan answered, then hesitated. "Come to think of it, I guess I don't know what a child that age understands. What is she? Two?"

"Two and a half," said Marsha, as Baron held out his arms.

"In that case, let me take her," he said. "We haven't finished our puzzle anyway."

"Want to sit on the porch?" Marsha invited, leading Logan back the way she'd come in. "It's so nice out."

"Sure," Logan said, taking a rocking chair. "This way Annabelle can see me."

"Ah, I didn't hear her," said Marsha, peering at Annabelle sitting alertly beside her dogwood. "She's quiet today."

"I see her reputation has preceded her."

Marsha laughed. "Small island."

"That's kind of why I'm here," Logan said, unsure how to broach the subject. "Small island life. I have a question about the intern committee. You said Connor funded the intern, so I can see why you asked him to help choose an applicant. But why was Liza Holland on the committee?"

Marsha looked perplexed. "I guess she volunteered."

Logan felt her neck flush. "What I was getting at is, did you invite her or did Connor?"

Marsha looked at her steadily, a bit of understanding registering. "They were already in place as committee members when I arrived," she said. She waited for a moment, then said gently, "But I don't think that's what you're really asking, is it?"

Logan looked away, then back at the young minister. "No," she admitted. "I want to know if Connor was having an affair with Liza."

Marsha's expression didn't change. "You probably know I can't tell you that, Logan."

"I guess I hoped that Connor's death revoked any clergy–parishioner confidence."

"Liza's not dead," Marsha reminded her. "But even if both of them were, even if I knew such a thing, I couldn't confirm or deny it." She looked pointedly at Logan. "What could it possibly do but devastate your mother?"

"I wasn't going to tell her," said Logan, feeling like a chastised teen. "I'm just trying to figure out the dynamics among the people in their house the day before Connor was killed."

Marsha looked at her in surprise. "People were there?"

Logan nodded. "Mother and Connor and Margot had a happy hour the afternoon before. The Satterfields and Fitzgeralds were there. Mother's editor Renata O'Steen. Liza Holland and Fred Manigault. Renata told me she thought Liza had a crush on Connor, but didn't know if she'd acted on it." Logan met Marsha's gaze. "Connor was a good man. I'm trying to find any reason someone would kill him."

Marsha rocked back in her chair. "I'm sympathetic, Logan. I really am. I admired and respected your stepfather very much and would love nothing more than for the police to find his killer. But anything I know about my parishioners is off-limits for me to discuss."

"Okay," Logan said. "It was worth a try."

"Do you really think something happened that day that led to Connor's murder?"

Logan shrugged. "It's more like I can't come up with anything else. Nor can the sheriff's office."

Marsha rocked for another minute. "So the authorities think it was someone Connor knew? Not someone passing through?"

Logan nodded. "Yeah. We saw the sheriff this morning, and he said they had ruled out the construction crews, anybody like that on both Isle of Palms and here. And nothing was taken, so it doesn't look like robbery. It's looking more and more like it was intentional. And personal."

"So not a robbery," Marsha repeated. "I hate to hear that."

Logan thought about Marsha's congregation – what it would mean if one member had killed another. Not everyone in the neighborhood went to Chapel by the Sea, of course. There were Baptist and Anglican and Presbyterian churches on the island. And how many in Charleston? This was not only the Bible Belt, but what folks called the belt's buckle – meaning that it often seemed there were as many churches as people. But it *could* be a case of one parishioner killing another and Marsha would have to deal with the fallout.

Logan was still lost in thought when Marsha bolted upright. "Where are my manners? Can I offer you some coffee or lemonade?"

"No, that's all right." Logan stood. "I need to finish walking the fearsome one."

"Well, come back to see me any time," Marsha said as Logan descended the steps and untied Annabelle. She re-entered the house before Logan left the yard. Logan walked around the side of the parsonage, preparing to enter the cemetery, when she heard voices from the Philpots' open window. She instinctively stooped to remove herself from the window's line of sight, pretending to tie her shoes.

"You didn't tell her." Baron's voice was a statement rather than a question.

The child starting laughing and calling to her mother, and Logan missed Marsha's answer.

But Baron's next comment came through clearly. "I see why you don't want to tell Connor's family. But maybe you should tell the sheriff he was having an affair."

Logan rose from tying her shoes, her eyes filling with tears. Annabelle whined softly. She stumbled forward, then veered toward Connor's grave. Fresh lilies filled a bronze vase. Who had put those there?

Logan stood at the graveside, tears slipping down her face. As if from a distance, she pondered whether they were tears of grief or anger. Was she crying for her stepfather? Or for her mother? Or for herself – that she didn't know Connor as well as she thought? She honestly didn't know.

Abruptly, Logan ripped the lilies out of their vase and hurled them across the graveyard. A few white and yellow petals broke away and floated through the rays of spring sunlight.

Chapter 15

When Logan arrived at the beach house, Margot was in the kitchen making a veggie burger. "Want one?" she asked.

"Sure." Logan found the potato chips and filled two glasses with iced tea. She peered through the French doors on to the porch. "Mother's writing?"

"Yep. She fixed her own lunch and told me to take the afternoon off. I'm heading out for my first official beach day. Want to come?"

Logan thought about the alternative, which was brooding in her room. "Yes, yes, I do."

When they had finished eating, the young women collected beach towels, sunglasses and books. Logan found a portable CD player stashed in her bedroom closet. "Margot!" She raised her voice to reach the length of the upstairs hall. "Are there any batteries in the house?"

"Check the laundry room drawers," Margot called back.

Logan walked downstairs in a two-piece navy and white tankini and flip-flops. The laundry room's second drawer yielded an unopened pack of large batteries that she fit into her ancient boom box. She popped in a CD she'd found in her room and the sounds of John Hiatt and the North Mississippi Allstars filled the house.

"Whoo hoo!" Margot yelled.

Logan felt a momentary twinge about the way she was spending her personal day. She turned down the volume and opened the doors on to the porch, but Julianna didn't look up. She crept behind her mother, peeking over her shoulder to read what was on the screen. Her mother was busily typing on page fifteen, something about Annette. Who was that? There was no Annette in the manuscript she had read.

"Mother?" she said softly.

Julianna whirled around in her chair.

"I'm sorry," Logan said. "I just wanted to let you know that Margot and I are headed down to the beach."

It seemed to take her mother a few seconds to focus, but then her face relaxed. "Yes, Logan, that's fine. You girls have fun."

"What are you working on?" she asked.

"Same novel."

"But I read the manuscript while you were away," Logan admitted. "I didn't see an Annette."

Her mother looked at her in bewilderment. "You read my manuscript? Where did you get it?"

"Your bedroom. I hope that's all right."

"Of course it is. Without Connor, I'll need another early reader." She paused. "Any notes to give me?"

"Only that it was awfully good to turn around and add an Annette at this stage."

Julianna laughed. "Annette is the former Alyx. Martin Engler's wife." She warmed to her topic. "It occurred to me in Scotland that her character was in the way. Martin was always having to work around her. So I had the idea to make her his accomplice. After all, she was the biological mother of Catherine, the endangered daughter. What do you think?"

Logan stood speechless. "I-I think you've never asked my opinion about your work before," she stammered.

Julianna smiled. "You never asked about it. Believe me, I'll talk to anyone who's interested. Ask Connor. " She caught herself. "I didn't mean that. Force of habit."

"Well, it's an interesting premise," said Logan, "that both Englers are involved. Are you keeping the son in the picture?"

"No, I thought it would be more powerful if they hadn't been able to have children after giving the daughter up for adoption."

Logan nodded. "I agree."

The women were silent for a moment. "But changing Annette

means a huge rewrite," said Julianna with a wave toward the laptop. "That's what I'm working on."

"Well, I'm glad you feel like working at all," Logan said. "That's wonderful." When her mother made a movement to turn back to her desk, Logan added, "If you get to a stopping place, you're welcome to join us."

Julianna turned back and eyed her daughter. "I might do that. How warm is it out there?"

"It's supposed to be in the mid-70s."

"Give me another hour," said Julianna. "I'll have Annette firmly ensconced into chapter two by then."

Logan and Margot unfolded their lightweight canvas chairs on to the sand and draped seashell-printed beach towels over them. A few people were walking in the distance, but no one else was in bathing suits yet. With the tide out, the afternoon wind hadn't picked up, and the sun felt gloriously warm on their skin.

"Now this is my idea of a beach," said Margot. "I'm telling you, I don't know what those Scots are thinking."

"Little chilly for you, was it?"

"Have you been there?"

"Only once, when I was a teenager. I do remember trying to wear summer clothes and giving up."

"I know it's probably healthier and all that," said Margot as she slathered sunscreen on her arms, then raised an umbrella on the back of her chair. "But no Carolina girl is going to be able to survive it."

Ignoring the books they'd brought, the women talked about their childhoods at opposite ends of the state. Margot was the adopted daughter of a schoolteacher and an engineer for the state Department of Transportation. "I have a younger sister who's getting her master's in early childhood education to follow our mom into teaching."

"How did they tell you that you were adopted?" asked Logan languidly.

"They were the type of parents who used the word 'adopted' long before my sister and I knew what they were talking about. It's true what they say. You're so accustomed to hearing the word that when you figure out what it means, it's no big deal."

"Did you ever go in search of your biological folks?"

"Never. I know how lucky I am."

The women sat in silence for a moment, listening to the waves hiss against the shore. "Can I ask you another personal question?" Logan asked. At Margot's nod she continued, "Do you like your work? Do you get to see people other than Mother? And before, Connor?"

"Yes, I do like it," said Margot, wriggling her toes into the sand. "I'm responsible for the speaking tours and liaising with the universities and bookstores and all that. Mr Burke did it before they hired me, but it had gotten to be too much. After I came, he worked more with her publisher and looking at the big career picture, and left the details to me."

Logan didn't know how to ask the next question. Margot broached the subject for her. "I'm not sure what's going to happen now, because Julianna said she didn't want to make any more appearances this year."

"She did?"

"Yeah. She said she has a window when people will understand if she stays out of sight."

"I guess that's true," Logan said. "But Margot, I know how much she relies on you. Without Connor, she's going to need you more than ever." She paused. "I don't mean to pressure you, but if you're worried that you might be out of a job, don't be. Your position might be different than it was before, but I'm sure Mother still needs an assistant. And I don't think it would be easy to find someone she trusts *and* that she can stand to have in close proximity."

Margot laughed. "Thanks. I think. To tell you the truth, I was hoping the job might morph more into the editorial side. That's what my degree is in. Well, English lit, anyway."

"You mean you want to make suggestions on her manuscripts?"

Margot nodded.

"I don't see why not," Logan mused. "I remember overhearing her and Connor when I was growing up. Mother always said that any writer, no matter how good they were, needed other eyes. If nothing else, to save them from stupid errors and typos."

The Hiatt CD ended, and Logan flipped in one by Leonard Cohen.

"Just in case we were having too much fun?" teased Margot.

"I guess he can be a downer," said Logan. "I do have one more question for you, and it's awful."

"Uh-oh. What?"

Logan hesitated, not knowing how to phrase it. "It's something Renata said that I haven't been able to get out of my mind."

Margot turned to give Logan her full attention.

"Was Connor having an affair?"

Margot gasped. "Renata said that? How would she know?"

"She didn't know," Logan amended. "And that's not exactly what she said. She said that someone had a crush on Connor. Someone at the happy hour."

"Who?" said Margot. "It wasn't me, was it?"

That brought Logan up short. "You? No." Logan wondered why Margot would've said such a thing.

But the assistant visibly relaxed. "Who then?" she asked. "That leaves Mrs Satterfield, Mrs Fitzgerald and Ms Holland." She smiled wickedly. "Unless Renata is claiming there was a gay vibe going on."

Logan snorted. "No, not that. Renata thinks Liza Holland had a crush on him."

Margot gazed out at the ocean. "Huh. I didn't catch that. But then I probably wouldn't." She thought for another minute and shook her head. "But Logan, I was probably around your mother and Mr Burke more than anybody. And I honestly thought he was devoted to her."

"You honestly thought who was devoted to whom?" Logan and Margot jumped as Julianna approached them from behind, a beach chair in one hand, a glass of wine in the other.

"Brad Pitt to Angelina Jolie," Margot said smoothly. "We're diving into old celebrity gossip."

Logan eyed Margot, grateful for the quick recovery but marveling at the young woman's easy lie.

"Well, it's time for me to get some exercise," Margot said, standing and brushing the sand off her thighs. "I'll go for a walk and leave you two to it."

Julianna settled into Margot's vacated chair and stretched her legs. "Ah, first beach day of the year. That's always special, isn't it?"

"Sure is," said Logan. "Did you get the newly murderous Annette insinuated into chapter two?"

"Yes, I did. Unfortunately for Renata, all this rewriting isn't going to add to the page count any time soon."

"Yeah, but the fact that you're writing again will thrill her. She knows what a pro you are."

Julianna looked at her daughter. "Why, thank you."

Logan plowed on. "Liza said something while you were in Scotland that surprised me. She said you didn't know if I read your books." She kept her gaze fixed on the watery horizon. "I thought I ought to tell you – I'm a huge fan."

"You are?" Julianna took a sip of wine. "Logan, I cannot tell you how much that means to me."

"Surely you knew. You're, like, the bestselling mystery writer in the country."

"But somehow it's different with your family," Julianna explained. "I really wanted you to like my books, but I was afraid to ask in case you didn't."

Logan laughed. "That's crazy."

"Yeah, maybe." Julianna smiled. "But don't you have some crazy ideas about your art?"

Logan waved a hand dismissively. "It's not the same thing."

"It's *exactly* the same thing," said her mother. "You are a talented artist. I promise I wouldn't say that if I didn't believe it."

"Well, okay." Logan was embarrassed. "Thank you."

"So tell me what's going on with your painting."

For the next quarter of an hour, as her mother followed up with questions, Logan chatted about shows and festivals she'd participated in, restaurants where her work hung, even the call she'd gotten from the owners of a restaurant that had branched out from Charleston to Greenville. They wanted to include three of her paintings in the Upstate location.

"That's marvelous," Julianna said. "And I believe you said you're working for a dentist? How's that going?"

"Internists," Logan corrected. "Drs Littlemeyer and Johns. Do you remember Gus Johns I went to high school with?"

"I don't think so."

"Anyway, that's how I got the job. He's an old friend."

"Do you like working there?"

"It's all right." Logan idly shoveled sand with her feet. "To be honest, I'm not sure I've found my passion other than not-very-well-paid art."

"As long as you have a passion, period, you're ahead of the game," her mother said, waving her wine glass. "Many people never find that. And if money follows, it's sheer coincidence."

"Well, you sure found your passion," Logan said. "And money did follow."

"Yes, it did," said Julianna. "I've been very fortunate." She gave a sad smile. "But look at me now. A fifty-eight-year-old widow with a broken heart and a memory like Swiss cheese. All of a sudden, the future doesn't look so bright."

Logan didn't know what to say. The women sat in silence as Julianna finished her wine.

"You're making me want some of that," Logan said. "Can I bring you another?"

"Yes, please."

"Will do."

Alone on the beach, Julianna luxuriated in the sun, feeling the tension drain from her shoulders after several hours at the computer. The wine was making her drowsy and she closed her eyes. Immediately, she heard Lance Royston's words from that morning – words she'd apparently uttered the night of Connor's murder. "Why don't you ask Dr Engler?"

Goodness, she was quite mad. Before they left his office, Lance had requested a copy of her manuscript. She emailed it to him as soon as she returned home, but it didn't include the scene in which Dr Engler killed his patient, asleep in his home office. Should she show Lance that scene too? Or would he arrest her on the spot, before she had a chance to figure out the truth?

She shuddered despite the sun's welcome rays. She pictured herself on that other warm day, walking from the porch to her office as she'd done a thousand times, eager to tell Connor something. But what? What had she wanted to tell him?

She'd been writing, Margot said. Or, based on the sorry output between November and February, sitting at her desk and *not* writing. She probably wanted to tell him something about Martin Engler. Or the patient, Edward. Or the daughter, Catherine.

If she could remember what she'd been thinking about that day, maybe she could remember what had triggered a question or comment for Connor. Was it about Edward, the father desperate to tamp down his lust for his daughter? Or was it about Catherine, oblivious, walking around the house in shorts and T-shirts as she had all her life?

Logan suddenly appeared at her side, honey blonde hair shining, sunglasses hiding those gorgeous eyes, well-shaped legs sprinkled with sand. She handed her mother a glass of chilled chardonnay, the glass sweating.

Julianna took the drink, unseeing, silent. Logan was, practically if not legally, Connor's adopted daughter. Was that where the idea for this novel had come from? She vaguely remembered a phone call from Logan, asking if they were spending Christmas together. She'd answered that she and Connor were going to Florida. "Oh," Logan had responded, "I thought since we weren't together at Thanksgiving…" Not Thanksgiving. Not Christmas. Why had she not included Harrison or Logan in their plans? Had she intentionally kept Connor and Logan apart? She struggled to recall if Connor had objected. She didn't know.

She began breathing harder, the earlier camaraderie between her and Logan forgotten.

"Mother, are you all right?" Logan asked.

"Yes, yes." She took a gulp of wine, then another. Her breathing didn't slow. She was anxious to be alone, to think. "I believe I'll go for a walk too. See you in a bit."

Logan watched her mother hurry away, and her heart pinched. For the first time, she thought that being Julianna Burke might not be such a great thing.

Julianna veered into the water, but it was cold, and she returned to the strip of hard packed sand where the tide had retreated. She walked rapidly, grateful to be away from Logan's curious gaze. What on earth had just happened? She had equated fictional Edward and Catherine with Connor and Logan. That was ludicrous. She had never, not once, suspected that Connor harbored anything but the purest affection for her daughter. If anything, he was a little more distant than she might have wished. Wasn't he? Well then, why had she not seen Logan – or Harrison, for that matter – for so long before Connor died? Was that Connor's idea? Or hers? She honestly couldn't remember.

She tried to recall starting her book. It was last spring, she thought, even later than now. April maybe, or May. She remembered productive days on the deck overlooking the ocean, stopping for huge salads or cut-up fruit stirred into vanilla yogurt. She remembered setting daily incentives – a cocktail with Connor, an outdoor concert, a walk on the beach, a Netflix movie. She worked best when she set deadlines and rewards. *A thousand words and I can take a walk. Two thousand words and we'll have dinner in Charleston.*

But where had the idea for the book come from? Her mind kept scrabbling away from the question. Why was she so afraid to face it?

"Julianna! Yoo hoo!" Julianna jerked to a halt, wondering if she'd really heard her name or if it was a trick of the rising breeze. She looked up at the row of houses and saw Liza Holland hurrying down the steps from her deck, Maxie leaping in front of her. She stopped and waved.

Liza had a huge smile on her face and grabbed Julianna in a hug. "When did you get back?" she said. "I thought you were staying in Scotland longer."

"We got home yesterday," said Julianna.

"How was it? How are you? Is everything all right?"

Julianna shrugged. "The trip was all right. But after a while, it felt too lonely there. I was ready to get back home."

Liza nodded in sympathy. "Maxie wants to walk. Is it okay if we come along with you?"

"Sure. Logan's already walked Annabelle. She's been a big help. Logan, I mean. Not Annabelle."

"She's staying with you?"

"Yes, she's taking some vacation days to help me get settled, bless her heart. We're having our first beach day of the year. She's back there," she said, waving toward her house, "and Margot is somewhere ahead of us."

"Fun!" Liza said. "I like Logan. We had a nice visit last week." She looked sideways at her friend. "You seem different, Julianna."

"How so?"

"I'm not sure. More vibrant, maybe? How are you?" she repeated.

"Do you mean my memory?" Julianna had a sudden vision of herself gliding through Liza's unfamiliar house in the dark of night, unthinking, unfeeling. She spun to look at the attractive blue house behind them. "I stayed with you," she said abruptly.

Liza nodded. "You sure did. The sheriff wanted everyone out of your house for a while."

"Thank you, Liza. That was kind of you."

"Don't mention it. The girls enjoyed it," she said with a nod at Maxie. "In fact, I think she's been lonely since Annabelle left."

The women walked in silence for a few moments. "Since you mentioned it," Liza asked tentatively, "how *is* your memory?"

"Better, I think. Especially in the mornings. I still get a little fuzzy at night."

"So Charlie's suggestion of gingko worked? I may begin taking it myself. I could use a memory boost."

Julianna opened her mouth to tell her that she'd been seven days without the pills, but hesitated. She wasn't sure what held her back. She still wanted to discuss it with Charlie, so Logan had made an appointment for tomorrow.

Instead Julianna nodded and changed the subject. "So what's going on with you? Still dating Frank? Wait, that's not right. I'm sorry, what is his name?"

"Fred," said Liza. "No problem. Yes, I see him once or twice a week." She chatted on about a fundraiser she and Fred had attended. "But listen to me prattle on. I'm more interested in how you're doing. Have you heard anything from the sheriff's investigators?"

"I saw Lance Royston this morning." Julianna cringed inwardly at the memory. *Did you ask Dr Engler?* "Apparently he was at my house right after Connor was killed and I didn't even remember it."

"Goodness knows you were in shock. No one could expect you to remember everything about that night."

"Yeah, maybe. But we all know it didn't end there."

"Give it some time," said Liza. "You already seem more… focused, somehow."

"Yes, I do feel more focused. That's a good word for it. I've been working on my novel again."

Liza stopped, a big smile on her face. "You are? That's amazing!"

Julianna was puzzled. "I'm not sure it's amazing. What else would I do?"

"I don't know. Sleep? Eat? Watch TV? Lie on the beach? It's amazing that you could be back at work after what you've been through. Isn't Charlie surprised?"

"I haven't seen Charlie yet. I have an appointment with him tomorrow. Logan is coming along to see about her doddering old mother."

Liza laughed and hugged her friend's shoulders. "I don't care what you say. I think you're amazing."

They walked a bit further, then turned around and headed back to where Logan waited.

Meg Fitzgerald dragged a beach chair in one hand and held a bottle of pinot grigio in the other. She wore knee-length khaki shorts and a flowing sleeveless T-shirt. "Happy hour?" she said gleefully, placing her chair next to Logan's.

"You bet!" Logan answered. "Where's your bathing suit?"

"This body doesn't do bathing suits any more."

"Ah. Can you actually decree that?"

"Honey, after fifty you make all new rules."

Logan laughed. "Good to know." She held out her glass to accept a generous pour.

"Where is everybody?" Meg asked.

"Margot and Mother went for walks. Must have been something I said."

The women sat in companionable silence. "This is why we live in South Carolina," said Meg drowsily. "While the Yanks are still digging themselves out of snow, we have a day like this."

"Amen."

"When you're finished listening to Leonard, I brought you some real music.

Logan grinned. "Lemme see." She took the plastic CD case with starbursts and banners across the cover. "*Best of Carolina Beach Music*, huh?"

"And that's saying a lot, my dear."

"Is this what you and Dr Fitz danced to?"

"It is indeed. Up north of here at Ocean Drive. We danced at an open-air, wood-floored bar called the Spanish Galleon. On the first week school was out, kids from all over the state crammed in there, but we had it the rest of the summer."

"That is so cool to have such a long history together."

Meg didn't answer. Logan looked at her. Meg took a long pull on her glass and looked away, but not before Logan saw her eyes suddenly shining. "Meg? Is everything all right?"

Meg brushed a hand across her eyes. "Sure. It's… nothing. Nothing at all."

Logan wondered if Meg knew about Charlie's philandering. To give her a moment of privacy, Logan turned her gaze toward the beach in the direction her mother had gone. She shaded her eyes with a hand. "Someone's coming back with Mother." She watched them approach, a dog prancing in front of them. "It's gotta be Liza and Maxie."

"Hmmm," Meg murmured under her breath.

"What?" asked Logan.

"Nothing."

"Meg – what? Do you not like Liza?"

Meg shrugged. "Not my favorite person."

Logan remembered what Fred Manigault had said about Liza and Charlie. Her hope rose a little. Maybe Renata was wrong. Maybe Liza was having an affair with Charlie, and not Connor.

Was that a horrible thing to wish?

"I hate to be provincial," Meg sniffed. "But she's got a big-city superiority about her."

"What big city?"

"Chicago. She ran a YWCA or women's center or something like that."

"I never knew that." Logan thought for a minute. "That wouldn't generate enough money to buy a house on this beach, would it?"

"I think she got a divorce settlement."

"She's divorced? I guess I don't know much about her. I don't think she and Mother were friends until they got those matching dogs."

Meg laughed. "Her husband was an attorney," she said. "So pretty good money, I imagine. She doesn't talk about him much."

"I'm surprised she never remarried, as attractive as she is."

"Hmmm."

Logan twisted around in her seat to face Meg. "You keep doing that. What is up?"

"Oh, don't pay any attention to me, Logan. I'm just a bitter old woman."

"You are most certainly not a bitter old woman. You are the kindest person I know. If you don't like Liza, I'd think there's probably a reason." She couldn't bring herself to ask if Meg suspected Charlie was having an affair with their neighbor.

"It's just…" Meg paused. "It's just that sometimes having a single woman around isn't easy. And I know that is dreadfully unfair and dreadfully anti-feminist and all the rest of it." She blushed. "And I am duly ashamed of myself."

Logan waited to see if she'd say something else, but she didn't. Her mother and Liza were almost upon them.

"Meg!" said Julianna warmly, coming around to hug her friend. "How good to see you!"

"Having Logan around is a bad influence," said Meg. "She's got me drinking in the middle of the day."

Logan hooted. "From what I hear, you guys don't need me for that."

"Midday drinking," said Julianna. "What a good idea. Who's up for happy hour one day this week?"

"Count me in," said Liza. "I could do Thursday or Friday."

"Any day's fine for me," said Meg.

"I've got to go back to work," said Logan, "but I can join you by 5:30."

"Then let's make it Thursday," said Julianna. "Logan, don't let me forget."

The women laughed. "None of us will," said Meg. "That's a promise."

Liza sat on the sand with Maxie at her side. "Liza, you're the only one without a drink," said Logan. "Can I bring you one?"

"Actually, I need to use the bathroom anyway. I can get my own if you tell me where it is."

"There's an open bottle of Chardonnay in the fridge," said Julianna. "Or plenty of reds in the rack above the refrigerator. Help yourself."

"Will do. Logan, I'm going to wrap Maxie's leash around your chair leg."

"Sure. Come here, Maxie. You are such a good girl. Unlike your buddy."

"Were that only true," said Liza.

Chapter 16

Julianna and Logan pulled up at Charlie Fitzgerald's medical office building five blocks from where Logan worked. His waiting room was more elegant than Littlemeyer and Johns' – with a coffee/cappuccino/hot chocolate dispenser and up-to-date *Coastal Living* and *Architectural Digest* magazines.

"I'm in the mood to go out after we finish here," said Julianna. "Would you prefer coffee and bagels or a fancy schmancy lunch?"

"Ooh, let me think about it," said Logan. "Both sound good."

They sat in the waiting room, passing magazines back and forth as they pointed out rooms they liked or hated. Logan showed her mother a spread about a four-story house with an infinity pool on St Simons Island in Georgia. "Here's what Harrison will do to your house if he ever gets his hands on it," she said.

Julianna laughed. "You're right. And I'm sure he could bring it in for under $15 million." She looked at Logan for a moment. "What about you? You used to want to spruce up the house too."

"Spruce up?" laughed Logan. "That house needs more than sprucing up." She thought for a minute. "I guess I've come to understand your attachment to it as it is. You really don't like being a celebrity, do you? I think maybe that house keeps you grounded."

Julianna looked at her daughter with gratitude. "I've never articulated it, but I think that's it exactly," she said slowly. "As long as I live there, I can still be Julianna Montague, not Julianna Burke. There's not a person on that street who cares one bit about what I do for a living. And that means everything to me."

"Meanwhile, everyone else in the world is fighting to gain celebrity," said Logan. "Irony abounds."

"I suppose so."

The nurse called Julianna's name and once they'd entered an examination room, asked her to step on to a scale. "You've lost six pounds since you were here, Mrs Burke."

"I've lost my husband since I was here too. I'm surprised it's not more than that."

The heavyset nurse blushed.

"She's eating pretty well now," said Logan. "I think the weight loss came in the first couple of weeks. Oh, I'm her daughter, Logan."

The nurse nodded. "Nice to meet you." She took Julianna's blood pressure, then left the room, saying, "Dr Fitzgerald will be right in."

She had hardly closed the door when Charlie Fitzgerald came in. He hugged Julianna and Logan, and sat on a rolling stool to look over her chart on his laptop. "Have I mentioned how much I hate this thing?" he said cheerfully, tapping keys.

"Oh yes, you've made that quite clear," said Julianna.

"Ah, you remember?"

"I do indeed. Which tells me you have mentioned it more than once."

He laughed. "I think most of my patients would tell you that. Now catch me up on what's going on with you. Gingko doing you any good?"

"Is it possible that it made me worse?"

His eyebrows shot up. "I don't think so. Side effects can be mild stomach upset, headache, dizziness, increased heart rate, but it shouldn't make your memory worse."

"Well, I was clearer in the morning and got progressively worse throughout the day after taking it," she said. "I know it's common to lose clarity over the course of the day, but this was awful." She shook her head. "Anyway, I finally stopped taking it about a week ago in Scotland. I've seemed to be a little clearer every day since."

Dr Fitzgerald and Logan looked at her in surprise. Logan was the first to speak. "I didn't know she'd stopped taking the pills, but she's definitely better now than when she left," she said. "Ten times better." She remembered her conversation with Harrison at The Mangrove. "Dr Fitz, is it possible that something you prescribed to help her sleep after Connor's death could have made her memory worse?"

"Now that *is* a possibility," he said. He looked to see what he'd prescribed. "I only gave you five pills though," he said doubtfully. "But if you're really, really sensitive to it, it could exacerbate confusion. As for the gingko, that's pretty subjective. Some people swear by it. Some say there's no improvement. So if you think you're better without it, by all means leave it off." He tapped at his screen for a moment. "Let's see what else you are taking. Blood pressure meds, right?"

"Right. And vitamins and calcium. And fish oil when I can remember."

He looked at Julianna curiously. "Talk to me a bit," he invited. "Tell me about the last few weeks." Logan kept quiet, rightly guessing that he wanted to test Julianna's coherency.

"If you don't mind," she said, "I'll go back further than that." He nodded assent. She drew a deep breath. "How many times have I visited you since Thanksgiving?"

He tapped for several seconds on his keyboard. "Let's see. You came in early November to talk about mild memory issues. That's when I suggested gingko and/or fish oil. But since Thanksgiving, only once – for a sinus infection. And if I'm remembering correctly – which isn't a given – Connor was with you both times."

"I do remember coming to you about my memory," she said, nodding. "And yes, Connor came too. I had been struggling with names and dates at book signings and speeches." She paused. "But I have no recollection of a sinus infection." She paused to gather her thoughts.

"Anyway, last spring I started work on a new book. Apparently I wrote 170 pages by mid-November." Julianna's face took on a puzzled look. "I would've told you I was working on the book right up until Connor died. But there's almost nothing to show for it." She shrugged helplessly. "I – I – don't really know where those last five months went." She looked as if she wanted to say something more but stopped.

Logan thought back to her phone calls to her mother at Thanksgiving and Christmas, asking – rather plaintively, she realized in retrospect – if the family was getting together, and hearing her mother's airy explanations that she and Connor would be traveling. Had her mother been trying to hide her worsening memory?

Dr Fitzgerald was studying Julianna closely. "You talked about the book the day we were at your house," he said. "You told us the title."

"I'm not sure I'd have any recollection of that day if Margot hadn't filled me in. Repeatedly." Again, Julianna looked as if she was on the verge of saying something else.

"What did you think of Mother that day?" asked Logan.

"I do remember thinking that she was a little slow in processing the conversation," he admitted. "Connor and Margot were quick to answer for her." He looked thoughtful. "Logan," he said, "I'm very glad you've come in because I'm a big believer in having everyone on board in cases like this. But is it all right if I talk to your mother privately for a moment?"

Logan was startled, but assured him it was and left the room.

When they were alone, Dr Fitzgerald got directly to the point. "I got the feeling you were holding back. Is there something you need to ask me?"

Julianna twisted her hands in her lap and gazed out of the doctor's window. "Anything I say to you is confidential, right?"

"Of course."

"You've heard me and Connor talk about my wanderings, haven't you? When I'm writing?"

The physician smiled broadly. "The secret to your success, according to Connor."

Julianna didn't smile. "There are gaps that day Connor was killed," she said so quietly that he had to lean forward. "Complete voids."

"Okay."

She licked her lips nervously. "Margot saw me earlier that afternoon on the porch and thought I might have been wandering. When I do, I have no idea where I've been or what I've done – only that I have new ideas when I come to."

He nodded.

"An hour and a half later I found Connor's body in my office." She hesitated over the next part that she'd shared with no one. "While I was in Scotland, I found a scene I'd written in my novel that was almost exactly the way Connor was killed. A man stabbed while lying asleep in his office." She couldn't bring herself to add the part about her fictional victim's feelings for his adopted daughter. How that might have become confused in her mind with Connor and *his* stepdaughter.

Julianna watched as Charlie put the pieces of her story together. She waited for his quick and explosive dismissal of the idea. It didn't come.

"And you think you might have acted out Connor's murder during a wandering," he said. It wasn't a question but a statement. "Whew!"

He twirled around on his stool and looked out of the window, as Julianna had done.

When she could stand the silence no longer, Julianna said, "I've been trying to work it out for myself before talking to Sheriff Royston. But for the life of me, I can't remember."

Dr Fitzgerald met her eyes. "Julianna, part of me – the longtime friend and neighbor part – wants to tell you there is no way you could have killed Connor. Absolutely, positively, no way on earth."

She smiled sadly. "But there's another part of you that says otherwise."

"The professional part of me has no idea what's going on in your mind," he said. "Medicine is not very advanced as far as memory and dementia and Alzheimer's are concerned. And what you have described for twenty years as your wanderings…" He held a palm up. "I have no answer for that. I'll be happy to refer you to a neurologist or a psychiatrist if you like."

"It may come to that," she said, "but not quite yet. Give me another couple of days to try to work it out for myself."

Logan was in the waiting room when Julianna emerged. "Everything all right?" she asked.

"Yes," said her mother. "I'm relieved that he was fine with dropping the gingko. I wasn't going back to it no matter what he said. I honestly think it made me hallucinate, among other things."

"Is that what he wanted to discuss with you? Your hallucination in Crail when you thought you saw him?"

"Oh," said Julianna. "I forgot to mention that."

Julianna stood in the middle of the waiting room. She was confident now that she hadn't seen Charlie in Crail. But why had her mind told her she had? Why that particular hallucination?

"Mother?"

Julianna looked around to see people in the waiting room sneaking glances at her. Embarrassed, she indicated the door. "Are you ready to eat?"

"You bet!" said Logan. "I've got a carb craving. Let's hit my favorite bagel shop."

Not wanting to face Charleston's lunchtime traffic, they walked several blocks to a street near Logan's office. The weather remained warm for March, and the women walked in the dappled mid-day sun, stepping carefully to avoid tripping on the broken concrete, passing an art gallery, a drugstore, a Subway shop, a vintage clothing store. Logan explained that a Jewish couple from up North had established Peninsula Deli a decade before bagels were widely known in the South. Now the couple's daughter and son-in-law ran the shop, but the feel of a no-frills kitchen remained.

Once they'd placed their orders at the counter, they took their coffee mugs and settled at a nicked laminate table, one of only two that were unoccupied. Julianna looked at the paper towel roll and made a face.

"You like slumming, I see," she teased.

"Wait until you taste the bagels," Logan promised.

"I noticed you didn't order meat or cream cheese or even butter."

"You don't mess with perfection."

A server brought Logan's pumpernickel bagel and Julianna's turkey sandwich on wheat bagel, with pickles and chips. Logan watched her mother take a bite.

"Oh my, you're right," she said. "This is delicious."

Logan sat back. "Okay, so tell me what you think about the visit to Dr Fitz."

"Truthfully? I don't think he knows a thing that we don't. I'll stay away from taking any more sleeping pills, obviously. And over-the-counter gingko, though it makes no sense that it could cause confusion in me and no one else in the world."

"You're one of a kind."

Julianna laughed. "Yeah, maybe that's it."

"But how do you feel?" Logan pressed.

Julianna sighed. "Still sad, obviously. But not so out of it." She paused. "And…"

"What?"

"It almost makes me feel guilty to say this, disloyal to Connor somehow. But I have to admit, I'm excited about finishing the book. There was a while there that I thought I'd never feel that way again." She looked squarely at her daughter. "Is that awful?"

Logan thought about all the times she'd felt second best to her mother's writing. Heck, third best, after her writing *and* Connor. But her mother had loved her in her mildly distracted way. Logan was an adult. It was time to get past blaming her mother for her own less than stellar career. She shrugged. "Nothing to feel guilty about. That's who you are." She was surprised to find that she meant it.

Julianna smiled. "If anything, the book will probably turn darker, sadder. But that's all right."

"In that case," said Logan, "I think I'll go back to work tomorrow."

"But you don't have to return to your apartment yet, do you?"

asked her mother. "I love having you at the beach house. And I'm sure Margot does too."

"And Annabelle."

"Ha! Yes, and Anna B. So what do you think?"

"I guess I can stay awhile longer. But you honestly do seem so much better. It's pretty amazing actually."

"Well, part of it may be that I'm around people I know. I haven't had to do appearances for several weeks. That's what unnerves me. And frankly, without Connor as a buffer, I don't know if I can ever resume that."

"What will your publisher say?"

"They won't like it. But maybe I'll bring up J. D. Salinger." Julianna smiled self-mockingly. "He somehow managed without speaking to the undergrads at USC."

Logan laughed and brushed crumbs off her lap. They talked awhile longer, refilling their mugs from a nearby coffee canister, gingerly aware of enjoying each other's company in a way that was new to them.

Finally, Logan looked around and saw a second-wave lunch crowd coming in. "Are you ready to go, or do you want more coffee?" she asked.

"I'm ready. Thanks for sharing your special place with me."

"My pleasure. Next time we'll hit a restaurant that's bought my artwork."

"I'd love that! It's a date."

Mother and daughter left the deli not speaking, but each wondering about the last time they'd had lunch together in Charleston. Julianna wasn't surprised that she couldn't remember. But Logan couldn't either.

Chapter 17

Logan returned to a hectic Wednesday in the internists' office. Gus and Dr Littlemeyer had a busy practice, and as the frontline receptionist, she sometimes felt like an air traffic controller. She not only oversaw patient check-ins, but when the office manager was called to the back – which was frequently – Logan directed the staff who were handling checkouts and payments.

Still, she was able to leave shortly after 5 p.m. She ran some errands, refueled the Jeep and stopped by a drugstore for more sunscreen in case the weather held to allow beach time this weekend. As she pulled into her mother's driveway, she saw Dick Satterfield in his yard, tinkering with lawn sprinkler heads.

She walked over to speak to him. "You're doing something right!" she called. "Best yard on Sully's!"

He straightened and smiled. "Hello, Logan. How nice to see you. How's your mother?"

"She's surprisingly well, thank you. You'll see her out walking soon, I'm sure."

"I think I saw her and Liza out this morning. But I was inside." He waved at his house.

Logan hesitated, unsure if she should bring it up. "How's Sunny?" she finally asked. "The last time I talked to her she seemed a little… nervous."

Dick adjusted his ball cap more firmly on his balding head, and didn't quite meet Logan's eyes. "She's taken your stepfather's death very hard," he said in an even tone. "Would you like to visit her? I'm sure she would like that."

"Um, sure," Logan said, though she had been looking forward to getting her scrubs off and taking a walk.

"I'll have to let you in," he said. "She's got everything locked up tight."

He tramped to the front porch, fishing a set of keys from his pocket. As he opened the door, Buster rushed to meet them and Dick let the dog into the front yard. "I know, boy," Logan heard him say softly. Then he raised his voice, "Sunny, it's me. Logan is here to see you." He waited until he heard an answer, then opened the door wide. When Logan was inside, he pulled it shut; she heard the bolt slide into place.

Sheesh, she murmured to herself. *What is this, Fort Knox?* "Sunny!" she called, not wishing to startle her neighbor. "It's Logan."

"Come on in," she heard a voice say from the back. "I'm on the porch."

Well, that's progress, I guess. Logan walked quietly through the living room and adjoining music room to a porch that ran the entire width of the house's rear. She found Sunny huddled on one corner of a sofa nearest the kitchen, a glass in her hand.

"Got a little jump on five o'clock," she said, her words slightly slurred. "Can I get you a drink?"

"No, no, I'm not…" Logan couldn't think of a reason to refuse a drink, but she didn't want one. Sunny didn't seem to notice there was no excuse forthcoming. Her blonde hair was stringy and unwashed, with a stripe of ashy gray at the roots. She'd lost weight she could ill afford to lose.

"Sunny, are you okay?" Logan asked gently.

"Where's Buster?" she asked, suddenly alert. "Where'd he go?"

"Dick let him out in the front yard where he's working."

"But you're here."

"Yes, I'm here."

"So I guess it's all right then."

Logan had no idea what she was talking about. "What's all right?"

Sunny looked suddenly sober, meeting Logan's eyes with intensity. "You knew him, Logan, didn't you? As well as anyone?"

"Who?"

A flash of irritation crossed Sunny's thin face. "Connor, of course."

Logan thought of Baron Philpot's comment that she'd overheard through an open window, his certainty that Connor was having an affair. She had assumed it was with Liza Holland. But Baron hadn't said that, had he? Did she know her stepfather? Clearly not as well as she'd thought.

"I knew him," she answered slowly. "But I wouldn't say well."

Sunny looked at her quizzically.

"He and my mother were pretty much a closed circle," Logan said, choosing a wicker armchair and remembering Dick's evading eyes a few minutes earlier. Now she peered closely at Sunny and recalled her neighbor as she'd been a month ago: vibrant, pretty, talented, perhaps a decade younger than Dick and Connor. *What has happened to you?*

"I feel like I need to tell you something, Logan," she said, taking a sip of her drink, something amber and unappetizing, its ice melted. "But I don't want to hurt your family."

Logan grew still. "Go ahead."

Sunny squeezed her eyes shut. "This has always been such a safe place, you know? This neighborhood. This island. Remember walking to Poe's after dark? We didn't think anything of it."

Logan nodded, remembering Meg and Sunny taking her and Britt to the popular tavern named for Edgar Allen Poe, who'd spent time in the area. Where had her mother been? She didn't know – only that she and Britt enjoyed pretending that Sunny was their big sister.

"But Sunny, we can still do that."

Sunny looked distressed. "Oh, no! Not on your life!"

Logan wasn't following Sunny's line of thought. What did that have to do with Logan's family? Or had she changed subjects in mid-thought?

"What did you want to tell me about my family?" she asked.

"Dick," Sunny said, pouting. "Dick travels all the time. Did you know that?"

"I thought he was retired."

"He is. Ob-tensibly. Or-tensively."

"Ostensibly," Logan provided with a sigh.

"He still piddles. He says that's why he has to fly to New York and LA and even Las Vegas. Though I'm not sure how seeing Elvis impersonators helps our portfolio."

Logan was lost. It didn't seem to matter what she said, so she said nothing.

"Your stepfather, now there was a kind man," Sunny said. Logan held her breath. "And handsome. And sexy." She giggled. "Your mama was one lucky woman. For a while there anyway."

Logan could scarcely believe what she was hearing. "Was he having an affair, Sunny?" She spoke so softly it was almost a whisper. She realized she didn't really want to know the answer.

Sunny's eyes narrowed, and she studied Logan through a squint. "Oh. I suppose that would hurt your family, wouldn't it?" She picked up her drink. "Ugh. Watered down." She rose to her feet. "I'm freshening this. Are you sure I can't get you one?"

Logan stood as well, fatigued by the cryptic nature of Sunny's conversation. "No, I need to go. I haven't even made it home yet."

She stood uncertainly in Sunny's kitchen, battling with herself. Her curiosity won. "Sunny, are you telling me that Connor was having an affair?"

"What?" Sunny looked at her vacantly, obviously having lost the thread of their conversation.

"You said my stepfather was handsome and sexy. Was he having an affair?"

"How the heck would I know? I'm not the adultery police." She cackled, then put her hands on the counter as if to catch her breath.

Logan gave up and let herself out of the front door. Dick was throwing a tennis ball to Buster, who seemed ecstatic to be outside. "So what do you think?" he asked.

"About Sunny?"

"Of course." Dick looked impatient. "Did she tell you what she's so anxious about?"

"No," said Logan carefully. "She mentioned not wanting to hurt my family."

"It's too late to worry about that," he said brusquely. "It's hurting my family too. I'm going to Sheriff Royston."

Logan's mouth opened in surprise. "Sheriff Royston?"

Dick nodded and drew uncomfortably close to her. "On the afternoon of the murder," he said, "Sunny saw someone at your mother's." He inclined his head to indicate the weathered gray house across the street, which, for the first time in Logan's life, appeared ominous. *Moby Dick*, she thought crazily. She gazed at the house's closed façade, not entirely wanting to hear what her neighbor had to say.

"Who?" Her voice sounded squeaky even to her own ears. "Who'd she see?"

"Your brother," he said. "Harrison."

Logan rushed across the street and into the house. Annabelle met her at the door with a soft yip. She could hear her mother and Margot talking on the porch, but she didn't want to see anyone. She ran upstairs and changed into biking pants, a long-sleeved T-shirt and tennis shoes, and let herself quietly out the front door.

In a storage room underneath the house, along with two spider-web-covered surfboards and a boogie board, she located her mother's old bike. She wheeled it to the driveway and hopped on. She'd had enough of this neighborhood and its secrets. She biked to Middle Street and followed it all the way to the bridge over the inlet, then veered down the crooked side streets to the Isle of Palms' beachfront road.

It was much cooler here, as the sun sank and the wind whipped between magnificent oceanfront mansions, many of them new since Hurricane Hugo devastated the island in 1989. She didn't want to think. She wanted only to ride mindlessly, her hair streaming behind her. But how could she avoid it? The thing she really didn't want to know – if Connor had cheated on her mother – seemed insignificant in light of Dick Satterfield's revelation. Harrison had been at the beach house on the afternoon of their stepfather's murder. And he had lied to the detectives about it.

She thought back to that Saturday morning with Detectives Giles and Lancaster. Was it only eleven days ago? "In your previous statements," she could hear Detective Giles say, "you indicated that you were at your separate homes on Friday evening, February 22." Plainly, that was Harrison's story. Her mind cast about for an explanation. Maybe Harrison *was* back at his place by evening. But he neglected to mention he'd been at his mother's that afternoon. That wouldn't fly.

And Sunny. Why would Sunny Satterfield hesitate to share what she'd seen with investigators? Was her loyalty to her neighbors that strong? Or was there a reason she'd protect Connor's stepson? Was she afraid of what else might come to light if detectives began looking at Connor's relationships too closely?

Logan rode hard, pushing her body in an attempt to quiet her mind. It didn't work. She zipped through the Isle of Palms' tiny downtown of sandy bars and beachwear stores, then out past a grocery plaza and Methodist church and back on to the beachfront road. She could picture Connor having an affair with the vivacious Sunny. Younger woman, professional musician. Yeah, if Sunny put her mind to it, Logan supposed she could have turned Connor's head.

And what? If Sunny told the detectives she'd seen Harrison at the house, they'd start looking more closely into Connor's private life? That made no sense. Detectives would automatically look into a murder victim's relationships, no matter what.

So why wouldn't Sunny tell them she'd seen Harrison? It had to be to protect Harrison.

Logan tried to recall interactions between her brother and their across-the-street neighbor. Where was he when she and Britt and Meg and Sunny walked to Poe's? Back home, expressing contempt for the idea of accompanying thirteen-year-olds to dinner. She saw Sunny, a newlywed, not much older than Harrison was now, standing in the doorway to his room. "Are you sure you don't want to come, Harrison?" And his seventeen-year-old face blushing furiously.

Logan reached the curve in Palm Boulevard that bent away from the beach and eventually led to the high-end golf course development of Wild Dunes. She pumped the old bike's pedal brakes, then dropped her feet to the sidewalk, breathing heavily.

Sunny and Harrison. Was it possible? She did the math. Sunny was at least eighteen years older than her brother, which seemed an eon in his teens, but now maybe not. It was hard for her to think of Harrison that way.

Or did she simply have affairs on the brain? Was there a reasonable explanation for why Sunny would lie to protect Harrison?

No way to know without asking. She looked around and assured herself that no one in the nearby houses could possibly hear her. She pulled her cell phone from a pocket, pushed her sweat-dampened hair out of her face and called her brother. "Harrison," she spoke to his voicemail. "Can you call me?" She paused, unsure of how much to say. "It's about Connor, and it's important."

She swiveled her bike toward Sullivan's Island and began the long ride back, realizing she'd be making most of it after nightfall.

Logan rode through the dusk, now facing the wind. She should have thought of that. What was an easy ride with the wind at her back was now grueling. She pumped and pumped to make headway, her legs growing weary even though the land was flat. She finally reached the popular Boathouse at Breach Inlet, its outdoor decks bare and diners ensconced warmly inside. She immediately mounted the bridge, the wind over the open water humming in her ears. From out of nowhere, car lights appeared behind her. She inched toward the bridge's railings, but the car didn't pass. She pedaled harder, but the wind rose against her, and she seemed hardly to move. She glanced behind her, but could see only the glare of headlights ten feet off her rear tire.

Logan had a moment's panic as she looked into the churning water below, beset with deadly currents. On the other side was the two-lane road, filled now by the looming vehicle, visible only by its blinding, full-beamed headlights. She gestured for the car to pass, but it slowed and settled in. She shook her head in frustration, and stood to pedal against the wall of wind. Her hair whipped into her eyes, and her leg muscles burned. She gasped for breath.

When she finally cleared the bridge, she swerved into a sandy yard and let the bike fall, her sides heaving. The car stopped, and Logan could see its black bulk under a streetlight. Still no driver emerged. She turned to the house in front of her, judging how much time she had to run to its front porch. But no lights were on, and she feared the porch could become a trap.

She tried to make out the house next door, through the hedges. Was there a light on inside? Her phone vibrated in her pocket and she snatched it.

"Who are you running from, little girl?" said a voice.

Logan pushed past her fallen bike and stomped over to kick the car's front tire. "What is wrong with you?" she shouted.

Harrison opened his door and got out, laughing. "I was answering your phone call. Why are you mad at me?"

"I just left that message twenty minutes ago," she said.

"I was in Wild Dunes and decided to drive over and see you in person. You sounded serious."

"Well, yeah, it is serious. Meet me in your old bedroom."

"The bachelor pad?" he asked. Logan laughed, both at the release of adrenalin and at the memory his words evoked. Even as a pimply teen, Harrison had called the downstairs bedroom suite his "bachelor pad". She and Britt used to spy on him through a salt-filmed window, and there was precious little bachelor action as far as they could tell.

"Yeah," she agreed, relaxing for the first time. "Meet me in the world's most pitiful bachelor pad."

He popped open his trunk. "Put your bike in here and I'll drive you."

"No." Why did she hesitate? Surely she wasn't afraid of her brother. Was she? "I'm almost home now and I don't want to get sand in your car."

"Suit yourself," he said, slamming the trunk and getting back into his Mercedes. "I'll meet you there."

She found him in the driveway of the beach house, leaning against his car. "I told Margot we were here so she wouldn't hear us and panic," he said. As Logan wheeled the bike into the storage room, Harrison pulled a key ring from his pocket and opened the door to the ground-floor suite.

They entered the vacant bedroom that smelled of mildew and something else Logan couldn't identify. A red and brown plaid comforter covered the double bed, but rather than the handsome pine floors found upstairs, this floor was covered in worn linoleum. The idea, Logan recalled, was that this level could be flooded during a storm surge – hence the building of the house on stilts. Her grandfather hadn't wanted good pine floors ruined.

The suite's one redeeming architectural feature was a ceiling cross of rugged beams. In the center, where the beams met, hung a fan with blades shaped like palm fronds. Harrison had bought it with his own money during a *Casablanca* phase. Logan recalled a teenaged Harrison flung face-up across the bed under the high-speed blades, trying to cool down after football practice in Charleston's punishing humidity. Looking at it now made her sad.

Harrison walked over to a shelf that displayed his high school trophies. "I haven't seen these in a while," he said, running a hand over the identical figures that had one arm extended, one arm tucked around a football.

"Haven't you?" she asked, settling into an armchair.

He ignored her question. "So what did you want to tell me about Connor?"

She studied his face. Even now when he hadn't exerted himself, it was flushed in a way she recognized as unhealthy. She guessed he wasn't the first high school athlete to run to fat. "I want to tell you that a neighbor saw you on the afternoon of Connor's murder. Right here."

The flush drained from Harrison's face, then flooded back. He looked about to bluster, then about to crumple. In the end, he did neither.

"Who?" he asked. "Who saw me?"

"So you *were* here?"

"I thought you said someone saw me."

"Yes. What were you doing? And why did you lie about it?"

Harrison sighed and sat down heavily on his bed. "I can't tell you."

"Well, you're going to have to tell Sheriff Royston. Your witness's husband is telling him."

Harrison stared at her. "How'd he find out?"

Logan shrugged. "She told him."

Harrison slumped. "That hag."

Logan looked at him in surprise. "So there *was* something going on between you and Sunny." She suddenly realized what the faint smell in the room was – coconut sunscreen. Sunny wore it year round. She waited a moment. "When's the last time you saw her?"

Harrison lay back on his bed and crossed his arms behind his head, sighing deeply. "That day. The day Connor died."

"Something's wrong with her, Harrison. Bad wrong."

"You mean, besides the fact that she's a loudmouthed hag?"

The words fell like blows, startling Logan. "Well," she said, "I'm assuming it wasn't a good break-up." When he didn't respond, she went on. "She's drinking around the clock, she's lost at least ten pounds, her hair is gross, and she's got herself locked up in that house like it's a fortress."

"And she felt it necessary to tell her husband, who will now blackball me all over Charleston?"

Logan's sympathy vanished. "Do you hear yourself? What the heck is wrong with you?"

Harrison turned his head to look at her. "What?"

"A witness has placed you at the scene of Connor's murder. She is scared to death of *something*, and all you can worry about is your business?"

Harrison seemed to consider that for a minute. He swung his legs to the floor. "So you think I'm going to be arrested?"

With her brother staring at her, Logan felt a tug of uneasiness. Had he really told Margot they were here? Would anyone know where to look for her?

"Maybe," she responded. "Dick said he was going to Sheriff Royston." She paused, curiosity winning out over her apprehension. "But back up a minute. How long have you and Sunny been an, um, item? Tell me it wasn't when you were in high school."

Harrison snorted. "I wish. But no. I had a crush on her back then. I mean, who wouldn't? But I hadn't seen her in years. Then I ran into her last summer at a bar in Charleston when she was out with girlfriends. One thing led to another, and I came home with her."

"Where was Dick?"

"Traveling. Whenever he left, she'd call. I'd pull my car directly into her garage after dark so Mother and Connor – or any of their nosy neighbors – wouldn't see."

"So why were you *here* that day in February?" Logan asked, with a wave of her hand to indicate the musty bedroom. "I'm surprised Sunny would agree to… this."

"Because Dick was home."

"But you'd been meeting only when he was gone. What changed?"

Harrison didn't answer.

"Harrison, what changed?"

For the first time, he wouldn't meet her eyes.

She changed tack. "Did you go upstairs? Did you see Mother and Connor?"

He stared at her and gave an almost imperceptible nod.

"Did you see them?" Logan persisted. "Did you talk to them?"

Her brother continued to watch her until Logan grew uncomfortable. Her eyes darted involuntarily to the door. Could Margot hear screams from this room? Should she make a run for it? *Sheesh*, she countered her own thoughts, *this is Harrison we're talking about.*

He ran his hands through his hair and looked at the floor.

"Harrison," she asked, her heart beginning to pound and her voice cracking, "did you kill Connor?"

That broke through his silence. "No," he groaned. "Heck, no. He was already dead, Logan. I swear."

Brother and sister stared at each other for what seemed like long minutes before Harrison's phone rang, its cheery ditty incongruous in the charged atmosphere. Harrison looked at the screen. "It's the sheriff's office," he said in a strangled voice. He looked at the phone as if he wanted to fling it away. Logan reached for it and heard the broad drawl of Sheriff Royston. He told her that deputies were sitting in front of Harrison's house in Charleston, and others were in front of his office.

"He's with me," she said. "We're on Sully's." She listened awhile longer, and said, "That won't be necessary. He can come to you."

She asked the question with her eyes, and Harrison nodded. "He'll be there in half an hour, Sheriff. I'll drive him myself."

"He's trusting us," Logan said, taking charge as she clicked off. "Your car or mine?"

Harrison shrugged, wearily handing over the decision-making to his sister.

"Okay," she said briskly. "Let's go." They locked up and walked to Logan's Wrangler. Unspoken was the thought that she might be returning to the island alone. As she pulled out of her mother's driveway, she said simply, "Tell me. Before we get there, tell me everything."

He sighed and again ran his hands through his hair in a gesture she recognized from childhood. "I don't know where to start."

"Start with why you and Sunny were so desperate to meet that you came to the house when Mother and Connor were home."

"At first, last summer, it was just about the sex," he began. "I mean, I was living out my teen fantasy. But after a while, as we walked around Sunny's *very nice* house, I realized she felt the same way I did about Mother's house. I mean, every time the Satterfields came out of their front door, there was that monstrosity."

"Oh, for goodness' sake," said Logan impatiently. "That's absurd."

"Well, you asked."

"Go ahead."

"So I had the idea to enlist Sunny in encouraging Mother and Connor to renovate the house the way the Fitzgeralds had done theirs."

"Or to let you handle a sale."

"Yeah, maybe. But anyway, Sunny was getting more and more into sex with a younger man. Complaining about Dick's age and how he was more interested in golf than he was in her. Stuff like that." He paused for a minute. "Then she started accusing *me* of being more interested in Mother's house than I was in her. To tell you the truth, I think she was getting ready for a full-blown mid-life crisis."

Logan made the turn off the island and headed over the inland waterway, dock lights reflecting eerily off the water.

"That still doesn't explain why you were at Mother's house. That strikes me as dangerous."

"It was Sunny's idea. Dick had been home for weeks, so we hadn't met. She called and asked if I could meet her in my old bedroom. She said it would be a turn-on to pretend she was having sex with the eighteen-year-old Harrison."

Logan couldn't see if he was blushing. "Ew. You're kidding."

"I kid you not. So I left my car at Poe's, which was already crowded because it was a Friday, and walked over. Dick was out playing golf, but we'd never had enough nerve to do it in their house while he was in town. She slipped over to the 'bachelor pad' and that was that."

"So at what point did you go upstairs?"

"Sunny left. I told her I would walk to my car when she was safely inside her house." He hesitated so long Logan was afraid he wasn't going to continue.

"You can't stop now," she told him.

"I know. But this isn't easy. I haven't told a soul. Obviously."

They were cruising on Interstate 26 West, and still had a way to go before reaching the sheriff's office in North Charleston.

"Why did you go to Mother's office?" Logan repeated.

"A friend of a friend had heard me talking about the property. I had an offer."

Logan turned to him in incredulity. "What part of 'someone else's property' do you not understand?" she demanded. "How could *you* have an offer on something you don't own? Are you insane, Harrison?"

"Do you want me to tell you this, or do you want to wallow in your self-righteousness?" he asked.

With an effort, she reined in her temper. "Go on," she said tightly.

"I wanted to talk to Connor, because clearly I'd made no headway with Mother. Heck, I hadn't even seen either one of them for months. I went up the side stairs to the kitchen and knocked, but no one answered."

"Wait a minute. Annabelle didn't come to the door?"

"No. I think she was on the deck with Mother. She must not have heard me."

"Okay."

"Anyway, I let myself in with my key. I could see Mother sitting at her desk on the porch, and also saw a light in her office. So I took a chance that Connor was in there. And he was."

Harrison fell silent. Logan waited while her brother breathed noisily beside her. She glanced over to see if he was crying, but she couldn't tell.

"And Logan, I swear to you he was already dead."

"But why didn't you call the police?"

"I don't know," he mumbled.

"Yes, you do," she said. "Why didn't you call the police?"

"It was everything," he said finally. "The affair with Sunny. The fact that I wanted to inherit and develop the property. Everything. If I called it in, all that would come out."

"And if you stayed quiet, you'd have Mother in a weakened state and you might get exactly what you wanted," she finished.

"Yeah."

"Of course, you realize you've made things a hundred times worse," she said flatly. "All of that stuff is going to come out, plus you're a murder suspect."

"But I didn't do it, Logan. I didn't kill Connor."

"Good luck convincing Sheriff Royston of that. Or Mother, for that matter."

Logan felt him looking at her. "You think Mother will think I killed him?" he asked, his voice gruff.

Logan was disgusted with her brother's lies and greed. "I imagine so. You said yourself the house was locked up. No signs of break-in, right?"

"Yeah, but I didn't look at the front door." He sounded hopeful.

"The detectives said it wasn't broken into either," Logan said.

There was a moment's silence as Harrison recalled the quiet house, the dark afternoon, the locked side door. "But Logan, don't you see? I know you don't trust me right now, and I can't blame you. But I *know* it wasn't me. So if there was no break-in, that leaves only Margot or Mother."

Chapter 18

Logan remained in the sheriff's spartan waiting room for an hour and a half before realizing that detectives could question Harrison all night or even jail him. She left word at the desk that she was leaving. Her brother could call her – or a taxi – when he was released.

Wearily, she drove to the island, aware that she'd missed dinner. On the long drive from North Charleston, she changed her mind several times about what to tell her mother and Margot. Harrison's Mercedes was in the driveway, and he'd spoken to Margot. She'd have to tell them something.

Her brother's last words haunted her. She wasn't sure which was worse – to think that he had killed Connor, or to think that Margot or Mother had. The thought of any of those scenarios sickened her. Maybe she was better off right now, grieving Connor but not knowing anything else. She was glad to drop the dilemma into the sheriff's lap.

Fortunately, by the time she returned, both women were in bed. Annabelle greeted her at the front door, whining loudly and jumping on her, but not barking. "You waiting up till everybody gets in?" Logan whispered, rubbing the dog's head.

She popped a bag of microwave popcorn and filled a large glass with ice and water, and settled in the living room with the TV turned low. But she couldn't concentrate on the screen.

Where did Harrison get the idea that someone owed him this beach house? she thought, gazing at the richly stained walls and the fishing net with its globes of colored glass shimmering in the low light. He was obsessed with getting his hands on it, that much was clear. Where did that sense of entitlement begin?

Logan had almost no memories of their father, but Harrison had been older when he left. Did he resent that? Julianna and Rivers Arnette had divorced when Logan was two and Harrison six, and though she and Harrison continued to see their paternal grandmother, their father disappeared from their lives. From hints their grandmother dropped, Logan knew he'd abandoned them for Atlantic City and Las Vegas, Reno and Biloxi, the haunts of sad gamblers.

Even in those days, beachfront property on Sullivan's Island was coveted – though not nearly so much as it became later. Julianna struggled as a single mother working as an elementary school librarian, but at least the house was paid for.

It was never enough for Harrison, however. Logan recalled silent suppers when he wouldn't speak to his mother because he didn't get the new track shoes or cell phone or polo shirt or other necessity *du jour*. It was only their mother's spaciness that kept her from being bullied by her son. She was already writing, though no one knew it. She seemed hardly to notice Harrison's silent treatment.

And then Julianna met Connor Burke at an art show opening that benefited her school. It wasn't long before they were inseparable on evenings and weekends. Logan remembered their simple wedding at Chapel by the Sea, officiated by one of Marsha Philpot's predecessors. Harrison was the only groomsman, and she the only bridesmaid. She could still see her mother's radiant face, her brother's surly one.

When Connor moved in, Harrison relocated to the downstairs maid's quarters, and Logan, at least, relaxed at the easing of tension. Connor struck the perfect balance with his new stepson, showing a mild interest in his sports teams but never so much that Harrison had anything to rebel against. It was clear that Connor accepted Julianna's children as part of his new life, but Julianna was his focus.

The family's finances improved immediately, because Connor was a public relations executive at a food products company with offices all over the Southeast. Harrison accepted the new bike, the new surfboard, the new clothes as his due. But when Julianna's writing career took off, the tap opened. She and Connor spent freely on both children, though Logan wondered if it was a substitute for their mother's attention, a way to prevent claims on her time and affection. As demands on Julianna accelerated, Harrison spent most of his time on his high school's football field and track. Logan spent most of her time at the Fitzgeralds' house next door.

After graduating from Clemson University at the other end of the state, Harrison returned to Charleston and began selling real estate. Logan knew that Connor and her mother directed business his way, and his success would have been enough for most thirty-five-year-olds. But Harrison seemed to have a bottomless pit of need – or greed. He had no idea what Julianna's publishing fortune was worth, only that he wasn't sharing in it.

Logan pushed her half-eaten bag of popcorn aside. Was she any better? Maybe she didn't think her mother owed her anything, but she didn't have much to show for her elite education at Duke University in neighboring North Carolina.

Like Harrison, she had returned to Charleston after graduation. Unlike him, she'd taken a string of low-paying jobs. She was proud of her art, sure, but did she do all she could to advance it? Or was she content to play the starving artist, bemoaning the fact that wealthy Charlestonians didn't appreciate anyone born in their midst, choosing instead to buy from the Midwest or Southwest or West Coast?

Or was it even more basic than that? Did a famous parent inevitably cripple her children by her very fame? But there, that very question, wielded blame. That sounded like something Harrison would say. She might have thought it once too, that somehow Julianna's blazing light overwhelmed her own. But she was past that now. She would make something of herself, or she wouldn't. But it had nothing to do with Julianna.

Logan felt her eyes growing heavy. She thought about stretching out on the sofa to sleep. But Margot and Mother would be up early.

She forced herself to stand, and Annabelle trotted beside her up the stairs. She still didn't know what she'd tell them about Harrison.

The next morning Logan walked into the kitchen to find notes from Julianna and Margot propped on the counter. Julianna was walking on the beach, and Margot had gone to get supplies for that afternoon's happy hour. Logan groaned. She'd forgotten that the neighbors were coming over. What had sounded like fun on Monday now sounded like a minefield. How could she tell them about Harrison's night at the jail?

She grabbed a cup of coffee from the pot Margot had made, and let herself out, glad that she didn't have to explain just yet. Before pulling out of the driveway, she punched Harrison's name into her speed dial. To her surprise, he answered, his voice scratchy.

"Where are you?" she demanded.

"In a taxi, pulling up to my house to catch a few z's," he said. "I'll pick up my car later."

"But what happened?"

"Royston and those two detectives questioned me all night. And I do mean All. Night. Long." He sighed.

"But they let you go."

"Yeah. I'm not sure they believed anything I said, but I guess they don't have any evidence. They told me not to leave Charleston."

"And you told them everything? About Sunny?"

"Yep, I threw her under the bus. So if she was trying to pretend she was simply standing at her window and saw me across the street, Dick will be disabused of that notion shortly. I'm sure detectives will be on her doorstep today. Serves her right."

Logan bit her lip. "Did you tell them your suspicions? About Mother and Margot?"

"Geez, Logan, what do you take me for? No." He paused, then relented. "But that's not saying they didn't make the leap themselves. They asked me repeatedly how I got in the house and if there were any signs of forced entry and where Mother and Margot were. Oh, and Annabelle – where Annabelle was."

"What did you tell them?"

"That I had my own key, of course, and the door was locked. Nothing was broken. That I didn't see anyone but Mother through the kitchen window, sitting at her porch desk. I never saw Margot or Annabelle at all. But I couldn't have been in the house more than ninety seconds, tops."

Logan rolled off the Ben Sawyer Bridge and headed for Charleston. "Did they ask you about finding Connor?"

"Yeah. The position of his body, the blood, the letter opener. All that. I don't think I was much help though, because I was in and out so fast."

Logan blew out a long breath. "So what's next?"

"I have no idea. I stay in town until they catch whoever did this. Or they end up arresting me because they don't catch her."

Logan ignored the implication.

"But Logan, I gotta crash. Talk to you later."

Logan drove the rest of the way to her office deep in thought. She would have all day to think of how to tell her mother about Harrison. She wondered if Sunny would show up for happy hour. She was sure Margot had invited her. She'd like to duck it herself, because she needed to talk to Julianna privately first. Maybe she'd say she had to work late.

When she pulled into her office's lot, she saw Gus Johns walking from his private parking space. He waved, and waited until she approached. "Are you free for dinner tonight?" he asked her. "I think it's my turn to buy, and there's a new Mexican place I want to try."

She made an instant decision to avoid her mother's neighbors. "Absolutely," she said. "When can you get away?"

"Probably by six. Want to meet there, or have me swing by your place?"

Upon learning that Sombrero was located in Mount Pleasant, she agreed to meet him at the restaurant so she wouldn't have to backtrack to retrieve her car. She texted Margot that she had to work late and wouldn't make the party. "Who's coming?" she typed.

"Meg, Marsha, Liza, Julianna, me," Margot responded. "We'll miss you."

So Sunny wasn't going. Logan wondered what excuse she had given Margot.

Logan stuck her head in Gus's office as she was headed out. He told her he could be at the restaurant by 6:30. "Oh, and I have some news for you," he said.

"Intriguing," she replied. "See you there."

She drove the few blocks to her duplex and let herself in. It was strange being in these familiar rooms after so much time away. Friends told her it was apparent that an artist lived here. Every room was a different color on the Rainbow Row palette. The living room was coral, the kitchen lime green, the bedroom periwinkle, the bathroom lavender, and the small study sunny yellow. Slipcovers and rugs and artwork with some or all of those colors pulled the rooms together into a pleasingly eclectic blend. The result was fun and vibrant without being jarring.

Logan kicked off her shoes and settled on to the comfy sofa striped in lime green and periwinkle to open her mail. Then she stretched out and allowed her mind to run over the events of the previous evening.

If Harrison was telling the truth, he and Sunny had been in the downstairs apartment of the beach house when Connor was murdered. That made four people who hadn't heard enough of a commotion to become suspicious. Could someone else have slipped in and out so quietly that none of them heard? Or was it more likely that Mother or Margot – the two with easiest access to the office – had committed the murder?

Logan forced herself to consider the possibility her mind had avoided for the past four weeks. Why would Margot want Connor dead? Either for career advancement or something personal between them that Logan didn't know about. She heard again Margot's surprising response to Renata's suggestion that someone at the February happy hour had a crush on Connor: "It wasn't me, was it?"

So *had* Margot harbored feelings for Connor? Undeniably attractive in a fresh-faced, all-Irish-American sort of way, Margot had lived with Connor and Mother for two years. And Connor had hired her. Was there something already between them at that point? Logan felt sick to her stomach. That was the most horrible thing about murder. It brought unfounded fears and doubts swirling up from a swampy muck.

And her mother? As fond as Logan was of Margot, it would be so much worse if Julianna had killed Connor. Logan pushed past her dread to probe the idea. For one thing, it undermined every single interaction she'd witnessed between the couple for the past twenty-two years. If two people were ever in love, it was them. Could something have happened to change that? Or was it something that had been hidden all along, something that had bubbled up? Something that would ruin Julianna's reputation?

Julianna's reputation. Logan let her mind meander into barbed territory. Her mother was a celebrated mystery writer, a genius of diabolical plotting. Could she have feigned memory loss to set an elaborate stage for murder? Could that be the reason Julianna had kept Logan and Harrison away at Thanksgiving and Christmas, indeed for the entire six months prior to Connor's death? Was there something she didn't want her children to see? Did she fear that they alone could unravel the plot she was setting in motion?

Logan groaned aloud. What was she thinking? This was her mother!

The alternative was that Julianna's memory impairment was real, and she had killed Connor for some murky reason in her alternate mental universe. That would be a little better, Logan supposed. She imagined the blow of a judge's gavel: "Not guilty by reason of insanity." She was surprised to feel a lump in her throat and sternly swallowed it down.

Of course, if Harrison *wasn't* telling the truth, he could have mounted the side steps after Sunny left, let himself into the kitchen and discovered Connor in their mother's office. Maybe they argued – over the house or something else – and Harrison, perpetually angry and aggrieved, stabbed his stepfather.

Would they argue over the house? Or was it something else? Logan sat up abruptly, remembering Harrison's proposal to have their mother declared incompetent and assume Power of Attorney. Who benefitted from Connor's death? She'd assumed no one to any great extent, but she'd never actually asked.

She had entered the number for the sheriff's office into her phone during her first interview with the detectives. Now she punched it, and within seconds was connected to Lance Royston.

"I've been meaning to call you, Logan," he said. *Ah-ve bin meanin' to cahl ya, Logan.* "I wanted to thank you for bringing in your brother last night."

"You're welcome, Sheriff. But I'm calling about something else. What can you tell me about Connor's will?"

"He left everything to your mother."

"That's what I thought. I don't know how to ask you this, but have you looked into my mother's will?"

The sheriff hesitated for a moment. "We have."

"Can you tell me about it?"

"No-o-o," he said. "I don't think that's my place. But it's pretty straightforward, and I imagine she'd be willing to tell you. And she hasn't revised it since Connor's death. She'll need to do that."

There was a moment's silence. The sheriff's voice was kind. "Was there something else I can help you with, Logan?"

Was there? Could anyone help her? "I… I don't know," she blurted. "I'm scared not to know, but I'm scared that when I find out, it may be even worse."

"Do you know something, Logan? Something that could help us?"

"No, I don't know anything any more," she said honestly. "That's the problem."

Before changing clothes, Logan wandered into the spare bedroom that served as her studio, and fingered the dried paintbrushes in an old mayonnaise jar. She hadn't been in here since Connor died, and she wasn't sure why. Landscapes, mostly marsh scenes, were propped along the walls. Two easels held still lifes of shells, wine bottles and flip-flops. One was pretty good, she realized, but the other wasn't quite right.

Her eyes jumped to a canvas turned against the wall in the far corner. She hadn't looked at it since she got the phone call in February. She hesitated and then walked over and flipped it abruptly. It was a portrait of Connor, intended as a Christmas gift for her mother. Seeing it fresh, she saw that she had captured her stepfather's strong jaw and kind brown eyes, his perpetually tousled hair. His reading glasses were shoved on top of his head, as they were in the photograph that lay on her desk. The painting, like the photo, caught the moment of his startled smile.

She'd planned to frame it so that it made a matched set with the portrait of her mother she'd created for Connor a year earlier. But she hadn't given it to her mother after all, because they hadn't spent the holiday together. Had she been peeved? Or hurt? She couldn't really remember.

It would've been good to display this painting at the memorial service, she thought. Pastor Marsha would have loved it. Should she take it to her mother now? Maybe. She'd think it over.

Logan changed into slacks with a wild print that reminded her of a Jackson Pollock painting, along with a sedate cream blouse and red sling-backs. Her hair swung freely, and she wore pounded silver metal earrings. When she reached the restaurant, Gus hadn't arrived, so she selected a booth and ordered a frozen margarita.

He came in a few minutes later, plopping wearily on to the burgundy banquette across from her. "Mrs Loquacious caught me as I was trying to leave."

Logan laughed, knowing he meant an elderly patient named Mrs Lokette. "Please don't tell me whatever she told you. We're getting ready to eat."

"I will definitely save you the monologue," he said, gesturing to a waiter for a beer. "So what's going on with you?"

"We've still got this murder investigation hanging over our heads.

It's frightening how it makes you question everybody and everything you thought you knew."

"Sounds rough," he said, his gray eyes sympathetic. "Anything I can do?"

"You're doing it. Saving me from a neighborhood gossip-fest and taking my mind off it."

"Well then, glad to be of service."

"And what's your news?" she said, sipping her drink.

"Oh, right. I think you'll be pleased. Ready?"

She nodded, perplexed.

"You know all that bad department-store art that came with our offices?"

Logan certainly did. Rainy street scenes in Paris, perfect gardens in some vaguely sun-soaked village, even a few attempts at Charleston's horse-drawn carriages.

"We've decided to chuck it all and support our local artists." He performed a drum roll on the table. "And who better than… our own Logan Arnette?"

"Really?" she said, delighted. "You want to hang one of my paintings?"

"Not exactly." His eyes twinkled as he tried not to grin. "We're buying and hanging eight of your paintings."

"What?!"

"Sam and his wife and I bought six from DeeAnn's. We thought you might want to select the last two. We could either buy them directly from you, or if your contract says they need to come through the gallery, we'll do that." He leaned back, smiling.

"Gus, I don't know what to say! That's amazing. Thank you."

He held up his beer and they clinked. "Well, quite frankly," he said, "we think it's an investment. You are incredibly talented and we figure we're getting in on your ground-floor prices."

The waiter brought salsa and chips, and they dug in hungrily. "Let's hope you're right," she said, already running through her inventory in her mind. "Let me see what you picked out and I'll try to select something complementary. Or even paint something new." A thrill ran through her. She wasn't sure if it was the thought of a permanent showing of her work in a public setting or the idea of getting back into her studio. She took another sip of margarita and shoved all thoughts of Harrison and her mother and Margot aside.

Chapter 19

It was Saturday morning before Logan was able to find Julianna and Margot together. The three met in the kitchen, where Margot had brewed a pot of coffee to go with fresh bagels from a shop on the Isle of Palms.

"We've got cut-up pineapple too, if you want it," Margot said.

"I need to tell you two something," Logan said, rummaging for a handmade pottery mug that she'd once given Connor for his birthday. "When's the last time you saw Sunny Satterfield?"

Julianna looked up from the newspaper. "I have no idea," she said. "She wasn't at the last happy hour, was she, Margot?"

"No," said Margot with a deliberate look at Logan. "What about her?"

Logan told them about their neighbor's affair with Harrison, and about the couple's presence downstairs on the day of Connor's murder. As Julianna and Margot stared at her wide-eyed, she added that Sunny had told Sheriff Royston she saw Harrison come upstairs after she left. "The sheriff had Harrison in for questioning all night on Wednesday. He claims Connor was already dead."

The two women were silent for a long moment. "But Lawrence didn't arrest Harrison?" her mother asked. "He believed him?"

Logan frowned. "You mean Lance," she said. "Lance Royston."

"What did I say?"

"Never mind. I guess Sheriff Royston believed him. But Harrison is not supposed to leave the area, for whatever that's worth."

"And Harrison didn't see anyone leave?" Margot said. She looked skeptical. "He must have just missed the killer."

Logan didn't answer – didn't tell Margot that her brother thought the murderer lived in the house. "Anyway, I wanted you guys to know," she said. "The media didn't get wind of it, thank goodness."

Julianna walked to the kitchen window and absentmindedly looked toward the ocean. She reached for her bottle of fish oil capsules and shook one out. "Looks like a nice day," she said. "I think I'll work on the porch this morning."

"How's the book going?" Logan asked.

Her mother frowned. "I'm still having some trouble with Alyx."

"I thought you changed her name to Annette."

"Oh, yes. Annette."

Logan glanced at Margot, but she was looking pointedly at the newspaper. Julianna poured a cup of coffee and headed to the porch. Once she was seated at her laptop, Margot mouthed, "Meet me in my room" and left the kitchen.

Logan gave her a minute, then slowly followed her upstairs, a sinking feeling coming over her.

Margot closed the door to her bedroom and got right to the point. "It's happening again," she said. "She's forgetting."

"Like what?" Logan asked.

"I first noticed it Wednesday. We went to the grocery store on the Isle of Palms, and I swear she got lost and panicked. She tried to laugh it off, but we left without buying what we went for.

"Then Thursday we had happy hour – which they've decided to have every Thursday, by the way. You know how loud everyone gets and several conversations were going at once. I could tell that your mother was floundering. I tried to do what Mr Burke and I used to do, sort of reframe a question or comment if it was directed at Julianna. It felt very much like it did all last winter."

Logan sighed. "Boy, I hate to hear this."

"But that's not all," Margot said. "You know she's been giving me pages to read. Last week, they were fine and she was making real progress with changing the character Annette. Then all of a sudden – like I said, around mid-week – she'd be at her desk all day and have almost nothing to show for it. Go out there in a few minutes, and I guarantee she'll be staring at the ocean."

"But she was so good there for a while. What could have happened?"

"I don't know. But I was hoping you and Dr Fitzgerald could look into it again. Maybe try a new medication?" Margot shrugged helplessly. "Something."

Logan nodded, frustration welling up. "I so hoped we were past this. Didn't you?"

"Yes," whispered Margot. "Logan, read those new pages and you'll see what I'm talking about. She was back to being Julianna Burke last week. Now… now I don't know."

Logan met some girlfriends for dinner in Charleston Saturday night, but excused herself when they continued on to a bar. She drove to her duplex and walked into a quiet so complete she knew her neighbors must be out. She turned on all the lights and found a music channel on TV. She was restless, and recognized the problem: she'd gone too long without painting.

She quickly shed her clothes and pulled on paint-spattered leggings and smock. She stood barefoot in front of an empty canvas, dripping water on to her palette colors and letting her mind meander. Her eyes kept being pulled to the portrait of Connor, smiling, tousled. She really had captured him.

Suddenly, she saw a younger Connor, with the same smile but longer hair curling down his neck. She began brushing in the blue sky, an emerald sea, white and beige streaks of sand. Already in her mind's eye she could see what would be in the foreground. A young girl in a one-piece, red-and-white-checked swimsuit, flat-chested, blonde hair a tangled mess, carefully carrying a yellow bucket of water to an elaborate sandcastle. The man crouched beside the castle, reaching for the bucket, smiling at the child, eager to show her how the watery moat would surround their creation. What color were his swim trunks? Oh yeah, navy, with white trim. What they called surfer trunks.

The painting would be a riot of primary colors, she realized. That was okay. It matched the scene in her mind. And afterwards, after that long day in the sun, they'd showered and gone out for seafood, all four of them: Mother and Connor and Harrison and her. She'd had crab legs, and the other three had waited patiently as she cracked and dipped and ate, everyone else finished while her appetite for the tender white morsels was nearly bottomless. Where had those details come from?

She worked fast, as watercolorists must, and was delighted to see the father and daughter taking shape. For the figures in this painting were obviously father and daughter. A viewer would never doubt it.

The painting began to blur, but not from running watercolors. Logan wiped her eyes on her sleeve, leaving mascara streaks. She stepped back, pleased with the canvas in a way she rarely was, but aching more than she had in years.

Leaving the painting to dry, she loaded up fresh canvases, brushes, paint and an easel to take to the beach house.

Julianna was asleep when Logan got in, and Margot was watching television. Logan sat with her for a few minutes, but feeling restless she made a cup of hot chocolate and wandered into her mother's study. She raised the window to let in the cool night air, and, remembering Margot's comment about her mother's rewrite, opened Julianna's laptop. It was set to open without a password, so Logan accessed her files.

She scrolled down until she found the tab marked "Seventh Novel" and began reading. Much of it was what she remembered, but the character of Annette Engler had moved seamlessly into the narrative. The couple's back story was new, and within minutes Logan was engrossed in their rather cavalier decision to give up their baby for adoption in their early twenties. She read on as Martin and Annette achieved professional success – he in psychiatry, she in law – followed by a decade of fruitless attempts to conceive. Gradually, it dawned on the couple they'd given up the only child they would ever have.

Still, the manuscript was nuanced. Martin and Annette were not crippled by their childlessness. It was simply a strong regret against the backdrop of an otherwise robust marriage. Until, that is, Edward Raisman entered Martin's office one autumn day and spilled his feelings about his adopted daughter.

Logan shivered, both in delight at her mother's masterful set-up and at the lowering temperature inside the room. She rose to shut the window, but as she neared, she heard voices. Instinctively, she slipped back and turned off the desk lamp so she couldn't be seen. Adjusting to the dark, her eyes searched the side yard and the Fitzgeralds' driveway, and finally located two figures on their lower deck.

The Fitzgeralds' voices were raised in a way that told Logan they'd been drinking. Dr Fitz, she could tell, was urging Meg to come inside. But Meg was having none of it.

"…could you?" she said shrilly. Then the wind took a few words and Logan could only hear "neighbors" and "New York". And then almost a howl, "That tramp!"

Logan froze. Who was she talking about? She strained to hear Dr Fitz's reply, but he had retreated to the French doors and was begging Meg to come inside.

Logan saw her stumble, then acquiesce. She shivered again, and pulled the window down and locked it.

For a moment, she sat in the dark, trying to decide whether to keep reading or go to bed. She felt sad for Meg. The fight sounded as though she had discovered an infidelity. Was Gus right about Dr Fitz's recent trip to New York being another opportunity for unfaithfulness? How must that feel to approach your retirement years and have the rug pulled out from under you? Or had Meg always known? Just because Logan hadn't suspected didn't mean Meg hadn't.

She sighed. Her neck and shoulders ached. She closed the document, then scrolled idly back through the menu. Just below the file she'd accessed was another, "Seventh Novel – Murder Scene".

Curious, Logan opened it. When she saw it was only two pages, she went to the top and began reading. Within just a few paragraphs, she was staring wide-eyed at the screen, weariness forgotten, racing through the depiction of Martin Engler stumbling upon Edward

Raisman asleep in his study. No! This was Connor's murder! Did Sheriff Royston have this? He couldn't, or her mother would be under arrest.

Logan read the last sentence, in which Edward died on the couch, the letter opener protruding from his chest. It sounded like the final sentence of a chapter, but she scrolled on to make sure there was nothing further, nothing about him staggering to the chair, nothing about him pulling out the letter opener. There was none of that, but there was a nearly blank third page. At the top was a single sentence in boldface, clearly not part of the original manuscript:

"No, no, no! Did he know it was ME?"

Chapter 20

Logan woke early Sunday morning, more tired than when she went to bed. She'd hardly slept, worrying all night about what she should do. Where did her loyalty lie? With her mother, who apparently had killed Connor? Or with her stepfather? She truly didn't know, and even now, seven hours after the discovery, her stomach convulsed at the thought.

If Harrison were in jail, she told herself, she'd tell Sheriff Royston what she'd found in order to get him released. But since he wasn't...

She dragged herself out of bed, her eyes gritty. Seeing her mother's admission in black and white like that – "No, no, no! Did he know it was ME?" – was shattering. Should she delete it? That was the conclusion she'd reached at least four times during the night.

She got into the shower, hoping it would clear her head. She'd spend the day with her mother, she decided, and maybe persuade her to turn herself in. Perhaps she would be sentenced to a psychiatric-style ward, not a prison. Still, the thought made Logan's stomach spasm, and when she emerged from the shower, she clutched the pedestal sink for support.

She dressed for church in a light blue sundress and a thin matching cardigan. She knocked on her mother's bedroom door, then pushed it open. Annabelle bounded to meet her, but Julianna remained a huddled mound beneath the covers.

"Mother?" she asked softly. "Do you want to go to church?"

The mound didn't stir.

Logan looked at her watch and walked closer to the bed.

"Mother?" she said more loudly. "If we're going to church, you need to get up now."

Julianna's eyes opened and roamed from Logan's face to the window to Annabelle's lounge chair and back. Logan could tell her mother had no idea who she was.

"Mother, it's Logan."

Her mother's eyes settled on her paintings and Logan saw understanding dawn. Julianna still didn't speak, but she looked at Logan and the dog by her side. "Annabelle," she pronounced.

"Yes. That's right." Logan paused. "Would you like to go to church?"

Her mother nodded.

"Then I'll get out of your way and let you get dressed. I'll see if Margot wants to come with us." Logan left the room and made her way downstairs.

Margot was sipping a cup of coffee in the kitchen. "Good morning," she said, with a wave toward the coffee pot. "Help yourself."

Logan perched on a stool across the counter from Margot and picked up Julianna's bottle of fish oil supplements. "You were right," she said. "She's worse. I guess I'll call Dr Fitz. He offered to refer her to someone who understands dementia." She popped a capsule in her mouth and took a sip of coffee. "Want one?"

"Nah. I know they're good for you, but they taste oily to me. It's probably all in my head."

"It is in your head. The capsule doesn't let you taste anything if you swallow fast." Logan poured cereal and milk into a bowl. "We're going to church if you'd like to come."

Margot raised her head from the newspaper. "Actually, I would. Let me get cleaned up."

She put her cup into the dishwasher and left Logan alone in the kitchen. Logan stared out of the French doors to the bright day and the sunlit ocean. She carried her bowl and coffee on to the porch, which was chillier than she expected. She pulled her cardigan around her and drank deeply of her scalding coffee. She had a decision to make about her discovery – what amounted to a confession on her mother's part. She didn't trust Harrison to help her with it. He had made it pretty obvious that all he cared about was the property. And Harrison.

Should she ask Pastor Marsha for advice? Or Dr Fitz? She remembered the shouting at the Fitzgeralds' house the previous night and didn't really want them involved. She felt alone. All of the anchors in her life had suddenly pulled away from their moorings, and she was adrift.

Through the open doors she heard the doorbell ring. Annabelle raced down the stairs and stood howling at the front door. "Stop that!" Logan snapped, her nerves rattled by the noise. She opened the door to Liza and Maxie.

"Does anybody want to walk?" Liza asked, as Maxie tried to nose her way inside.

"Everyone's getting dressed for church," Logan said, opening the door wide to invite Liza and the Shiba in. "Aren't you going?"

"I went to the early service," she said.

"Then come join me for coffee," Logan said. "I'll walk Anna B this afternoon."

"Are you sure I'm not holding you up?"

"No, I'm ready and the other two will take a while. I'd love the company."

"So how is everything?" Liza asked, taking a seat at the counter and accepting a mug. Her silver hair was pulled back into a ponytail, which made her look youthful despite the crow's feet around her eyes. Logan was struck again by Liza's calm demeanor. She so needed a confidante. It occurred to her that she didn't know much about Liza.

"I've never heard you say. Do you have children?"

Her neighbor smiled sadly. "No, when I was married, my husband and I weren't able to have them. One of my great sorrows."

"I'm sorry."

"Don't be. It was a long time ago." She took a sip of coffee.

"Meg said you ran some kind of women's center in Chicago." Logan put her bowl and spoon in the dishwasher and sat across from Liza.

"That's right. You could say I had thirty children at a time during those years." She smiled. "The mothers on my staff assured me our work was very much like parenting. Or re-parenting anyway."

"What brought you to Sully's?"

"Oh, not a terribly interesting story. My husband and I basically grew apart and finally divorced. I wanted a fresh start, so I got out a map. I'd lived in landlocked areas all my life and thought I'd like to try a coast. So I visited northern California, Oregon, Cape Cod and Sullivan's Island, staying two weeks in each place, hiking, beach walking, eating seafood. I loved how laid back this beach was and, of course, it had months more warm weather than the others. I wasn't sure I'd like the endless summer, but after one year I was hooked. I never plan to leave."

"And you didn't miss your work?"

"I did not. I thought I might, but I never did. I volunteer at the homeless shelter in Charleston and with Sunny at the symphony and at the church. Add in gardening and reading and Maxie, and it's been enough."

"I'm glad. I'm always intrigued by how people carve out new lives in a whole new place away from family and friends."

"I won't ever be mistaken for a native," Liza laughed. "Not like a Montague or a Fitzgerald. But people have been pretty welcoming."

Logan wondered why she didn't mention Fred Manigault. Did he not figure in her life? Maybe he was too recent. Or… there was that creeping feeling again. What had Renata called him? A decoy? Was it Connor she was really after? She'd been a good friend to Julianna after Connor was killed. Was guilt driving her friendliness?

Liza's voice jerked Logan out of her reverie. "And what about you guys?" she asked. "Julianna still getting better?"

Logan's face clouded. She'd thought so as recently as yesterday. How could she tell Liza that she was pretty sure Julianna had killed Connor?

"Logan?"

"I wouldn't say she's getting better," Logan hedged. "Margot says she's slipped back to how she was in the winter. I've noticed too." She clamped her lips together, unwilling to voice the worst of her fears.

"Oh, no. I'm sorry," Liza said gently, reaching out to cover Logan's hand with her own. "And her writing?"

Logan shrugged. "Margot says the pages have pretty much stopped too."

Liza sighed. "You know, I sometimes think our world is simply too much for artists," she said. "Too ugly, too demanding, too cold."

They heard footsteps on the stairs. Liza rose and placed her coffee mug in the sink. "I need to let you get to church," she said. "Pastor Marsha wouldn't appreciate me holding you up. Sure you don't want me to take Annabelle?"

"Thanks for the offer, but I need a walk this afternoon anyway. I can do it."

Liza spoke to Margot and hugged Julianna on her way out. Logan heard Margot enunciate Liza's name and wondered if her mother would have known the neighbor without her assistant's nudge.

The day had warmed by the time the women exited the church at noon. Julianna smiled politely at her fellow congregants, but avoided conversation. Logan and Margot could tell she was eager to get home.

During the walk Logan tripped on the edge of a pothole.

"You okay?" asked Margot. "You almost fell asleep in church."

"Yeah, I feel a little loopy. I didn't sleep well."

"You must've stayed up reading last night. Your light was on late."

After Logan had changed out of her church clothes and into shorts, she knocked on Julianna's bedroom door. Her mother was sitting on her bed, staring vacantly at the wall.

"Mother, did you want to change out of that skirt?" Logan asked.

"Yes, I will," she said, but she didn't stir.

Logan didn't know how to bring up her discovery of the previous night. "I looked over some of your writing last night," she said.

Julianna looked at her dully and didn't respond.

"It was good – the changes you made to Annette." Logan waited, but again got no reaction. "Do you remember writing ahead to the murder scene?"

That got her mother's attention. Julianna looked wildly around the room, as if she wished to escape.

"Do you?" Logan asked.

"I've seen it," she said.

Odd answer, Logan thought. "You wrote something at the end. Do you remember that?"

"I… I… the writing wasn't very good," Julianna said. Logan looked at her mother in surprise. "It was jerky. Not very good." The effort of speaking seemed to drain her.

"I don't mean the writing itself," Logan pressed. "I mean the very last line. What you added."

"I changed the ending?" Julianna finally asked.

"No, it was more like a note to yourself. Do you remember writing it?"

Julianna tried to concentrate. "Sometimes I jot down ideas that are for later in the book. I don't want to forget them."

Logan tried not to show her annoyance. "No. That's not what this was. Focus, Mother. Your murder scene was set in a study and the victim was stabbed to death almost exactly like Connor was." She searched her mother's eyes, but they were guileless. "At the end you wrote, 'No, no, no! Did he know it was me?'"

Julianna jerked back in horror. "Me? No, that can't be right. You're wrong, Lorraine."

"You wrote it, Mother," Logan said gently. "And I thought you might want to tell Sheriff Royston about it."

"*Sheriff Royston!?*" Julianna began breathing rapidly, and Logan feared the onset of a panic attack like the ones Margot had described. "Why would I tell the sheriff about it?" She laughed hysterically. "Maybe someone else wrote it. Maybe *you* wrote it."

Logan stepped back as if she'd been slapped. "Mother, the last thing I want to believe is that you hurt Connor," she said. "I thought maybe by writing that, you wanted to tell someone. I apologize."

"You should apologize!" Julianna shrieked. "I would never hurt Connor. I've been racking my brain to figure out who did." Julianna stopped speaking and cocked her head, as if listening to a voice. Then, much calmer, she asked, "Why would I say it was me?"

Logan didn't know if her mother was addressing her or a voice inside her head. Sputtering another apology, she backed out of the room.

Later that afternoon Logan picked up her phone to call Sheriff Royston. But she couldn't make herself do it and put the phone down again.

Chapter 21

Julianna hooked Annabelle's leash on to her harness as the dog whined deep in her throat and shivered in anticipation of a walk. The Shiba's antics usually made her laugh, but she felt heavy and dull this morning and didn't smile. Two cups of coffee had done nothing to dispel the tendrils of fog laced through her mind. Julianna wondered if she'd made decaf by mistake.

It was still early, the sun barely purpling the ocean as she watched from the deck, but Connor had already gone. If he was out for a run, maybe she'd meet him on his way back.

Annabelle bounded down the side stairs, pulling her extension leash to its full twenty feet and getting it wrapped around the shrub at the bottom. Julianna bent to untangle her, and they set out along the sun-cracked boardwalk that led from the side yard to the beach.

Her father had built this walkway one summer, inexplicably choosing the hottest, most breeze-free weeks she could ever recall. She could still see John Hewer Montague, his black hair soaked with sweat, his shirtless back dark as tobacco, hammering the fragrant new wood into place. It was a memory of her father she didn't usually have, not a whole lot older than Harrison was now. She saw her mother walking out with a pitcher of ice water, saw her father gulping gratefully from a real glass, all they had in those days, then swatting her mother playfully on the backside. She saw her mother smile and look up to catch Julianna's eye, checking, always checking, to see where her daughter was. She tried to picture her three- or four- or five-year-old self, the one her mother was looking at, but couldn't.

She crossed between the dunes and turned left, drawn toward the inlet between Sullivan's and the Isle of Palms. The breeze coming off the ocean was cold, and Julianna wrapped her thin sweater more tightly around her. It did little to block the chill, and she picked up the pace.

She reached Breach Inlet within fifteen minutes, and Julianna stared at the whitecaps whipping between the islands and the open ocean. Even without all the warning signs, it was easy to see the deadly currents swirling in this place where ocean tides met tidal marsh. Julianna was surprised to see a figure ahead of them: a man with black hair and a deep tan. He turned. "Daddy?" Julianna was shocked.

"These waters are treacherous, Julianna," he warned. "You must never, ever come here without your mother or me. Do you understand? Can you remember?"

She nodded. She did remember.

"There's not been a generation on these islands that hasn't lost someone to this inlet," he said, flinging an arm out to encompass the far ocean. "Many a boat got sucked into open water before they knew what hit 'em."

Julianna nodded silently. She was cold. The wind that whistled under the inlet bridge knifed through her sweater. She wished she'd worn a sweatshirt. "Why didn't you wait to build our walkway until you had weather like this?" she asked, her teeth chattering. "When it wasn't so hot?"

He laughed. "Good question, my dear. That was one miserable job, wasn't it? Come on."

He beckoned her to round the point, and they walked under the bridge to the quieter marsh. Here she found some protection from the wind, and the water ceased its fearsome churning. A sliver of sand was available for walking, and now her father held a fishing pole over the water. Julianna knew it was baited with a chicken neck, and he was after crabs, not fish.

He laughed again and yanked the pole. A large blue crab clung to the line, and he whisked a bucket under it a second before it let go. "Gotcha!" he yelled. "Think your mother can cook this guy for us?"

"No, Daddy," she cried. "Let it go."

He looked at her in astonishment. "Really?"

She nodded her head vigorously. "Well then, all right," he said, turning the bucket upside down and watching the crab scuttle back to the water. "You're the boss, Jules."

Jules. Julianna snapped her head around to find Annabelle looking up at her. Who called her Jules? Her father, of course. But someone else.

She shook her head in bewilderment. Above the marsh she saw a white heron sail majestically until it landed across the canal from where she stood. She turned to point it out to her father, but he wasn't there. Of course not. Julianna looked down at the veined hand that held Annabelle's leash. It was hard to tell the difference between its freckles and brown age spots. But it was not the hand of someone with a youngish father. It was not even the hand of someone with a living father.

But that name – Jules. Someone else called her Jules. She strained to remember and couldn't. The heron took to the air again, which sent Annabelle into a barking frenzy. Julianna looked at the dog. "Come on, you," she said finally. "Let's get home."

They walked back the way they had come until Julianna became uneasily aware that they'd walked further than they should have. Even Annabelle was staying at her side rather than running ahead. Julianna raised her gaze to the beach houses. They looked vaguely familiar, but which was hers? She'd been cold earlier, but now a trickle of sweat dripped down her back. She yanked the sweater off and tied it around her waist. Her breathing came faster, more shallow, and her heart fluttered a warning.

She turned and started back, afraid she'd missed her house. She and Annabelle trudged for another ten minutes, and she grew increasingly panicked. Which one was hers? Unwelcome tears blurred the dunes and sea grasses and rickety wooden structures that led to the houses. Then she saw a blue two-story with white trim that looked familiar. A figure waved from the deck. Simultaneously, Annabelle spied a twin

Shiba and raced toward it until the leash reached its limit and jerked in Julianna's hand.

She crossed the wide expanse of beach and mounted the wooden stairs. She knew the silver-haired woman at the top as well as she knew Margot, but the name wouldn't come. *Libby. No, Lisa.*

"Hi, you two!" the woman called. Julianna smiled and responded to the greeting, listening for a clue as Connor and Margot had taught her. The woman's dog jumped up onto Julianna's sweatpants, tail wagging. "No, Maxie, down," the woman said, and Julianna had it. "How are you, Liza?" she said smoothly.

"I'm looking forward to our happy hour this afternoon," she said. Julianna must have looked blank because she added, "That's right, isn't it? Every Thursday?"

"Oh, yes, of course," covered Julianna. "I was thinking today was Wednesday. I'm sure Margot has everything we need."

"Can I get you some coffee?" asked Liza. Suddenly Julianna knew she couldn't make small talk for another minute. "No, no," she said, flapping her hands. "I think I've worn my dog out. I need to get her home."

Liza peered at her. "Are you all right?"

"Yes, just fine. Connor will be wondering where I am."

A shadow passed over Liza's face that Julianna caught even in her agitated state. "What?" she asked.

"I, ah… nothing. Is Logan still staying with you?"

"Well, she's at work, but yes, she's still here at night." Julianna knew it was true, but was struck by the oddity. Why was Logan staying at her house?

"I'm looking forward to seeing her this afternoon," Liza said. "That's all." She paused for a moment. "Let Maxie and me walk you back to your house."

"No!" Julianna bolted down the staircase to the beach, desperate to be relieved of following a conversation. Annabelle yelped as Julianna stumbled over her. "No, we're fine," she shot back over her shoulder. "See you later."

Leaving Liza staring after them, Julianna headed back the way she'd come, looking closely at the island houses, tears threatening again. Where was hers? Why couldn't she recognize her own house?

And then she saw him, standing at the end of the boardwalk he'd built, a cigarette in one hand, waving at her with the other. She heaved a sigh of relief that became a sob and made her way through the shifting sand toward her father.

Logan finished promptly at 5 p.m. and the office manager took over for the last patient who was with Dr Littlemeyer. "You go on," she told her. "You've stayed late too many days recently."

"Gladly," said Logan, shedding her office sweater and grabbing her purse. "I've got a girls' night on Sully's – at my mother's, of all places."

Logan stopped by her duplex to change into jeans, a heavy fisherman's sweater and flip-flops. The day had never really warmed and gray storm clouds hung over the city. She shook her hair out of the ponytail she favored for work, changed her earrings to gypsy loops and added lipstick. She grabbed more underwear, socks and yoga pants, and stuffed them into a plastic grocery bag, promising herself she'd exercise this weekend.

She pulled into the vacant spot under her mother's house, hoping to give the Wrangler some protection from the expected rain. She carried her extra clothes up the side stairs to the kitchen, and found the party in full swing. Margot was at the sink stirring up a purplish red concoction in a cut-glass pitcher. Rum punch, Logan guessed. Meg was perched on a stool talking to Marsha Philpot.

At the little used breakfast table, Logan saw that Margot had put out crackers and cheese, a fruit tray, pita chips and hummus. Two women were helping themselves. Logan recognized Liza because she was facing her, but who was that with her back to her?

Then she heard a distinctive laugh.

"Renata?" she cried. "When did you get here?" Renata spun around and put down her plate to greet Logan with a hug.

"Early this morning," she said. "Flew into paradise to check on my girl." Her voice was light but her smile looked forced. "We'll talk later," she murmured.

Logan smiled a welcome at Liza, then popped her head into the living room, where an old Van Morrison CD was playing. She returned to Margot's side. "Where's Mother?"

"I haven't talked to her all day," said Margot, rinsing her hands. "She took Annabelle for a walk before I got up. Then I had to leave for a dentist's appointment, a haircut and the grocery shopping. When I got back, she was sleeping. Do you want to check on her, or do you want me to?"

The women exchanged a knowing look.

"I'll do it," said Logan, with a sense of dread.

Grasping her bag of clothes, she mounted the stairs and found Annabelle waiting at the top. The dog barked half-heartedly, her drooping tail signalling anxiety. "You don't like all these people in your house, do you, girl?" Logan stopped to pet her.

She walked through the empty master bedroom and knocked on the bathroom door. "Mother?" she said loudly. "You've got company."

Julianna's voice came back buoyant and bright. "I'll be right out," she called. For a moment Logan's hopes rose. Then she heard the voice again from behind the door. "What company, Mama? Who's here?"

Logan stood unmoving in her mother's bedroom. Julianna opened the bathroom door, smiling. She was dressed in a short pink and green Lilly Pulitzer skirt with a long-sleeved pink T-shirt. Her hair was attractively mussed and her eyes shone. "Ready!" she pronounced. But when she saw Logan, her smile faltered. Logan saw her eyes dart around the room, searching. Both women were silent.

Logan could see the struggle on her mother's face. Finally, she asked quietly, "Did you think Grandmother was here?"

Julianna nodded, the eyes that shone with happiness a moment before now shining with unshed tears. "She's dead, isn't she?"

Logan nodded.

"And my father's dead."

"Yes." And then Logan added gently, "And Connor."

Julianna's intake of breath was sharp. Tears spilled down her face. "And Connor." She listened for a moment. "But I heard Mama's music…" Van Morrison's "Brown-Eyed Girl" drifted up the stairs.

"We have a bunch of neighbors downstairs for happy hour," Logan explained. "Meg brought all that music that you love."

"Meg," said Julianna. She squared her shoulders.

"Do you want me to send them home?"

At first Julianna's gaze was so pleading that Logan was sure she'd say yes. But then she saw a look of determination cross her mother's face. "No, I can do this." Then, smiling at her daughter, "*We* can do this. You, me and Margot." She stopped, a look of confusion replacing the determination like a cloud passing over the sun. "Is Renata here?"

"Yes," said Logan. "Have you talked to her?"

"I think so." She paused. "Logan, after this whing-dig…" She stopped. "That's not right. What's the word I'm looking for?"

"Whing-ding," said Logan. "Or shindig. Easy mistake."

"After this *party,* we're going to have to talk. Maybe see that doctor Charlie mentioned. I'm getting worse, aren't I?"

"Maybe." Logan shrugged helplessly. "But the fact that you know it may mean there's still hope. I don't think dementia and Alzheimer's patients know they're losing their memories."

"Lucky them."

Logan smiled at her mother's plucky attempt at humor. "Ready to go down?"

"Ready." Julianna looped her arm through Logan's and they made their way down the stairs, Annabelle running ahead to check out the commotion. Everyone turned with smiles when the women entered the kitchen.

"There's our hostess!" cried Renata, hoisting her drink aloft. Margot's questioning eyes met Logan's, and Logan grimaced. Margot turned back to the blender.

"I've made your favorite, Julianna," she called. "Banana daiquiri!" She poured the thick drink into a tall glass and added a paper umbrella and straw. "Who else wants one?"

"Not a banana fan," said Renata. "But keep those pina coladas coming. Or rum punch – either one."

The others agreed, so Margot poured the remaining banana concoction into a royal blue antique pitcher and made a new batch of pina coladas. Logan saw her mother and Marsha head to her office, so she supposed they wanted to talk quietly. She hopped on to a stool to join Renata and Meg and Liza at the kitchen counter. "Guess I'll join the rowdy bunch," she said.

Renata leaned in, her voice low. "What have you heard about the investigation?"

"We met with Sheriff Royston last week," Logan replied. "He's convinced it was personal, someone deliberately after Connor. Or after Mother."

Three shocked faces stared at Logan. Finally, Meg spoke. "He thinks someone was after *Julianna*? Why?"

A silence descended as Margot paused to listen as well. Logan thought of the undercurrents humming beneath the surface. Meg disliked Liza. Was it because Charlie was having an affair with her? Renata distrusted Liza too, but thought she had nursed a crush on Connor. Had she? Margot wanted more editorial input on Julianna's writing, and Connor had stood in her way. And when Logan suggested that Renata thought someone had a crush on Connor, Margot's immediate response had been, "It wasn't me, was it?"

Logan looked at Margot's open face, hating the suspicions Harrison had raised in her mind. An unsolved murder was like an ugly comment that a "friend" passed on to you. You didn't know who had said it, so it made you question every friendship. Every person in her life but one was innocent of Connor's murder. Yet it tainted her thoughts about everyone.

Logan looked again at the expectant faces momentarily sobered by her pronouncement.

Should she reveal that Julianna had introduced the possibility of herself as the intended victim by directing Sheriff Royston to her book: "Why don't you ask Dr Engler?" Could her mother, that master mystery writer, have introduced a red herring to hide her own guilt? *Harrison, I wish I'd never heard what you said!*

For some reason she couldn't have articulated, Logan held back on telling the women about her mother's comment. Instead, she said simply, "It happened in her office. Sheriff Royston thinks someone was looking for Mother and ran into Connor instead."

There was a moment of stricken silence, then several of the women began talking at once.

"But why?" asked Meg. "Why would anyone want to hurt Julianna?"

Renata's face drained of color. "That's why he let her go to Scotland, isn't it? Everyone at Ironwater thought that was strange."

"Where is Julianna anyway?" asked Liza.

"I think she's talking to Pastor Marsha," said Margot, walking over with the blender's heavy pitcher. They heard footsteps, and Marsha and Julianna entered the kitchen.

"How does a girl get a drink around here?" Marsha asked.

Logan got a fresh glass and Margot poured. "You can't wait politely," Logan told her. "You gotta grab whatever you want."

"I'll remember that," Marsha laughed, then took a sip. "Oh, Margot, this is delicious. Now I understand what all the fuss is about."

Margot took a mock bow. Meg put an arm around Julianna and whispered in her ear. Julianna nodded. "'Brown-Haired Girl'. I knew that had to be you."

"'Brown-Eyed Girl'." Meg smiled. "But close enough. I do believe I've got some Tams here too."

"Go right ahead," said Logan. "You're in charge of the music."

Meg disappeared into the living room. In a moment came the sounds of "Be Young, Be Foolish, Be Happy".

"Ooh, my mother taught me to dance to that song!" said Margot, heading in to join Meg.

The other women followed. Logan held back, looking over the food table. Grabbing a handful of pita chips and deciding she wasn't going to get much in the way of a healthy dinner, she located Julianna's vitamins on the counter near the sink. She shook a tablet into her palm, then added a fish oil capsule from the next bottle. She chased them with a sip of rum punch and joined her mother's friends in the living room.

Chapter 22

Julianna awoke to the sun in her eyes, reflecting off the North Sea. She reached blindly for Connor's arm, but found his side of the bed empty. She listened to see if she could hear him banging around the kitchen, but the house was silent. He must have gone out for an early golf game.

She squinted at the wall opposite the bed and saw something that shouldn't be there. A marsh scene. A Lowcountry marsh scene. Wait. That was Logan's watercolor. She was in her bedroom on Sullivan's Island. She turned her head to the window and, sure enough, there was Annabelle lying on her lounge chair, watching, waiting to see if they were getting up or sleeping in a while longer. That meant the sun streaming in the window was bouncing off the Atlantic.

Why was she so groggy? Mornings were supposed to be her best time. She was cognizant enough to be disappointed by her lack of lucidity.

She thought back to the night before. Had she been drinking? Yes, that was it, she thought with relief. That ol' demon rum. She almost laughed out loud. Now it was coming back. She and Logan and Margot and who else? Meg and Liza and Marsha. They'd made a girls' night of it.

Margot had made Julianna's all-time favorite drink, a frozen banana daiquiri. No one else had liked it, so Margot had emptied the entire blender into a pitcher for Julianna. While everyone else drank pina coladas and rum punch, Julianna had polished off the entire batch of daiquiris.

She rose off the pillow and was greeted with an aching head. As chagrined as she felt, it was something of a reprieve. A hangover was preferable to memory loss, that was for sure.

But it was hard to separate the two. Her mind ran back over the evening. Someone else had been there. *Connor? No, silly, it was a girls' night.* Connor had probably gone out with Dick and Charlie.

A friend of Logan, maybe? There'd been a younger vibe going on, what with Margot and Logan dancing to her old sixties beach music in the living room: "You Lied to Your Daddy", "Sixty Minute Man", "Under the Boardwalk". Meg had joined them, dancing with a drink in one hand, the other hand waving in the air. And someone else. Liza? Pastor Marsha? She couldn't quite make out a face. Someone had said that it was the worst music they'd ever heard. Who would've said such a thing?

Renata! Well, of course. Renata had been here. Probably still was. Julianna glanced at her bedroom door, as if expecting Renata to pop her head around the jamb. She needed to get up and make breakfast for her house guest.

She swung her feet to the floor, groaning as her head protested. Annabelle joined her, whimpering in sympathy. "You know better than to get into the rum, don't ya, baby girl?"

She crossed the hall and looked out of a window on to the driveway. Renata's rental wasn't there. Had she imagined her editor's presence? Surely not. Suddenly Julianna was uneasy. What else wasn't she remembering? She needed to talk to Connor. He could always calm her, persuade her that her memory lapses were simply that, nothing to be overly concerned about. She was the writer, Julianna Burke. A creative mind like hers got overloaded. Something had to give. And it was the everyday, inessential matters that went. Not a bad trade-off. Connor always said that.

But something was off. The thought of Connor usually filled her with pleasure. Now there was a creeping dread when she thought of her husband. Where was he, anyway? Maybe there'd be a note in the kitchen.

She tiptoed down the hall. Logan and Margot's doors were open, but the girls weren't there. She reached the yellow and blue guest room where Renata usually stayed, and peeked in. The editor's overnight bag lay open on the bed. So she wasn't totally mad, she thought grimly. Not yet, anyway.

She made her way down to the kitchen. No notes. Maybe Renata and Logan and Margot were on the beach. She walked on to the porch but couldn't tell anything from this distance. Oh well, she would need coffee and headache medicine before she was remotely ready to see anyone.

She turned and glanced at the door that led to the side hallway and her office. The reason for her earlier dread hit her with the force of a rogue wave. Her office. Connor was dead. Connor was dead. Connor was dead. She doubled over, her breathing ragged, then stumbled to her office doorway. *Here,* she thought, *here is where it happened.*

All the doubts and fears of the past few days crashed in on her. Martin Engler found the patient he distrusted asleep on his office couch. If he killed him, Martin's biological daughter would be protected *and* would be spared from knowing the sickness of her adoptive father.

Julianna had found Connor asleep on *her* office couch. Had she, deep in the throes of her plot, killed him, believing him to be Martin's patient? She met Annabelle's bottomless black eyes. "You didn't bark," she said helplessly. "Why didn't you bark?" But Julianna already knew the answer. The Shiba didn't bark because no one entered the house. She had murdered her own beloved husband. There was no other explanation.

Something akin to relief flooded through Julianna. At least she knew. The answer was horrible, but it was an answer. Now she had two choices. She could call her old friend Lawrence Royston. Wait, that wasn't right. Lance. Lance Royston. Or…

As if in a trance, Julianna turned and walked through the kitchen, down the wobbly side steps to the sandy ground beneath the house. She thought she heard a distant ringing, the church bells maybe or a doorbell, but she had reached a place where she no longer trusted her senses. Annabelle barked but didn't leave her side.

Julianna reached into the ground-floor storage room and fumbled for the key that hung on a rusted hook. She entered the single bedroom suite, what was called a maid's quarters in her parents' day, though no maid had ever stayed there. Harrison had made it his teenage hangout, and it still held his football trophies, and posters of bands she'd never heard of. More importantly, it sported a steel chin-up bar across the closet doorjamb.

She wandered through the bedroom and adjacent sitting room, touching long forgotten items, looking for things Connor had brought to Harrison from their travels. There was a golf ball hit by somebody at the British Open. Connor had gotten excited about it, but she couldn't have recalled the golfer's name on her best day. There was a bottle of Scotch in a decorative decanter, a golfer in a kilt, purchased from a brewery in Scotland and given to Harrison on his twenty-first birthday. She idly wondered why Harrison hadn't drunk it, then lifted it and found it empty. Connor had been a good stepfather, she thought. Yes, she'd done all right in that department. Which was why she couldn't live with what she'd done.

She glanced at the wall of shelves that held Harrison's books – high school yearbooks, old college texts, a full shelf of novels from high school English classes. Something prickled the back of her neck, something about those novels. One was sticking out, the heavy dust disturbed. She came closer and sneezed. Something was familiar about this shelf… She pulled out *Lord of the Flies* and saw a flash of pink. She reached in behind the books and extracted a rose-colored binder. Of course. She had hidden this here – when? Last week? Two weeks ago?

She opened it and old newspaper articles slid to the floor. She retrieved them and looked at the headlines. Something about a psychiatrist killing a patient. Oh, yes! Her novel! But why had she removed these clips from her office and concealed them down here?

Logan's voice floated into her mind, accusing her – had it really been an accusation? – of writing at the end of her murder scene, "No, no, no! Did he know it was me?" Had she written such a confession? Logan wouldn't lie. Unless there was something between Logan and

Connor, something vile and ugly. But no, her mind couldn't go there. But had it once? Was that why she had killed her beloved Connor?

She returned the articles to the folder and slipped it back into its hiding place behind Harrison's books. She didn't need the clips now, because she wouldn't be finishing the book. A wave of regret passed over her. But then the guilt returned, and the guilt was stronger than the regret.

Unwavering now that she was sure, she turned into the bathroom and opened its linen closet. Rather than linens, it held a jumble of plastic beach toys, a cooler, a tool box, a plunger, half-empty paint cans. And yes, exactly where she thought it would be, a coil of rope. She reached for it.

The ringing came again, echoed by Annabelle's staccato bark. She could tell it was the doorbell directly above her. Footsteps hammered the outdoor staircase. "Julianna?" called a voice.

Julianna turned, irritated at the intrusion, her agitation mounting, her breath growing shallow. Surely no one would search for her in these unused rooms. She stood unmoving and hushed Annabelle.

But she heard the bedroom door scrape open, and waited transfixed. As the bathroom door creaked open, she tried to shove the rope behind her, back on to its shelf, but it fell to the floor. Her visitor took it all in, comprehending in a flash. "Yes, I can see how you might do that."

The voice came at Julianna as if from a distance, as if from a dream: a trusted voice. So why did it send a chill up her spine? Her visitor moved her aside, almost gently, and grabbed the rope.

And then Julianna comprehended too. She nearly laughed out loud at the irony, at how the great mystery writer had so misread everything that had happened, all the way back to last autumn. She had a crazy desire to sit down for a chat, to demand details, to figure out how it had all come together – how she, of all people, had fallen victim. But of course, it was too late. Much too late.

Her visitor ushered her into the bedroom. Julianna watched as the rope was cinched tight around the chinning bar, seven feet off the floor to accommodate Harrison's height. She fought to focus on one final question, but her mind was splintering. She closed her eyes, oblivious to the danger, fighting only to frame the query. Finally she heard it, though she couldn't tell if it was in her head or spoken into the musty air: *Why Connor? Wasn't it me you wanted?*

Her visitor dragged a footstool from Harrison's closet and placed it under the bar. "Step up," came the command. Julianna looked mutely at the stool. It occurred to her to be afraid, and then to protest, to fight, to kick, to scream. But her arms were pinned to her sides and she was being half pushed, half lifted on to the stool.

She was so tired, so very tired, and her limbs were impossibly heavy. Perhaps it would be easier to succumb. She scrabbled on to the stool, falling to one knee. She felt the rope around her neck. "Tell Logan," she gasped. "Tell her she's an art—" Her voice choked to a stop. Her final thought was of Pastor Marsha's funeral sermon, and her promise that one day she'd join Connor.

PART III

Chapter 23

Standing in the cemetery propped between Harrison and Margot, Logan was numb. The day was as unlike the bleak February day of Connor's funeral as it was possible to be, yet the brilliant sunshine did nothing to melt the icy knot in her chest.

She'd heard of couples so in love that when one died the other immediately followed. But that wasn't really the case here, was it? Julianna hadn't died of a broken heart. She'd hanged herself. But the result was the same. Apparently she couldn't go on without Connor. Her son and daughter weren't enough. They had never been enough.

Pastor Marsha asked the huge crowd to join in reciting the twenty-third Psalm, and their hypnotizing rumble rose in the jasmine-scented air. Would this never end? Logan thought they'd been through the worst of it inside the church – Marsha's eulogy, Scripture readings by Meg and Dr Fitz, hymns by the chapel choir, a second eulogy by Renata dealing with Julianna's literary legacy. When Marsha had asked earlier in the week if Logan or Harrison would like to speak at the service, Logan had recoiled in horror. This latest loss had unmoored her, and there was no way she could pretend otherwise. She'd left the service to Marsha and the Fitzgeralds and Renata, though Dr Fitz's voice had cracked and Meg cried openly during her reading.

Now Marsha was finishing up with the "ashes to ashes, dust to dust" liturgy, foreseeing a day when Julianna would join Jesus in the final resurrection. All Logan wanted to do – all in the world she wanted to do – was run on to the beach and scream and scream and scream into the wind. It would be the most exquisite release, and yet she had to stand here, stoically, silently. She felt a moan burble up in her throat and coughed to disguise it.

Logan raised bleary eyes and stared across the burial plot at the neighbors standing directly behind Marsha. Meg and Dr Fitz stood slightly apart, looking dazed. Sunny Satterfield was all but unrecognizable beneath a wide-brimmed straw hat and oversized sunglasses, leaning like an invalid into Dick. Leo and Peggie Oswald from next door shared his walker, their frail arms helping to support their weight. Liza Holland held lightly on to Fred Manigault with one hand and dabbed at her eyes with the other. She'd been on Annabelle-walking duty for the past five days, as Logan had refused to leave the house.

Renata O'Steen stood with the New York contingent, every single one dressed head to toe in black, not understanding that bare arms and legs were acceptable in this part of the South in April. Behind them stood rows and rows of Sullivan's Island neighbors and church members and Charleston society denizens and literature lovers and the media. Baron Philpot had spoken to the journalists and helped them find vantage points, and for the official service at least, they hung back respectfully. Margot had issued a press release that the University of South Carolina would host a memorial event in the fall, hoping to cut down on visitors to this service. It may have helped, though many in the crowd had not been able to get inside the chapel and had stood waiting in the graveyard.

Off to one side, Logan saw Sheriff Royston, his eyes not on Pastor Marsha or the casket but on the mourners. *At least his job is done*, she thought. *He must be relieved.*

Logan heard Marsha's cadence change. She closed her eyes for the benediction but felt her knees buckle. She grabbed for Margot, and Margot slid an arm around her waist. *Please, please, please, let it end.*

And then it did, and the New Yorkers were upon her, eager to discharge their duties and hurry to the airport. Logan got a taste of her mother's life as stranger after stranger spoke to her, hugged her, patted her, whispered in her ear. A couple of them cried – something Logan had been unable to do.

She'd also refused to speak to the media – Margot had become the family spokesperson – or to have people come to the house after the service. When the food trays and cakes and casseroles arrived, Margot carried them next door to Meg, who had volunteered to host the reception.

Now the crowd was blessedly breaking up, walking in the mid-day sunshine to the Fitzgerald house, their hushed silence giving way to muted murmurs and bursts of laughter. Margot headed straight for the reporters in an attempt to keep them from Logan.

"You coming to Meg and Charlie's?" Harrison mumbled.

"In a bit," she said. "I'm going to stay here for a minute."

Marsha unzipped her robe right there in the cemetery, then walked over to Logan, her auburn hair glinting red in the sun. "Shall I stay with you, or would you rather be alone?" she asked.

"Thanks for everything, Marsha, but I'd like to be alone," she said.

Marsha nodded, and joined her husband and daughter to follow the neighbors to the Fitzgeralds'. Logan felt woozy, so she walked to a nearby bench and sat. She held both arms over her stomach and rocked, a soothing motion surfacing from her childhood.

"You look like you're seven years old." The voice came from behind her, but she'd know it anywhere. She leapt up with a half-laugh, half-cry to greet her childhood friend, Britt Fitzgerald. Britt's brown hair was cut in a short, no-nonsense style, and her body had settled prematurely into her mother's build, stocky and broad hipped. She gathered Logan into an embrace exactly the way Meg always had.

"When did you get in?" Logan asked. "Your folks didn't say a thing about you coming."

"I wasn't sure I would get here, so I told them not to tell you. But the gods were smiling and I made it with ten minutes to spare in my trusty Honda."

"So you heard the service?"

"Yep. Mom sneaked me in."

"Britt, I felt like they were talking about somebody I didn't even know. I mean, Marsha did a good job, but it was surreal. I don't know how to explain it."

"I imagine you're still in shock," Britt said calmly. "You've lost two parents in less than two months. Speaking of which, did Number 3 show his face?"

Logan smiled in spite of herself at the mention of their nickname for Rivers Arnette. "No, haven't seen him and don't expect to. You were right. I lost my real father in February."

Britt hugged her again. "I can't believe you're going through this. How are you even standing? Has Dad got you on drugs?"

Logan laughed. "I didn't know that was an option." She wiped her eyes. "I can't believe you're making me laugh."

"Sorry," said Britt, who clearly was not sorry at all. She looked into the gaping hole that held Julianna's casket. Two workers stood well away to give the women space before filling it in. "Do you want some time alone, or do you want to go to Mom and Dad's, or Poe's for a beer, or none of the above?"

"None of the above if you think that's not too rude. I'd love to have a glass of wine with you on our deck."

"Consider it poured."

Logan started to walk with Britt, then stopped. "They're going to throw dirt on the casket," she said helplessly, waving toward the workers. "I do need another minute."

"I'll wait for you on the church steps," said Britt. "Take all the time you need. I've got my Kindle and a Julianna Burke novel I've been meaning to read."

Logan smiled. "You're awful."

Logan returned to the bench, and Britt sat on the church steps within her peripheral vision. Logan found it comforting to have her friend nearby.

There were so many things she wanted to ask, but no words came. Was her mother conflicted about their relationship, or had the rough patches dissipated in the clouds of her memory? She was curious about her mother's last thoughts. Had she thought of her daughter at all?

Or had she simply been consumed by guilt? Logan saw again her mother's note on her laptop, possibly the last words she ever wrote. "No, no, no! Did he know it was ME?"

Whether Connor knew or not, Julianna certainly did. That was the coroner's interpretation when she ruled Julianna's death a suicide. Or, more accurately, a murder/suicide with a five-week lapse in between.

Logan shook her head, scarcely able to believe that both her mother and Connor were gone. She remembered Julianna standing in her bedroom last Thursday, scanning the empty room for her long-dead mother. She remembered her gamely facing the neighbors and Renata, struggling to follow their quick conversations when her mind simply couldn't make the leaps. She remembered starting for work the next morning and tracing Annabelle's whimpers to the stale ground-floor rooms.

And then time had stopped as Logan's mind grappled to make sense of the scene, of the body hanging motionless from Harrison's chinning bar, of an overturned footstool, of the sad-eyed Shiba keeping vigil. Logan had stared for the longest time, unable to process what she was seeing, before bursting into the wails that brought the Fitzgeralds and Renata and Margot running.

With her friend sitting nearby, Logan let her mind linger on the painful images she'd avoided all week. She prodded at them like a sore tooth, and she rocked and she remembered and she hurt. And then, for the first time, she cried.

When she joined Britt nearly half an hour later, Logan felt light and hollow.

"All better?" asked Britt.

"Some better. Thanks for staying."

They walked in silence down Middle Street, cutting across Station 21 to Atlantic Avenue and passing Joan Agerton, already on her way back from the Fitzgeralds'. She beamed at the young women. "It's good to see you girls back home," she said, touching Logan's arm. "I'm so sorry about your parents, dear. And Britt, I hope you're going to stay with us for a while."

"I'm thinking about it, Mrs Agerton," Britt responded.

News crews were filming the crowds going in and out of the Fitzgerald house, so the women tiptoed up the side steps to the Burke kitchen to avoid being seen. Annabelle greeted Logan with anxious barking, shivering all over. With Julianna gone, she followed Logan from room to room and slept on her bed.

Logan rubbed the dog's head and slipped off her heels. She pulled a bottle of chilled pinot grigio from the refrigerator. "This all right with you?" she asked.

Britt discarded her suit jacket and pumps. "If you don't have a beer, that'll do."

"Actually, we do still have Connor's beer, and I'd love for somebody to drink it."

The women walked on to the porch and slumped into chairs. Logan felt as weary as she'd ever been. "I am *so* glad that's over," she said, resting her head on the chair's back.

Britt looked around the gray splintered deck, with Annabelle on the lumpy couch at one end. "Nothing ever changes here," she observed. "I love that. Every time I come to Mom and Dad's, they've remodeled, renovated, updated, improved. Makes me nervous."

"Nothing makes you nervous," Logan said languidly.

"Well, if anything *were* to make me nervous, it would be their endless renovations."

"So what's up with you anyway? Meg said your residency is ending?"

"Yup. Dad has asked me to join his practice. He—"

But Logan had shot straight up in her chair, weariness forgotten. "*You're coming back here?!*"

"Maybe. Dad and I could *not* work together indefinitely, but he's looking toward retirement. So I'm thinking about it."

"Oh, Britt, that would be so great." Logan was embarrassed to find that she was near tears again.

"I've got a lot of decisions to make. But I'm not here to talk about me. You're the one we need to be talking about." Britt eyed Logan over her beer bottle. "For instance, are you going to live here? Or sell? Or what?"

"I honestly don't know. There was a time I dreamed of inheriting and renovating. Then there was a time I might have left it just like Mother had it. But now with both of them dying here, I don't know that I *could* stay." Logan shuddered. "Not to mention that people have been driving by day and night to see 'the murder/suicide house'. I'm not sure how long the neighbors will stand for that."

"Too bad for them," said Britt. "You haven't done anything wrong. Besides, you're a Montague."

"I think you've been away too long."

"What does Harrison want to do?" asked Britt.

"He may already have the house on the market for all I know."

Britt snorted. "He couldn't do that without you."

"Yeah, we'll have to go through probate and all that. Mother's attorney advised me not to do anything for a while. It's not like the price will go down. He said sit on it until I'm very sure what I want to do." Logan smiled. "I have a feeling he dislikes Harrison."

"Who doesn't?" Britt took a drink. "What's Margot going to do?"

"She's staying a few more weeks to work with Renata and cancel contracts and stuff like that. Then she's heading back to her parents' house in the Upstate to look for a job."

"Well, I'd be glad to stay with you too, if you need me."

Logan turned to face her friend. "Really? Your folks won't mind?"

"I'd be right next door. They'd see me plenty. And if I *do* go into Dad's practice, I sure don't need to be coming home with him too. I'll need to find myself a place, pronto, probably in Charleston. But I could hang with you for a while first."

"If you're serious, there's nothing I'd like better." Logan found her throat closing up again. She stood. "But if you don't mind, I need to lie down. I feel queasy. You probably need to show your face at the reception anyway, don't you?"

Britt stood as well. "Probably."

"Can you make excuses for me?"

"Yep, I'll tell them you're over here dead drunk."

"That'll work. See you later."

Britt gathered her in a long hug. "Later, my friend."

Chapter 24

The morning after the funeral, Logan, Margot, and Britt slept late, and as if by tacit agreement wandered into the kitchen mid-morning. Logan, her eyes puffy and hair tangled, brewed a pot of coffee, then went to peer out of the living room window. A single car drove slowly past, its occupants pointing.

"How's the traffic?" asked Margot.

"I only saw one car. Maybe it's finally thinning out." Logan reached into the refrigerator and got the cut-up berries and pineapple that Britt and Margot had brought from the reception. In fact, there was enough leftover food and frozen casseroles to keep them fed for weeks.

"Pastor Marsha tells me that a funeral is for the family," she said, pulling her head out of the fridge. "But I found it brutal. I never want to go through that again."

"I think when it's a celebrity, it's harder on the family," Margot agreed.

"Not to mention it's harder when you've had another one five weeks before," Britt said, yawning and absently spiking her brown hair with her fingers.

"So how was everything at your folks' house?" Logan asked, grabbing Julianna's vitamins and fish oil tablets and shaking them into her hand. "I'll have to apologize for not making it."

"You'll do no such thing," Britt said. "Mom knows everyone grieves in their own way. Don't worry about it."

Margot popped a slice of wheat bread into the toaster. "Did I hear one of you getting sick during the night?"

Logan winced. "That would be me. Honestly, I felt like I had a hangover, but I only had half a glass of wine." She stopped her coffee cup halfway to her lips as a thought hit her. She'd felt that way three times over the past two weeks – at church, then after Thursday's happy hour, then yesterday at the funeral. The first two times she'd put it down to too much alcohol, though the fogginess and queasiness were unlike any hangover she'd previously suffered.

She thought back, trying to identify anything out of the ordinary she'd eaten or drunk. She'd taken no medication. Pregnancy was out of the realm of possibility. She looked at the tablet and capsule in her hand. Hadn't she taken them on those days?

"Dr Britt," she said, "can a vitamin or fish oil make you loopy or sick?"

Margot jumped in. "I always have to eat when I take a multivitamin," she said. "If I forget and take one with only coffee, I feel nauseated within minutes."

"Have you had one of these?" Logan asked her. Margot shook her head.

Both women looked to Britt, who had a mouthful of pineapple. She motioned for Logan to hand her the bottles and read the ingredient lists. She shook several vitamin tablets into her hand, then put them back. Then she shook several of the fish oil capsules into her hand. She squinted at them for a moment. "Do you have any reading glasses down here?"

Margot rummaged in a kitchen drawer and pulled out a pair with a red plastic frame. Britt perched the glasses on the end of her nose and looked at the capsules in her palm for several minutes. "I see little bumps in these things that could be pinpricks that have sealed back over," she said.

Logan and Margot looked blank. "What do you mean?" Margot asked.

"I mean there are tiny imperfections in each one of these." She shook a few more into her hand and ran a finger over them. "They're in separate places." She looked up. "I can't imagine this being part of the manufacturing process. If it was, they would be in the same place on each capsule."

The three women looked at each other. Finally Logan spoke. "Do you mean they've been tampered with? Like that Tylenol case you told me you learned about in med school?"

"Yeah, but this would be a syringe prick into the capsule. I'm pretty sure it's pliable enough to re-seal itself." Britt slid the capsules back into the bottle. "Let me send them to Dad's lab."

Logan felt a twinge of unease as she watched Britt drop the bottle into her purse. "No, wait."

"For what?"

"I think I'd rather give them to Sheriff Royston," said Logan. "He'll have lab access. And what is it they call it? Chain of evidence? If we put them in other people's hands, it could mess that up."

Britt stopped. "You don't think it's a drugstore tampering, do you?"

Logan shrugged. "I don't know what I think." She reached into Britt's bag for the bottle. "The only thing I know for sure is I trust the sheriff."

Britt eyed her friend but said nothing. She nodded slowly. "Fair enough."

Sheriff Royston and Detective Giles and Logan were crowded into Julianna's study. They had gone through all the bathrooms in the house, collecting vitamins and medicines, and labeling them according to Logan's explanations. Connor had had nothing but antacids, but Julianna had blood pressure pills, gingko capsules, calcium tablets and multivitamins in addition to the fish oil.

The officers had talked for a while in the living room with Britt and Margot, but then the sheriff asked to see Logan privately. He and the detective took seats on the office's vibrant floral couch, and Logan turned to face them from her mother's desk chair. The rugged sheriff looked out of place in the Laura Ashley-dominated room, his gold-flecked eyes tired, his kind face lined. They were so close that Logan could smell his aftershave, the same as Connor wore. A wave of grief swept over her, making it hard to breathe.

"I don't want to get too far ahead of ourselves before we get the lab report," said the sheriff, "but I'll be honest with you, Logan. The coroner's report didn't sit well with me."

Logan swallowed. "You don't think my mother killed herself?" she whispered.

"Well, that part seems pretty cut and dried," he admitted, leaning forward. "But I cannot get my mind around her killing Connor. I can't make sense of it yet, but something's not right."

He stood to pace, but there wasn't a lot of room to do so. Detective Giles motioned toward the bookshelf. "Your mother's titles?" she asked.

Logan nodded, and the detective stood to study them. "Have you read all these, sir?"

"I have."

"Could there be something in them that could help us?"

"Couldn't hurt," he mused. "But those are first editions. We'll buy copies on the way back to the office, and you can get started on them. Fresh eyes will be good." He turned to Logan. "I've read Julianna's unfinished manuscript and the separate murder scene you sent. So, number one, even if she did kill Connor, as that murder scene notation indicates, we may find that she was impaired. And number two, we want to find out who was drugging her, if that turns out to be the case."

Logan kept quiet, as the sheriff seemed to be thinking out loud.

"And I keep going back to the night of Connor's murder, when your mother told us to 'ask Dr Engler'. Do you see a connection between Dr Engler and anybody you know?"

Logan stiffened, and glanced involuntarily out of the window at the house next door. "Is that why you asked Britt to leave?" she replied.

The sheriff stared at her unflinchingly. "Maybe."

"I would say absolutely not, except for Mother thinking she saw Dr Fitz in Scotland," she said softly. "That makes me think there was some misfired synapse or *something* in her mind." Logan closed her eyes. "But I gotta tell you: that *cannot* be true. That would be almost as bad as losing Mother and Connor in the first place."

Sheriff Royston reached down to pat her shoulder awkwardly. "Yeah, I know. I've known Charlie for years, and it's hard to imagine." He sighed. "I'm glad Britt and Margot are here for you."

Detective Giles was writing down the titles of Julianna's books. "Should I read them in any particular order?" she asked.

Logan idly picked up *The Palm Rustler*. "No, they're all stand-alone," she said. She looked at the cover again and remembered the crazy opossum/squirrel story that her mother had borrowed. Her eyes roved to *A House Built on Sand*, and she remembered finding the newspaper article that had provided its skeleton.

"Oh! I didn't think of that!" she cried, opening her mother's file drawer. The officers looked puzzled as she extracted the Mail/Ideas folder.

"What?" asked Detective Giles. "What have you remembered?"

Logan was flushed and spoke rapidly. "When I came to stay with Annabelle after Mother went to Scotland, I was poking around in here. And I found a file of newspaper articles that people had sent her. Some of them she used as kernels for her book plots. I found two that she had used, and several she hadn't. But I didn't read them all."

The sheriff reached eagerly for the folder. "So there might be something in here that tells us where Dr Engler's story came from," he said.

He carefully divided the stack and handed half to Detective Giles. The two settled on to the couch to read.

Logan sat watching them. She didn't want to interrupt, even to ask if they'd like coffee. She simply remained in the desk chair and opened *The Palm Rustler*.

"Hey, I heard about this one when I was at a conference in Kansas City," said the sheriff, passing a clipping to the detective. "Wife hired a teenage neighbor to kill her husband. I would've loved to see what Julianna could do with that."

They read for another half-hour until Sheriff Royston slapped his last article down with a sigh. "We'll go over these more carefully at the station, but I don't see anything here like the unfinished manuscript I read."

"Me neither," said Detective Giles.

"Did you read the new pages too?" Logan asked.

The detective nodded. "So did Brad Lancaster. Like the sheriff said, he wanted lots of eyes on it."

Sheriff Royston let out a frustrated sigh. "Well, as I cautioned, let's not get ahead of ourselves. It may be that those capsules tell us nothing." He slapped his thighs. "Logan, we're going to get out of your hair, but I'd like to take your mother's files if it's all right." She nodded her assent, and he carefully took the folders from Julianna's drawers, handing a stack to Detective Giles and tucking the rest underneath his arm.

Logan led them down the hall and through the living room. They said goodbye and made their way down the rickety front stairs. After Logan had closed the door, the sheriff hit the wooden railing with his fist, hard enough to make it quiver. Startled, Detective Giles looked back at him.

"Damn it, Detective," he said, "we're missing something."

Chapter 25

By the time the officers left, Britt had gone home to visit Meg and work out a schedule to be in her father's office. Logan paced the living room, Annabelle at her heels. The second time she tripped over the dog, she went to get the leash and yelled to Margot that she was going for a walk. "Want to come?"

"Yes!" Margot called from her bedroom. "Let me get my shoes on."

Storm clouds were moving in as Logan locked the front door behind them. They stepped into a stiffening breeze. "Have you been setting this alarm?" Margot asked.

"Not once since you and Mother returned from Scotland. Have you?"

"No. I was more afraid of your mother setting it off than of any outsider coming in. Do you think we ought to start?"

Logan thought of Harrison and all the neighbors who had keys. And Britt, who wouldn't know the code if she set off the alarm. "Yeah, we probably should. But I don't want to. Is that stupid?"

"Well, it means looking differently at everyone we know," said Margot. "Maybe we should after you give the code to Britt."

The women noticed the rusted Camaro creeping by the house at the same moment and grew quiet. Four teenagers hung out of the car windows and stared up at the Burke house. "Hey, ladies, is it haunted?" yelled a boy in the back seat. They all laughed and ducked inside as the driver sped off.

"Lovely," said Margot. "At least the reporters asked intelligent questions."

"They did?"

"Yeah, most of them had done their homework or were Julianna fans to start with. They were doing their jobs. You haven't read anything online?"

Logan shook her head at the thought of stories about the famous mystery writer who committed murder, then couldn't live with what she'd done. "Can't make myself. But that..." she pointed at the Camaro as it raced up Station 22, "that's just ridiculous."

"That's probably exactly what the rector of All Saints Church said when we ran around Alice's grave backwards," Margot said about the Pawleys Island cemetery popular with teens. "It makes me see things in a different light."

"You did that too?" Logan shot her a tired smile. "I thought it was just us locals. We scared ourselves to death in that graveyard." Her smile faded as she thought of the nineteenth-century marker that read only "Alice", and the stories of the young woman's ghostly return in search of her engagement ring. For the first time, she considered how the Flagg descendants must have felt at the sight of the marker encircled by hard-packed earth, worn bare by the feet of drunken teenagers.

Annabelle pulled left, so Logan let her. "Margot, I want to ask you something. Do you know of any other place that Mother might have kept newspaper clippings?"

"What kind of clippings?"

"You know how she had that file of articles and used some of them for books? Like *The Palm Rustler* and *A House Built on Sand*?"

Margot nodded. "Yeah."

"Sheriff Royston thinks her mention of Dr Engler on the night of Connor's murder means something. So he went through that file to see if there was one that gave her the idea for this latest manuscript. He couldn't find one. It made me wonder if she could've kept it anywhere else – especially as she was writing."

Margot thought for a moment. "You could try her bedside table – and Mr Burke's. And there's an old chest on the porch that has some drawers. There are also some junk drawers in the kitchen. I guess if she wanted it nearby when she was writing, any of those might do."

Annabelle tugged hard on her leash, diverting Logan's attention. Up ahead, they saw an older woman with a dog that looked like Annabelle. Both dogs began straining toward each other.

"That's Mrs Agerton," said Logan. "With Maxie."

They reached their neighbor, who appeared relieved when Maxie stopped pulling and nosed Annabelle.

"What are you doing with Maxie?" asked Margot.

"Liza went to see her sister in Chicago," said the elderly lady. "So I'm keeping Miss Maxie."

"But *we've* always kept her!"

Mrs Agerton looked embarrassed. "I… I'm sure she didn't want to bother you with all you've got going on, dear. Maxie's a sweet thing. No trouble at all."

Logan smiled with an effort. "That's very nice of you, Mrs A. These Shibas need a lot of exercise. If you need any help, let us know."

"Thank you, Logan. I will." Mrs Agerton pulled Maxie toward her large house. Annabelle gave a final bark.

Margot turned on Logan. "Do you think Liza doesn't trust us to keep her darn dog?"

"Surely that's not it. She probably didn't want to ask us the week of the funeral."

Margot tightened her lips. "I don't know, Logan. Sullivan's Island is not like Columbia or Greenville. With rubberneckers driving by the house and the funeral all over the news, you may start getting frozen out."

Logan stared at her. "Are you serious?"

"I am."

Logan gazed at the familiar houses on the street and wondered if Margot could be right. Would the longtime neighbors prefer to let Harrison erase all evidence of the house where the murder/suicide took place? That would take care of the awkward problem.

At that moment a tan Buick passed them, slowing as it reached the Burke house. Margot pointed. "See what I mean?"

"Well, it's already down from what it was earlier in the week. People may lose interest by summer." Even to her own ears, Logan's argument sounded weak.

"I hope so, for your sake." A flash of lightning ripped the sky, followed by a crack of thunder. Annabelle yelped.

"We'd better get back," Logan said. "That storm came faster than I expected."

The women turned and hurried back to the house, making it to the driveway before the drenching rain began.

A few hours later, Logan sat in the living room, not seeing the competitive cooking show blaring at her. She turned the volume down when Margot came into the room.

"Logan, would you mind if I went to Columbia for the weekend?"

"Of course not," Logan replied. "But you don't need to ask my permission."

"I know, but I hate to leave you here by yourself."

"I won't be by myself. Britt's coming back."

"Where is she anyway?"

"I imagine she's at her father's office, trying to decide if she's going to join his practice. I need to spend this weekend trying to decide some things too."

"I thought you were intentionally trying *not* to decide anything for a while."

"Well, not the big stuff like whether to sell the house. But some stuff, like am I going to stay here or go back to my duplex? Am I going to keep my receptionist job or paint full time? Am I going to keep Annabelle or send her with you?"

"Ha ha. I can answer that one for you." Margot smiled. "But you do have some choices now, don't you?"

"Yeah, I do. It's a shame I'm not happier about it."

"That'll come. You're still in shock."

"Anyway, have fun in Columbia. Are you staying with a friend?" Before Margot could answer, Logan interrupted herself. "Wait a minute. You need a car. Take the Jeep."

"Are you sure you don't mind? My friend, Cheryl, was going to come and get me tomorrow. But I'll drive up tonight if you're serious about the Jeep."

"Yes, it's fine. I can use Mother's Lexus if I go anywhere. In fact, I want to get it all cleaned and vacuumed and the deed transferred, because I'm giving it away."

"That's nice. To whom?"

"To you."

"*What!?*" Margot shrieked.

"If you want it, that is. I was trying to think of an amount of money to give you for all you've done and then I thought you might prefer the car. What do you think?"

Margot rushed to the couch and hugged Logan. "I think that's perfect. I was going to have to buy something when I got home, so this solves everything. And it's such a nice car! Thank you, Logan. Really."

She ran upstairs to pack.

It was past 10 p.m. Margot was gone, and Britt still wasn't back. Logan hoped she and Dr Fitz hadn't gotten into a quarrel. She had been surprised to hear that Britt was considering joining his practice, because the two had always butted heads. She hoped nothing had happened to derail her friend's plans to return home.

Logan was restless. She tried to watch television, but couldn't make herself care about what was happening on the screen. She drifted into the dining room, where she'd left her art supplies. Did she feel like painting? She propped a canvas on the easel, and picked up a brush, then put it down. She tried to picture quitting her job and painting full time. Would she be too isolated? And would Gus and Dr Littlemeyer go forward with the purchase of her paintings if she was no longer on staff? She needed to wait at least until the sale went through.

She corrected herself. She might *want* the sale, but she didn't *need* it, not financially anyway. The truth was, she was rich. No matter what she and Harrison did or didn't do with the house here and the one in Scotland, her mother's attorney had shown her bank and stock accounts that totaled in the millions. Like so many good writers, Julianna had preferred to write, even when she no longer needed to.

As rain pummeled the roof and windows, and the wind screeched off the ocean, Logan walked around the familiar house, remembering her nervousness at being alone after Connor was killed. Yesterday all she'd felt was a deep and dark despondency. But now, with the possibility that her mother had been drugged, apprehension returned. Why would anyone do such a thing?

She now understood Sheriff Royston's frustration with the island habit of sharing house keys. Almost anyone could have come in and tampered with her mother's supplements. Even someone *without* a key could have walked into someone else's house and gotten the Burke key. But why would they?

She picked up a magazine, then slapped it down on a side table. The worst part was the suspicion – of knowing that someone she knew from church or happy hours or block parties – someone who had been welcomed into this house, someone who'd been part of their lives – had betrayed them so cruelly. *If* her mother had been drugged, she reminded herself. That wasn't a fact yet.

She thought about going to bed, but knew she couldn't sleep. Would she ever be able to sleep alone in this house again? She thought about Connor's stabbing and Julianna's hanging, and her stomach lurched. Maybe she would move back to her duplex and leave this gloomy place behind.

She needed to *do* something, *accomplish* something. Should she start packing? Even if she waited to decide about selling the house, she needed to pack Julianna's and Connor's clothes. She slowly climbed the stairs to their bedroom and walked in, eyeing her mother's laughing portrait and making her way to their shared closet. She ran a hand over Connor's golf shirts and khaki slacks and crisp blue dress shirts, her touch releasing the faintest scent of his aftershave. Dread pressed down on her, and she wanted to sink to her knees. But even more, she wanted to be out of there, to be away from these physical and olfactory reminders. She slammed the closet door, startling Annabelle, and fled to her own room.

Still restless, she looked around the familiar space, what had been a sanctuary for the teenage Logan. The ballerina jewelry box, the framed certificate that pronounced her Most Artistic in her senior class, the shelves of paperback mysteries. There was no sense in packing all this until she knew where she would live.

Maybe Harrison's things. She'd realized when she was downstairs last week that he'd left a lot of junk. No matter what happened, he wouldn't be moving back into this house. She could pack his stuff and make him take it away. Did she really want to go down there? Of course not. Which was why she would force herself.

She took a deep breath and walked down the stairs, Annabelle at her heels. "Afraid we're going to get wet, girl," Logan said.

She found an umbrella leaning in a corner of the laundry room and opened the kitchen's side door. When Annabelle saw the punishing rain, she backed away, whining far back in her throat. Or did she know where they were headed?

"Come on," Logan coaxed. "Don't make me go down there alone."

But the dog continued to back up, bumping the far wall of the kitchen. Logan considered carrying her down the steps, but figured a wet and irate Annabelle would be worse than no company at all. "Okay," she said. "Suit yourself."

She pulled the door shut behind her and locked it, aware there was a time she would've left it wide open without a thought. She hurried down the stairs, the umbrella giving minimal shelter from the sideways-driving rain. She ducked under the ground-floor overhang, retrieved the key from the storage room and opened the door to the downstairs suite.

She stood for a moment, her eyes flitting to Harrison's closet, illogically fearing that she might see a body hanging there. Her stomach clenched and she had to force herself through the doorway. How could a single house harbor so much happiness and so much pain? Because she knew, she *knew,* that no matter what else had gone on, what currents she was oblivious to, what infidelity may or may not have occurred, Julianna and Connor had loved each other. Loved each other not with a ferocity that evoked jealousy and violence, but loved each other with kindness and mutual delight. So how to explain what happened? Logan shook her head and drew a shaky breath. She would not let fear paralyze her. She would not.

She dragged a stack of cardboard boxes from the all-purpose bathroom closet and began packing Harrison's trophies and sports equipment, quickly realizing that she needed a trash box as well. She ripped his band posters off the walls and threw them into the trash, her irritation growing that he hadn't taken care of this. But then she remembered the high school paraphernalia in her bedroom. She didn't have room to talk.

In the silence, she was aware that the rain had let up slightly, or maybe the upper levels were taking the brunt of the storm. She looked around for a radio or CD player to provide some sort of comforting noise. Damn that Annabelle for not coming with her!

As if reading her thoughts, the Shiba burst into a frenzy of barking, so loud that it easily pierced the ceiling. Logan flinched, banging her knee against the closed cabinets that lined the bottom of Harrison's shelving.

She bit her lip to keep from crying out, listening for sounds above her. The dog kept up her howling, but now Logan heard footsteps. Her heart began to race. She peered out of the ground-floor window and saw no car but Julianna's Lexus. *It must be Britt*, she realized. Logan had given her a key, and Britt had probably left her car at her parents' house.

Annabelle stopped barking. She'd seen Britt enough to know her. Logan's heart slowed, and she went back to work. She'd need to let Britt know where she was in a minute, but she wanted to empty this one last shelf of paperback novels – everything from *Lord of the Flies* to *The Water is Wide*. The county library held an annual book sale, so she'd take the books there. She pulled out *Lord of the Flies* and saw a flash of pink, just as headlights swept through the film-smeared window. Logan peered out, but the lights were aimed directly at her eyes, blinding her. Her anxiety returned. Were some thrill-seeking teens trying to see the "haunted house" on a stormy night?

She flattened herself against the wall beside the window, waiting to see what the car's occupants would do. The headlights went dark, and she heard a single door open. Then someone was climbing the stairs. Logan waited for the ringing of the doorbell, but it didn't come. Had she set the alarm? Of course not! She was waiting for Britt to get back.

Annabelle's barking started up again, tinged with the hysteria that greeted any visitor. Logan turned off the lights in Harrison's room and, as her eyes adjusted, looked out of the window again. Britt's Honda Accord sat in the driveway.

Logan bolted from the room and hit the front stairs two at a time, screaming her friend's name. She slipped on the wet landing and fell. Britt stood in the foyer, the front door open, confused by the noise coming at her from both sides. "What?! *What?*" she cried.

"Somebody's here!" hissed Logan, springing up and limping through the doorway. "Somebody's in the house."

Britt's eyes widened. Annabelle stopped barking and leaped on Logan, pawing her legs. Logan pushed her away, searching for a weapon. There was absolutely nothing – no metal sculpture or heavy ashtray or fireplace poker.

"Wouldn't Annabelle go after anyone who was here?" whispered Britt.

Logan didn't answer. She crept through the living room, flipping lights on as she went. "Who's there?" she called. "We know you're here."

They were met with the drumming of the rain. Only when they stepped into the kitchen did they hear a loud crash from the screen door. Both women jumped. With a hand on her chest, Britt said, "It's the wind. That door's open."

Logan ran to the side door, but the outdoor pool of light revealed nothing. "Yeah, but I locked it half an hour ago," she said, closing and locking it once more.

"What a way to come home," said Britt, sinking on to a barstool. "What the heck is going on?"

"I'll explain, but first we need to search the house. Someone could still be here." The women stayed together and, closely followed by Annabelle, retraced their steps through the living room, then the rarely used dining room, to the game room and the porch. Logan paused in her mother's study, where the desk light was on. "This wasn't on when I left," she said. "I'm sure of it."

She opened Julianna's empty desk drawers, remembering that Sheriff Royston and Detective Giles had taken the files. Was that what someone was after?

She and Britt climbed the stairs to the upper floor and looked through the bedrooms. Logan got on her knees and looked under each bed and peered into every closet, tub and shower. She knew she'd never be able to sleep otherwise.

They made their way back to the kitchen, where Britt put on a kettle and searched for tea bags. Logan put out sugar and honey, and leaned shakily against the counter. "I probably need to lock up downstairs," she said.

"Can't it wait till morning?" Britt asked. "Is there anything down there to steal?"

"You're right. That's why I was down there, to get rid of every single thing."

"So talk," said Britt, sliding a mug of tea toward her.

"Well, Margot left to spend the weekend in Columbia. I let her take the Jeep. And I decided to start packing up some of the junk from the 'bachelor pad' that's going to need to go, no matter what we decide to do with the house."

"Ah, that explains it," Britt said.

"What did you think?"

"I didn't know," she said, her eyes searching Logan's. "I was afraid you wanted to be where your mother died. Or something like that."

Logan snorted. "No. It was all I could do to make myself go down there. And the cowardly Annabelle Burke wouldn't go with me."

Britt reached down to stroke the dog's head. "You've got more sense, don't you, girl?"

"Thanks a lot," said Logan. "Anyway, I was putting stuff in boxes and throwing junk out when I heard her bark and heard footsteps overhead. I was sure it was you – that you had left your car at your folks' and walked over."

Britt shook her head. "No, I've been in Charleston all this time. After the office closed, Dad showed me the equipment and a bunch of back office functions. Then we went for a drink. I followed him home, and since it was so late, I came straight here."

"Well, I was sure it was you, and I was trying to hurry back up so you wouldn't worry about where I was. Then your car pulled in. And you know the rest." Logan rubbed her backside. "I literally risked my butt to save your life."

The women broke into whooping laughter, the tension finally breaking. "Glad you can joke," said Britt, her brown eyes growing serious. "But any idea who was here?"

"No, but they had a key," said Logan. "I locked the front door earlier and I locked that side door when I went downstairs."

"And they thought you weren't home because the Jeep was gone. So what were they looking for?"

"Maybe something in Mother's office," said Logan. "I know that light wasn't on in there before."

"If we look, do you think you could tell if anything is missing?"

"It's worth a try, I guess."

They took their tea and went to the office. Britt stared at the blank space beneath the window where the chair had been. "Ugh. Is this where it happened?"

Logan nodded.

"Poor Connor," said Britt. "He was a good guy." She ran her fingers across the books on Julianna's shelf. "Boy, do these bring back memories."

Logan stood with her hands on her hips, surveying the room. "The thing is, Sheriff Royston took all of Mother's files. I can't imagine there would be anything to find."

"But whoever broke in didn't know that," Britt reminded her.

"True." Logan opened a cabinet beneath the bookshelf, and a pile of newspapers and magazines spilled on to the floor.

"Uh-oh," Britt said. "Are those more clips that the sheriff should have?"

"No, these are reviews of Mother's books," Logan said. "He already went through them and didn't need to take them."

Britt held up one of the articles, scanning it. "This isn't a review," she said, reading for a while longer. "It's a story about a case in Raleigh that relates to *A House Built on Sand*." She looked at Logan. "I didn't know Julianna's books were based on real cases."

"I think some are and some aren't," Logan said, reaching for the article. "I only found out myself when I moved in here." Logan sat down cross-legged in front of the cabinet and skimmed the article, then pawed through the scattered clips to locate several follow-ups. "So the reporters in Raleigh rehashed all this *after* Mother's book came out," she mused. She stared at the picture of the mother who was serving a life sentence for killing her daughter.

Britt looked at her blankly, and Logan explained. "I found a file of stories that readers from all over the country sent Mother about murder cases. A few she used and changed characters, genders, locales, all that. Most she didn't use. I gave the file to the sheriff. But these," she waved the articles she'd pulled from the pile, "were written after *A House Built on Sand* came out, when journalists linked the book *back* to the North Carolina case."

Britt grinned. "Life imitates art imitates life."

"I suppose." Logan frowned. "But the sheriff didn't leave these papers in such a mess. All Mother's files were organized, and as you can see, even her office supplies are." She pointed to the neat stacks of copy paper, manila folders and translucent binders in rose, lime green and powder blue. In contrast, the newspaper articles were wrinkled and a couple of them ripped.

"So you think someone else went through these?" Britt asked.

"Maybe," Logan said. Her eyes returned to the colored binders.

She'd seen one earlier that night. "Will you come downstairs with me for a minute?"

"I thought we were going to wait and lock up tomorrow."

Logan picked up a rose-tinted binder. "There was one of these on Harrison's shelf," she said. "It was wedged behind a bunch of books. I glimpsed it but didn't get to it because you drove up." She looked at her friend.

Britt nodded. "Okay, then. Let's go."

The rain had let up and a fine mist wet their faces when they opened the front door. This time Annabelle charged ahead of them down the stairs. The women walked into Harrison's bedroom, stepping over cardboard boxes filled with trophies. Logan went straight to the shelf she'd been working on and retrieved the supple pinkish binder from where it'd fallen, released from its hiding place behind Harrison's books. But unlike his old volumes, this folder was dust-free.

Logan opened it, Britt peering over her shoulder, and stared at a bundle of newspaper clippings. *Psychiatrist Charged in Patient's Murder*, read the headline on top.

"This is it," Logan breathed. "The real Dr Engler."

Chapter 26

As soon as it was daylight, Logan and Britt crept from the Fitzgeralds' house, carefully avoiding Charlie and Meg, and let themselves back into the Burkes'. They'd slept fitfully in Britt's renovated room with its twin beds, unwilling to spend the night in Logan's house. Logan slept with the rose binder under her pillow, Annabelle curled at the foot of her bed.

Britt made a pot of coffee as Logan left messages for the sheriff and Detective Giles. By 8:15, they received a return call that the officers were on their way. "Oh, and Logan?" said Lance Royston. "We got a confirmation on the drugs. Those gingko capsules were laced with crushed lorazepam. And the fish oil capsules were spiked with midazolam."

Despite herself, Logan gasped. "Are those tranquilizers?" Britt spun from the counter to listen. "I'm putting you on speaker phone, Sheriff," said Logan.

"Who's there? Margot?"

"No, just Britt."

"Okay." His voice crackled. "Our lab tech tells me they are anti-anxiety drugs in a class called benzodiazepines." He pronounced it as if the technician had written it out phonetically. Britt was nodding, but said nothing. Tears sprang to Logan's eyes. Even after everything that had happened, the cruelty staggered her.

"Needless to say, in a lot of people the drugs mess with memory," he said. Logan was silent for so long that the sheriff paused. "Logan? You there?"

She swallowed. "Someone was purposely making Mother think

she had dementia," she said. "Who could be so, so…" She couldn't finish.

Britt stepped closer to the phone. "Sheriff, Britt Fitzgerald here. We'll be waiting for you."

"Thirty minutes," he said and clicked off.

"Sheesh," Britt said. "That's serious stuff. Benzodiazepines are what anesthesiologists use during surgery. No wonder Julianna was whacked out."

Logan could hardly speak. Britt looked at her sympathetically. "Are you all right?"

"Not really. I guess on some level I knew this was possible, but the reality is worse than I imagined." She turned to gaze out at the ocean. "Britt, someone came into this house to erase my mother's memory." She sagged. "How could that happen?"

Britt poured another cup of coffee and slid it to Logan. "Well," she said briskly, "let's look at the possibilities. The obvious people, access-wise, are – or were – Connor, Margot and Harrison. I'm going to leave you out of the mix, because if it's you I don't want to know."

Logan couldn't make herself smile in response. "I think we can rule Connor out," she said.

"Why?"

"Because I'm pretty sure it started with those gingko pills. When she stopped taking them, her memory cleared. I watched it happen. And she was still taking the fish oil with no effect. I think someone added the drugs to the fish oil – *because* she'd stopped the gingko."

"Oh, man," said Britt. "That means someone's been watching you guys." She looked around, as if eyes might be on them still. "You know, Logan, you probably know things you don't even know you know."

"The sheriff thinks that too." She opened a junk drawer and located a pen and notepad. "We need to make a timeline." She tapped the pen on the counter. "Mother said she went to your dad in early November about her memory. She described having 'mild problems' with remembering people's names at her events. In retrospect, it doesn't sound like it was all that bad. That's when Dr Fitz suggested gingko and fish oil." Logan glanced at her old friend.

Britt met her eyes. "Surely you don't think..." Britt didn't finish her thought. "I mean, Dad..." She looked away, her lips forming a tight line. "You're right," she said, slamming her mug on the counter a little harder than necessary. "The worst part is suspecting everybody and everything you've ever known. My dad can be a world-class jerk, but he didn't do this." She drew herself up. "But you can't know that. Go ahead."

"Mother had 170 pages of *Murder, Forgotten* written at that point," Logan continued. "Then from November to February was a blur. She wrote only twenty more pages. She refused to see me or Harrison for Thanksgiving or Christmas, so we didn't know what was going on. Could that have been intentional?"

Britt shrugged. "Hard to say." She took a sip of her coffee. "Hand me that folder again."

Logan placed it in front of her friend. The folder held thirty-seven articles written over a fourteen-month period in the *Albuquerque Journal* of New Mexico. The first, written eighteen years previously, was a routine murder story about police investigating the shooting death of a local school board member. His wife and teenage daughter were out shopping, and at first authorities thought it might be a gang-related home invasion. Subsequent stories showed that theory petering out. Several more stories rehashed details of the murder, and featured interviews with the family, neighbors and fellow school board members. Clearly the investigation had stalled.

Then, five weeks later, the newspaper erupted with the front-page banner headline that Logan and Britt had seen the night before: *Psychiatrist Charged in Patient's Murder.* Dr Marissa Eskew had been arrested and charged with the shooting death of her patient in his home study. As details emerged in ensuing stories, Logan felt as though she'd already read them. As indeed she had.

Marissa Eskew had given up a baby for adoption sixteen years earlier. When a man came to her, confessing lust for his adopted daughter, he shared the girl's picture. A shocked Dr Eskew took one look at the lovely redhead, the distinctive chin, the blue eyes so like her own, and suspected that the teenager was the child she had given up for adoption. As a professional colleague of the lawyer who had arranged it, she had no trouble finding out what she'd not allowed herself to learn before – the name of the baby's adoptive parents.

"Marissa Eskew," Logan said, "became Martin Engler. The shooting became a stabbing. Albuquerque became California wine country. Mother always changed the details."

"Let me look at the photos again," Britt said, flipping through the clips.

"For what they're worth," said Logan. She walked around to stand behind Britt, looking at the newspaper photos over her shoulder. In one, Dr Eskew was turned away from the camera. In another, she wore a floppy hat and huge sunglasses. In the third, she was mounting the stairs to the Albuquerque courthouse, surrounded by her legal team and holding a purse in front of her face. It was almost as if she had planned it ahead of time – to disappear before the trial was over.

Another six articles rehashed the story of her escape from the courthouse and a disappearance so complete it confounded authorities. They knew she'd had help, but her ex-husband, a veterinarian, denied any knowledge of her whereabouts.

Britt tapped the useless newspaper photographs impatiently. "Let's say someone learned that Julianna was writing a novel based on these articles. If the purpose was to confuse her so much that she couldn't finish it, we've got to figure out who would've known what she was writing."

Logan counted on her fingers as she spoke. "Connor. Margot. Renata. Other editors at Ironwater. And whoever she might have told in conversation." She threw up her hands. "Given that this place was happy hour central, that includes the whole darned neighborhood."

Britt nodded solemnly. "This is definitely one possibility," she said, rapping the newspaper articles with a blunt fingernail. "But before the sheriff gets here, can I ask you something without making you mad?"

"Sure."

Britt looked uncomfortable. "Let me start by saying I'm not judging. While I was in med school, I learned that my father had been having affairs. For years."

"Oh, Britt. You knew?"

"Wait. You mean you knew too?"

Logan shook her head. "I literally heard a couple of weeks ago and didn't want to believe it."

"Well, believe it. One of my professors happened to be at a conference and saw Dad with a woman. Of course, he assumed it was my mother, but when he described her I knew it wasn't. The jerk. Dad, I mean."

"I am so sorry for you and Meg. It makes me feel like I've been kicked in the stomach, so I can imagine how you feel."

"Yeah, I'm pretty sure Mom knows, though I haven't gotten up the nerve to talk to her about it. But anyway, I digress. I brought that up as a segue." She took a deep breath. "Could there have been anything like that in Connor and Julianna's relationship?" Britt made a face as if awaiting a blow.

Logan sighed. "No, I'm not mad at the question. It so happens I've been asking it myself."

Britt looked relieved. "What happened to make you suspect?"

Logan related Renata's comment that Liza was interested in Connor. She told about asking Pastor Marsha and getting stonewalled, but then overhearing Baron Philpot say that Connor had had an affair.

"Wow. Who knew Sully's was such a *Peyton Place*?" commented Britt.

"What's that?"

Britt waved her hand dismissively. "A book from the fifties about affairs in a small town. I read it in a college class on pop culture."

Logan straightened abruptly. "Oh, I can't believe I forgot to tell you this!" She told Britt about Harrison and Sunny, and their rendezvous in the "bachelor pad" on the day of Connor's murder.

Britt screamed with horrified laughter. "Oh, my gosh, was there something going on when Harrison was a teenager?" She shrieked again.

"He says not. It began in the past year."

Britt shivered in revulsion. "Sorry, Logan. No offense to you. But that is so – let's see, what's the medical term? – yukky. Does Dick know?"

"I imagine so. Sunny reported to Sheriff Royston that she saw Harrison enter the house the day of the murder."

"She did not!"

Logan shrugged. "She did. So I assume Dick learned the whole story during the fallout. And Harrison got hauled in for questioning."

"So what do you think?" Britt asked. "Were Renata and Baron Philpot right? Were Liza and Connor having an affair?"

"I have no idea. I asked Margot and she seemed to think Connor and Mother were as devoted as they appeared. And I kind of danced around it with Liza and she claimed to be sincerely interested in her boyfriend, a man named Fred Manigault." She hesitated a beat. "So is your point that this whole thing could be a tawdry sex scandal?"

"See, I knew you were going to get mad."

"No, we do need to look at everything. *Was* that your point?"

"Well, yeah. Before we go down the road that is Julianna's writing, could it be simpler than that? Connor fell in love with someone else and tried to eliminate Julianna with the benzos. Maybe she would have been institutionalized and he would be free to carry on." Britt looked apologetic. "I know it's far-fetched, but he did have access to the gingko pills. Of course, someone else would have had to follow up with the fish oil." She thought for a moment, then plunged on. "But if the affair was with Margot, you have double motive and double access."

Logan groaned and put her head in her hands. "And what? Mother found out and killed him? And then herself?"

"Or he told Margot it was over and Margot killed him and convinced Julianna that she'd done it. I keep coming back to that note your mother left at the bottom of her murder scene. 'No, no, no! Did he know it was ME?'" Britt grimaced. "There's no getting around that."

Logan looked up, her eyes hardening. "Britt, you are undermining everything I thought I knew about everyone I ever loved."

Britt ran a hand through her hair and jutted her chin out with a stubbornness Logan knew well. "I'm sorry, Logan. But you do know, don't you, there's no way this is going to turn out well?"

Chapter 27

Logan threw open the front door to Sheriff Royston and Detective Giles, noting the balmy spring morning. A few palm fronds torn by the previous night's storm littered the driveway, but the air was freshly washed and sweet. Her heart pinched at the memory of such flawless mornings when the house was filled with the sounds of coffee percolating, and her mother and Connor murmuring in the kitchen.

A late-model BMW cruised slowly down the street. Logan remembered a time when tourists irritated her. Now she hoped they were people renting for the weekend, and not more rubberneckers titillated at her family's expense.

She thrust the rose-colored folder at the sheriff as he crossed the threshold. She had arranged the news articles from Albuquerque in chronological order, so he and Cynthia Giles settled on the living room couch and began reading. Britt and Logan fidgeted in armchairs, watching their expressions. "Dr Marissa Eskew," muttered Detective Giles. "That name mean anything to you?"

The sheriff shook his head. "I remember hearing about the case, but I couldn't have come up with the name. Or even where it happened." He placed the last article on the coffee table and looked at Logan. "So you found these in the room where your mother died?"

Logan nodded. "She had hidden them behind Harrison's old paperbacks."

"There was a letter in the file you gave us from a town in New Mexico," he said, "but there were no news clips. It was a fan letter and didn't even mention this case. We'll go back and take a closer look to see if the letter-writer could have sent these." He grew quiet for a moment. "Julianna knew something," he mused as if to himself. "If she'd merely been using the articles to write from, they'd be in the place where she wrote, wouldn't they?"

"If she was thinking logically, yeah," Logan answered. "But you should have heard her during her last days. She thought her dead mother was here. I wasn't sure she recognized me. Or anybody, in fact, except maybe Annabelle."

"I understand that," he said. "Still, she *hid* these. She was cognizant enough to hide them." He looked at his colleague.

"The question is," said Detective Giles, "*when* did she hide the articles? Early in the writing of the book? Or did she take them downstairs the day she hung herself? Was she trying to tell us something?"

"I don't think so," Logan said slowly. "We might easily have never found that folder. It was a fluke that I started packing up Harrison's room."

The sheriff slapped his thighs. "Well, let's go have a look."

Britt slipped away to her guest bedroom, and Logan trudged down the front stairs with the law officers. Inside Harrison's old room, three sets of eyes swung to the bar at the top of the closet. Logan tore her gaze away and pointed to an adjacent shelf, empty now of everything but clotted dust balls. "It was tucked behind books there," she said.

Out of habit, the officers clasped their hands behind their backs, eyes scanning the remaining shelves. "Let's get a team back in here," Royston said. "Since they were thinking suicide, they weren't looking for anything else."

Logan's head jerked up. "You don't think it was suicide?"

He punched his cell phone. "I think we need to look at everything with fresh eyes."

Logan felt a flutter in her chest and realized how much she hoped that her mother had not left her voluntarily. The thought surprised her. The rising hope surprised her.

Detective Giles interrupted her thoughts. "Logan, do you have contact information for Margot? Where she's staying?"

"No, but I'm sure she has her cell phone."

"Do you know how old she is?"

Logan frowned. "Thirty-four, I think. Why?"

The detective ignored her question and walked to one side of the room to place her call as Sheriff Royston ordered a forensics team on his phone. Then he looked up the police department for Albuquerque and placed a call. Even from five feet away, Logan could hear the clatter of early morning in the Southwestern police station.

It took several minutes for the chief to come on the line, but when he did, she could hear his booming voice easily. Sheriff Royston held his phone away from his ear and put it on speaker for Logan and Detective Giles. "Chief, Sheriff Lance Royston here, from Charleston, South Carolina. I believe we met once at a conference in Lincoln, Nebraska." *Ah be-lieve we met wuh-unce atta con-fer-ence in Lee-cohn, Nubraska.*

"You bet. How are things in North Carolina, Sheriff?"

"South Carolina. But not bad. Not bad. I'm calling about a cold case of yours that may be impacting us here. It's still a little murky."

"And what cold case is that?" Logan wasn't sure, but the chief's voice may have stiffened. Cold case meant *unsolved*, and he probably didn't want to be reminded of that.

"Marissa Eskew."

"Hooeee. Worst boondoggle in Albuquerque, I can tell you that." The chief's voice grew perceptibly warmer. "I'm glad to say that was before my time. Yes, I'm very glad to say. That little filly gave our boys the slip like nobody's business. Ain't seen hide nor hair of her since."

"It looks like the case might have some bearing on a murder here. Could you fax or scan the files to us? Whatever's easiest."

"Sure. I can get Miss Belinda on it today. But I gotta warn you. There's a ton of it."

"I figured. You been following up tips over the years?"

"Not as many as you'd think. The lady didn't leave a trace." He hesitated for a moment. "But Sheriff, you're not the first from your neck of the woods to call about this."

The sheriff grew still. "No? Can you tell me who else was asking?"

"Hell, you're taxing my memory. I don't know if I wrote it down."

"Could it have been Julianna Burke?"

"The writer? Hell, no. I'da remembered that." He paused. "But that last name, Burke – that rings a bell. Hold on. Let me see if I put a note in the file. *Belinda!*" Sheriff Royston cringed as the chief bellowed at his secretary.

They waited almost four minutes, knowing they weren't cut off because they could hear banging file drawers and chatter in the background. Finally, the police chief's voice rumbled through the phone. "Well, I was right, Sheriff," he fairly shouted. "It was a Burke who called. On February 20 of this year. Connor Burke."

Sheriff Royston flipped the speaker off, grabbed a notebook and pen from his colleague, and began taking notes. When he hung up, he repeated what Detective Giles and Logan had already heard. "Connor Burke," he said, still surprised. "Connor called about Marissa Eskew two days before his death."

The three were silent, their minds working furiously. "What was he looking for?" asked Detective Giles, her brown eyes alert.

"He was trying to get a description."

"And?"

"A little on the heavy side, redhead or maybe strawberry blonde, always well dressed in suits and heels. Connor asked the chief if he could send a photo, and the chief had intended to send Dr Eskew's booking photo. But he never got around to scanning and emailing it. He said it probably wouldn't be very helpful anyway, because he'd seen the real Dr Eskew and wouldn't have recognized her from that photo."

"Going back to that description," said Giles, "all those things could be changed. You gain or lose weight, you color your hair, you change your wardrobe."

The sheriff nodded. "You could even have plastic surgery so you don't look your age."

"But the age wouldn't change," said Logan. "How old would Marissa Eskew be?"

"Fifty-three." He paused, and seemed to consider whether he should speak in front of Logan. "There's one more thing," he said slowly. "The ex-husband upped and left Albuquerque ten years ago. The authorities have no idea where he went."

The sheriff and the detective walked out from under the house, carrying the folder with the newspaper articles. Logan ran after them, stopping them before they got into the car.

"One more thing I forgot to tell you," she said. "Britt brought it up this morning." She hesitated, not wanting to voice it, not wanting to release the idea into the universe. The officers waited. "It may be nothing," Logan stumbled. "It probably *is* nothing. But I don't trust what I know and don't know any more."

Detective Giles looked quizzically at her boss. He nodded encouragingly at Logan.

"It's something I heard before Mother died. I was outside Marsha Philpot's house. The pastor of Chapel by the Sea?"

Now Detective Giles was openly frowning, one hand on her hip.

Logan blushed. "I had gone to talk to Marsha, and I asked her if Connor was having an affair with another church member before he died." Sheriff Royston raised an eyebrow. Logan plowed on. "She couldn't, or wouldn't, say. But they had their windows open. And as I was leaving, I heard Marsha's husband Baron tell her she might have been right not to tell me, but shouldn't she tell *you* that Connor was having an affair? Did she? Tell you, that is?"

The sheriff was quiet for a long moment. "No," he said at last. "She didn't say anything about that." He stood for another moment, as if lost in thought. "Did Mr Philpot mention a name?"

"No," Logan said honestly. "He didn't."

The sheriff peered at Logan. "But you think you know who it was?"

Did she? "Not really. Pure gossip and speculation."

The sheriff waited for another moment, then briskly opened the passenger door of his vehicle. "Thank you, Logan. You never know what may be helpful."

Detective Giles slid into the driver's seat of the sheriff's car and buckled her seatbelt. "Well, that came out of left field," she said. "But are you thinking what I'm thinking? From earlier?"

"About a certain redhead who's been living in this house?" he said. "What did Lancaster turn up when he interviewed her before?"

"She grew up in Greenville, came here for college, worked for a wedding planner until Connor Burke hired her two years ago."

"Find her parents," the sheriff ordered. "See if she was adopted and if so, where."

Chapter 28

Logan went to the guest bedroom and dropped into the room's only armchair, a beautifully skirted piece upholstered in cheery blue and yellow checks.

"What did they say?" Britt asked.

Logan looked shell shocked. "Connor must have suspected something," she said. "He called the police in Albuquerque about Marissa Eskew."

"You're kidding!"

Logan shook her head in silence.

"Do they think that's why he was killed?"

"They didn't say. Obviously he knew about the articles Mother was writing from. Something must have triggered his interest in the real Marissa Eskew."

"Wow. When was this?"

"Two days before he was killed. He was asking what she looked like."

Britt held up her hand to quiet Logan. "Someone's in the house," she whispered a moment before Annabelle charged out of the room and down the stairs, barking at full volume. The women froze. The barking didn't stop, and if possible grew more shrill.

"Maybe the sheriff came back?" asked Britt softly.

Then they heard an irritably raised voice. "Logan! Are you home? Get this stupid dog!"

Logan's shoulders slumped in relief. "It's Harrison," she said. The women walked down the stairs, Logan calling for Annabelle. But Harrison wasn't alone. Standing beside him in the living room was

Fred Manigault. Logan introduced Fred to Britt, then turned to her brother. "So what's up?"

"I just wanted to show Fred the inside of the house." He glared at Annabelle. "Is that dog going to live with you?"

"I guess," said Logan. "But why does Fred want to see the house?"

Harrison looked at his feet, obviously uncomfortable. Fred jumped in, his voice jovial. "Why, in case you two decide to sell, Logan! Nice little piece of beachfront you got here."

"I thought you'd been inside when you and Liza visited," Logan said.

"Oh, I was in here, I was. But I wasn't looking as a possible buyer back then. Whole different thing, you know?"

Logan looked at Harrison in disbelief. "Mr Manigault, I don't know what my brother has told you, but the property is not out of probate, and we've been advised not to make any decision for at least a year."

"Oh, call me Fred, Logan. And I know how lawyers are. They always say, 'Wait, wait,' don't they? But I have found that when it comes to beach property, you can't wait until everything is all neatly tied up, or it'll be gone out from under you. Just like that!" He snapped his large fingers.

Britt was scowling at both Fred and Harrison, but Harrison reached out to his former neighbor as if she held a lifeline. "Britt, we'll have to take you to Fred's restaurant," he said. "Your folks have been there. You'll love the flounder and crab cakes."

"You sure will, little lady!" Fred said. "Ol' Charlie and Meg have been there with Connor and Julianna and some of your neighbors." He glanced at Logan to see if he'd overstepped, then blundered on. "Yessiree, you bring your boyfriend; we'll fix you right up."

Harrison began to ease Fred toward the kitchen. "Well, let me show you the porch," he said.

"Ah no, no, that's not necessary," boomed Fred. "We can do that another time. We don't want to inconvenience your sister and her guest." Logan realized that with her Jeep gone, Harrison had assumed she wasn't home. She wondered exactly what he'd told Fred.

"Well, Mr Manigault, I think it's premature to look at the house," she said. "We haven't decided if we're going to sell." Harrison shot her a murderous look, which Logan ignored. "Harrison, I've been packing up your old trophies and books. You can't take them now, because the sheriff is sending a forensics team back, but pretty soon you'll need to get the boxes out."

Harrison looked at her, hopeful once more. "You're clearing out the house?"

"Just stuff that needs to go no matter what we decide. Connor's and Mother's clothes. Your and my old things."

Harrison made a move toward the front door, then seemed to process her earlier remark and turned. "Wait a minute. Why is the sheriff coming back? I thought all of this was over."

Logan didn't want to get into the details in front of Fred Manigault. "We can talk later," she said.

"But downstairs?" Harrison persisted. "He's going over the downstairs? Where Mother… where it happened?"

Logan watched her brother's face and could almost read his thoughts. He feared that Sheriff Royston wasn't looking into their mother's suicide but returning to his earlier suspicion that Harrison had walked upstairs and murdered Connor. "What's he after down there?" he demanded.

Logan shrugged. "He didn't share his suspicions with me."

Scowling, Harrison escorted Fred out of the front door.

When the door closed behind them, Britt looked at Logan. "What the hell was that?"

Logan plopped on to the couch. "Harrison didn't think anybody was home. He is going to sell this house come hell or high water."

"Not without you, he isn't," Britt said firmly. "There's not a thing in the world he can do until you agree. Don't let him railroad you."

Logan let her eyes roam around the stained pine walls, the glass balls and starfish and sand dollars ensnared in the fishing net on the wall. What once was soothing and familiar had become unknown and frightening. "I don't know, Britt. Remember how we felt last night?

We were too scared to sleep here. Maybe I should get out from under this thing."

"If that's what you ultimately decide, okay," Britt said. "But don't let Harrison or anyone else run you out." She snapped her fingers. "I know. Let's get the locks changed. Today."

Logan smiled. "Now there's an idea."

Britt found her phone and looked up Charleston locksmiths. "Here," she said, handing it to Logan. "They offer same-day service."

True to his word, the locksmith finished by late afternoon and gave Logan the four sets of keys she requested – for herself, Britt and Margot to start, and maybe later, depending on how she felt, for Harrison. Logan also showed Britt how to set and disarm the alarm, and they vowed to begin using it.

"Now," said Britt. "How would you feel about dinner out? My treat."

"I think that would be great. Somewhere close by or downtown?"

"You choose."

"There's a new restaurant in Mount Pleasant. Shrimp and Tomatoes."

"That sounds vile."

Logan laughed. "Yeah, but it's really good. The Mangrove is too, actually, but I don't want to run into Fred Manigault again."

"Okay," said Britt. "I need about thirty minutes to get spruced up."

Logan smiled sadly, remembering her conversation with her mother about sprucing up the house. That was one of the last good days they had.

Britt squeezed her shoulder. "You know, I'm torn about whether it's better for you to stay here or not. It may have too many memories, good and bad. You might never be able to be your own person as long as you're here." She shrugged. "I can see why the grief professionals say to wait a year. I'm sure things will look very different in a year's time."

"You're probably right. I just know I'm tired of thinking about it."

As dusk fell, Britt and Logan pulled into the parking lot of a cedar- and glass-fronted restaurant set well back from the road into Mount Pleasant. On one side a large deck was built around soaring oak trees, tiny white lights winding up the trunks and shining through newly sprouting leaves. On the other side was an ancient red brick church with a worn sign, Legacy AME.

"Quick quiz," said Britt, recalling the game Meg had played with the girls. "What's AME stand for?"

"Don't insult me," answered Logan. "African Methodist Episcopal."

"Ding ding ding," sang Britt. "Give the girl a free dinner."

"I thought I already had that."

The women walked into the cheerfully noisy restaurant. Logan could almost feel the dread and sorrow from the past few weeks lifting. They ordered glasses of chardonnay and shared an appetizer of fried green tomatoes before placing their orders – shrimp and grits for Logan, a seafood platter for Britt. They caught up on the last few years – Logan's string of jobs and her painting, Britt's residency and plans to practice in Charleston, friends who had married, divorced, had children, gotten fat. They enjoyed the singer/guitarist playing folk rock across the room and called out requests.

When the waitress brought the loose-leaf menus back to let them look at desserts, Logan idly flipped to the last page. At the very bottom was a single line: *On every day except Sunday, our customers may park at Legacy AME next door.*

"Boy, that's one bad acronym for a church," she said. "L.A.M.E."

"Amen," laughed Britt.

Logan continued to study the page so intently that Britt finally asked, "What are you looking at?"

"M.E.," Logan said slowly. "What if Mother didn't write, 'No, no, no! Did he know it was ME?' but 'No, no, no! Did he know it was M.E.?'"? She looked up, the blood draining from her face. "She was using initials. Marissa Eskew."

Britt stared at her.

"She used capital letters," said Logan. "That's it. M.E.! Not 'me'!"

She began to laugh, a trace of hysteria in her voice that made the people at the next table halt their conversation. "She didn't kill Connor. Britt, she didn't kill Connor!" Now the other diners were openly gaping. "She was asking if he knew his killer was Marissa Eskew!"

Britt spoke in a low voice, trying to encourage Logan to do the same. "And that's why she told the sheriff to 'ask Martin Engler'," Britt surmised. "As drugged as she was, something in her mind was trying to make the connection."

Half laughing, half crying, Logan fished for a tissue in her purse. Until this moment, she hadn't realized how much her mother's innocence meant to her. That in the midst of all the horror of her parents' deaths, she hadn't been wrong about the love they shared. That twenty-two years of watching their love story hadn't been a lie. She wiped her eyes, smiling at her friend.

Britt waved for the bill. "What are you waiting for?" she asked. "Call the sheriff."

Chapter 29

It was late when Logan and Britt pulled into the driveway of the beach house. The first thing they noticed was the Jeep. The second thing was the figure huddled on the stairs.

"Margot! What are you doing back so soon?" Logan called, stepping slowly out of the Honda.

"Let me in and I'll tell you," she said. "It got cold sitting out here."

"Sorry. We changed the locks," Logan said, unlocking the door. She paused, surprised to feel a slight reluctance at the thought of giving Margot new keys. But she still lived here. How could she *not* give them to her? "I have a set for you." She punched in the code for the security system as Annabelle jumped on her legs in greeting.

Margot's face showed surprise. "And you're using the alarm. Did something happen?"

Logan filled her in on the events of the night before. "But why are you back so early?"

"Detective Giles called and asked me to come in tomorrow for more questions," Margot replied, "so I decided to drive on tonight."

"I'm sorry your weekend got ruined," Logan said.

"Turns out I wasn't in the mood for partying anyway." Margot headed to the kitchen. "But I left without dinner and I'm starving. Do you want to keep me company while I make a sandwich?"

"Sure," said Britt. "And I'll have one more glass of wine. How about you, Logan?"

"Okay." She prised off her shoes and followed Margot.

"So someone was in the house last night and left when Britt drove up?" Margot asked, as she pulled bread and peanut butter out of a cabinet, and a banana from the refrigerator.

"Yeah, someone with a key."

"As we told the sheriff, that's a big group," Margot said. "Harrison. The Satterfields. Pastor Marsha. Britt's folks. Mrs Agerton. The only ones it couldn't be are Liza Holland because she's in Chicago, and Peg and Leo Oswald next door because you would've heard the clump of a walker." She pulled a face at her bad joke.

"And you," said Britt, opening a bottle of pinot noir, "because you were in Columbia."

Logan and Margot looked at Britt. "Well, yeah," Margot agreed. "Plus the fact that I'm here all the time and have no need to break in."

The women took their food and drinks to the breakfast table in front of the porch doors, now slates of black. Britt took a sip of wine and leaned back in her chair. "Logan realized something this evening and has already called Sheriff Royston to report it," she said. "She realized that the note on Julianna's murder scene wasn't what we thought."

Margot looked up from her sandwich. "What do you mean?"

Britt was silent, letting Logan explain. "You remember the line that stood alone on the third page, 'No, no, no! Did he know it was ME?'"

Margot nodded.

"The M and E were capital letters. Mother meant Marissa Eskew."

Margot stopped eating, and looked from Logan to Britt. "Who's Marissa Eskew?"

"Sorry," said Logan. "So much has happened since you left." She told Margot about finding the folder of newspaper clippings regarding the real-life psychiatrist in Albuquerque who had killed her daughter's adoptive father.

Margot sat still, her supper forgotten. "Julianna's novel," she breathed. "So it *was* from a true story."

"You didn't know?" Britt asked. "I would've thought Julianna would tell her assistant something like that."

"That wasn't my job," Margot said. "I set up appearances, interviews, speeches, things like that. Mr Burke and Renata did everything on the editorial side." She picked up her glass of iced tea and gulped from it, not noticing the trickle that spilled on to her shaking hand. "Is this why Detective Giles wants to see me?" Margot asked. "To see if I knew about this? I didn't!"

"I don't know," said Logan. "We didn't know she wanted to see you until you told us."

Margot's lower lip quivered. "But if Julianna thought this Marissa Eskew killed Mr Burke, she wouldn't have killed herself," she said. "It doesn't make sense."

"You're right," Logan agreed. "Unless Mother was so addled from the drugs that she kept forgetting, kept boomeranging to thinking she did it." She paused. "That night before, that happy hour, she was in bad shape. She thought my grandmother was in the house. In a lucid moment, she agreed we needed to go back to Dr Fitz and have him recommend a neurologist."

Britt looked at them with steely eyes. "When all she really needed was a good family practitioner to recognize that she was over-medicated." She stood with a scrape of her chair and walked to the sink with her empty glass.

Logan looked at her friend. Britt seemed angry, but at whom? Her father? Margot?

"I'm going to bed," Britt said. "See you two in the morning."

Logan and Margot sat in silence, Logan twisting her wine stem between her hands, Margot fingering a spiraling red curl.

Finally Margot spoke. "Did I miss something?" she asked. "Is Britt mad at me?"

Logan shrugged. "I wouldn't think so. But something's up. It may be about her dad. She's thinking about going into practice with him, but I believe there are some issues between them."

Margot murmured noncommittally. After another long moment, she asked, "Without getting all psycho-babbly, how do you feel now that you know Julianna didn't confess to killing Mr Burke? Thinking she did had to be hard on you."

"You're right," said Logan. "I guess I feel relief, not only for my mother but for my sanity."

Margot cocked her head. "How so?"

"That everything I thought I ever knew about the two of them is still true."

"Oh," Margot nodded. "Yeah, me too."

"Really?"

"Oh, yeah. Even though I only knew them for two years, they seemed to be truly, genuinely in love, almost to the exclusion of everyone else." She smiled. "And I know what that looks like. My parents are like that."

Logan smiled sadly. "Do you think that's why neither of us is married?"

Margot considered, her eyes roving to the French doors and the black night. "Could be. I keep waiting for the one perfect guy because I've seen it's possible."

Logan stood with her empty glass. "Are you glad to be headed back home?"

Margot wagged her hand to indicate indecision. "I don't plan to stay long. I'm sure they're enjoying their empty nest."

She got up to discard her half-eaten sandwich. "Thanks again for loaning me the Jeep. I would've hated for Cheryl to make two trips so quickly."

"No problem. See you in the morning."

Logan stood for a moment at the kitchen sink, turning off the lights so she could see the roll of moonlight across the ocean. She glanced at the empty counter where Julianna's bottle of tainted fish oil supplements once rested. She was torn about remaining in this house, because it could never be rid of its memories. She remembered the lifting of trepidation when she entered the clatter of the restaurant earlier in the evening. Had that trepidation returned now that she was in the beach house again? Her shoulders drooped. Yeah. It had. New locks and an activated alarm could keep intruders out. But what if the evil had settled within? What if the very pine boards that her great-grandfather and grandfather had so painstakingly laid had absorbed something bad, something malevolent?

She rubbed the back of her neck. Now she sounded like the teenagers driving by, or at least how she heard them in her head, scaring one another as they pointed to the house where two violent deaths had taken place. She should go to bed, she knew. But with Britt and Margot already upstairs, the prickling of the hairs on her neck and arms returned. She recalled Britt's comment about somebody watching her family. Somebody *had* been watching to know that her mother had stopped taking the gingko and was regaining her clarity. That's how she – if it was Marissa Eskew – or he – if it was an accomplice – knew it was time for a new drug, a different benzo, to carry her mother deep into confusion once more.

Something bumped her leg, and Logan jumped. Annabelle's dark eyes shone in the moonlight. "Sorry, girl," Logan said. "You scared me."

Annabelle whimpered, probably wanting Logan to come to bed. But suddenly Logan couldn't stand to be in the house another minute. "Come on, you want to walk, don't you?"

The dog ran to the laundry room where Logan grabbed her leash and snapped it on to her harness. She rolled up her pants, pulled a jacket from the hall closet, and left by the kitchen door, carefully locking it behind her. Annabelle ran down the side steps, excited to have this unexpected walk in the middle of the night. The moon reflecting off the ocean provided light, and Logan walked gingerly on the creaky boardwalk, wary of getting splinters in her bare feet. At its end, she jumped on to the sand.

She breathed in the bracing air and heard the familiar rumble of the waves. It was low tide, so the beach was wide and fragrant with salt and seaweed. Logan remembered her mother's funeral – how she had wanted nothing more than to stand on this shore and scream into the wind. She raised her voice and did so now, not at a volume that would carry back to the dark houses, but loud enough to purge herself of sorrow and loss. She was an orphan, she realized with a start. Well, not technically. Number 3, Rivers Arnette, was out there somewhere. But practically speaking she was. She would never bring her children to visit their grandparents for Sunday dinner or Thanksgiving or Christmas.

She thought of what Margot had said about the great love between her mother and Connor. You'd think growing up in such a household would provide a good model. That's what all the TV psychologists said, didn't they? All the books on marriage. But did it set children up to expect too much of their own relationships? Did they think their loves would never measure up? There it was again, that self-pity, that blame. Why couldn't she let go?

She turned and faced the old beach house. Maybe Harrison was right. Maybe the thing to do was take the money and create new lives for themselves – lives far removed from the shadow of Julianna's fame and Connor and Julianna's love. Sell the darn thing to Fred Manigault. That New England-esque façade would be gone in no time, replaced with ivory stucco and Spanish arches or some other Mediterranean-style monstrosity. Maybe she could move on more easily without the house as a reminder of her past.

Her mind went back to the afternoon visit from Harrison and Fred. The restaurateur had to know that Harrison didn't have the authority to sell the property yet. And he'd seen the inside of the house numerous times. Could he have been after something else? Something that was thwarted by Logan's presence?

Logan was tired of thinking, and certainly tired of suspecting everyone of ulterior motives. She began to jog along the beach, Annabelle running ahead. All the houses were dark, the Oswalds', Joan Agerton's, Liza Holland's. "Maxie's having a sleepover at Mrs A's," Logan told Annabelle, who barked in response.

With the exercise invigorating her, Logan's mood lifted, as it had earlier in the evening. She did love this island, she thought. The open beach, the palm-sheltered houses, the interior streets with their Spanish-moss-laden oaks. If she sold her little piece of it, would she regret it for the rest of her life?

After half a mile, Logan turned and started back. She pulled off her jacket and tied the bulky sleeves around her waist. She lifted her face to the cool breeze, happy that summer was almost here. She caught herself. Happy? Was that possible? Would she ever be happy again?

She let herself into the house quietly, and walked through the dark, hearing the linoleum squeak. She mounted the stairs to her bedroom, and beside her Annabelle's nails clicked on the wood planks. Logan felt the presence before she saw the shadow cross the hallway. She stopped, scarcely breathing. Why wasn't Annabelle barking? She looked down, scarcely able to make out the brown dog in the blackness of the stairwell. A streetlight reflected light into the hallway above, which allowed her to see the shadow gliding from her bedroom.

Britt? Margot? It disappeared, but she couldn't tell into which room. She reached the top of the stairs and flipped the light switch. No one was there. She strode to Britt's door and swung it open. Her friend was a huddle beneath the blankets. She opened Margot's door, and found her sitting up in bed, reading.

"Were you in my room?" Logan asked.

"What? No." Margot held up a Ruth Ware paperback. "I got this from Mr Burke's room." Margot looked at her, puzzled.

"I thought I… Never mind." Logan looked at Annabelle, who was settling wearily on to Margot's rug. "Come on, you. Margot doesn't want you in here. Goodnight."

Logan walked into her own room. For the first time in her life, she locked the door.

Chapter 30

Logan was awakened abruptly Saturday morning by the sound of sirens, unusual on this quiet stretch of beach. Even when Connor and her mother were killed, there had been no sirens. But the electronic screams were jarringly close. She bolted out of bed and ran down the stairs and on to the front stoop in her pajama pants and tank top. She saw a fire truck up the street, but it was hard to tell from this angle which house it was.

She ducked back into the house to grab flip-flops and ran squarely into Britt. "What's going on?" Britt shouted. Then the siren stopped, and there was blessed quiet.

"I'm not sure," Logan answered, too loudly. "Come on."

The two walked up Atlantic Avenue, nodding to neighbors who were stepping into their dew-drenched yards to see what was happening. As they neared Joan Agerton's elegant house, they could see that firefighters had entered, leaving the door wide open. There was no sign of smoke or fire, but now there was the sound of another siren in the distance. As Logan and Britt stood watching, Marsha Philpot hurried from the opposite direction.

"Is it Joan's heart?" she asked.

"No idea," said Logan. "But those sirens are getting closer. It may be EMS."

The women stood without speaking as an ambulance appeared and skidded into the driveway behind the fire truck, spattering oyster shell fragments. Two paramedics hurried to the front door, their arms full of equipment. A blur of brown and white flashed by the medics, and Logan dashed forward.

"It's all right!" she shouted to the young man who hesitated in the doorway. "I've got her."

"Come here, Maxie," Logan called to the frightened dog. Maxie took one look at Logan and bounded toward her, huddling between her and Britt. Logan knelt and hugged her. "It's okay, girl. Nobody's after you."

Maxie whimpered and wagged her tail enthusiastically. "She likes you," Marsha observed. "What's she doing at Joan's?"

"Apparently, Liza is visiting her sister in Chicago."

Marsha nodded. "Yeah, she goes there a good bit."

The women turned to watch as paramedics rolled Joan Agerton out of the house, her face pinched and her eyes closed. The young man asked them, "Next of kin?"

"None here," Marsha answered, "but I'm her pastor. Shall I come with you?"

"Why don't you bring your own car?" he suggested. "She may be in the hospital awhile."

"Will do." The pastor turned to Logan and Britt. "I'll go to the hospital if you can take care of the dog. Sound fair?"

"I think we got the easier part of this deal," Logan said. "Come on, Maxie. I know someone who's going to be glad to see you."

Logan and Britt's progress home was slow, as they had to keep stopping to update neighbors about Joan Agerton. Dick and Sunny Satterfield stood in their yard, but something in their rigid stance stopped Logan and Britt from approaching. They waved, and the couple turned aside.

"What the heck is going on with them?" said Britt.

"Well, apart from all the trouble my brother has caused, do you think they're upset about the traffic?" Logan asked.

"It's Easter weekend," Britt said. "I don't think they can blame you for that."

Logan spun to face her friend. "It's Easter weekend?"

Britt laughed. "Heavens, I'm having second thoughts about staying in your house. My memory may be gone by summer."

Logan gave her a withering look. "You're developing a mean streak."

Britt halted, stung. "Am I?"

Logan watched as Maxie ran up the front stairs. She steeled herself. "Last night you sounded mad at someone. Was it your dad? Or Margot? Or me?"

Britt assumed a stubborn look that Logan knew well. "Not you. But I'm not too fond of those other two right now."

"Because… "

"Well, my dad because of what we talked about earlier. I swear he's gotten worse as he's grown older. Trying to prove his virility or something. I'm wondering if Mom is going to leave him."

"Oh Britt, no. Really?"

"Yeah, the tension over there is pretty bad."

"That breaks my heart. But what about you? Can you work with him?"

"Not for any length of time. If he agrees to retire in six months, maybe. But I'm not sure taking over his practice is a good idea anyway."

"So you have about as many decisions to make as I do."

"Yep."

"And Margot? What's your problem with her?"

Britt worried the crushed oyster shells with the toe of her flip-flop. "I'm not sure exactly. But how much do you know about her? I mean, she showed up here two years ago, right? When all is said and done, both of her employers are now dead. She could have put the drugs in Julianna's pills more easily than anyone. She could have stabbed Connor. And where was she when Julianna supposedly committed suicide?"

Logan's face turned ashen. "She said she went to get bagels."

"Did she bring them home?"

"I… I… don't know. That's the last thing I was thinking about." Maxie barked, eager to get inside the house. Corralling her thoughts, Logan said, "But what possible reason could she have, Britt? She's out of a job. She's walking away with a few months' severance and Mother's SUV."

Britt frowned. "Didn't you say she wanted to get into the editorial side of your mother's books? Maybe she wants to take over as the next Julianna Burke. You know, like that woman with the *Gone with the Wind* sequel, and that Swedish guy with *The Girl with the Dragon Tattoo* series."

Logan looked at her friend in horror. "Who says Mother's books are going to continue?" she asked. "I can't imagine such a thing."

A horn honked, causing them both to jump. They stared at the unfamiliar white Camry pulling into the driveway. Logan feared for a moment that it was someone who wanted a close-up view of the "death house". Then the driver's window rolled down and she caught a glimpse of raven hair and sunglasses.

"Don't worry!" called Renata O'Steen. "I'm not crashing in on you. I've got a hotel room."

The women gathered in the kitchen over a pot of coffee, vanilla yogurt and granola, and some leftover strawberries and grapes from the funeral reception. "What brings you back so soon?" Logan asked, sliding a cup of coffee and a plate to Renata.

Renata spooned fruit onto her plate, then liberally covered it with yogurt. "Two other editors and I have spent the past two days huddled over Julianna's manuscript," she answered. "We agree it's too good to abandon."

Logan and Britt looked at each other.

"What?" said Renata.

"We were just talking about that," said Britt.

"So what does that mean – 'too good to abandon'?" asked Logan.

"It means we want to come up with a way to finish it," said Renata. "We want to talk to whomever Julianna talked to about it. Find any notes she made. Any scenes she might have written ahead. I know she did that sometimes."

"And then what?"

"Then find the best writer we can to see if he or she can carry those ideas to conclusion. It'll be a throw of the dice. But we think it's worth trying." She took a bite of fruit.

"Who are you thinking about as a writer?" asked Logan, frowning.

"We haven't gotten that far," said Renata. "I came down here to speak to you and Margot and anyone else Julianna may have talked to as she wrote."

"Margot, huh?" asked Britt with a pointed look at Logan.

"Well, yes. She was Julianna's assistant. And as I understand it, she was moving into the editorial side of things after Connor's death."

"She's the only one who *would* know anything," Logan admitted. "Mother didn't talk to me about the book."

"How about Harrison?"

Logan and Britt laughed. "Even less," said Britt.

"Okay, so Margot it is. Where is she?"

"I guess she's still in bed," said Logan, "though how she slept through those sirens, I don't know."

"What sirens?"

Logan told her about Mrs Agerton and Maxie. "Did you not notice we have double the number of Shibas?"

Renata looked around to see the dogs sitting quietly in case someone spilled granola on the floor. "I guess I didn't," she said. "I'm a little out of it. I feel like I'm living in northern California with Julianna's characters."

"You don't have to stay in a hotel," Logan said. "You're always welcome here."

"Thank you, Logan. I know I am. But I also know you've got a lot on you right now and you don't need another house guest."

Britt carried her dishes to the sink. "I'm going to head over to help Mom with Easter dinner," she said. "Logan, she told me to invite you and Margot. She's already called Harrison. Renata, you are certainly welcome too. It'll be after church tomorrow, around one o'clock."

"That's nice of you," said Renata. "I'm not sure right now, but I may take you up on it."

After Britt left, Logan poured more coffee for Renata. "Tell me what you're thinking for *Murder, Forgotten*," she said slowly. "I'm having trouble imagining anyone else finishing Mother's manuscript."

"And it may not work," admitted the editor. "It's a long shot. But your mother is just about the biggest name there is in commercial fiction. I don't mind telling you that her loss has sent Ironwater reeling. Both professionally and personally." She sighed. "And the thought of a Julianna Burke thriller sitting here, even if it is only half-finished…" She trailed off and held up her palms. "Well, it's tempting."

"I've read what she had so far," Logan said. "And you probably know she was making changes to add Martin Engler's wife, Annette, as his accomplice."

Renata nodded, interested. "Yes, she sent me new pages from the first few chapters." She hesitated. "And Margot texted me that you found the newspaper articles that inspired the book."

"So you know about that?"

"Yes. Julianna told me about the real case a long time ago. But I never read the articles. Now I'd like to."

"To give you an idea of how to finish the book?"

"More likely to give me an idea what to stay away from."

"How so?"

Renata shrugged. "Julianna's books are clearly fiction. She changes names, genders, locales, time periods. I like to know the real facts of the case so I can make sure we don't accidentally veer too close to the real thing. It's not worth the threat of a lawsuit and all that."

Logan was about to tell her of her fear that the real Marissa Eskew was indeed aware of Julianna's book. But if there was one thing she'd learned over the past few weeks, it was that she didn't know whom to trust. She remained silent, and slid the sugar bowl toward her guest.

Chapter 31

Easter morning dawned cold and blustery, but Logan didn't mind. The weather matched her mood. She and Margot sat, not talking, reading the newspaper, occasionally glancing at the whitecaps riffling the gray waters beyond the dunes.

Margot sighed. "Coming to church?"

Logan nodded. "Yeah. Oh, and I almost forgot. Meg invited us to dinner afterwards."

"And I almost forgot to tell you – Detective Giles said the sheriff has gone to New Mexico."

"Really? Wow." Logan thought for a minute. "How did your session go with her?"

Margot wagged her head. "Hard to tell. Her questions were all over the place. What do I know about benzos? Do I aspire to write novels? How did Mr Burke come to hire me?" She flushed. "And at the end, some rather insulting questions about me and Mr Burke. I think she knew I'd get upset about those, so she held them till last."

Logan wanted to ask more, but Margot was clearly uncomfortable. She rose to put her dishes in the sink, ending the conversation.

The women went back to their winter clothes, layering grays and blacks and searching their closets for closed-toe pumps. They met in the living room and smiled. "We don't look much like an Easter parade, do we?" Logan asked. "I don't even want to walk. Let's take the Jeep."

Chapel by the Sea was crowded even though there had been a sunrise service to accommodate the crush of attendees. The music director had added a trumpeter and a saxophonist to the morning orchestration, but even the grand music couldn't lift Logan's spirits.

Pastor Marsha referred to the difficult months the congregation had faced with the loss of two beloved members. She interwove it with the sadness faced by Jesus' followers during the last week of his life. "But death does not have the last word," she said. "Because of our faith, death has lost its sting."

Easy for you to say, Logan thought, looking at Alana perched on Baron's knee. *Your family is intact.*

The child reached up and put her hands on either side of her father's face. It was a gesture so innocent and trusting that Logan's eyes filled with tears. She wasn't sure whom she missed more, her mother or Connor. She drew a shaky breath, glad the service was ending. At least she'd spend the afternoon with the Fitzgeralds, the closest thing to family she had left.

As she and Margot stood, she saw the entire Fitzgerald clan in a pew across the aisle. Britt's twin brothers Blake and Batson, and younger sisters Mary Carol and Emily, waved at her. "See you at lunch?" mouthed Mary Carol, and Logan nodded.

"Are you sure I won't be in the way?" Margot asked as they walked to the Jeep.

"There's no such thing at the Fitzgerald house," said Logan. "I'm sure Harrison and Renata will be there too. Britt says other people actually help her family get through a meal civilly."

Margot laughed. "So it may be awkward, but it won't be because of me."

"Exactly."

They stopped at Liza's and Logan left a note on the door, telling her they had Maxie. Upon arriving back home, the women selected three bottles of wine from Connor's rack and walked next door. The house was loud and filled with the delicious smell of roasting pork loin. Britt's brothers and sisters descended on Logan, hugging her and meeting Margot. "Harrison's in the den with Dad," Emily reported. "Watching NASCAR or golf or baseball or Frisbee-throwing-from-a-deepsea-fishing-boat."

"Jock heaven," Logan said. "Some things never change."

"Is Renata coming?" asked Britt as she accepted the wine. "We're getting ready to unleash the Bobbseys to set the table." Logan smiled at mention of the nickname they'd long had for the twins.

"Emily brought some crazed Easter bunny decorations we have to use," said Batson, grabbing two beers from the refrigerator and tossing one to his brother.

"Beyond frightening," added Blake.

Meg shoved a final casserole into the oven. "I'll have some of that wine," she said with a nod to Britt. "Did Connor bring it from Napa?"

"He did," said Logan. "I can't think of a better time to enjoy it."

"That's the spirit," said Meg.

The doorbell rang and Logan accompanied Mary Carol to the door, thinking it must be Renata. But it wasn't.

"Hello, Mary Carol, Logan," said Dick Satterfield, holding out a loaf of warm grain bread. His other hand gripped Sunny's arm tightly, as if she might bolt. Sunny allowed Mary Carol to hug her, but she looked so stiff and forbidding that Logan didn't feel welcome to do the same.

Logan smiled at her longtime neighbor and lightly touched her arm. "It's good to see you, Sunny." Sunny pulled off her sunglasses and tripped as she crossed the threshold. Logan caught a wave of bourbon fumes as Sunny passed, unspeaking.

Mary Carol arched an eyebrow at Logan as the couple entered the kitchen. "What the heck was that?" she whispered.

Logan smiled. "You are the spitting image of your big sister," she said. "Ask her when everybody's gone."

Before they closed the door, they saw Renata's rented Camry pull into the driveway. Logan walked out to meet her. "So glad you decided to come."

"I need to talk to Margot anyway," Renata said, pulling a bakery box from the back seat. "I figured I'd find her here."

Thirteen people were seated around the polished mahogany table in the Fitzgerald dining room. The formal room was at the front of the house, painted a deep red that Britt once told Logan had taken nine coats to get right. Twin chandeliers hung over the table, and massive sideboards hugged the walls. Only the paintings reflected the house's island location in vivid watercolor landscapes.

The pork loin and mashed potatoes, asparagus and squash casserole were delicious, and the wine flowed liberally. Logan felt herself relax after two glasses of cabernet sauvignon, but could sense the tensions among the others. Dr Fitz and Meg did not speak to each other directly, but traded barbs through their children in what she now realized was a long-practiced dynamic. Dick and Harrison studiously avoided eye contact. Sunny was silent, though at the rate she was drinking that might not last long. But there was plenty of loud chatter as Britt's brothers sparred with their sisters and caught up with Logan and Harrison.

"Mom says teenagers are driving past your house, Logan," said Emily. "Are they bothering you?"

Logan shrugged. "Not me so much. But I worry about the neighbors." She glanced at Dick and Sunny, who were studying the tablecloth.

"Is it bothering you guys?" Emily asked bluntly, looking from her parents to the Satterfields.

No one answered, but Mary Carol chimed in. "Speaking of ghost stories – sort of – remember when you took us to Alice's grave, Sunny?"

Startled, Sunny looked up, then giggled. "Sure do." She looked aggressively at Harrison. "Everybody except Harrison. He was too mature for us."

Logan glanced at Harrison and Dick. Harrison's lips had disappeared into a thin line, but Dick was looking at his wife incredulously. The others didn't notice as Batson and Blake and Mary Carol and Emily shouted their memories of the trip, laughing and talking over each other.

When they'd settled down, Dr Fitz addressed Logan. "Harrison tells me he wants to sell the house, but you're undecided."

Logan nodded. "Yes, Mother's attorney advised us not to make a decision for a year."

"A year, huh? That's probably good advice." He hesitated. "But I would like to ask that you let me know if you decide to sell." Meg looked up in surprise, but Logan could tell from Harrison's bland expression that he and Dr Fitz had already discussed it.

"That would be quite expensive, Charlie," Meg said, breaking their unspoken rule about addressing each other.

Dr Fitz took a swig of wine. "I'm sure it would. I don't know that we could swing it, but we'd like to have that property if we could."

Logan looked from him to Meg. "Well, of course," she said slowly. "If we sell, we can certainly give you first crack at it."

"The Montagues have held that property since before I was born," said Dr Fitz. "We'd want to make sure that whoever goes in there would be the same kind of neighbors."

Britt caught Logan's gaze and rolled her eyes. "Don't want no crackers moving in, do we, Dad?" she drawled.

Her sisters laughed, but her father frowned. "When you're a homeowner, you'll understand," he told her, shutting down the exchange.

In the lull, several conversations resumed. Logan noted that Renata and Margot were huddled at one end of the table. Were they discussing *Murder, Forgotten*? She wasn't sure how she felt about a stranger finishing her mother's book. And regardless of Britt's suspicion of Margot's ambitions, there was no way Ironwater would hand over the project to an unproven writer. They'd go after a mid-list name, someone not as big as Julianna – who would have no incentive – but someone for whom attachment to Julianna's legacy would be a career boost.

Across the table she heard Batson trying to engage Sunny in conversation – something about a hot-air balloon festival he planned to attend.

Sunny's head jerked up and she looked at him with bleary eyes. "I used to go to those every year," she said. "I loved them."

"In Atlanta?" he asked. "Isn't that where you're from?"

Batson and Dick looked at Sunny, waiting for her to answer. But she returned their gazes with a blank stare. To fill the silence, Batson chatted on about his upcoming trip to Decatur, Alabama, and how different cities held their festivals in spring and fall, seeking just the right mix of clear skies and temperature and breeze.

Logan took a sip of wine and tried to pretend she wasn't listening. But if there was one thing she knew about Albuquerque, New Mexico – and indeed, there was only one thing she knew about Albuquerque – it was that the city hosted a huge international balloon festival. *Sunny?* Was it possible Sunny had lived in Albuquerque?

Finally Sunny spoke, ignoring Batson's explanations and going back to his question. "Yeeah," she slurred. "In 'lanta. Tha's where I saw balloons." She went to pick up her wine glass and knocked it over. It clanged loudly against her plate and sloshed red wine on to the ivory tablecloth. "Oh no!" she cried, as Batson and Meg leaped up to contain the spill. Sunny rose and, apologizing, fell heavily against the sideboard.

"Do you want to lie down for a bit?" asked Meg, signaling Britt with her head to show Sunny to a bedroom.

"Yeah, maybe tha'd be good," she said, allowing Britt to lead her from the dining room.

Logan turned to Harrison, who was ignoring a story Blake was telling him. Harrison's eyes narrowed as he watched Sunny stagger down the hallway, Britt's arm around her waist. Logan wondered what her brother was thinking – if it had occurred to him that maybe Sunny wasn't quite as obsessed with sex as he'd thought. Maybe she'd wanted to get into the Burke house for an entirely different reason.

Chapter 32

Logan was glad to end her walk with Annabelle and Maxie. The only people on the beach that cold Easter afternoon were other dog walkers. The Shibas, barking uproariously, strained to reach a boxer and a golden retriever. It was all Logan could do to hold them in check and give the other dogs a wide berth.

She kicked off her sandy tennis shoes and socks on the side landing and walked barefoot into the kitchen. "I have had it with you two," she told them, unsnapping their leashes. They raced to hop on to their favorite couch on the porch. Logan found a single packet of instant hot chocolate in the cupboard and heated water in the tea kettle. On her way to the porch, she saw a note propped on the table. It was from Margot, saying she had gone to the hotel to work with Renata and would be late. Logan glanced next door and saw no one on the Fitzgeralds' decks, but assumed Britt was still there. She and Britt and Mary Carol and Emily had sent Meg off to relax and had cleaned up after dinner, the sisters gossiping about what had gotten into Sunny Satterfield.

Logan sank into a cushioned wicker chair on the porch, pulling a blanket over her shoulders and relishing the warmth of the mug in her hands. "I guess it's just us girls," she told the dogs.

As dusk fell, she tried not to think about the decisions ahead, instead letting her mind roam over the events of the weekend. She wondered what Sheriff Royston was learning in Albuquerque and if Ironwater would push through the writing of *Murder, Forgotten.* If so, would it meet her mother's standards?

Of course, any new writer would have a 190-page start and the murder scene. But what was it her mother had said about the murder scene? Logan had dismissed it at the time because she was focused on the notation at the end, "No, no, no! Did he know it was ME?"

But her mother had picked up on something else. "The writing wasn't very good," she had said. "It was jerky. Not very good."

That was odd. Her mother didn't remember writing the scene, nor did she think it was well written. The laptop showed that the scene had been created on February 21, the day before Connor died, the day all the neighbors were there for happy hour. Could someone else have written the scene? And why?

Well, the why was pretty clear, Logan realized. To point to her mother as the confused murderer.

She got up and went to her mother's study. Her laptop was still on the desk, and Logan turned it on, swiveling in the desk chair while she waited for it to power up. Presumably Renata and Margot had copies of the manuscript on their own laptops. Renata and Margot. Mother's closest confidantes and biggest fans. Professionally speaking, her mother's death impacted them more than anyone. But what if they were able to resurrect this book? Or what if they were to change its direction?

Renata had said she wanted to veer away from the details of the real murder in order to avoid a lawsuit. But could it really be to eliminate any connection to the actual case?

Would that accomplish what the elusive Marissa Eskew had wanted all along?

Logan bolted upright. *Renata?* She was in her early fifties, she'd been in the house multiple times, including the day before Connor's death and the day of her mother's death. She had supposedly flown back to New York hours before Connor was killed, but had anyone checked?

Renata? Sassy, loud-mouthed, opinionated Renata*?* And now she and Margot were collaborating on her mother's final book. Her legacy book. Could they change it enough so that no one would ever connect it to Marissa Eskew of Albuquerque? So that no journalist would ever raise the questions that would threaten Dr Eskew's anonymity?

Certainly, if they altered the book enough, Marissa Eskew's story would remain forever buried in a cold case file in New Mexico.

Logan turned back to her mother's computer and scrolled through the menu until she got to "Seventh Novel – Murder Scene". She called it up and read through the familiar text slowly, looking not for the content that had so shattered her in previous readings but for style. For structure. For cadence.

Her mother was right. It didn't have the Julianna Burke flair. A couple of sentences were wooden, a few pronouns confusing. Logan remembered Connor's favorite toast as he'd clink a beer bottle against her mother's wine glass: "The hardest thing about good writing… is to make it look easy."

Logan thought back to what the neighbors had told her about that last happy hour in the beach house. Renata had left the room, giving Sunny enough time to ask Connor about the title and plot of her mother's latest book. But did Renata have enough time to write the murder scene? Surely not. But then Logan realized something: she didn't need the time then. She'd spent the night. She could've slipped down to the study any time after her mother and Connor had gone to bed.

Logan picked up her cell phone, but her call went to voicemail. "Sheriff," she said hesitantly, "I have a thought I want to share. Call me when you can. Oh, sorry, this is Logan Arnette." The doorbell rang and within a heartbeat Annabelle's high-pitched barking rang out from the porch. "Oops, gotta go." Logan clicked off.

She heard the dogs race across the kitchen and into the living room, Annabelle's baying jangling her nerves. She walked to the door, calling out "Just a minute!" as she tried to shush Annabelle. Maxie sat quietly, her eyes fixed on the door.

Logan paused, her eyes flitting between the Shibas, one so calm, the other raging at the very idea of a visitor. A thought tried to push its way to the forefront of her mind, but it was too slippery to take hold. She opened the door and froze. *Renata.*

Renata pushed her way into the living room, her black hair unusually messy, her make-up smudged as if she'd been running her hands over her face. "I was able to get a plane out tonight," she said, "but I didn't want to leave without telling you goodbye." She grabbed Logan in a tight squeeze. "I don't know when I'll see you again."

"Where's Margot?" asked Logan, her voice muffled against Renata's shoulder.

"She stopped for ice cream, but I didn't have time." Renata flung herself on to the sofa. "Plus, I'm too tired to eat. Words I never thought I'd utter."

Logan felt her face flush, and her mind bounced to the study she'd just left. Was the window open? Could Renata have overheard her phone call to the sheriff? No, that was crazy. Anyway she hadn't actually mentioned Renata's name. Had she?

The editor's black eyes studied Logan curiously, and she grew silent, prompting Logan to prattle. "So what did you two work out?" Logan asked. "You and Margot?"

Renata appraised her for a moment. "Well, I tried to pick every stray thought Julianna had ever voiced out of Margot's brain. Now it will be a matter of finding a talent as brilliantly twisted as your mother's." She smiled tiredly.

Logan frowned.

"What?" Renata's smile faded. "Do you not want the book finished?"

"It's not that," Logan said slowly. "At least, it's not only that. I'm not sure how I feel about someone else writing Mother's book." She paused nervously. "But what you said earlier. About making sure it wasn't too close to the real case in New Mexico. Is that really an issue?"

Renata's face tightened. "Well, as you know, anybody can sue anybody for anything. Whether they have a case or not, a lawsuit can be a nuisance. Believe me, we see it all the time in New York." She peered at Logan. "Why?"

How much could she say without raising suspicion? "That real case. The psychiatrist who killed her patient. She's still… out there somewhere."

Renata rose to her feet. "Yes."

"So… so she wouldn't be suing anybody. She's in hiding."

"Oh. I see what you mean." Renata picked up a magazine and put it down. "But the other family members. Her ex-husband. The daughter. The adoptive mother. We've seen people come out of the woodwork when they smell money." She ran her hands through her hair. "But I really don't have time to talk about this now. I imagine this will be my last trip down here, and I wanted to say goodbye."

She reached for Logan again, but Logan stiffened. Renata noticed and cocked her head. Annabelle gave a nervous bark.

"Logan, is something wrong?"

"No. I mean yes, of course, everything. Everything's wrong." She met Renata's eyes and saw confusion. *And something else.* She stumbled on. "I guess Easter with the Fitzgeralds reminded me… reminded me of all I've lost."

Renata relaxed. "My poor girl. Yes, you have lost a great deal." She reached inside her handbag. "And I am truly sorry for that, Logan."

With her hand still inside her handbag, Renata's grimly lined face was suddenly illuminated and she jerked her head to look out of the window. It took Logan a moment to recognize the source as headlights pulling into the driveway. "That must be Margot," she said, surprised at her relief. From the corner of her eye, she saw Renata withdraw her hand and hoist her purse strap on to her shoulder.

Hearing footsteps on the stairs, the dogs leapt up from where they'd been lying, Annabelle howling ferociously at a second disturbance and Maxie sitting up alertly. Again, the thought from earlier flew across Logan's consciousness, something she was missing. *Something obvious.*

She threw the door open to Liza Holland. Liza thrust a bottle of wine in Logan's direction, even as she addressed Maxie. "There's my girl!" she crooned with delight.

Annabelle stopped barking and switched to a squeal deep in her throat, the ear-splitting Shiba scream. "Annabelle, stop it!" Logan cried, her nerves on edge. Still, Maxie only wagged her tail, and it occurred to Logan that she'd never heard Maxie make the breed's namesake cry.

"I got your note," Liza started, stepping into the foyer and pausing when she saw Renata. "Oh, I'm sorry. I didn't know you had company."

"I'm just leaving," said the editor, pushing past Liza with the barest acknowledgment. "Goodbye, my dear."

Liza looked puzzled at Renata's brusque departure but said nothing. Logan took an unsteady breath. Her head was beginning to ache from Annabelle's near constant yelps and the swirl of things said and unsaid during Renata's visit. She needed to talk to Sheriff Royston. She'd call him again as soon as she could get Liza out of the house.

Her neighbor bent to hug Maxie, who shivered in delight at seeing her mistress. Logan looked from Maxie to Annabelle, and the elusive thought finally snagged in her brain long enough for her to examine it. The Shibas. Two Shibas that looked exactly alike but behaved differently.

"Tell me what happened to Joan," Liza said.

Logan felt she was on autopilot, with one half of her mind telling her neighbor about Joan Agerton being taken to the hospital and the other half leaping to a day in February.

Liza smiled. "It's lucky you and Britt were there," she said. "We're so grateful, Maxie and I, aren't we, girl?"

As Liza nuzzled the dog, Logan's mind raced. Annabelle barked when anyone came to the door. Maxie didn't. Was that how she managed it? Could it be?

"So how is Joan now?" Liza asked.

Logan's thoughts clanged inside her head, and it took her a moment to focus on Liza's question. "At church today, P-Pastor Marsha said she's 'resting comfortably'," she managed.

Liza rose slowly. "Is everything all right, Logan?"

"Sure." She attempted a smile, but it felt like a gruesome crack across her face. "How was your trip? Chicago, wasn't it?"

"Yes, my sister lives in Chicago. I go there quite often to visit her."

Logan tore her eyes away from the dogs and feigned interest in the wine. A pinot noir. Her favorite, which of course Liza knew because she'd been in this house so often. "You know me well," she said brightly. "Connor introduced me to pinot noir. It's so much lighter than merlot and cabernet sauvignon. That's what I like about it."

She knew she was babbling. What she didn't know was if Liza was buying it. She sneaked a glance at her neighbor, her silver hair pulled into a stylish chignon for travel, her black slacks and champagne blouse expensive and understated. Liza's eyes narrowed, and she watched Logan's face.

Logan didn't allow her eyes to return to Maxie, but she couldn't stop her mind. *Maxie would never bark if her own mistress came in.* The last unknown clicked into place in Logan's mind, and Liza watched it happen.

Desperately Logan continued her chatter. "I've always wanted to go to Chicago. Does your sister live on Lake Michigan?" Could she reach the office and lock herself in? She'd left her cell phone there.

Liza reached behind her to shut and lock the front door, her eyes never leaving Logan's face. "I'm sorry, Logan." Her words were similar to Renata's, but this time the meaning was clear. She reached for the wine and almost tenderly extracted the bottle from Logan's grasp. "I hoped you wouldn't have to know."

Logan raised her eyes, still too surprised to be afraid. That would come later. "You took Annabelle and left Maxie here," she breathed. "That's how you killed Connor without anybody hearing you."

Liza nodded, almost sadly.

Logan closed her eyes, unable to believe that this neighbor she'd thought so helpful was behind her family's misery. "Are you…" she whispered, "are you Marissa Eskew?"

Again Liza nodded. "That was so long ago," she said. "But Julianna wouldn't leave it alone." She walked deeper into the living room, motioning for Logan to sit. "Where's Margot?" she asked, looking up the stairs.

"Picking up ice cream. She'll be back any minute," Logan lied.

"Then we'd better get things settled." Liza smiled, and oddly it was as warm as Logan remembered. *But then she was a psychiatrist, wasn't she? Practiced at compassion and empathy.*

"Sit, Logan," she demanded, brandishing the wine bottle like a club. "I need to think. I was just coming over to get my dog, you know."

Logan made a move to grab the bottle, and Liza whirled, smashing it against the edge of the coffee table. Logan leaped back and watched incredulously as the red wine spattered on to the floor and the crisp stripes of her mother's sofa. The bottle's jagged edges gleamed and dripped in Liza's hand

"I said *sit*!" she commanded.

Logan sank on to the sofa, feeling the wet spots soaking into her pants.

Liza began pacing, holding the broken bottle tightly. "If I had it all to do over," she said, "I suppose I would've disappeared again. But I thought all Julianna needed was a nudge to make her stop."

"You knew all about benzos," Logan said slowly. "And she told you what she was writing."

"She talked about it while we walked. She'd mentioned the articles years ago when some *Albuquerque Journal* reader sent them. I tried to tell her the case didn't sound that interesting, point her to other stories people had mailed. But she kept coming back to that one. And then last spring she started writing it." Liza gave a sad smile as if to say she'd had no choice.

Logan felt her throat constricting. "But why Connor?" she pleaded. "You wanted to stop Mother."

"As you and I talked about before, they were a team." Liza shrugged. "So he knew all about the Albuquerque case. The benzos worked to stop Julianna's writing, and Connor was distraught that she was sinking so fast. Fortunately, you and Harrison were nowhere around, so he confided in me."

Logan's heart lurched, recognizing the truth of the statement.

"I suggested a nursing home, but he was having none of it. I still thought the whole book might go away. Then Connor mentioned that he had called the Albuquerque police to find out what Marissa Eskew looked like. He was grasping, but he managed to hit the nail on the head." She shrugged. "I was afraid it was only a matter of time until he figured out my identity and connected it to Julianna's downhill slide." She flung out a hand to indicate she was finished talking, sending blood-red drops of wine across Logan's face. "No sense messing with success. Like mother, like daughter. Where do you keep your rope?"

Logan tried to stand, but her rubbery legs gave way. "The de-detectives took it," she stuttered.

Liza wielded the sharp-edged bottle to force her to remain seated. "Surely you have more." She glanced at the fishing net on the wall. "Or I guess we could improvise."

Logan's heart pounded so loudly she could scarcely hear herself speak. "You hanged my mother," she said, the truth landing like a punch to her stomach.

Liza shrugged again. "She was going to do it anyway."

But Logan knew better. "No," she said, breathing hard and standing despite her trembling legs. "She never would – not if she knew it was you who killed Connor and not her. She wouldn't leave me."

Again Liza waved the menacing glass. "Take that net off the wall," she ordered. "That will work just fine."

"No," Logan said. "Maybe you could overpower a woman you drugged to the point of oblivion, but you're not—" Without warning, Liza lunged. Logan flinched away, but the sharp edges of the serrated bottle sank into the skin above her collarbone. Logan's eyes opened wide in disbelief, and she dropped heavily on to the couch, blood gushing between her fingers as she grabbed her neck. Annabelle bared her teeth and growled, and even in her confusion Logan was aware that the low-pitched rumble was unlike anything she'd heard from the dog before. Maxie's head swiveled from Annabelle to her mistress.

Logan closed her eyes, feeling the room spin. A wave of nausea gripped her and she leaned forward to gag. Through a haze of pain, she saw Liza readying to spring again, and she raised her arms to fend off the wicked shards. But rather than the expected blow, she was assaulted by an explosion of sound, if possible even more agonizing. Logan fought to identify it and blearily recognized the blast of sirens like those that had screamed through the neighborhood the previous day. Liza's gaze flew to the windows where a blue light pulsated.

Already the sirens were alarmingly close. Annabelle burst into panicked barking as the cacophony grew louder. Had something happened at the Satterfields' or the Fitzgeralds'? Could Logan signal to the responders that she needed help?

If possible, the clamor grew even louder – outside with the wailing sirens, inside with Annabelle's furious barking. Logan was woozy with the pain and noise. Liza stood immobilized, her eyes seeking escape. As the sirens shrieked, Logan felt as well as heard footsteps pound up the wooden stairs and fists batter the door. It felt as if the whole house was shuddering.

"Open up!" a voice shouted. "Sullivan's Island Police!"

Logan fought through her dizziness, managing to stand and stumble for the door. With a screech, Liza swiped at Logan again, the bottle slashing her upper arm. Logan crumpled to the floor just as Annabelle launched herself at the older woman, ripping into an arm with a sickening crunch. Liza cried out again and fell back across the coffee table.

When police broke down the door, they found two severely bleeding women and two identical dogs, tearing at each other's throats.

Chapter 33

Britt brought Margot a cup of coffee.

"Where's mine?" asked the figure in the hospital bed.

"Look who's awake," smiled Britt. "If you sit up, I'll give you mine."

"It's a deal." Logan groped for the buttons, groggily hitting several and causing the bed to buck.

"Let me do that," said Margot. "I'm no doctor, but I can handle this part."

When Logan was sitting upright, Britt handed her the coffee. "Boy, am I sore," Logan croaked, her voice raw as she fingered the bandages on her neck, shoulder and arm. "What happened?"

You've got twenty-four stitches under there," said Britt. "That wine bottle did some damage, but luckily it was more on your shoulder than your neck."

"Liza," Logan rasped. "Who called the police?"

"Sheriff Royston," said Margot. "He heard the doorbell ring on the message you left him. He was still in New Mexico, but his detectives had been questioning everyone who had a key to the house, trying to figure out who had come in on Friday night. And he had just learned that Liza Holland had *not* been on the plane to Chicago like everyone thought."

"That made him start looking at her timeline for arriving on Sullivan's Island," Britt added. "It matched Marissa Eskew's timeline. So he got scared that Liza was still around the Charleston area and *still* wanted those articles that would link her to Julianna's book. He was putting it all together when he got your message."

"And I called to tell him I suspected Renata!" Logan said, shaking her head. "Ouch. I can't move my head."

The women heard a knock on the door, and without waiting for an invitation, Sheriff Royston pushed it open. His uniform was rumpled and spattered with what looked like coffee stains. "Coming from the airport," he explained. "Pardon my appearance." He walked over to examine Logan's upper torso, swathed in bandages.

"Logan, I apologize," he drawled, pulling a chair close to her bed. "It took us too long to realize you were in danger. Liza Holland fooled us as completely as she fooled the Albuquerque police. And switching those dogs. I'm not sure we'd ever have caught on to that."

"I guess she'd walked Annabelle so often that Anna B was used to her," Logan said, trying to remain still so her head and shoulder wouldn't throb. "Liza must've taken her earlier on the day she planned to kill Connor and left Maxie at Mother's house. Mother was in no condition to realize that Maxie wasn't Annabelle. And Maxie wouldn't have made a peep when Liza let herself back in."

Margot spoke up. "May I ask you a question, Sheriff?"

"Sure."

"I've been getting calls from my parents and friends about detectives contacting them. Did you think I had something to do with Mr Burke's murder?"

"Well, it did occur to us that you were the right age and the right coloring to be Marissa Eskew's biological daughter. *And* you were adopted. *And* you'd been living in the Burke house for two years. But Detective Lancaster found out that you were born in Georgia and adopted in South Carolina. You'd never been near the Southwest."

Margot turned to Britt. "You suspected me too, didn't you?"

Britt grimaced. "Sorry, but I thought it was possible."

The sheriff continued. "That's why it took us awhile. We weren't looking only at women Marissa Eskew's age. Dr Eskew's ex-husband had disappeared from Albuquerque, as had their biological daughter and the adoptive mother. Albuquerque officers suspected that all three had helped Dr Eskew escape during the trial. Apparently she was pretty convincing about the murder victim's predatory intentions. But the authorities couldn't prove anything, and all three denied it.

"The daughter and adoptive mother, by the way, moved to Chicago after the trial, and Marissa Eskew's ex followed years later. That's why she visits Chicago."

The four were silent for some minutes until Logan realized she'd forgotten to ask something. "Annabelle," she said, eyes darting in agitation. "What happened to Annabelle?"

"Sully's officers took her and Maxie to a vet," Britt said. "But once they got them cleaned up, it turned out it was more of Liza's blood on them than theirs. They each got a few stitches." She grinned. "Liza, on the other hand, has a broken wrist, radius and elbow."

"I need to make Annabelle a K-9 officer," said the sheriff admiringly. "She's a pistol."

"Except she'll go after all your other K-9s," said Britt.

"Who's going to take Maxie?" Logan asked.

Margot spoke up. "The Philpots have her for now. But Shibas aren't great with kids. I'm going to ask them if I can take her to Greenville."

Logan lay back on her pillow, exhausted. "Okay, then. I'm going to officially stop worrying."

"Oh, and Logan," said the sheriff, "a couple of things have already turned up from Liza Holland's questioning. When Julianna was staying with her the week after Connor died, Liza got on her laptop and found the murder scene. Liza deleted your mother's version and wrote a scene to reflect how she'd actually killed Connor, hoping to cast suspicion on Julianna. Which it did – even in Julianna's own mind."

"That explains why Mother thought the scene was badly written," said Logan. "Even in her confusion she could tell something was off."

The sheriff continued. "Liza began contaminating the gingko pills back in December. She was in and out of Julianna's house so much, it wasn't hard to make the substitution. But then right after Julianna returned from Scotland, she ran into all of you on the beach. She said that Julianna was doing so well it scared her. She knew she must have stopped taking the gingko. Liza went up to your house, supposedly to get something to drink. That's when she found the fish oil capsules and decided she could inject them with midazolam. It was easy enough for her to come back and do it while you and Julianna and Margot were out."

Britt interrupted. "But why was Liza so scared of Julianna's book in the first place? Couldn't she have laid low and gone on with her life?"

"Possibly," said the sheriff. "But when *A House Built on Sand* came out, reporters in Raleigh resurrected the case Julianna based it on. That woman was in prison, but they still focused a spotlight on the story again. Liza was afraid that if *Murder, Forgotten* was published, Albuquerque reporters would re-ignite interest in her case and lead authorities to her ex-husband and the girl and her adoptive mother, and link them to their frequent visitor from South Carolina." He shrugged. "Who knows? Coulda happened that way."

He rose and stretched. "I haven't pulled an all-nighter in a while. Better get home to bed."

Logan stopped him. "You'll think I'm being silly," she said, "but I need to know one more thing." She looked at Britt and Margot, gathering her resolve before addressing the sheriff. "What Baron Philpot said. Was Liza having an affair with Connor?"

Logan held her breath. His answer would have no bearing on the prosecution of Liza Holland, nor on the devastation Logan felt at the loss of her mother and Connor. But it would color the memories she had. It would tell her if she knew love when she saw it.

Lance Royston smiled ruefully. "Liza did try to start an affair with your stepfather in order to follow the progress on Julianna's book. Baron overheard them in the church. But apparently he didn't hear it all. Connor refused." Logan allowed herself to breathe as the sheriff continued. "But he kept her as a friend and confidante. When she discovered he'd called Albuquerque to inquire about Marissa Eskew, she panicked. She was afraid he was closing in. Whether he was or not, we'll never know."

"But I found lilies on his grave."

"Julianna and I brought those," Margot said. "We didn't think to mention it to you."

Logan bit her lip and looked down at the sheets, then back at the sheriff. "Thank you for telling me."

"Sometimes our heroes need to keep being heroes," he said.

The next Saturday, Logan and Britt sat on the oceanfront porch of the Burke house, sipping coffee and spreading walnut cream cheese on toasted bagels. Logan's stitches had been removed, though her shoulder and upper arm itched with their reminder. She had the scars covered with a long-sleeved shirt and scarf to prevent sunburn.

Margot and Maxie had departed for the Upstate two days previously, Margot's work with Renata complete. It was now up to Renata and Ironwater to find a writer who was equal to Julianna's story.

A spring breeze swept through the screens and promised a perfect beach day. Annabelle lay on her couch, loudly chomping a squeaky toy given to her by Detective Giles.

"Last vacation day," said Logan, swallowing a bite.

"Um-hmm," Britt nodded.

Tomorrow Logan would move back to her duplex in Charleston, and Britt to a condo in Mount Pleasant. They planned to return to work on Monday, Logan in her internists' office, Britt in her dad's. Neither was ready to make a permanent decision, but figured that getting into a work routine would help them choose their paths.

"You all packed?" Britt asked.

"Yep, I didn't bring much out here. Jezebel's got more stuff to move than I do."

"I saw that you're taking that portrait of your mom. Which is crazy good, by the way."

"Thanks. You haven't seen the one of Connor, but I'm going to hang them both in my living room. Keep them together."

"Good idea."

They ate in silence and looked at the beach, which was dotted with chairs and umbrellas.

"I'm sorry if you thought I suspected your dad in all this," Logan said.

"I didn't blame you. I swear when he started talking at Easter dinner about buying this house, I wondered the same thing. He's such a jerk."

"But your folks are staying together?"

"Yeah, see no evil, hear no evil, speak no evil."

Logan couldn't help laughing. "I'd offer some sage advice about forgiveness, but my relationship with Number 3 is way worse. Or rather, non-existent."

"At least you had Connor. He was the real thing, wasn't he?"

"Yeah, he was."

"Is that why you're having such a hard time deciding whether to keep the house?"

Logan turned to her friend. "I suppose," she said, looking around at the splitting beams, the warped screens, the rickety boardwalk. "I feel like I'm abandoning him. And Mother. But the house is just too sad." She flapped a hand and sent crumbs flying. "I kept thinking I didn't want to be scared away, that in time I'd feel differently, that it'd feel like the old days. Especially when warm weather came." She attempted a smile. "But there's a huge hole in my chest. It may never go away, but it sure won't as long as I'm here." She paused and looked at her friend from the corner of her eye. "But I *have* come up with a new possibility."

Britt twisted to look at her. "Something to do with Harrison's visit this morning?" Britt had slipped away to her bedroom to give them privacy.

Logan nodded. "Sort of. I'm thinking of a compromise."

"Go on."

"I think it's the house itself that holds bad memories. The rooms. The very floorboards. But I think that I would regret losing the land and the neighborhood and the beachfront." She drew a deep breath. "So I'm considering tearing the house down and building something modest for me to live and work in."

"What does that mean, 'modest'?"

"No offense to your folks, but more like Joan Agerton's house. You know, traditional, stately but smaller, not a McMansion."

"And Harrison agreed to that?"

"Well, he's thinking it over. It means I would take this house, and he'd get the place in Scotland free and clear. He was already eyeing it for the golf market. We would split everything else. I could see his greedy little eyes light up."

Britt laughed. "Would you start right away?"

"No, I'll still wait and see how I feel in a few months. As you said, he can't do anything without my okay."

"I have to admit, it sounds like a win-win. You get a great new place. And there is nothing for people to drive by and gawk at. Brilliant, my dear."

Logan stood and swiped more crumbs from her lap. "Ready for a final beach day?"

"Ready."

They left their dishes in the sink and grabbed towels, sunscreen and an umbrella from the laundry room. Without a look back at the old house, they walked arm in arm across the yard to the sand.

Book Club Discussion Questions

1. When the book begins, Logan has mixed feelings about her mother. How do those feelings change over the course of the book?
2. Why is Logan so obsessed with finding out if Connor had an affair?
3. How has Julianna's fame affected Harrison and Logan? Was she a good mother to them?
4. Logan pondered that "an unsolved murder was like an ugly comment that a 'friend' passed on to you. You didn't know who had said it, so it made you question every friendship. Every person in her life but one was innocent of Connor's murder. Yet it tainted her thoughts about everyone." Is that what it must be like for the families of victims of unsolved murders?
5. Do you think Julianna would have gone through with suicide had she not been interrupted?
6. Do Julianna's last words – "Tell Logan, tell her she's an art…" – give the reader new insight to her as a mother?
7. Some readers think it's somehow "against the rules" to have a major protagonist die in a murder mystery. What did you think when this happened?
8. Logan contemplates the marriage of her mother and stepfather in this way: "You'd think growing up in such a household would provide a good model. That's what all the TV psychologists said, didn't they? All the books on marriage. But did it set children up to expect too much of their own relationships?" Did Julianna's marriage represent an impossible ideal for Logan to attain?

9. Have you ever been around a Shibu Inu? Did the author capture the breed accurately?
10. The mother–daughter relationship is as important to *Murder, Forgotten* as uncovering the murderer. Near the end, Logan asks the sheriff a final time if Connor had an affair, then "held her breath. His answer would have no bearing on the prosecution of Liza Holland, nor on the devastation Logan felt at the loss of her mother and Connor. But it would color the memories she had. It would tell her if she knew love when she saw it." Why is the truth of their relationship so important to her?
11. Logan thinks the old beach house holds memories in its very floorboards. Is that possible?